River's Edge

Also by Marie Bostwick

FIELDS OF GOLD

River's Edge

MARIE BOSTWICK

KENSINGTON BOOKS
http://www.kensingtonbooks.com

KENSINGTON BOOKS are published by

Kensington Publishing Corp.
850 Third Avenue
New York, NY 10022

All Kensington titles, imprints and distributed lines are available at special quantity discounts for bulk purchases for sales promotion, premiums, fund-raising, educational or institutional use.

Special book excerpts or customized printings can also be created to fit specific needs. For details, write or phone the office of the Kensington Special Sales Manager: Kensington Publishing Corp., 850 Third Avenue, New York, NY 10022. Attn. Special Sales Department. Phone: 1-800-221-2647.

ISBN 0-7582-0991-6

First Kensington Trade Paperback Printing: September 2006
10 9 8 7 6 5 4 3 2 1

Printed in the United States of America

For my mother, Margaret McCormick,
a woman of humor, generosity, optimism,
and the creator of Something Good.

Prologue

I don't trust memory—not really. My mind is a storehouse of wordless snapshots from childhood, pictures without context or captions, still frames of silent movies that seem so true but whose veracity cannot be counted upon.

I remember sitting in the back garden near a bush heavy with blooming lilacs, holding a white kitten in my lap, giggling with delight as the kitten extends a tiny sandpaper tongue and begins licking my hands. The picture is clear in my mind, but I do not trust it. Did I have a kitten? Father never mentioned it, and in the photographs of our garden in Alexander Platz there are no lilacs, only serviceable shrubs and rows of spiny rosebushes, blooming in season exactly as they were supposed to. I cannot imagine Father allowing anything as unruly and independent as lilacs to take root in his garden.

I remember, too, a day in the park, Father smiling and humming as he carries me in his arms. I feel the brass buttons of his dress uniform pressing circles into my chest as I snuggle close to him. Mama and I are in matching white linen dresses, her eyes bright and her face glowing with good health, her figure shapely, a bit plump even. Her hands soft and teasing, her fingernails pale pink ovals as she playfully slaps Father on the wrist in scolding response to a joke I don't understand but laugh at anyway. If I close my eyes, I can conjure the picture into being, but I do not trust it. Were we ever so happy? Was there a time, when we were as carefree as any other young family strolling in the park on a sunny afternoon? I suppose it is possible, but I can't quite bring myself to believe it. I may have imagined the whole thing.

But there is one childhood memory that I am certain of. I was very young, but I remember the day of my first piano lesson with utter clarity. I always loved to listen to Mother play. Sometimes I sat across from her, rapt and still, in a chair of tufted green velvet, watching her hands float above the keys, graceful and fluid as swimmers moving through clear water. Other times I would lie stomach-down on the floor, as close to the foot pedals as possible, to feel the notes rumble through every part of my body. Every day I spent hours listening to the music Mother made, but until that day, I never so much as touched the piano myself, not because anyone had said I mustn't, but because somewhere inside me lay a belief that Mother was a magical being and only her touch could make the heavy black box sing so beautifully.

Her cough was worse that day. Sitting in the green chair, I grew impatient as she stuttered through my special song, "Für Elise," starting and stopping to clear her throat. Finally her shoulders started convulsing, and she pushed the piano bench back and leaned down, coughing violently, her handkerchief held tight to her mouth. I jumped up from my chair and ran to her side, thumping her back with my little fists, trying to free her from the invisible obstruction, but my efforts seemed to make no difference.

"Mother!" I cried and thumped her back even harder than before. "Are you all right? Tell me what to do!" I begged.

She just shook her head silently and waved a hand to motion me back to the green chair, but I wouldn't leave her side. Finally the fit passed, and her shoulders dropped more evenly as she took in deep breaths of air, becoming herself again. She sat up and pulled the cloth away from her mouth to show a ragged circle of red, cruel and unseemly against the ladylike linen and convent-made lace of her handkerchief.

"Mother! You're bleeding!"

"No, darling," she murmured, folding the hankie quickly to hide the stains. "I'm fine. I was just coughing too hard, that's all. It brought up a little blood. Nothing to worry about, Elise."

"Are you all right?"

"Yes. I'm just a bit tired, that's all. Playing the piano is hard work, and I get tired more easily these days." She smiled so sweetly and reassuringly that I didn't think to ask her why that was. She chucked me under the chin playfully. "I can't always do all the work, you know. You've watched long enough, my love. It's time for you to start playing and me to start listening."

She walked slowly to a bookshelf, chose a couple of thick leather-bound volumes that she stacked on the piano bench, and perched me on top of them so I could reach the keyboard. Then she sat down next to me and let her hands hover over the keys. "Watch," she said and gave me my first piano lesson.

Completely bypassing nursery songs and scales, Mother began teaching me Beethoven's "Für Elise." She played through the entire composition. Urging me to watch her fingers carefully, she played through the first eight bars twice more, then told me to try.

Surely that first attempt was halting and punctuated with mistakes. After all, I couldn't have been more than four years old, but in my memory the music flows from my fingers unbidden, unerring, an untapped spring of music gushing from my fingertips, spilling into the room and quenching a thirst I'd never known I had.

Somehow I understood that it didn't matter if I never spoke again, because the piano would always be able to express what I felt more completely than words. Words, like memory, can't be trusted. You can never be sure that you've chosen the right ones or that they were heard correctly. Music isn't like that. It cannot ring false. Music doesn't try to describe the heart: it is the heart. It says exactly what it means. It cannot dissemble or be misunderstood.

This was a revelation as my fingers rocked rhythmically from ebony to ivory and back. I finished the phrase, beaming with the joy of my discovery and looked to Mother for approval and her acknowledgement that, like her, I, too, was a magical being. She rewarded me with a smile and a rare, delicious peal of laughter, silver and bright, a sound like pearls and new coins pouring a generous stream into my open palms. Her pale, delicate face was suddenly unlined and glowing—mysteriously, there seemed to be more of her, as if a new layer of flesh had suddenly been added to her thin frame. She was the Mother of my memory again, pink and healthy and strolling through a park where every day was happy and gilded with promise.

I laughed too, giddy with my newfound power—the power to banish sickness and age, the power to make Mother well again. I played through the phrase again without being asked. It was even easier than the first time. Mother laughed again, and I joined in, the sounds of our shared delight filling the dark corners of the room and making them light.

"That was beautiful, *Liebling,*" she said in the soft, breathless voice I still hear in my dreams. "I was right. You could only be called Elise. When Herr Beethoven sat down to compose this, he surely had you in mind."

I believe in destiny, but not in fate. Maybe that sounds contradictory, but in my mind they are two completely different things.

Fate says that whatever happens is meant to be, and nothing you can do will change it. If I believed that, I'm not sure I'd be able to get myself out of bed in the morning. What would be the point? Destiny is different. It is a place. Once you arrive there, you understand that this is precisely what and who you were created to be. Fate is resignation and defeat. Destiny is peace and discovery. If you are lucky, sometimes you stumble upon clues to your destiny—riddles that, after you have reached your destination, are suddenly so obvious you wonder why you didn't see the answer to begin with.

Before I was born, my parents agreed that if I was a boy I would be named Herman Braun, the name my father shared with the previous four generations of firstborn Brauns. There was not much thought given to the possibility of my being a girl. However, in the extremely unlikely case of such an embarrassing occurrence, my father declared I should be named Helga, after his own mother.

On the day of my birth, mother held me in her arms and, in a rare and surprising display of independence, insisted that my name was Elise. Father protested briefly but indulged my mother, chalking it up to female inconstancy. When his son followed, he would have to be firm, but why not let Mother have her way this time? I was, he reasoned, only a daughter. It was of little importance what I was named. Mother knew better.

Of course, destiny does not always leave a trail for us to follow. Sometimes, if you are fortunate, you stumble upon it by accident. I was born in Berlin in 1925, a link in the chain of an ancient Prussian military family that stretched back to the days of Frederick the Great. There was never any reason for me to suppose that my destiny lay in the tobacco country of the Connecticut River Valley, but it did. At the age of fourteen, the seemingly accidental tides of history carried me across the sea. I fought against the current, and yet, at the moment I stood on the edge of the valley and saw the ribbon of river at my feet, a great peace descended upon my heart. I understood my arrival in that spot was meant to be.

Someone once told me that the Connecticut River is the third most beautiful river in the world. I don't believe it. There cannot be any place more beautiful than this. Here, just outside Brightfield, Massachusetts, the river is generous, and paradise lies on both banks. It is like the Jordan that we must cross to enter into the bounds of heaven, except this crossing is unnecessary, for whichever side you rest on, you are already home.

The river moves slowly. There is no reason to hurry, and it seems even the fish linger a time before swimming downstream to the sea. The river valley is lovely in every season. In summer, the fields fed by the river are dressed in swathes of green velvet and fine white linen; the swaying leaves of the tobacco plants and the cotton tents that are erected to shade the growing plants protect the best of them from the harsh summer sun. In fall, the meadowlike intervales are brown and rich, their scent ancient and sure. In winter, snow blankets the landscape, stretching pristine white to the edge of the world, unspoiled and chaste, unblemished by human contact. In spring, the soil is soft and stoneless, so tender the blades of the plow cut through it like butter. So rich you might think planting almost an act of egotism—as if you could toss the seeds in the air, come back a few weeks later, and find a jungle of green had sprung up. It's a cunning disguise, but I know the truth.

The ground is fertile and yielding, but tobacco is a fickle mistress. She requires coaxing and care and sometimes life blood before she'll give up her favors—if she chooses to give them up at all. Still, if you come to the valley and it speaks to you, there is no other place for you on the face of the earth.

I had no more asked to come to the valley than the tobacco seeds had asked to be planted. Someone brought those seeds from the jungles of Sumatra, and against all odds they flourished in the river-washed soil of a New England valley, just as I did. We'd both been brought from foreign shores and climates, transplanted exotics, moved by forces beyond ourselves, but once planted we took root and became as much a part of the landscape as the life-giving river that fed us both, that made us grow and thrive in a country that was ours not by birth but by destiny.

Chapter 1

My eighth birthday party, January 30, 1933, was a small one, as always. The same five people were in attendance every year: Mother, Father, Uncle Wilhelm, Cousin Peter, and me. Mother's health did not allow her to entertain large groups, and even small adult celebrations were taxing for her, leaving her weak for days afterward. Inviting other children was simply out of the question. Even if I'd had any little friends to include in the festivities, their parents would have forbidden them to attend. They were afraid of contagion. I don't blame them. If Mother hadn't been consumptive herself, I am sure she would have felt the same way.

Captain Wilhelm Canaris, whom I always called Uncle, was my nominal godfather. Father had served under him on his first posting, as a midshipman aboard a U-boat. Like Father, Uncle Wilhelm came from a distinguished German family, and though Father was then only a young officer in training, just sixteen years old, Captain Canaris had taken a liking to him. Over the years, they had become good friends. In 1935 Uncle Wilhelm would become Admiral Canaris and head of the *Abwehr,* the German military intelligence office. He made Father part of his staff.

Though Uncle Wilhelm came to our home only rarely, I looked

forward to his visits. He was very prompt and always arrived for my birthday dinner at precisely the appointed hour; yet I came downstairs fifteen minutes early to wait for him just the same. I sat dressed in my very best on the bottom step of the staircase, hugging my knees in close as I rested my chin on them and stared at the face of the old grandfather clock, willing it to strike seven.

When at long last the magical hour arrived, the heavy brass knocker sounded waltz time, one-two-three, on the front door. I rushed forward to open it, only to be impatiently pushed aside by the uniformed housemaid who had been hired to serve for the evening. Uncle came in the door smiling, murmuring inconsequential complaints about the cold to the housemaid, and bearing a simply enormous and extravagantly wrapped gift in his hands. Though I knew I wouldn't be permitted to open it until after dessert, it was difficult to keep my eyes off the beribboned box. Guessing what was hidden inside gave me a way to occupy my mind during the long, dull meal and grown-up conversation that I was expected to endure as the silent guest of honor. Uncle always insisted on bringing my present into the dining room and placing it on the sideboard, directly across from my place at the table. I think he knew how gazing at it helped me to pass the time.

Upon handing his coat and hat to the maid, who hung them up and then went to announce the arrival of Captain Canaris to my parents, Uncle pretended to suddenly notice me perched on the stair where I had retreated after being pushed aside by the maid.

"Well, well, well!" he said cheerfully, drawing his considerable eyebrows together into a single, bristly bunch, like a well-used scrub brush. "What do we have here? A mouse hiding on the stair? Come here, little mouse, and let me see how you have grown." I stood up, and he kneeled down, so we were eye to eye as he looked me carefully up and down, declaring, as he did every year, that I must have grown a meter since he last saw me.

I smiled timidly in response, but before I could say anything, Father emerged from his study, wearing his full dress uniform, complete with highly polished shoes and rows of shining medals. Mother followed slowly behind, using a cane to steady her uncertain steps. She was beautiful, dressed in one of the dozens of elegant evening gowns that hung in her dressing room, a glittering reminder of the gay life she had led before I was born, before she first became ill.

Uncle rose from his knees to clasp Father's outstretched hand. The room always seemed smaller when Father entered it, and, not for the first time, I reflected that it was a good thing Mother and I were so petite or there wouldn't have been room in the house for us.

"Lale, my darling," Uncle purred as he leaned down to kiss Mother on the cheek, "You are looking radiant, my dear." It was true. Mother's face was always radiant. Her cheeks were twin flames in her thin face, feverish reminders of the specter that haunted us all.

The welcoming rituals having been observed, we filed into the dining room and sat down at the table, Father at the head, with Uncle at his right hand and Mother at his left. I sat next to Uncle. This left an empty place next to Mother where Cousin Peter was meant to sit, but he was late. The grownups talked quietly of things that did not interest me. From time to time, Father looked impatiently at his watch. Finally he said, "I don't know what is keeping Peter. He is always late."

"I am sure he is not *always* late," Mother disagreed gently, but I knew she was wrong.

Whenever Cousin Peter came to dinner he was at least ten minutes late and would enter the dining room breathless and beaming, full of good cheer and complicated explanations. Unlike Uncle Wilhelm, Cousin Peter was an actual relative, descended from our common ancestor, General Yorck, hero of the Napoleonic wars. Father was very proud of our connection to the great General

Yorck. When expounding on the shameful state of the German military, as he did tonight to Uncle, he often quoted Yorck's 1813 speech to the troops in which he declared that the chief virtues of a Prussian soldier were courage, endurance, and discipline.

"And then," Father said, fixing his eyes skyward and stabbing the empty air with his index finger to emphasize his point, "the Great Yorck said, 'but the Fatherland expects something more sublime from us who are going into battle for the sacred cause—noble, humane conduct even towards the enemy.' "

Finishing the quote, his hand dropped to the table and his lip curled in disgust as he complained to Uncle, "These Allied generals know nothing of the honor that should exist between warriors, both victor and vanquished." Uncle nodded in agreement as he sipped wine from his glass. "But, neither do we anymore," Father continued. "We have forgotten our tradition and honor. That is our shame."

Father put a great store on honor and tradition. Although Cousin Peter was an actual count, titled, and more closely related to the great Yorck than we were, he was far less Prussian than Father, lacking the stiff formality that was the mark of a German military aristocrat. They were nearly the same age, but Peter seemed much younger than Father. Peter was handsome and fun-loving, and I was a little in love with him. I suspected that Father disapproved of his cousin taking up the law, just as he disapproved of his habitual lateness, but he still liked Cousin Peter. However, Peter's lack of punctuality rankled.

"Whatever can be keeping Peter?" Father growled as he pulled out his pocket watch to confirm that his cousin was now late by a full quarter-hour.

"I am sure he has good reason for his tardiness," Mother said gently. "You know what the traffic is like this time of night, Herman."

Father grunted. "Captain Canaris had to deal with the same traffic, and he is not late. I don't think it is fair to keep everyone waiting for their dinner just because—"

But before Father could finish his sentence, the door to the dining room burst open and Uncle Peter was in the room, pushing past the housemaid, who looked irritated that he had not given her a chance to announce him properly, kissing Mother on the cheek, shaking hands with Father and Uncle, winking at me as he put his birthday gift on the sideboard next to Uncle's, all the while offering his profound apologies, saying it simply couldn't be helped, the shop assistant who had wrapped his gift had taken forever and . . .

"Well," Father said gruffly but not unkindly, "you are here now, and that is what is important. Please, sit down." He got to his feet and motioned toward the empty place next to Mother. Turning to the maid, he inclined his head slightly to indicate that she could begin to serve.

The meal consisted of three courses and two wines and one birthday cake. I ate my slice of cake with relish and thought with pleasure about what was to come next.

When the plates were cleared I would finally be allowed to open my gifts. What would I find in those boxes? A bright-eyed Steiff bear? An elegantly dressed doll? One year I received a hand-painted miniature tea set imported from England. What about this year? Uncle Wilhelm and Cousin Peter never failed to give me the perfect gift, and I never needed parental prompting to bestow sincere kisses of thanks on their cheeks. Afterward we would retire to the music room, and the grownups would sip sherry from tiny crystal glasses while I played the piano for the prescribed half-hour, always opening the concert with my favorite, "Für Elise," and closing with Uncle's favorite, "The Blue Danube" waltz. When the clock struck nine, Mother would suggest that it was time for me to go to bed. With my bedroom door left slightly ajar, I would fall asleep to the sounds of pleasant, rumbling male voices punctuated by Mother's tinkling laughter and occasional cough.

Certainly, my birthday celebrations were quite subdued and predictable compared to many other children's, yet I liked them just the way they were. Growing up in the shadow of my mother's illness made me cherish the tradition and regularity of the occasion, as though observing our little rituals with exactness and precision would keep anything from changing. But it didn't work that year, my eighth. I didn't realize it yet, but that was the year when everything began to change—for me, for my family, for Germany, for the entire world.

As I scraped the last bite of icing off the plate and onto my fork, I heard a faint murmur of voices outside that grew in strength and volume as the moments passed, like a distant sound of rushing water that grows and swells when a current carries you to the edge of the falls. I saw a flicker of candlelight that became a glow through the darkness, illuminating the white lace curtains of the windows, bathing them in heat and yellow light. I looked around at the faces of the grownups to see if they'd heard it too. They had. The stiff, uncomfortable set of Father's jaw and the studied indifference of Uncle's expression told me that they were as aware that something was happening outside as I was. Mother started making aimless small talk with Cousin Peter about the cake, commenting that she didn't think it was as moist as it should have been. They were all working so hard to ignore the noises outside that I somehow sensed I should do the same, but when the swelling voices began to sing, I couldn't help myself. I jumped out of my chair, pushed open the French doors, and ran out onto the dining room balcony. The grownups followed me, slowly, and stood framed in the door behind me.

The street below was crowded with young people, singing and carrying torches, marching in the direction of the Brandenburg

Gate. There were so many of them that the sky glowed orange-red with the light of the torches they carried. The air was electric with their excitement, and, for one silly moment, I was excited too, thinking that the parade was somehow connected with my birthday. The marchers finished singing, and a handsome young boy dressed in a brown shirt with military-looking braid, no more than fifteen or sixteen years old, saw me leaning over the balcony railing and grinned at me. Raising his arm at a stiff, sharp angle, he shouted, "Heil Hitler!" and, as if in answer to his call, the other marchers shouted lustily, "Heil Hitler!" They began singing again, even more loudly and enthusiastically than before. The sound was so powerful and the atmosphere so thick with their expectation that I could feel the hair standing up on my neck.

I spun around to face the grownups, too excited to take much note of their serious expressions. "Mother! Father! Look how many people there are!" I exclaimed breathlessly. "There's no end to them!" I pointed down the street in the direction that the marchers had come from. It was true; the crowds of people stretched down Wilhelmstrasse as far as the eye could see, as though the parade stretched to the horizon and the marchers had been mysteriously summoned from the bowels of the earth.

"What are they so excited about?" I asked. I was young and knew nothing of the political turmoil of recent days. "Who is Hitler?"

"He is the new chancellor," Mother answered without offering further explanation.

Father snorted derisively at her simple description. "He is a thug with delusions of grandeur. He is a former wallpaper hanger and a former *corporal.*" He spoke this last word with a sneer. Worldly I was not, but I was an officer's daughter, and even at the age of eight, I knew that corporals ranked very low on the list of persons one must concern oneself with. Corporals were not people who merited parades.

Father's eyes narrowed as he scanned the columns of torches advancing past him. "Stupid sheep," he commented to no one in particular. He shook himself as if in response to a sudden chill. "Come, Lale," he said. "Elise. Come inside. It's cold. Come inside before you catch a chill."

Mother and I did as we were bid. Father and Uncle followed behind, and I heard Uncle say, "Flash in the pan, Herman. Nothing to worry about. He may be chancellor, but the strength of Germany still lies with the military. He needs us more than we need him. He can be managed. You'll see."

"I am not so sure about that," interjected Cousin Peter. "He becomes stronger every day. Two years ago, or even one, could anyone have imagined that this would have happened? He may only be a former corporal, Cousin Herman, but now he is chancellor of Germany. He is powerful, cunning, and ambitious. A year ago you might have been able to manage him." He turned his head and scanned the crowds of chanting young people streaming by, their eyes unnaturally bright and fixed, as if they were gripped by some feverish delirium. A cloud of concern passed over Peter's normally cheerful face. "He doesn't need you anymore. He has them."

For a moment the adults were silent. I could feel the tension among them, and I drew close to Mother, leaning my head against her hip. She looked down at me and smiled. "Peter! Herman!" she remonstrated cheerily. "Have we forgotten? It's Elise's birthday! This is no time to discuss politics. Not when we have a gifts to open and a lovely evening of music planned!"

At Mother's prompting, we all adjourned to the music room. I was finally allowed to open my presents—a charming Victorian dollhouse complete with five rooms of furniture and a family of tiny dolls from Uncle, and from Cousin Peter, a truly exquisite book, *The Children's Encyclopedia of Animals,* filled with lifelike illustrations and information on animals from all over the world. I was delighted.

"Now, my little mouse," Uncle said, pinching my cheek playfully, "you must give us something in return. A song. Yes?"

I sat down on the piano bench and began, but I had to strike the keys more firmly than usual to be heard over the singing outside. It threw off my timing. For the first time in my life, my fingers stumbled across the keyboard and I had to begin again.

I didn't realize it at the time, of course, but this day was the beginning of the end of my childhood. In a few short years my town, and my nation would be transformed. The map of my world ended a few hundred meters from our house on Alexander Platz, and my country was Mother's bedroom. However, even that private land was soon to change.

Her cough got worse. There were no more parties, not even small ones. She almost never left her room. She liked to hear me play, said the music eased the pain and the fits of coughing more than all the doctor's pills and powders, so Father had the piano moved to her room. I spent my afternoons playing to her. If she was awake she would applaud weakly after each piece, her hands delicate and so pale they might have been carved from ivory, fluttering like the wings of a dove. When she fell asleep, I continued to play, never lifting my foot from the soft pedal, the notes a quiet accompaniment to her dreams. In those early days, when Mother would go through a particularly bad spell, I would play longer and more intensely. Time and time again, she rallied in response, and I came to believe that the music healed her and that as long as I kept playing, Mother would live. For a long time it was true, but one winter she was worse, and nothing I played seemed to help.

Each morning, when I would pull aside the heavy drapes that covered the bedroom windows, she seemed a fraction smaller, her skin a shade paler. She was quietly disappearing, and as the months passed, I grew more and more afraid that one day I would tiptoe into the thick blackness of her darkened bedroom, pull back the curtains to let in the morning sun, and find that she was simply gone.

I convinced Father to allow me to leave school and study at home. In our hearts we both knew the end was coming, and we both tried to deny it. For Father that meant removing himself from the hurt by working longer and longer hours, staying as far away as possible from Mother's little room, a room that smelled like camphor and secrets. For me it meant staying as close to Mother as possible, knowing that while my music urged her not to leave me, she would fight to live as long as she could.

How well I remember those years, sitting on the floor near Mother's bed, studying quietly when she was asleep, reading to her from my textbooks when she was awake, playing music to distract her when the pain was worse. It was a private play in which Mother and I acted out the only important parts, with occasional cameo appearances by Father, doctors, nurses, and housemaids.

Father spoke to me about Mother's illness only once. He called me into his study to say he'd heard of the Schatzalp sanatorium in Davos, Switzerland. It had a wonderful reputation. Many of its patients came home completely cured after months of exposure to the resin-scented pine forests and healthful climate. Mother was awfully sick. She could not sleep at night because the coughing never stopped. Father explained that after Uncle had pulled some strings with a Swiss cousin who knew one of the doctors at Schatzalp, he had been able to secure a bed for Mother.

"She will be leaving for the sanatorium tomorrow," Father said. "I will take her there myself."

"No!" I cried, surprising both him and myself with this outburst of protest. I had never contradicted him before. "You can't send her away! Those places never do any good, anyway."

In the past, Mother had gone to various sanatoriums for short periods of time and always came home improved, but not cured.

"Elise," Father began gently, "you must understand—"

"She will get better," I insisted. "You'll see. She always gets better. I am the only one who knows how to take care of her. Mother says that no one but me knows how to make her tea properly. There won't be any pianos there, and no one to play them if there are! You'll kill her!" I shouted. Father stared at me hard, as if he didn't quite recognize me. I took a deep breath and forced myself to speak more calmly.

"Please, Father. Don't send her away. She needs me," I said pleadingly. "I can make her better. I know I can! I've been working on a new sonata. Mozart's C Minor. Her favorite. It is very difficult, but I'm practicing as hard as I can. Soon I'll have it, and then . . ." Father's eyebrows drew together, and he studied me with a mixture of concern and confusion.

I stopped in midsentence, knowing I wouldn't be able to make him understand. As Mother's illness progressed I had forced myself to learn more and more difficult pieces, believing that somehow only the sacrifice of my time and effort would satisfy the greedy god of tuberculosis. So far it had worked. Each time I stretched myself and mastered a more difficult piece, Mother rallied just as she had the day I'd first played for her. Well, not quite like that. She was never as well as that again, but she was still alive. The Mozart was the hardest composition I'd ever attempted, not because of its technical difficulty, though it certainly was a challenge, but because it required an emotional depth that seemed beyond me. Mother loved it for just that reason. "It is so impulsive! So personal!" she would say. "As if he is finally daring to reveal the complexity of his own nature."

Maybe that was why I didn't care for the piece despite my love of Mozart. My favorite was the third movement of the Sonata in A Major, the "Alla Turca," which I loved to play as fast as I could, which is to say much too fast. But I didn't care for this piece. The structure was unlike anything else Mozart had written, with unpredictable pauses, and sections that seemed almost improvisational in nature. Try as I might, the notes sounded pedantic and planned when I played them. This was a piece that required drama and intensity and, most of all, maturity. That was something no amount of practice could give me.

In my frustration I felt like tearing the sheet music into a hundred pieces. But I forced myself to keep going, convinced that if I could learn it, Mother would live. I practiced every spare moment and had taken to getting up in the middle of the night to practice silently, my hands suspended over the keyboard but not actually touching it, my fingers stretching silently over an impossibly complex landscape of sharps and flats, in a race against death. I was making progress, but not quickly enough.

"Father, you don't understand. I've almost got it," I explained urgently. "I just need more time!"

For the first time in my life, I saw tears in Father's eyes. He swallowed hard. "Come here, Elise." I walked across the carpet to the wing chair where he was seated. He pulled me onto his lap, a thing he had never done before. "You have done a wonderful job caring for your mother. A wonderful job," he repeated. "But she is very sick, and she is getting worse. You must be brave. This isn't like the other times, Elise. It is much worse. There is nothing more you can do. Schatzalp is the only chance we have. If she doesn't go, she will certainly die."

I sat on Father's lap, blinking back my tears just as he had. I knew he was telling me the truth. I couldn't save her. I was not good enough. I had not practiced hard enough, and the race was lost. It was my fault. Everything in me wanted to lean into Father's broad chest and sob, but I couldn't. I didn't want Father to know how I had failed us. I had to be brave so no one would ever know. Like Father. "All right," I whispered my reluctant assent.

"There's a good girl," Father said, patting me awkwardly on the back. "Run upstairs now, and help Mother to get ready. You will know exactly what she needs. If you leave it to the maid, who knows what she will pack?"

I slid off Father's lap and walked to the door. Turning back to inquire what time the train was to leave, I saw him sitting with his head buried in his hands, his shoulders jerking silently as he fought to suppress his grief. I wanted to run to him, to climb back into his lap and cry with him, to call him *Vati*—Daddy—the way other little girls addressed their fathers, to share our fears and find solace in bearing the unbearable together, but I couldn't bring myself to do these things. I did not know him well enough. I swallowed my questions and climbed the stairs alone to Mother's room. Our moment of intimacy passed.

The next day I stood on the railway platform and waved goodbye to Mother and Father as the train pulled out of the station. I could see Mother's pale hand waving farewell, but her face was obscured by steam from the locomotive.

Children weren't allowed to go to Schatzalp. Father went to see her occasionally, but his visits were short. He never said much about them except that he was sure she was getting better, or at least no worse. Mother wrote me letters weekly, at first in her own hand, describing the lovely mountain scenery, or the funny doctor whose eyebrows were so thick they grew into one straight line that raised up and down like a curtain when he was confused or irritated; or the way the nurses would wheel all the patients out into the afternoon sun, wrapping them so tightly in layers of blankets that they couldn't move their arms but just lay there like rows of pink and white sausages baking in the sun. Later she began dictating her letters to a nurse. They still came as regularly as before, but they weren't as personal. She always asked how I was, assured me that the alpine air was doing her a world of good and she was growing stronger every day. It wasn't true. She died at the Schatzalp sanatorium in the spring—May 14th, 1938.

Father went to Switzerland alone to "see to the arrangements." The night he returned, he drank too much at dinner and told me about his trip.

"The director met me at the door with a sad face and a bill. He said he had taken the liberty of contacting a minister who would meet me later that afternoon so we could discuss the funeral arrangements. Sanctimonious little priss," Papa mumbled before draining his glass and pouring himself another.

"I told him that wouldn't be necessary. No ambassadors of God were wanted—thank you just the same. If there is a God—which I think, given our recent experiences, there is much reason to doubt—" Father said in a voice slurred by wine and sarcasm, "if there is a God, He certainly didn't help me when Lale was alive. I have no intention of praying to Him now that she is dead. There will be no funeral. A simple burial will do. There is no point in doing more."

He picked up the glass and took another drink, drawing the liquor into himself with greedy gulps like a man desperate to quench an unquenchable thirst. The man sitting in front of me was nothing like my fastidious, tight-buttoned father, and yet there he was, sitting in Father's chair, wearing his clothes, speaking in Father's voice. I asked permission to be excused and go to bed. He looked up at me with a surprised expression, as though he suddenly realized that I was in the room and how this all must look to me. His eyes softened, and for a moment I thought he was about to apologize. Instead he nodded his head once, granting my request. I placed my napkin next to my nearly untouched plate and pushed my chair back from the table.

"She was very beautiful," Papa said as I was leaving. "She was everything to me, Elise, but I never knew how to tell her so. You are very like her. Very like her."

I waited for him to say more. To cry. To hold me close, but he didn't. He couldn't, and neither could I.

"Good night, Father."

"Good night."

At breakfast the next morning, Father sat in his usual chair, wearing his uniform with the knife-edged crease in the trousers and drinking strong black coffee while he read a report. I ate my breakfast rolls in silence, every now and then tearing a piece off a roll and dipping it into my cup of hot chocolate. Everything was exactly as it had been before. It was easy to imagine that nothing had changed at all—that Mother was upstairs in her room still asleep and Father and I were eating breakfast alone in the silent dining room just as we had for so many months before. But we knew the truth. Mother was gone, and she would never come back. We didn't speak of her, but there was nothing unusual in that. There were so many things we did not speak of. It had been that way for such a long time.

The clock on the hall struck half past seven. Father gathered together the loose papers and stacked them neatly before taking a last sip of his coffee. "The car will be waiting. I must go. Frau Finkel is coming later to help you with your lessons." He paused and wrinkled his brow. "I suppose we must enroll you in a proper school again next term. There's no reason for you to stay home anymore. Don't wait for me at dinner, Elise. There is so much I must catch up on. So much time lost."

"Yes, Father."

He bent over to kiss the top of my head and left. I sat alone at the long table and finished my bread and chocolate.

A year later I waved good-bye to Father and to the shores of Germany from the gangway of the *SS Deutschland* as she prepared to weigh anchor and sail to America. Actually, that isn't true. I didn't wave good-bye.

New political developments in Germany meant that Father was busier than ever, but Uncle Wilhelm had insisted that Father borrow his car and personal driver to take me and Frau Finkel, who was to be my chaperone, to the dock in Hamburg. Our conversation during the drive was uncomfortable and confined to questions regarding what I had and had not remembered to pack.

When we reached the port, he escorted me to the gangway, told me to be a good girl, shook my hand, and kissed me quickly on the forehead. Then he shook hands with Frau Finkel and disappeared into the waiting staff car. He didn't turn back to look at me. I didn't expect him to. He had already made it clear that his decision was final. "I am an officer, Elise. When war comes, it is my duty to go into battle. You have your duties as well." And well did I know what my duty was—to board the ship with Frau Finkel and follow Father's orders without complaining or questioning, at least not out loud.

Frau Finkel was an old friend of Mother's family. Once she had been wealthy, but the war had left her widowed, and the depression had left her broke. Father hired her as a sort of governess, to help me with my lessons. She'd earned enough to pay for most of her passage to New York. Father paid for the rest in return for having her look after me during the voyage. After delivering me to America, Frau Finkel planned to go and live with her married daughter in Buffalo. I liked the sound of the word *buffalo* and the look of the enormous shaggy beast I had found pictured in *The Children's Encyclopedia of Animals,* but I did not like Frau Finkel. She treated me like a child, and she never stopped talking. As the days passed, the ship seemed smaller and smaller to me because Frau Finkel filled every empty space with the sound of her chatter. By the third day I had simply stopped talking to her.

"Elise! She looks just like your mother! Don't you think so? Her eyes are so deep. So caring. They see right into your soul!"

Frau Finkel was standing behind me and squeezed me tightly as we gazed out past the prow of the ship at the Statue of Liberty. Then she clamped her hands on my shoulders and turned me around to face her, her eyes dripping with sentimentality—and the remains of the cold that had plagued her for the whole of the trip. Leaning down so her brow was level with mine, she said, her voice raspy and confidential, "You must remember this day, Elise. I know you don't want to be here, but you are lucky. You understand? Your father did right to send you to America. You'll be safe now, and you'll be part of a family, a real family. I know you miss your dear mother, but in some ways"—she sighed to herself—"who knows? Maybe it was a blessing . . ."

I glared at the old woman, but she ignored me.

"Anyway, your mother wouldn't want you to go on like this, so angry and silent." Extending a gnarled finger, she pointed toward the mist of the harbor. "When you miss her too much, maybe you can think of that lady out there and you won't feel so lonely." The old lady smiled to herself and sighed theatrically. "The eyes. So caring. Just like dear Lale's."

She is ridiculous, I thought. They were all ridiculous. Soaking wet, with not an umbrella among them, the passengers cheered like schoolboys when they caught sight of her, but Lady Liberty was unmoved by their adulation. She stood her ground, a judging expression on her face as she looked over these newcomers, not sure if she welcomed yet another boatload of uninvited guests to her shores. I couldn't blame her. They were fools, and Frau Finkel was the biggest fool of them all.

The statue was gray and cold and flat. Eyes, hair, dress . . . all the gray-green of seawater. Mother's eyes had been blue, the blue of meadow flowers, so much prettier than my own, which I thought too large and too dark, of a color like melted chocolate. Her hair was dark brown and thick, the same as mine, but she'd worn her braids wound around the back of her head in a coil instead of hanging loose down her back like mine did. She had smelled like the lavender soap she had sent to her from England and menthol lozenges. Her eyebrows were a thin, dark line above her lashes, and the rest of her face looked like . . . I could not remember, anymore, exactly what she had looked like. I could remember pieces of her. Her nose, short and turned up a little at the end. Her lips, fuller than mine. The texture of her skin, white and smooth and delicate as that of a wax doll. Though I remembered each little part of her, I could no longer knit those parts into the whole picture that was my mother, but one thing I knew for certain. She looked nothing like the statue in the harbor.

I turned my gaze away from the water and back toward Frau Finkel, who was still eyeing me hopefully.

"I see no resemblance," I said coldly.

The old woman's left eyebrow shot upward and transformed her syrupy expression to one of irritation. "You are a hard girl, Elise. Stubborn."

She glowered at me, and I glowered back until she grew tired of trying, unsuccessfully, to move me to shame. "Well," she harrumphed. "At least you're finally speaking, though I'm not sure it's an improvement." She eyed me critically, her attempts at establishing a motherly connection between us apparently abandoned. I continued glaring at her stonily.

"Come on," she said with a sigh of resignation, "we might as well go below and pack. I hope Herr Muller is there to meet us. I wish him better luck with you than I've had."

Frau Finkel shuffled off toward the staircase that led to our stateroom. I followed behind but hesitated for a moment before going inside. It suddenly occurred to me that today was May 14th—the same day that Mother had died, the day I would set foot on American soil for the first time. I looked out once more at the face in the harbor, and it stared back at me as though knowing something I did not. The next chapter was beginning.

Chapter 2

1939

"Mr. and Mrs. Muller? Mr. and Mrs. Carl Muller?" The social worker called in a flat, nasal accent that refused to acknowledge the existence or need of the letter R.

She gripped my hand tightly, as though concerned that I might try to run, which meant she was a good judge of character. The idea of bolting away and somehow escaping into the street had crossed my mind, though only briefly. There was no place to run to, no ship that could take me back to the life I had known before. I had no choice but to let go of the social worker's hand and approach the couple who emerged from the crowd of anxious, waiting relatives to greet me—Mother's third cousins, whom she'd never met, from the distant branch of the family tree whose great-grandparents had left Germany decades before.

The man was tall and muscular and approached us in big, confident strides, as though he were crossing a stream by leaping across a path of stones. His eyes were deep brown and flecked with green. His gaze held maturity and intelligence in spite of his boyish grin and loping gait. His suit was clean, but he wore it carelessly, and I could see he'd forgotten to button the bottom button of his vest. He wore a clerical collar, which instantly made me suspicious of him. Father hadn't told me that Mr. Muller was a minister.

Father always said religion was a fine thing for women and children, but that no true man could possibly embrace such superstition. Frau Finkel was an enthusiastic converted Catholic. That alone convinced me that religion was a waste of time and the people who practiced it were mere sheep. But I didn't know what to make of the broad-chested masculinity of the man who approached, whose appearance was a direct contradiction of all my ideas on what clergymen looked like—skinny, bookish, and bespectacled, knowing nothing of industry or discipline. It was all very puzzling.

Except for a smile that was equally broad and warm, the woman beside him was his complete opposite—petite and polite-looking. Her blue suit was simply cut, but she wore it well. The bar pin on her lapel was shiny and polished, and her gloves were beautifully white. She had penciled her eyebrows, just as Mother always had, into a careful arch, and her red lipstick had been perfectly applied. I did not yet know that she had "put on her face," as she called it, just to come to the city and collect me. On the farm there was no time for such vanities, and she only put on lipstick and powder for Sundays and special occasions.

Standing side by side, they were complete contradictions, only their welcoming smiles making them a matched set. They were keeping up appearances, I thought. I didn't want to leave my home and come to America to live with the Mullers, and I couldn't think of any reason they would have wanted me there.

"Yes. Hello. I'm Reverend Muller, and this is my wife, Mrs. Muller." The husband kept looking at me from the corner of his eye even as he tipped his hat to the social worker, revealing a shock of thick red hair that seemed to spring out from all directions when released from under the brim of his crushed homburg. His accent was pleasant to my ear, even though it lacked the soothing vowels of German, those lovely *u*'s that oozed out like thick cream from between layers of sweet pastry, or the preciseness of Germanic consonants.

"You must be Frau Finkel?" he said doubtfully to the social worker, and though my face was a perfect mask of indifference, I smiled inwardly to think that anyone could mistake this pretty, youngish lady with her quick step and starched manner for the ancient and bent Frau Finkel.

"I'm Miss Barnett," the social worker corrected him politely. "I work with the Department of Immigration. Mrs. Finkel came on the ship with the little girl, but she seems to be a bit ill. She'll be kept in our hospital for a few days." Mrs. Muller looked concerned and started to ask a question, but Miss Barnett continued before she could interrupt. "I'm certain it's nothing serious. Most likely just a bad cold, but she must be kept under observation for a few days before we can be certain she is well enough to enter the country. We've notified her family in Buffalo. They'll come and get her just as soon as she is well and can travel."

This time it was Reverend Muller who began to interrupt her, but Miss Barnett was not a woman who was easily steered off course. "You mustn't worry. It's all being taken care of. Besides"—she smiled artificially, anxious to be rid of me and move on to the next case—"I understand that you are here to meet this young lady, aren't you?"

She turned to me and smiled even wider. "Elise, these are the Mullers," she said in broken German that was positively painful to listen to. "You are to go with them now. Do you understand?" She nodded at me helpfully, but my only response was an aloof blink.

"I don't think she speaks any English," Miss Barnett said to the

Mullers. "In fact, she hasn't said a word since she arrived. It must all be very confusing to her."

"Or maybe she hasn't found anything worth saying?" said Mrs. Muller with a knowing smile, addressing her comments to me as though asking a question. Her voice was soft and a bit deep for a woman's. Though her English had none of the musical lilt of the British English my mother had learned from her tutors and had in turn taught to me, I liked the sound of it. This was partly because of the gentleness of her tone, but mostly because, unlike the social worker, she did not talk about me as if I couldn't understand her, even though she had no reason to suppose I could.

"Come, Elise," she said, holding out her hand to me as Reverend Muller picked up the trunk that contained everything I owned. "Let's go home."

Home. Where was that now?

The second I stepped out onto the street from the comfortable limbo of the immigration station the world changed. I have often heard the word "bustling" used in reference to New York City, but that is too pleasant a phrase to describe what I saw that day. Chaos. Pandemonium. Bedlam. Any of those words would do.

Horns honked incessantly, and people talked too loud in an English that was so fast as to be beyond understanding. The buildings were huge—ten times, a hundred times taller than any I'd seen in Berlin. They were awe-inspiring, but only because of their sheer size. I saw no beauty in their construction, only mass. They rose around me like the walls of a vast, inescapable canyon, a valley of shadows that blocked out the sun.

I was terrified. As we waded into an ocean of people, I clutched Mrs. Muller's hand like a sinking swimmer grabbing a rope. All the people were moving—all walking fast and in the same direction, and it seemed to me that we were carried along by the force of the crowd's current. They were all so sure of themselves. A thought flashed in my mind, as bright and clear as the streetlights that were blinking around me: *I am the only one here who doesn't know where he or she is going.*

Suddenly I was conscious of the clothes and faces and manners of everyone around me. Everything about me was different from everything about them, and I realized that they knew this just by looking at me. A man walked by eating what I later came to understand was a hot dog. I thought he was very vulgar to be eating as he walked on the street, and I stared at him. He stared right back. His eyes swept over me, with my long braids and woolen stockings sticking out beneath my skirt, which I suddenly realized was too long. He threw me the same amused and superior smile I had reserved for the country visitors to Berlin. I hated him for his arrogance even as my face colored with shame at this revelation of my own lack of sophistication.

Mrs. Muller must have sensed my discomfort. "It's simply enormous, isn't it?" she said. "I have been to New York several times, and it still makes me feel so small and out of place. It is exciting in a way, but I am always glad to get back to Brightfield."

I was relieved to learn that we would not be staying in New York. There was a whispered conversation between them about there being a train to catch, but it was decided that there was enough time to get something to eat first because they guessed I must be very hungry. I did hear Mrs. Muller mumble under her breath something about not having enough to pay for a restaurant meal in New York, but Reverend Muller said we could go to the Automat and that wouldn't be much. Hearing this exchange made me realize that the Mullers were poor. In my childish self-absorption I wondered, not at their kindness at taking me in despite their own financial strains, but if they had always been poor or had recently become poor. The difference in my mind was important—it marked the boundary between gentility and peasantry.

Many people in Germany, people of good family, had become poor after the war. The cost of everything rose so high and so fast that a loaf of bread that cost a bucket of marks one week might cost a barrelful the next. At least that was what Father had told me. I don't remember it myself. Though we lived in the great house that other Brauns had built in grander days, we were no longer wealthy. But Father made me understand that no matter what happened, I was a Braun, the last in a long and distinguished line of military aristocrats, and I had every reason to be proud of my heritage.

Brauns had occupied our beautiful home on Alexander Platz for five generations. The house was like a museum of our family history. Portraits of generations of Brauns looked down at me from the walls, wondering if I measured up to the family name. Nothing ever changed in our house. Worn fabrics weren't replaced. Chipped china was ignored. Growing up, I thought it was out of respect for history, but now I realize there were other reasons for this. Mother was simply too ill to oversee the care of such a large home, and the cost of her medical care must have been significant, forbidding any possibility of remodeling or refurbishing. In spite of our reduced circumstances, however, Father insisted we maintain our standards and our dignity. Our home was always ordered and formal. How shall I explain it? It was very German, just like Father. Things were run predictably and efficiently with a minimum of emotion and drama, utterly different than the chaotic world I now found myself plunged into.

Yet, in spite of my fear and confusion, there was something exciting about finding myself carried along on a tide of scurrying New Yorkers. The streets vibrated with an urgency completely unknown on the tree-lined boulevards of Berlin. Everyone here seemed to be in hot pursuit of something terribly important.

The Automat was the first thing I truly liked about America. In every space that wasn't taken up by tables were shiny white machines with glass fronts and rows and rows of food, each in its own separate, lighted compartment, sitting on a clean white plate. All you had to do was put in some money, pull a lever to choose what you wanted, and a door would open, so you could take your food out, all ready to eat. It was as though in America people simply wished for food and it appeared before their eyes like magic. As if just thinking about a thing would make it so.

I was fourteen, too big to believe in fairy stories, but I couldn't help myself—I wished on a piece of chocolate cake. *Let me go home,* I thought. Then I remembered the realities of the situation and the cold kiss Father had planted on my forehead as he said good-bye. Going home was impossible, at least for a while. I added a codicil to my wish, which at the time seemed only slightly less probable than my leaving America soon. *Or let me like it here.*

We took a train to Hartford, and when we arrived at the station, Reverend Muller carried my trunk himself rather than paying a porter to do it. He had a black Ford truck that was far from new. I had never ridden in a truck. I did not think Father would approve of me doing so, as though I were some sort of delivery person, but I had no choice. Reverend Muller boosted me up into the cab. The engine sputtered rather than hummed, and the ride was bumpy. I sat wedged between the Mullers, watching the scenery go by.

At first I did not like New England. The buildings in Hartford seemed as devoid of ornamentation and artistic sense as the skyscrapers of New York. The edifices I saw out of the passenger window of the Mullers' Ford were utilitarian at best.

I despaired to think that the whole of America might be like this, but as we reached the edge of the city and headed north, the landscape began to change. Buildings were spaced farther apart and gave way to houses that boasted small gardens and trees. We passed a sign that said "Welcome to Massachusetts" and drove into a land of farmhouses and fields, canopies of oaks, and pastures enclosed by miles and miles of stone walls. I could not help but crane my neck to get a better view. The scenery was beautiful, though it lacked the order and settled look of German farmland. In spite of the stone walls that stood as a solid, ancient testament to man's long struggle to tame the land, there was a wild, almost junglelike quality to the scene. The battle between man and nature was still very much in progress here, and it was anyone's guess as to which side would prevail.

In the village of Brightfield—it could not in all honesty be called a town—man had clearly gained the upper hand. Nothing could have been more settled and orderly-looking. Though I later came to realize that in architecture and design it was much like any other small New England village, it seemed to me that day, as it still does, to possess a unique charm.

The houses stood side by side on small town lots that were perfectly equal in size, and there seemed to be only one acceptable color for any dwelling—white. More latitude was granted on the subject of shutters. Here the owner could have a choice, black or dark green or any color within that narrow spectrum. The whole effect was enchanting and deliberate, as welcoming as a table set with matching china.

The center of town was a parklike rectangle of grass ringed on three sides by gnarled apple trees that had long since ceased to produce fruit. The park's fourth side was dominated by a monument to the dead of various wars. Although I still had not spoken to her, Mrs. Muller explained that the park in the center was fittingly called "the green." The streets of Brightfield extended from the green like spokes on a wheel, with the oldest inhabitants occupying the houses closest to the center and the newcomers residing on side streets in concentric circles around it.

"Not that there are many circles," she said, laughing gaily, her blue eyes twinkling. "I don't suppose there are more than a thousand people living in town, perhaps three thousand including the outlying farms.

"The church is here on the green, of course, but our home is a farmhouse outside the center of town. It is small and cozy, but we've got plenty of land for the children to roam, nearly fifteen acres on the river. There are some lovely views, and when the weather gets just a little warmer, you can go swimming."

Though I did not even nod my understanding or look in her direction, Mrs. Muller continued her monologue in a tone that was calm and informative, nothing like the mindless chatter of Frau Finkel. Reverend Muller spoke not at all but seemed content to serve as a smiling chauffer on our tour of Brightfield. I wondered silently where the school was and, as if reading my mind, Mrs. Muller answered the unspoken question.

"The school is on the outskirts of town. You'll see it soon enough. We are lucky, as it is only a short walk from the house. Even when the snow is deep, it won't take you more than ten or fifteen minutes to get there." Snow? It was strange to think that snow could ever fall here. Though it was only late spring, the air was already hot and sticky with moisture.

"We'll get a lot of snow when winter comes. The children have great fun sledding." She smiled at me in the mirror before continuing the tour.

"As you can see, the green is surrounded by four streets. Main and Meadow are there on the long sides of the rectangle. Main is where the shops and businesses are—not that there are many of them, but we do have a few stores. Meadow is all houses, and, as I said, the oldest families in town live there. 'Yankees,' we call them. That big stone building to the south on Washington Street is the town hall. It has a couple of offices, a courtroom, and a lending library in the basement that is open three afternoons a week. And here on the north end of town on Duke Street is our church. Reverend Muller is pastor here."

As she finished speaking, Reverend Muller pulled up to the curb. We stepped out of the car. The church sat dignified and firm at the end of a short expanse of lawn, the green anchored by its stately presence. The steps leading up to the wide black doors were balanced by two sets of gothic columns, pristine with white paint, as was the church's clapboard siding. The steeple was not really that tall, but in relation to the rest of the landscape it was a commanding presence, pointing skyward, a finger that existed to turn men's attention to heaven. All my life I had lived in the shadow of great monasteries and cathedrals, but none of them possessed the elegance or simple grace of this plain, white clapboard church standing at the edge of a New England village green.

As we entered the sanctuary, I felt a great sense of peace. Inside, there were no impressive stone carvings or gilded statues with mournful faces, only rows and rows of waxed and shining wooden pews glowing in the light that spilled in through the tall, arched windows. The air was perfumed ever so faintly with a scent of lemon oil and old floral arrangements. The view of the tree canopy outside the window and the outline of the hills in the distance was much more beautiful than any scene in stained glass could have been. The Mullers watched as I walked up the aisle toward the simple altar with its plain, unadorned wooden cross.

I saw the piano sitting to one side, clean and curved and gleaming ebony black. Without thinking, I reached for the keyboard. The lid lay open, revealing lovely carved hammers clothed in green velvet and touches of brass. Without striking a note, I knew how rich and full the tone would be, how quick and light the action of the keys.

"It is so beautiful," I breathed in English. "May I play it?"

Reverend Muller grinned at his wife and bounded toward me, swept me off my feet, and deposited me on the piano bench. "Of course you may," he said. "You may play as much as you want."

Chapter 3

Seven pairs of eyes fixed upon me as I descended the stairs into the Muller kitchen the next morning. The whole family was seated around a big table in the kitchen. There didn't seem to be a dining room. There was a smell of bacon lingering in the air, but the plates were all cleared except for two cups of coffee that sat before Reverend and Mrs. Muller.

Clearly I had slept through breakfast. I was embarrassed to be so late and to feel the eyes of the Mullers' five children following my every move with as much curious interest as if I'd been an animal on exhibit at the zoo.

True to his word, Reverend Muller had let me play as long as I wanted, piece after piece, Beethoven, Brahms, Purcell, and, of course, Mozart. I played all the music my mother had taught me. Then I played everything I'd taught myself after she became too ill to sit at the bench beside me, when I had played to ease her pain and my own because it was the only remedy I knew, then or now. I played furiously, giving myself up to the music, pouring all my frustrations into the keyboard.

The Mullers listened patiently, never urging me to finish up, never looking at their watches. They just sat in the front pew and listened.

By the time I'd finished and we left the church, the trees were making lacy shadows on the ground. I was exhausted. I must have fallen asleep in the truck because I didn't remember the drive to the Mullers' house or getting into the small bed with the strange coverlet decorated with multicolored stars that I later learned was called a quilt.

In the morning I woke to the sound of cutlery clinking against plates and the murmur of conversation. I heard many different voices downstairs and supposed I must be the only one who was still in bed. I got up, rebraided my hair as quickly as I could, and put on the blouse and skirt that were laid out for me at the end of my bed.

Mrs. Muller was the first to spot me standing tentatively at the foot of the stairs. "Good morning, Elise. Did you sleep well?" she asked cheerily. I nodded. "Good. You were so tired last night that we didn't bother to wake you for supper. You must be hungry. I'll get you an egg and some toast."

I looked around for a maid or cook, but apparently Mrs. Muller intended to make my breakfast herself. She reached for an apron that hung on a hook near the stove and started pulling bowls and plates off a shelf. "Carl, why don't you make the introductions."

Reverend Muller drained the last of his coffee in one gulp and held out the empty cup for his wife to refill. "All right. Let's start with the oldest," he said, gesturing to the boy on his right, who was, like his father, tall and well-muscled, but the resemblance ended there. In fact, he looked almost nothing like his father or any of his siblings. In place of their unruly, reddish to auburn curls and blue eyes, this boy had serious dark eyes and a head of thick, straight hair in a shade of brown that was close to my own. The other Mullers were light-skinned and, except for the girl, freckled. Spring had only just begun, yet this boy was already bronzed by the sun. I thought he must be at least seventeen, but I later learned he'd only turned fifteen a few weeks before. "This is Carl Muller the third, but everyone just calls him Junior. It's less confusing that way." Junior nodded his head in greeting, but his eyes darted away when they met mine. He seemed shy.

"Next is Coral, our only daughter. You two are just about the same age."

Coral's hair was done in two long braids down her back, but that was the only girl-like thing about her appearance. She wore blue denim coveralls, just like her brothers and, like them, had her father's red hair and her mother's heart-shaped face and blue eyes. In spite of her red hair, she didn't have a single freckle. Her complexion was china-doll pink.

She smiled at me easily, "Nobody calls me Coral except Papa. Just call me Cookie. You're fourteen, too?" she inquired. Then, without waiting for an answer, said, "We'll be in the same class at school in the fall. We'll have Miss Gleason as our teacher next year. She is the nicest in the school. You'll like her." The girl was so friendly and outgoing that I couldn't help but smile back at her even while I wondered at her strange clothes and even stranger name. What in the world did "Cookie" mean?

Reverend Muller continued with his introductions. "Those two troublemakers sitting near the stove are the twins, Charles and Chester, but everyone calls them Chuck and Chip." The two boys looked as much alike as two bookends. It would not take me long to realize that the twin who was talking was probably Chip, and the one who stood by nodding in agreement was probably Chuck. However, at that time I wondered how I would ever be able to tell them apart, and if anyone in this country was actually called by the name they'd been born with.

"Watch out for the twins, Elise," their father said with mock seriousness. "They are always into some kind of mischief. Speaking of which, where is my new screwdriver? I can't find it anywhere."

"We needed it to tighten up the wheels on the go-cart," said Chuck or Chip through a mouthful of eggs.

"Well, it had better be back in my toolbox where it belongs before supper tonight," said Reverend Muller, examining the boys over the top of his eyeglasses. "Do I make myself clear?" The twins assured him in unison that he had. The reverend turned his attention to the smallest boy, who was sitting at the end of the table nearest to his mother.

"This is Curt. He'll be six years old next month. Won't you, Curt? Can you say hello to your cousin Elise?" Reverend Muller said hopefully. He spoke more gently than he had to his other children. The little boy didn't answer, just looked at me with wide, wondering eyes. In spite of his silence, there was something wise and curious in his gaze. I liked him. "Curt isn't much of a talker," his father explained to me.

"That is all right," I said, smiling at the little one. "I don't talk much, either. There is so much to learn by listening."

"There certainly is," Mrs. Muller said as she set a plate piled high with eggs and bacon in front of me. The whole family cheered in agreement, then proceeded to talk all at once, with no one listening to anyone else. I ate my breakfast silently, keeping my eyes on my plate, but after a few minutes I sensed someone's stare and looked up to see Junior's distrustful gaze boring into me.

The empty bed that I'd seen next to mine turned out to belong to Cookie. Until my arrival she'd had the whole room to herself while her brothers shared a long, low room lined with beds that stacked one upon the other, like a dormitory in a boarding school.

Being an only child, I'd always had my own room, but Cookie

said she didn't mind sharing with me—in fact, she seemed to welcome the company. "It's been nothing but boys around here forever!" she exclaimed, "I've always wanted a sister."

She was a great talker and as friendly as everyone else in the family. The Mullers were all as nice as could be. Even little Curt, who rarely spoke, gave me a shy smile whenever I looked his way. Only Junior seemed a bit cold and aloof, but that didn't bother me. Besides, with so many people trying so hard to get me to talk to them, it was a relief to have at least one who seemed content to maintain his distance.

I knew the Mullers were very kind to take me in, yet I couldn't help but feel that their manners and way of life were awfully crude. There were no servants of any kind. Mrs. Muller did all the cooking and housework. She seemed always to be in the kitchen. The children helped her, and they all had jobs to do every day, but Mrs. Muller didn't assign any tasks to me, and I didn't offer to help, not sure what I should do. Once I heard Junior ask his mother why he had to help Cookie hang out the wash when I was just sitting around reading, but Mrs. Muller shushed him and said something about giving me time to get my bearings. Junior scowled in my direction as he carried the laundry basket outside. I pretended not to hear or see him.

Cookie spent more time in the kitchen than the boys, but they all were expected to take their turn clearing the dinner table and washing the dishes. I'd never washed a dish in my life and was embarrassed for the Muller boys to be caught drying pots and pans, especially since they didn't seem to have the good manners to be embarrassed for themselves. Such a thing would never have happened in my home, and I knew if Father had seen the careless way the Muller boys were being brought up, he would certainly have disapproved.

He would also have disapproved of the way all the children were allowed to run wild. They were forever shouting and jumping, playing tricks on one another, sliding down the banisters instead of walking politely down the stairs. Cookie was more like a boy than any girl I'd ever met. True, she was always available when her mother needed a hand in the kitchen and seemed very capable, too, but she never wore a dress unless she was going to school or to church. She played baseball along with her brothers, sliding into the bases just as they did and getting just as dirty.

A few weeks after my arrival, I sat under a nearby oak tree reading while the Muller children engaged in their daily baseball game. The game seemed silly to me, and I couldn't understand why the Mullers loved it so. One of the twins, either Chip or Chuck—I still couldn't tell the difference between them—ran over to where I was sitting and offered to teach me to play. I said no, thank you, and that I preferred to read.

"Aw, c'mon, Elise," he urged. "If you played outfield, we'd have enough people so I could play catcher. It would make the whole game go a lot faster."

Cookie ran over to add her plea to her brother's. "Oh, yes, Elise! Come and play. It really isn't hard at all. You'd catch on in no time. Besides, nobody ever hits anything into the outfield except Junior, and even when he does, we don't really keep score, so it doesn't matter."

"That's not true," the twin objected, giving his sister a shove with his elbow. "I hit it there all the time. Last week I hit it clear over past the barn, and it took you so long to throw it in, I coulda walked to homeplate,"

"Chip, that wasn't a fair hit, and you know it," Cookie argued. "The right side of the barn is the foul line, but you ran in anyway. Junior said it didn't count."

Chip scowled. "It did too. What does Junior know, anyway? Who died and made him the ref?"

"Well, I guess he knows more about baseball than you do," Cookie returned sourly.

"Does not!" yelled Chip, giving his sister a shove.

"Does too!" shouted Cookie and shoved him even harder. They kept shouting and shoving with increasing ferocity until it seemed they were on the verge of an out-and-out fistfight. Mr. Muller heard the noise and came out onto the porch to investigate, but Junior ran over to break his siblings apart just as Cookie bit into Chip's hand, which was pulling on her braid.

I was shocked. At home a girl would never even dream of pushing a boy, let alone biting him.

"What's going on here? Knock it off, you two hotheads!" Junior pried the combatants apart. Chip and Cookie backed away as their brother stepped between them, but they were still panting with emotion. Cookie was the first to speak,

"Chip wanted to teach Elise to play ball, and I said she should, too. I said she could play outfield because nobody ever hits it out there except you,"

"That's not true! I hit one way past the barn last week!" Chip shouted, lunging for Cookie's braid again. For a moment it seemed like the fight was on again until Junior wedged himself between his siblings.

"Stop it, Chip!" Junior commanded, and, amazingly, Chip did. "That hit you had last week was foul, and you know it," he added.

Chip scowled, and Cookie stuck her tongue out at him in victory, but Junior froze her with a look. "It's not true that nobody hits into the outfield but me. Last summer Chip must have hit eight or nine homers. It's just the beginning of the season. He'll start clobbering 'em any day now. He's just in a slump. Happens to all ball players."

He ruffled the hair on the top of his brother's head, and Chip looked at him with half a smile, then shot a triumphant look at his sister.

"Well," said Cookie, trying to recover her command of the situation, "that's no reason Elise shouldn't play outfield. We could use the extra player."

Just as I opened my mouth to decline the offer, Junior interrupted. "She can't play," he said, shaking his head as though they were crazy even to think it.

"Why not?" Chip and Cookie asked simultaneously.

"Well, just look at her!" Junior spat contemptuously. By now the other children had moved off the field and stood nearby, watching the conference. They all turned to look at me studiously, trying hard to catch a glimpse of whatever had made me defective in their brother's eyes.

"She's no ballplayer! She's hardly even a kid. Never plays. Never runs. Never hollers. Just sits reading her book and thinking how much better she is than the rest of us. She thinks she's too good to talk to us, never mind running after a ball. She might muss her dress or something. Isn't that right, Fraulein Perfect?" he said, laying on a thick imitation of my German accent.

Five sets of eyes bored into me, four of them questioning, one judging. I felt my cheeks go scarlet with embarrassment that quickly turned to irritation. "I should hope I'm not a 'kid,' as you call it. Isn't that another name for a goat? That just about fits you! My parents brought me up to behave like a young lady, not a wild Indian. I am not perfect. I never said I was, but at least I know I'm a girl!"

As soon as I spoke, I saw the wounded expression spread across Cookie's face and I wished I could take back my words.

"What's that supposed to mean?" asked Junior, his eyes narrowing.

Searching for something to say and knowing that every answer was the wrong one, I opened and closed my mouth like a landed fish, gasping for air.

"I know what she means," Cookie said softly, her eyes filling with tears. "You mean me, don't you, Elise? You think I don't know I'm a girl."

Before I could protest or explain, she ran into the house, dropping her baseball glove on the ground. I felt awful.

Chip, who had been ready to knock his sister into the dirt only a few minutes before, cast a look of pure hatred in my direction, picked up Cookie's glove, and followed her into the house. The remaining Mullers trailed behind in a line of hostility with Junior taking up the rear.

"A properly brought up young lady?" he sneered. "Yeah, and I'm sure your Herr Hitler is a real gentleman. Your father is an officer in the German army, isn't he? I'm sure all those Austrians whose country you invaded think real highly of German manners." He laughed derisively. "I've already seen enough of the manners of proper German young ladies to last me a lifetime. If that's what you are, give me a plain old American girl any day of the week." He marched off with the rest of his siblings and left me standing alone.

I was furious with Junior for insulting Father and confused about his reference to Germany invading Austria. We'd freed the Austrians, not invaded them. At the school I'd attended after Mother died, I'd seen a film showing crowds of Austrians cheering the German troops and giving them flowers. I simply didn't understand what Junior was talking about, and the more I thought about Junior's cutting words, the angrier I became.

But I was also genuinely and deeply ashamed of myself for hurting Cookie's feelings. That was the last thing I wanted to do. Even though she was such an odd girl, she had never shown me anything but kindness and generosity.

I was suddenly and deeply homesick.

I didn't understand these strange children and their strange ways. I longed for a good German meal with sausages and sauerkraut and chewy rye bread, or a strudel dripping with the juice of sweetened apples. My head ached from the effort of speaking and listening to English all day long. I would have given anything to turn on the radio and hear a song by Erna Sack or Lale Anderson . . . or one more glimpse of Mother.

Somewhere a screen door slammed, and the noise frightened the birds roosting in the oak tree. They took to the sky in a sudden furious flutter of wings and startled chirruping, sounding exactly like the birds that lived in the tree outside my window at home. I turned my head to follow them as they flew away. A tear seeped from the corner of my eye. Father would have been ashamed of me, but I couldn't help myself. Just then, a hand thrust a clean white handkerchief in front of my face. It was Reverend Muller.

"Here," he said shoving the handkerchief into my hand. I took it, quickly wiped my eyes and nose, and returned it to him, ashamed that he had caught me crying.

"Wonderful thing about the sky," he said as his face turned to follow the flight of the sparrows. "It looks the same everywhere. Landscapes are different, they are so variable, but if you are in Brightfield, or Berlin, or Bangkok, heaven is the same clear blue." He stood looking up for a long time before speaking again. "I've been to Europe, you know. France."

"You have? When?" I asked in surprise.

"During the war. I was a soldier, but I didn't see much action. I had sort of a desk job."

I didn't know what to make of this. I liked Reverend Muller. He seemed so nice, but it was hard to think of him as a soldier, fighting Germans.

"Junior hates Germans," I said gloomily. "He hates me."

"No," Reverend Muller replied. "Junior is just young, and he gets easily fired up. Fifteen-year-old boys are very passionate and very righteous."

I didn't really understand what he meant, but I knew he was trying to make me feel better. "Do you hate Germans?" I asked. "Do you think we are invaders?"

"Of course I don't hate Germans," he answered easily, as though the question was too silly for serious consideration. "Half the people in my church are of German ancestry. My own father was born there. Even if I don't agree with German politics, I certainly don't hate Germans. It's wrong to hate anyone, and it's especially wrong to hold a little girl responsible for tides of history that are beyond her understanding or control."

I wasn't sure I liked being called a little girl and was about to say something to that effect, but I thought that would be rude. Instead I studied a bank of white clouds suspended in the sapphire canvas above us.

We stood there a long moment before the reverend took up the conversation again. "When I was in Europe and homesick, it made me feel better to look up and realize that the clouds and sun and stars and sky there looked just the same in Brightfield. It was as if God wanted to remind me that no matter how far from home I was, He was watching over me. "

"My father doesn't believe in God," I murmured.

"Hmmm," Reverend Muller rumbled distractedly, his eyes still scanning the horizon. "What do you believe?"

"I'm not sure. I never really thought about it."

"Lots of people never do," he said simply. "I guess it's the sort of thing a person has to decide for themselves. You can't just rely on the opinions of others. Now, for me, when I look at the sky and the trees, the river as it flows by nourishing the earth, the faces of my children, and your face," he said, turning to me with a smile, "each so unique and precious, no more alike than any two snowflakes and each one a miracle of creation, I just know that God exists and that He is good."

"Is it that easy for you?" I asked, surprised and genuinely interested. This was a brand of theology that bore no resemblance to the dull litany of saints, church history, and confusing theories that Frau Finkel, who was devout and insistent in her attempts to convert me, had recited to me.

Reverend Muller tilted his head to one side and paused for a moment before answering. "Not quite so easy, at least not all the time, but a beautiful sky helps. It gives me faith that God is in heaven and things will turn out all right in the end."

I didn't know how to answer him, or even if he expected me to. I looked at the sky again. It did look just exactly the same as it did at home. I felt a little better. I stood admiring the view for several moments before I remembered with dread that I couldn't just stay there. It was almost lunchtime. At any moment Mrs. Muller would be calling me inside, where I would be forced to face an undoubtedly stony reception by the children.

"Elise," said Reverend Muller, "I need to finish my sermon for Sunday, but it's too noisy to work at home. Far too many battles going on outside the window of my study," he commented with pretended seriousness. I couldn't help but blush a little at his observation. "I have just decided I'm going to the church where I can finish my work in peace. Would you like to come with me? Maybe we'll drive by the river on the way. Have you been down to the river yet?"

"No."

"Well, you've got to see the river! We won't have time for a swim today, but you should see it. It's just beautiful. Then we could stop off at the café for an egg cream. After that you could go to the library and check out some more books, or you could sit in the sanctuary and play the piano. Nobody's there on a Tuesday, so you wouldn't be disturbed."

I didn't know exactly what an egg cream was, but my heart leapt at the thought of being able to play that beautiful piano again. Even so, I was hesitant to accept his invitation. "Wouldn't I be bothering you?" I asked doubtfully. "You said you couldn't work with so much noise going on."

He grinned. "Elise, listening to my children argue about foul balls is noise. Listening to you play . . . Well," he said, his tone softening slightly and his grin fading, "that is inspiration. I'm not sure I've ever heard anything like it.

"This will probably be the best sermon I've ever written." His eyes twinkled. "What do you say? Are you coming to town with me, or are you going to spend the rest of the day standing under this tree?"

I couldn't help but laugh. "I think I'd rather go with you, Reverend Muller."

"Good! I'll get the keys to the car. " He turned to go but stopped short as if remembering something. "Elise, you know, you might be with us for a while, and it seems awfully formal, calling us Reverend and Mrs. Muller. If you want, you could call us Papa and Mama, same as the other kids."

I hesitated for a moment, trying to imagine how Reverend Muller had looked when he was young, dressed in a soldier's uniform, carrying a gun that could kill another young soldier, but I couldn't conjure up the image. All I could see was a kind man with a kind face.

"Yes," I said slowly. "I would like that. If you are sure you don't mind."

"I don't mind at all. In fact, I'm pleased," he said, grinning as if he really was. "Now you wait here, and I'll be back in a jiffy."

I watched him walk toward the house with his long, loping strides and made a mental note to ask him what a "jiffy" meant when he returned. As the screen door slammed behind him, the few sparrows that had returned to the oak tree were startled again and fluttered from the branches. I watched them rise over the treetops and wondered what time it was on Alexander Platz and if the skies were blue there, too.

I stood on the hill, with the landscape laid out before me like an impressionist painting—an idea of a river at the center of the canvas, a collection of colors blending one into another, a melted sunlight dream of a river that twisted and turned, making its own way wherever it pleased. Its banks were littered with branches and streaked with swatches of gray sediment where the waters had become impatient within their boundaries and spilled over onto the land, just to prove they could. The riverbank rose gradually, in steplike grades, until sandy shores gave way to mile upon mile of green velvet fields, flat and fertile, stretching to the edge of the valley floor, where they suddenly met the tree line. At that point the land sloped sharply higher, and trees in a hundreds of shades of green, from moss to sage, olive to emerald, stood row upon row. Each tree gazed over the head of the one in front of it, like spectators in a stadium peering at the spectacle below.

"People say it is one of the three most beautiful rivers in the world, but I can't imagine how there could be a river more beautiful than this." Papa pointed to the green valley floor. "Those are tobacco fields. One way or another, nearly everyone in Brightfield depends on tobacco for their living. The Indians were growing it when the Pilgrims landed, though not in any great quantity or quality. Yankee farmers have cultivated tobacco as a cash crop since the early eighteen hundreds. Immigrants, like my father and Mrs. Muller's grandparents, came later to work in the fields as laborers and then stayed on and bought farms of their own. We're mostly German stock here in Brightfield, but Connecticut River Valley tobacco has attracted a whole melting pot of people looking for a chance: Poles, Czechs, Russians, Jamaicans, to name a few."

Papa paused and smiled to himself. "I used to work in these fields when I was a boy. It's hard work, let me tell you, but this tobacco is some of the best in the world for cigars. See those long tents in that field over there?" He pointed east. I saw an enormous rectangle of what looked like fine, white linen surrounded by a sea of green tobacco plants, as though an alpine ski run and a tropical forest sat side by side and you could choose your climate by crossing from one to the other whenever you grew too hot or too cold.

"Those are shade tents, where they grow tobacco for cigar wrappers. Those tents protect the leaves from the sun and make the climate inside as moist and warm as it is in the tropics. Shade-grown wrappers fetch a high price, but they are expensive to cultivate and an awful lot of work."

"Now, farther out on the edge of that same field," he continued, and my eye followed where his finger was pointing at several long, narrow houses without windows, "is a tobacco shed. These plants are just starting to grow. When they are ready for harvest they'll stand taller than I do. The plants will be cut, sewn onto lathes, and hung in those barns to dry. The walls of the shed look solid, but they actually open up to let the air in, something like a shutter that can be louvered open to let in the light. That helps the tobacco dry at the right speed and temperature."

When Papa finished speaking, I climbed to the very crest of the hill for a better view. The valley spread beneath my feet like a gift, so lovely and serene it seemed almost a thing imagined rather than seen. Papa let me look for a long time. Finally he said, "It's pretty, isn't it."

"Oh no," I breathed in wonder, "pretty isn't nearly word enough for it. It's . . . it's . . ." I searched my brain for just the right word, but every one I thought of seemed pale and colorless when laid against the scene below. "It's like . . ."

"Heaven?" Papa offered.

"Is it?" I turned and asked hopefully, searching his face, wanting it to be true, wanting him to know the truth.

"I have read a great deal about it. Christ spoke of heaven as an exquisite place, a place of peace, in the very presence of God. A place of eternal satisfaction and ultimate fulfillment, lovely beyond imagining. I don't know what it will be like," he admitted and lifted his eyes to the horizon. "No one does. But it must be an awful lot like this."

Chapter 4

The summer seemed endless. The other children spoke to me only when it was absolutely necessary, which is to say just often enough to keep from being lectured by their parents. I am sure the Mullers were aware of the tension between us, but the children were perfectly polite to me in their presence, so they could hardly complain of their behavior. Once or twice Curt, who was really too little to understand what the disagreement was about and too sweet to hold a grudge for long, made a friendly overture to me, but whenever he would smile or try to speak with me, one of his siblings would glare at him and his face would freeze in a solemn, slightly perplexed expression.

I was not invited to play in any more baseball games, which certainly didn't bother me. I much preferred taking long walks by the river. Sometimes I ran the whole way because I was so curious to see how much higher the fields had grown since the day before. When I got there I would strip off my shoes and socks to wade in the cool, welcoming water. When the wind moved through the trees, the whole valley was alive. The leaves of the trees lifted and fell in rhythm with the whistling wind, like breath rising and falling in the body of the earth. It was lovely and secret and awfully lonely.

Reverend and Mrs. Muller, whom I now called Mama and Papa, as they had requested, were very kind to me. Papa took me to Brightfield every Tuesday so I could go to the library. After selecting my books, I would walk across the green to the church and play piano until Papa emerged from his study and said it was time to go home. I played the songs my mother had taught me, all the pieces I had played to help her forget her pain, and while my fingers floated across the keys, I was able to forget, too.

I did everything I could think of to win my way back into Cookie's good graces, even trying to help with the household chores, but having grown up in a house run by servants, I was hopeless at anything domestic. When setting the table, I could never remember where the silverware went, so Cookie would have to redo the whole job. Wet dishes seemed to leap from my hands every time I tried to dry them. Once, after I'd broken yet another glass, Cookie glared at me and said, "Just leave them! If you keep helping, we won't have any left."

After that I just sat in the parlor and read after supper. Mostly I read books that I had borrowed from the library and newspapers that seemed to be full of nothing but war and rumors of war. The papers presented Germany in such a completely different light than I was accustomed to that I sometimes wondered if I was mistranslating the words. They spoke of German aggression and of the German invasion of Austria and the occupation of Czechoslovakia, operations that my teachers at home had called liberations. I didn't understand how these American newspapers could be so ill informed. Still, I continued to read the papers because, as upsetting as they were, they provided me with some idea of what was going on at home—certainly more than Father's letters did.

His letters read like field reports, noting the date, followed by a vague but always positive assessment how his work was progressing, his health, the weather conditions, and closing with an admonition regarding my behavior, and the words, "Your Father, Herman C. Braun."

The formality of his postscript always made me wonder if he was trying to remind himself or me of our paternal relationship. His letters left me disappointed and adrift. After reading them I would sit silently, staring out the parlor window, hearing the laughter of the children as they played "kick the can" in the evening shadows and wishing the sun would set so I would be through with one more day.

I was sitting just like that one evening in mid-August when Mama stuck her head around the parlor door frame looking for me. "There you are, Elise. What are you doing hiding in here? If you want to read, you should go outside on the porch where it's cool."

"Oh . . . I don't mind," I stammered unconvincingly, folding up Papa's letter quickly and stuffing it into the pocket of my skirt. "I am more comfortable in here."

Mama sat down next to me on the sofa and laid her hand on my shoulder. "Elise, I know it must be terribly hard for you, being so far away from your family and having to adjust to a whole new culture. I want you to know that I'm glad you're here, and if you ever want to talk, I'll always be ready to listen. And if the other children are giving you a hard time, you should come to me and tell me. All right?"

"Thank you, but I'm fine. Really. Everyone has been very kind to me." Mama was well intentioned, but the last thing I was going to do was tattle on the other children. That would only make things worse.

Mama drew her brows together for a moment, not believing me, but then she smiled, looking suddenly younger. I could see that once she had been as pretty as Cookie, even prettier. "Oh, I almost forgot what I came in to tell you!" she said excitedly. "Run get your hat. We're all going to the movies!"

The theater was like a cathedral. The walls were decorated with murals of angelic creatures floating in a sky that was bluer and more brilliant than any sky could be. Nymphs danced with arms upraised toward a celestial ceiling that soared forty feet overhead, pricked with stars that glinted gold and silver on a field of midnight. The front of the theater was a large proscenium arch carved with serpentine waves and flanked on either side by more angels, carved from wood and painted with what looked like layers of melted gold, their necks straining forward as if to catch the wind on their faces, as though they were leading the prow of a great ship.

The lobby was filled with laughter and conversation as people worked out the arrangements of who was to sit where or decided what candy to buy, but a hush came over the crowd when they entered the splendor of the auditorium. They passed quietly through the aisles that parted the sea of red velvet upholstery and meekly chose their seats.

We wore our Sunday clothes and manners. Even Chip and Chuck were perfectly well behaved and settled quietly in their seats, waiting for something wonderful to happen. The scent of hot butter and popcorn seemed incongruous in the semi-sacred surroundings, but the smell was irresistible. People quietly munched stolen bites from the paper boxes of popcorn and held whispered conversations with their neighbors as they waited for the picture to begin.

There must have been a thousand people in the theater and all the seats were filled, but even the whispering ceased and the audience became dead silent when the lights dimmed. Then the spots in front warmed the red velvet and gold braid of the proscenium curtain, which levitated smoothly from the stage in heavy scallops to display still another curtain, this one of white silk, which parted to reveal the opening scene of the film. The screen was filled by a breathtaking cloud-swept sky stretching twenty feet high and twice as wide, made even more splendid by the music of the orchestra that swelled and ebbed like winds across a plain. I was entranced.

I've since heard people say that the *Wizard of Oz* was about the Depression, or populism, or American isolationism in the face of war. Maybe it was. For me, it was about Dorothy.

She had been carried away from everything she knew by forces she couldn't control. She wanted to go home, yet was trapped in a world full of people and customs she didn't understand. Dorothy was alone and lost, just like me. She sang about the world that she came from, the past she couldn't recapture, in a land so far away that its only address was "over a rainbow." She sang the song I couldn't sing for myself. Instead, I wept the tears that my celluloid soul mate was too brave to shed. I could, because it was dark in the theater, and I didn't have to be brave if no one was watching. I cried silently so no one would know what I was feeling.

I reached up carefully to lay my hand against my wet cheek in a gesture that I hoped would seem casual and unrelated to the scene on the screen. I saw a teardrop seeping from Cookie's eyes, too.

Chapter 5

That year it seemed as if nature itself shared my confusion. It wavered between hot and cold, unable to settle on a plan and stick to it. One August night we went to bed sweltering and woke up shivering. It was still dark when an urgent knock sounded on the door of the room where Cookie and I were sleeping. Mama handed us sweaters thick with the smell of mothballs and in a voice that was brusque and worried, told us to put them on quickly.

"Hurry downstairs and eat your breakfast, girls. Papa and the boys are already up and dressed. We're all going over to the Schollers' farm to see if we can't help bring in some of the tobacco before it's too late." The darkness and cold left us dazed, and we moved slowly, still not quite understanding why we were being roused from sleep. Mama turned sharply and snapped urgently, "Hurry, girls! We need every set of hands. The Schollers took out a mortgage to build shade tents. If they lose their crop, they could lose the farm, too." She rushed out of the room and down the stairs. We pulled on our warm clothes and followed behind.

As the Mullers' truck made the turn down the dirt road to the Scholler farm, I felt nervous, afraid I was about to embark on yet another occupation that would make me look foolish. If I couldn't manage to dry a dish without dropping it, I could only imagine what a disaster I'd be at tobacco harvesting.

We arrived at the Schollers'. It was decided that everyone should work on the broadleaf fields first, trying to harvest what we could before the frost ruined the leaves, and then tackle the job of harvesting the shade-grown tobacco, which was only about a quarter of the total crop.

Papa gathered us around him to explain the plan while Mr. Scholler, who wore a dirty plaid shirt and a worried expression, began bringing tobacco carts into the fields.

"It's warmer under those shade tents than out in the open. That should protect the plants from the cold for a while at least. We can tackle that tomorrow or the next day, after we finish working in the open field. If we can salvage a good portion of the broadleaf and then safely get in the shade-grown, which will bring in more money, the Schollers should make enough to pay back their loan. A fair amount of the crop is already lost, but if we're quick enough, we might be able to help them save enough to pay back the bank, plus a little extra."

Junior listened to his father and then measured the field with a critical eye. "He's got at least forty acres here, Papa. There's only eight of us, plus the Schollers. Shouldn't we try to get more help?"

"There is no one else to help," Papa answered. "The Schoellers' sons are grown and have crops of their own to tend. All the farmers have the same problem, and those that don't farm are helping their neighbors that do. We're racing against time and the odds, I know, but it's all we can do. Let's give it our best. Are you ready?"

We went to work. Mama showed Cookie and me how to spear cut tobacco plants onto long wooden lathes and then place the lathes loaded with tobacco onto carts, which, when full, were driven to the drying sheds. Then Papa and Junior unloaded the prepared lathes and climbed ladders that reached into the rafters and hung them, row upon row, with as much tobacco as the shed would hold.

Mama, Cookie, and I started spearing the pile of plants that Mr. Scholler had cut before we arrived. Chip and Chuck, who were smaller and better able to move through the rows of tobacco without bruising the tender leaves, worked at harvesting the standing crop, cutting the grown plants off at the base, then tossing then into a flat box with a long rope handle.

Little Curt's job was to drag the loaded boxes over to where Mama, Cookie, and I were working, but he was really too small to haul the big boxes. I saw him struggling and straining to pull a heavy box across a field, and making progress, but slowly. I jumped off the cart, ran to Curt, put my hands next to his on the rope handle and pulled. Together we were able to haul the box much more quickly. After we reached the carts, Curt grinned up at me. "Th-th-thanks, Elise. Th-those boxes are heavier than they l-l-look."

"That's all right, Curt. I'm sure you could have done it without me, but it goes more quickly with two, doesn't it?" Curt grinned wider with pride and set to unloading the boxes while I returned to my job of spearing leaves onto the lathes.

We worked from dawn until dark, only taking a short break in the middle of the day to eat the sandwiches and drink the coffee that Mrs. Scholler brought out into the field. My earlier worries about my potential ineptitude were unfounded. Though hopeless and clumsy around the house, when it came to working the land, I was suddenly able and confident. I found the earthy smell of the soil and the serenity of the field calming. The cold snap in the air made me feel sharp, quick, and wonderfully alive, although as the day wore on, the temperature rose steadily. By the time we'd finished our lunch it was hot enough that we took off our sweaters and ate in our shirtsleeves, enjoying the feeling of the warm sun on our skin.

"The weather has certainly turned," Mama commented. "It feels downright humid. Maybe we'll beat the frost after all."

Papa squinted up at the sun, now sitting high above our heads. "You might be right," he said through a mouthful of sandwich, "but we'd better keep up the pace. The temperature could drop just as quickly as it rose. You never can tell."

As the afternoon wore on, it got hotter and stickier. The boys took off their shirts entirely. I had never seen a man's bare chest before; I had rarely ever seen my own father wearing anything more revealing than a shirt, vest, and tie. Seeing the Muller boys shirtless was somewhat shocking, but it was impossible not to notice how muscular Junior's shoulders were. I blushed, lowered my head, and tried to concentrate on my work.

I quickly picked up the knack of spearing leaves without damaging them. It wasn't long before I was hanging five finished lathes to Cookie's three in spite of the fact that I took regular breaks from my work to help Curt with the hauling. Not that I was counting exactly, but I could see that for the first time since coming to Brightfield, I was more a help than a hindrance. Mr. Scholler, who passed by as he was getting ready to take a full cart to the shed, noticed my work.

"Hey, she's a quick one, ain't she?" Mr. Scholler remarked to Mama, who smiled in agreement. Then, turning his attention to me, he said, "You sure you han't worked tobacco before, girlie?"

I ducked my head and my cheeks colored. "No sir. Never."

Mr. Scholler cocked his head and made a clicking noise with his tongue as though he couldn't quite believe it. "Well, I never saw a girl pick it up so quick. Listen, if the reverend an' Mrs. don't treat you right, you can move over here with us. The wife and I could use some help. Bet you're quick in the kitchen, too, eh?"

Cookie let out a derisive little "Ha!" My cheeks flushed a deeper shade of scarlet, and Mama raised a warning eyebrow that Cookie would be sure to notice.

"Elise is more of an outdoor girl, " Mama said.

"Yeah, she is that," agreed Mr. Scholler, nodding approvingly. "Never saw a girl take to the tobacco so quick. Well, we'd better get back to it, eh? Sure appreciate your help, Mrs. Muller. You too, girls. Seems like now the weather has turned warm again that we'll have plenty of time to finish this up. If it keeps up like this, we probably won't need you tomorrow, but if the frost had come we'd 'a been in a fix without you folks."

"We're always glad to help a neighbor, Mr. Scholler. It's our pleasure," said Mama, and she was right, at least as far as I was concerned. We worked outdoors as long as there was light, and then we worked by lamplight in the shed until we hung the last of the prepared lathes. Arriving home under a night that was blanketed with a gray coverlet of fat clouds, we ate cold chicken and potatoes. Cookie and I stumbled up the stairs, stupid with fatigue. I was asleep almost as soon as my head hit the pillow, but not before I had a chance to remember Mr. Scholler's kind words and approving expression. I slept fitfully, dreaming of giants drumming on the roof, trying to get inside.

I expected to wake in darkness to the sound of Mama's knock at the bedroom door, but instead I was stirred from sleep by a beam of sunlight in my face. Cookie was still asleep in the bed next to mine. I leapt into my clothes and ran down the stairs to the kitchen, still buttoning my blouse as I went, afraid that Mama had been unable to waken me and had left for the Schollers' farm without me. Instead I found Mama, Papa, and Junior sitting at the kitchen table, drinking coffee and eating breakfast. The room was heavy with silence and the smell of baking apple pie.

"Where is everyone?" I asked. "Shouldn't we be getting ready to go to the Schollers'?"

"They're sleeping," Junior replied. "Look outside. There's no point going now. There never was," he said, shooting his father a slightly accusing look.

For the first time that day I looked out the window and realized why the sun had been so bright on my eyes. The earth was covered in white, and the sunbeams reflected brightly off the surface of the ground.

"Is it snow?" I asked. "How can that be? It's so warm outside."

"It's hail," Papa said. "Big as golf balls. All the shade tents fell under the weight of it and crushed the plants inside. The broadleaf was beaten flat and bruised. Anything that was standing in the fields is lost."

"What about Mr. and Mrs. Scholler?" I asked quietly. "What about their mortgage? Are they going to lose their farm?"

Papa sighed and smiled doubtfully. "Maybe not," he said. "We'll see. At least we helped them get some of the crop in. Maybe they can pay part of the loan now and the bank will give them another year to make up the rest." But I could tell from his tone that this was not likely. He reached for the sugar and stirred it into his coffee with an air of defeat.

"Isn't there something we can do?" I asked quietly, looking first to Papa and then, when he offered no response, to Junior, who seemed to eye me with curiosity.

"There's always something we can do," said Mama definitively, who had gotten up from the table to pull a freshly baked pie from the oven. "Carl," she said to Papa, "this pie should be cool by the time you shovel the snow off the car. I'll drive to the Schollers' and help you deliver it, if you want."

Papa raised his head up and smiled at his wife. The look they exchanged was so filled with unspoken understanding of one another and the certainty of two lives shared as one that it was almost too intimate to watch, but I couldn't help myself. I wondered if my own mother and father had ever looked at each other like that, or if anyone would ever look at me that way.

"I'll get my coat," Papa said with a renewed energy in his voice. "But we're going to need more than one pie," he mused. "Just about everybody lost their crop last night, or a good part of it. We've got lots of visits to make."

"I already put together a hamper of the peaches we canned last week," said Mama, pointing to a basket that was sitting by the back door. "That should be enough."

"Junior, bring that out to the truck for me, would you, please?" asked Papa. Junior got up from his place at the table and carried the peaches out the door. I offered to clear the table for Mama, who was already standing at the sink getting ready to scrub the breakfast skillet.

Papa pulled on his coat and headed toward the door but then, thinking no one was looking, he turned back to his wife and leaned down to kiss her on the cheek. "Sophia, you are a wonder," he said.

Mama just smiled and wrung the water from her dishrag.

Chapter 6

The hailstones melted before the day was out, leaving puddles and flattened fields in their wake. The whole landscape looked forlorn, defeated, and weary. But in spite of the ruined crops, the annual harvest supper at the church went on according to schedule.

For the entire week before the supper the Muller kitchen was a hub of activity, constantly buzzing with committees of white-haired women, some plump and friendly, with soft, sponge-cake figures; some thin and sharp-tongued, with bodies that seemed to be made entirely of bony angles covered with skin.

One group sat in the corner of the kitchen sewing a beautiful quilt that was stretched tight over a wooden frame. These ladies met together every Thursday morning during the winter to stitch the quilt top together, and now they were hurrying to finish it in time for the drawing that would take place at the harvest supper. The holder of the winning ticket would get to take home the quilt, and the money raised from ticket sales would be sent to missionaries in Darkest Africa. It was a simply breathtaking quilt, all done in shades of blue, red, and green and covered with flowers, birds, vines and hearts that one of the ladies said was a Baltimore style. I would have loved for one of the women to show me how to make those tiny stitches for myself, but I didn't have the courage to ask any more than I had the courage to ask what Baltimore was.

While the group in the corner sewed and gossiped, the rest of the ladies peeled basins full of ripe apples, baked pots of beans, mixed countless bowls of cake batter, and gossiped. The whole atmosphere was one of happy and industrious female companionship.

Members of the church congregation were always stopping by the house. Sometimes it was an official occasion, such as Papa's monthly meeting with the elder board, which meant we were all expected to dress in our best, greet the elders politely as they filed into Papa's study, and then spend the rest of the evening being as quiet as possible. Sometimes it was Mama's weekly women's Bible study or a ladies' committee meeting, but more often than not, people just dropped in unannounced for advice, to complain, or just to talk. These uninvited guests were invariably asked to stay for a meal, and nine times out of ten they accepted. Breakfast was generally the only meal of the day that didn't include visitors.

Mama and Papa always made a point of introducing me to people, and I was welcomed politely, but no one took much notice of me. I was just as happy not to be the object of anyone's attention, though I enjoyed it when Mr. Scholler dropped by. He always greeted me with a hearty handshake, called me "the best hand I've ever had on the place," and said that any time I decided I wanted a job on his farm there was one waiting for me. I liked him very much and would have liked to ask him what happened after the hailstorm and if he was going to lose his farm, but it seemed a very forward question, so I kept silent on the subject.

Although it seemed rude to me for people to drop in without a formal invitation, in the short time I had lived with the Mullers, I had become accustomed to the endless stream of guests and now accepted it as one of the many things about Americans that I would never understand. However, in the week before the church supper the stream of visitors became a flood. It was tiring having so many people around, but there was something exciting about it, too. It amazed me how all the women seemed to know their way around the Mullers' kitchen. Upon their arrival each woman poured herself a cup of coffee from the pot sitting on the back stove burner, donned the apron she'd brought with her from home, and set to work on some task seemingly preassigned to her, though I never heard anyone give anyone else instructions.

Cookie moved about the kitchen with an aura of capability and maturity that I envied. She seemed to know just what to do and was able to pull out just the right size mixing bowl without being asked or refill a lady's coffee cup just at the moment she realized it was empty. Cookie was clearly a great favorite with the ladies of the church, and she talked to them easily and comfortably, something I was simply unable to do. They asked her questions about how she'd spent her summer, patted her on the cheeks, and thanked her for assistance, saying she was a credit to her mother. I wanted to help, too, but remembered my earlier clumsiness and the resulting broken glasses, so I hung about the edges of the kitchen, just hoping to stay out of the way.

Mama noticed my discomfort and set me to work peeling apples, taking the place of Mrs. Walsh, who had been working at the task all morning and was ready to do something else. I was glad to have been given a job in which I couldn't possibly break anything and started peeling with enthusiasm, determined to make the mound of Mrs. Walsh's already peeled apples into a mountain. I started off well enough, but ten minutes into the operation, the paring knife slipped in my hand and I cut my thumb and the heel of my left hand.

A thin red line appeared against my skin and quickly widened to a bright gash, dripping blood into the bowl of newly peeled apples, mixing with the apple juices and turning the whole bowl a disturbing shade of pink. The wound was painful, but I was so horrified knowing that I'd ruined an entire morning's work that I sat at the table speechless and frozen while my hand continued to drip more and more blood.

Cookie, who was standing at the sink washing pots, was the first to notice what had happened. "Mama!" she shouted, "Look at Elise!"

Mama turned from the counter where she was measuring flour and sugar carefully into a bowl and gasped, "Oh my Lord! Cookie, quick! Get me a towel!"

Suddenly the whole room of women sprang to their feet, buzzing and clucking. A towel was located, and someone ran upstairs for the first-aid kit. There was a brief discussion about the need to call the doctor, but Mama, who held my bloody hand in her lap, declared that the cut was not deep enough to require stitches. Before I really knew what was happening, my cut had been washed, thoroughly slathered with rusty-colored iodine, and bandaged with clean white gauze. I don't know why, but the sight of all those concerned, motherly eyes focused on me was suddenly overwhelming, and I burst into tears.

My weeping brought on a fresh wave of scurrying among the women and a collective "there, there" and patting among those who were standing nearest to me. Mrs. Jensen declared that what I needed was a nice cup of tea and put a kettle on to boil. Mrs. Scholler decided that I probably had a headache and started rifling through the drawers, looking for a towel suitable to make a cold compress.

Mama, who had overseen the bandaging of my hand and was now seated on a chair next to me, put her arm across my shoulders and started rubbing my back. "You'll be fine, " she said in a soothing sing-song voice, the way one speaks to a frightened animal or a very young child. "You've just had a scare, that's all. Sit quiet for a few minutes and you'll feel better. You need something to eat.

Cookie, cut a piece of pie for Elise." She nodded her head toward the counter where several freshly baked pies were cooling. "And see if we have any of that nice cheddar left to go with it."

Cookie's face clouded over with annoyance. "We need to save these pies for the harvest supper," she said. It was the first time I'd ever heard Cookie contradict her mother. Mama's eyebrows raised, and she shot her daughter a pointed look that Cookie ignored.

"We were far enough behind as it is," Cookie grumbled, "and now that Elise has ruined a whole basin of apples, we won't have enough for Saturday night."

It was true. The thought caused fresh tears to well up in my eyes. "I'm sorry," I whispered to Mama. "I wanted to help, but every time I try, it ends in disaster. I've spoiled everything."

"Nonsense!" barked Mrs. Ludwig, the oldest lady in the church and the one I found the most intimidating. It seemed like half the people in the church were named Ludwig, and Milda Ludwig was the matriarch of that clan, mother of eleven sons. She was thin and sharp as a tree branch, with eyes that seemed to take in everything around her from behind thick glasses. She was a commanding presence, rarely speaking, but when she did, every woman in the church deferred to her. I suppose this was partly because four score years of living had made her wise, but also because she was mother-in-law, grandmother, or great-grandmother to a good portion of the ladies assembled in the Muller kitchen.

"Baking a few extra pies won't take much time. When my boys were little, I'd decide to make pie for dessert about the same time I put the stew on the stove. Before it was done simmering I'd been in the orchard to pick the fruit, washed it, mixed up the filling, rolled out the crust, and had four pies cooling on the sideboard before I rang the bell for supper," she croaked.

"People today make too much fuss over something as simple as a pie. Problem with young women today is, you're lazy," she declared authoritatively, nodding at Cookie, who blushed bright red at the accusation.

"Don't you feel bad about the apples," she said, turning her attention to me. "Won't take half an hour to peel up another basin." I knew she was lying, but appreciated her kindness in wanting to make me feel better.

"You know," she continued, "I'm feeling hungry myself. Maybe it's time we all sat down and sampled some of these pies." She turned to Mama and gave her a questioning look. I had noticed that Mama was the only woman to whom Mrs. Ludwig deferred. Possibly her position as the minister's wife gave Mama an elevated status in the old woman's eyes.

"Milda, that's a very good idea," Mama replied. "If we all took a break and had something to eat, I'm sure we'd be so refreshed that we'd be able to work more quickly for the rest of the afternoon. At the very least"—she smiled—"we'd know if the pies are any good." This comment was met with light female laughter and a scuffling of chairs as the ladies started to move about the kitchen in cheerful anticipation of warm pie and hot coffee.

Wanting to be of some use, I started to get up to help with the table setting, but Mama placed her hand firmly on my shoulder and pushed me back down into my chair. "No, you just sit still, and I'll bring you a piece of pie," she said gently. "Cookie, would you please get the plates out of the cupboard while I find a knife?"

Cookie, whose face was still slightly pink from her earlier chastisement by Mrs. Ludwig, murmured a soft assent and moved toward the pantry but not before casting a resentful look in my direction.

After the pies were cut, eaten, and declared a success, the ladies rose from the table and went back to work with renewed vigor. Mama tied an apron around her waist in preparation for washing up the dishes.

"Elise, you should go upstairs and lie down."

"But I'm feeling much better now," I protested. "At least let me help dry the plates."

"No," she said firmly. "I don't doubt you're feeling better, but you had quite a scare. It would be better for you to rest this afternoon. Go on now, and try to take a nap. I'll be upstairs to check on you in a few minutes."

I felt deflated, certain that she was banishing me from the kitchen just to keep me from stirring up yet another disaster. No matter what Mrs. Ludwig said, Cookie was right—I had cost the women a whole morning's work. I trudged up the stairs to my bedroom and lay down, but I couldn't sleep. I left the door open a crack so I could hear the ladies talking down in the kitchen.

Until that day, none of the ladies had taken much notice of me; no one in Brightfield had. There were so many Muller children that the appearance of an extra cousin coming to stay for the summer was not an event of much consequence. Now the women were suddenly curious about my history. Mama seemed to be filling them in on the details. I couldn't hear everything that was said, but I knew that the conversation was about me from the fragments that I could hear every now and then.

"And you don't know how long she might be here?"

"Doesn't her family ever write? What about her mother?"

"Oh, the poor little dear!"

"You wouldn't expect her to, would you? She never had anyone to teach her."

"You and Herman are perfect saints to take her in!"

I heard a generalized rumble of agreement among the women followed by a croaking but unintelligible voice that I recognized as belonging to Mrs. Ludwig.

It was humiliating to lie in bed listening to them discuss me as though I were a stray cat the Mullers had rescued from the roadside. Father, I knew, would have been furious to hear his daughter being discussed as an object of pity by a roomful of women who back in Germany would never have been received in our home unless they in came by the servants' entrance. A few months before I would have felt the same way, but now my anger was all directed at Father. He was the one who had abandoned me and shipped me off to live with people who, though tied to our family by the thinnest of genealogical threads, were complete strangers. Half the blood that flowed in my veins, the blood that had spilled into a bowl of New England-grown apples, belonged to Father, but he had left me orphaned.

These women hardly knew me, yet they were fussing over me, binding my wounds, and mothering me as if I were one of their own. How often I had heard of the long and noble heritage of the Brauns. But what was nobility, anyway? Was it something you were born with, or something you aspired to? At that moment it seemed to me that any one of the women working in the Mullers' kitchen had more nobility in her little finger than we Brauns had in our whole family tree.

The thought made me angry and dried the tears that had been threatening to well up in my eyes only moments before. Leaping up off the bed, I crossed the room with long strides, closed the door tightly, and climbed back under the covers, pulling the quilt over my head to shut out the noise of female voices. Mama came upstairs later, but I stayed still and quiet under the blankets, pretending to be asleep.

In spite of the culinary setback created by my presence in the Mullers' kitchen, when Saturday arrived, the ladies had finished the quilt, baked twenty-five pies, fifteen cakes, two dozen loaves of dark brown bread, another dozen loaves of white, prepared gallons of smoky-smelling baked beans, plucked and dressed and roasted three huge turkeys, an equal number of hams, and a score of stuffed chickens, all of which were accompanied by a dizzying array of side dishes, relishes, and jams. Most of the food had been transported to the church early that morning, but the Mullers' tables and counters were still crowded with platters and baskets of food waiting to be taken to the church, along with one final spice cake still rising in the oven. The kitchen was enveloped in good, warm, homey smells, and everyone was in a festive mood, rushing to get ready for the big event.

When I finally got my turn in the bathroom, the air was thick with steam and the mirror was clouded with vapors except for a clear oval in the center. I looked in the glass. My reflection peered back at me framed in mist like an old-fashioned portrait taken in a world of dreams. Cookie's reflection in the mirror, I was certain, had made her look like an illustration from a fairy tale—a sweet and pretty princess with bright blue eyes, fresh pink cheeks, and rosebud lips that invited kisses from handsome princes. By comparison, I felt my own reflection to be more in line with the poor little match girl or the ugly duckling. My eyes were too large for my face, and my cheekbones and chin were all angles and bones. My forehead was too high, my lips too curved, and my complexion was pale as parchment, with none of Cookie's rosy glow. My dark brown hair, which I'd always considered my best feature because it was just like my mother's, seemed dull and ordinary when I compared it to Cookie's bright strawberry-blond locks. I turned the knob on the faucet hard, filling the washbasin with steaming hot water that rose and fogged over the rest of the mirror, hiding my image behind clouds and mist.

The church basement had been transformed. The gray cinderblock walls were hidden behind false fences of white lattice that served as a backdrop for an autumn scene, complete with piles of pumpkins, bales of hay, and pots of mums in orange and yellow. In one corner a scarecrow with a mischievous-looking stuffed raven perched on his shoulder leaned lazily against a bundle of dried cornstalks. The scarecrow was dressed in one of Papa Muller's cast-off shirts and stiff white collars. I supposed it was one of Chip and Chuck's creations, because I saw them standing across the room grinning broadly as they watched people's amused reaction to the straw stuffed man's clerical costume.

Along the opposite wall stood a long row of tables groaning with so much food that their red checkered tablecloths were barely visible under the serving platters crowded onto every inch of available space. A line of people snaked around the edges of the walls. After piling their plates high with mounds of food, the diners moved to the center of the hall and chose places at one of the empty tables. They sat in groups, talking and laughing and eating, and then, when their plates were empty, went back to the end of the buffet line to fill them again and find a seat with a different group of neighbors. The women seemed to take turns, some sitting and eating with everyone else, others running back and forth between the kitchen and the serving tables to refill empty platters. Even the ladies who were working had big smiles on their faces and chatted amongst themselves.

I was amazed to see how happy everyone was. Most of the people in that room had lost much, and in some cases all, of their crop to the hail, but before the meal began Papa stood at the front of the hall and said grace, thanking God for the blessings of harvest and for His generous abundance. When he finished, all the people responded with an enthusiastic "Amen!" It made no sense to me.

After a spring and summer of sweat and hope and hard work, they'd found themselves even poorer than when they'd begun. Still, they declared themselves thankful, and, as I looked around the hall at the smiling faces, I had to admit they seemed sincere. I stood, leaning against the cool cinderblock walls of the church basement, watching the scene, trying to figure it all out. My reverie was interrupted by a tug on my skirt. I looked down to see Curt gazing up at me seriously. Knowing he didn't like to speak aloud outside of the circle of the Muller family, I leaned down within whispering range of him. "What is it, Curt? Do you need help with something?"

"You better get a plate or there won't be nothing left. You don't know these people like I do," he advised solemnly. "They'll eat it all and not leave you a bite."

I was so amused by his concern and impressed that he had delivered his entire speech without stuttering that I didn't have the heart to correct his grammar. Grasping his outstretched hand, I followed him obediently to the end of the serving line, reflecting on the truth of his observation. I didn't know these people like he did. I wondered if I ever would.

Though I only took a small sample of each dish, carefully avoiding Mrs. Jensen's mincemeat after the alarmed look on Curt's face warned me off it, my plate was soon piled high with food. We found two empty places at the end of a long table and ate in companionable silence. Now and then Curt smiled, examining me with his bright blue eyes as though wanting to make sure I was enjoying myself. I smiled back, surprised to realize I was.

But my enjoyment was short-lived. As I bit into a piece of ham I felt a bony finger stab at my shoulder, as if someone were poking me with a stick. Curt's eyes were suddenly wide, and he slumped down in his chair, looking smaller than he had a moment before. I turned around and saw old Mrs. Ludwig staring at me.

"I heard about your mother," she croaked, not bothering with the niceties of a greeting. "That's too bad. I'm sorry for your loss, but a girl your age ought to know her way around a kitchen, no matter what happened to her mother. You come to my house on Saturdays and help me. Eight o'clock. Don't be late. We'll start tomorrow."

My mouth was so full of half-chewed ham that it was impossible to respond. Noticing Curt cowering in his chair, Mrs. Ludwig narrowed her eyes and glared at him. "Curtis Muller, sit up straight," she commanded. "You keep slouching like that and you'll grow up with a hump on your back!" Curt's eyes grew even wider than they had been, but he obeyed.

Before I could say anything, the old lady hobbled off in the direction of the kitchen, mumbling something about the women not watching to make sure the empty platters were refilled and having to do things yourself if you wanted them done right.

"Sh . . . sh . . . she sc-scares me," Curt stuttered nervously after Mrs. Ludwig had gone. "Sh . . . sh . . . she looks like the p-p-picture of the witch in my *Hansel and Gretel* b . . . book."

"Don't be silly," I said with more conviction than I felt. "There is no such thing as witches."

Just then someone shouted, "Time to get the music started! C'mon, men! Let's get these tables pushed back!"

The hall sparked with new energy as the men and boys moved tables and chairs to the edges of the room and the women sprang to their feet to clear the last of the dishes and start setting out pots of steaming coffee.

Mr. Scholler walked by with a violin in his hand, giving me a smile and a wink as he passed. Two of his grown sons, Erwin and Jim, followed behind him, one carrying a guitar and the other a box with an assortment of tambourines, rattles, and some other instruments I didn't recognize. They set themselves up on chairs in the corner of the room and began warming up, and before long they were playing a tune in waltz time—but it didn't sound like any waltz I'd ever heard.

At first I didn't care for it. When Mr. Scholler sawed his bow across the strings of the violin, the result was raw, and grittier than anything I'd heard before, but when the high notes of the violin combined with the low bass accompaniment of the guitar and the regular thumping of a hand on the drum of the tambourine, the song took on an energy and life that seemed appropriate to the occasion. It was impossible not to tap my toes in time to the music.

Before long the floor was crowded with couples, mostly married men and their wives dancing and chatting comfortably. I also noticed one tense-looking younger man had worked up the courage to ask a blushing girl onto the floor. They seemed out of place amidst the laughing married folks that spun around them keeping perfect three-four time to the music. The ease of the husbands and wives in each other's company was in sharp contrast to the awkwardness of the young couple moving stiffly to the music and continually glancing at their own feet for fear of stepping on their partner's.

Papa and Mama Muller took the floor. Papa Muller was such a big man that I was surprised to see how well he moved. Unlike the chattering pairs of dancers around them, the Mullers were silent as they spun around the floor, smiling, with their eyes fixed on each other. They moved as one person, gracefully and harmoniously, as though they spent their lives doing nothing but dancing.

Across the room I noticed Cookie watching her parents with admiration. Her eye caught mine and I smiled at her. She smiled back.

Again I felt a tug on my skirt, and when I looked over at Curt, he whispered, "Elise, would you dance with me?"

"I don't really know how, Curt."

"We could dance here in our corner alone. Just for practice. I never learned, either."

"All right," I agreed. After some trial and error we arranged ourselves with Curt reaching his hand up to put it on my waist while I leaned down a bit, grasping his left hand in my right and resting the other on his shoulder. We shuffled about awkwardly in a simple box step. I suddenly understood why the young couple kept looking at their feet. Dancing was harder than it looked, but Curt seemed to think we were doing splendidly and beamed up at me with a big grin on his face.

"I like you, Elise. I'm glad you came. Promise you won't ever go back to Germany. Junior says it's bad there and that the people are bad,too."

It made me angry to think of Junior criticizing my country to his little brother, but I knew Curt was too little to understand.

"I like you, too, Curt," I replied without making any promises.

I looked up to see Papa standing behind Curt. He tapped him on the shoulder and said, "May I cut in?" Curt didn't protest as Papa guided me toward the dance floor, but I did. "I can't dance!" I whispered urgently, feeling as though every eye in the room was on me, and certain that I was about to make a fool of myself.

"Nonsense!" Papa said. "I just saw you dancing with Curt."

"That's different," I protested. "Please! I don't want people to notice me."

Papa smiled. "Well, that's a funny thing to want," he said. "Elise, you are a pretty girl, and you are going to be a lovely young woman." I blushed and felt a little pleased, even though I was sure he was just saying it to be nice.

"People are going to notice you whether you want them to or not. Before you know it, lots of young men are going to be begging you for dances. It's time you learned how to dance."

"Ready?" he asked, and off we went. At first I felt almost as awkward as I had with Curt, but Papa guided me gently around the floor.

"That's it," Papa said encouragingly. "Don't look at your feet. They'll move just fine without you watching. Feel the music. Try closing your eyes."

I did, and the music washed over me like a purifying flood. Suddenly my nervousness disappeared. Suddenly I wasn't thinking about dancing, or left feet and right, or in which direction I was to move next. I wasn't thinking at all. The music led, and my body followed, while my mind sang the piano accompaniment that no one else heard.

I opened my eyes to see Papa smiling at me. "Better?" he asked. I nodded, feeling happier than I had in months. We circled to the right, and I saw Cookie standing in the corner glowering at me with Junior next to her, his face as hard and blank as a block of stone.

The day was Friday, September 1, 1939. I did not know it yet, but while I was in Brightfield, eating and dancing and wondering why Cookie and Junior disliked me so much, my father was crossing the border into Poland.

Chapter 7

I tapped on Mrs. Ludwig's front door at five minutes before eight on Saturday morning. She answered my knock with a shout. "Come around to the kitchen! The door is open!"

The floorboards on the porch creaked as I walked around to the south side of Mrs. Ludwig's farmhouse, a house which had probably once been painted a bright and cheerful yellow but was now faded and peeling in spots. I opened the door and peered into the kitchen. A kettle whistled impatiently on the stove. There was no sign of Mrs. Ludwig. I hesitated, not sure if I should go in or not, when a loud voiced cracked behind me, giving me such a start that I let out a little yelp of surprise.

"Well, don't just stand there with your teeth in your mouth!" Mrs. Ludwig snapped. "Take the teapot off the fire. There's a potholder hanging on the hook near the sink. Be careful you don't burn yourself on the handle." I did as I was told, not even waiting to take off my coat before seeing to the kettle whose cheerful whistle had now become an impatient shriek.

"There's cups on the shelf. No," she said as I my hand reached toward a cupboard that held a collection of bowls, jars, and vases of cobalt blue glass, "the open shelf on the wall. Next to the plates." I took down a white ceramic teacup and saucer.

"Get one for yourself, too," she commanded. "The tea is in that mason jar. I don't take sugar, but if you want some, you can get it out of the canister. Not too much. It'll rot your teeth." Then, "You don't need to put in so much tea! Do you think I'm made of money?"

I placed the cups on top of the scarred wooden table and sat down in the chair that Mrs. Ludwig, using a curt nod of her head, indicated should be mine.

"Have you seen this?" she asked, pointing to the newspaper that was spread out of the table. I shook my head no. The old woman stared at me, then looked at her lap for a moment as though considering what she should say next.

"Yesterday, on Hitler's orders, the German army invaded Poland. They haven't done so yet, but it seems inevitable that England and France will declare war on Germany. It is the beginning of a second world war." She sat silent for a moment, allowing the information to sink in.

Of course, I said to myself. *Of course.* I had known this could happen for a long time. That was why I was in Brightfield—because Father had said there was going to be a war. But somehow his words had not seemed credible. To me, the possibility of war seemed a convenient excuse for sending away an inconvenient daughter. I had never really thought his predictions would come true. For an instant I was pleased to know that he hadn't just invented the whole thing as a way to get rid of me, but then I remembered what this meant.

"Do you think my father is in Poland?" I asked Mrs. Ludwig, my words a bit halting from the effort of holding my emotions in check.

"If the paper is to be believed, and I think it is, the entire

German army is in Poland. I suppose your father must be with them." She searched my face with her quick, beady eyes. "The newspapers say the casualties are light so far. I imagine your father is fine, but *your* life is about to get much harder.

"I have lived a long time," she went on, "through wars, floods, famines, and every type of calamity that can befall a woman. If you live to be as old as I am, though I don't recommend it, so will you. Drink your tea," she commanded.

I sipped at the hot, sweet liquid. It felt soothing going down my throat, which felt suddenly raw.

"Do you understand why I say your life is about to get harder?" she asked.

"Because I will always have to be worrying about my father now," I answered.

"Yes," she nodded, "that's true, but there is something more. Up until now, most people in town have felt sorry for you, a poor motherless girl fleeing from a dangerous place. Folks have had nothing but good feelings toward you, or at worst, they've simply ignored you."

Ducking my head down, I made a wry face as I took another sip of tea. She obviously hadn't talked to Junior, Cookie, Chip, or Chuck.

"Now it is going to be different. Germany is the aggressor in another world war, and that will make it hard for anyone who is German."

I opened my mouth to protest, but she barked, "Hush!" before I could say anything.

"I don't care what kind of National Socialist hogwash they taught you in Germany. Austria, Czechoslovakia, Poland—these are separate, sovereign nations populated by Austrians, Czechs, and Poles. They are not Germans. They have no interest in becoming Germans. Hitler is using that as an excuse to start another war. He is making an aggressive grab for power. Hitler and his wretched army are not liberators. They are invaders bent on grabbing as much land as they can while they can. They have no purpose other than to exploit the conquered resources and peoples for their own benefit and to serve their own twisted ideas of German superiority. "

When I left the house that morning, Mama had said to be polite, but this was too much to bear. "What do you know about it?" I spat at her. "I don't like Hitler any better than you do—Neither does my father, but you've no right to say such awful things about my country. I don't care what Mama says, I don't have to sit here and listen to this!"

I leapt from my chair to grab my coat off the hook, but I accidentally knocked over my teacup and Mrs. Ludwig's. Steaming hot tea spilled from the cups onto the table and Mrs. Ludwig's lap. She gave a startled yelp and shoved her chair back from the table. She winced in pain.

Horrified, and worried that she was really hurt, I ran to the sink and started searching frantically for a towel, apologizing over and over as I opened and closed drawers unsuccessfully trying to find something to clean up the mess with.

"It's all right," she mumbled grudgingly, her irritation evident in her tone. "It was an accident. I'm fine. Sit down. I can clean it up myself," she said, dabbing at her skirt with a napkin.

"No," I protested. "I'll take care of it. I just can't find—"

"Elise Braun, sit down this instant!" the old lady commanded in a tone that reminded me very much of my father.

I obeyed.

"I'll tell you what I know about it," she said evenly, folding her tea-stained napkin into a tidy square and placing it on the table. "Everyone in Brightfield calls me Milda Ludwig, but that's not my real name. The name I took when I married my second husband is Ludwiczak, Matylda Ludwiczak. Polish. I grew up in a little village just outside of Serokomla. When I turned fifteen, just a little older than you are now, my family married me off to the local baker, who was nearly seventy. He wasn't a bad man. He was kind to me. We were married for seven years, and then he died. We never had any children. Not surprising, considering his age. Still, everyone in town thought I was barren, so no one wanted to marry me. At twenty-one I was considered a dried-up old widow. For five years I ran the bakery by myself, and I thought that was how I would end my days."

"One day my mother came to the shop carrying a letter from her sister in Gdansk, my Aunt Grazyna, that told her about a man she knew who had emigrated to America and was writing to see if she knew of any girls who might be willing to emigrate and be his bride. Mama showed me his picture. Jozef Ludwiczak, age thirty-five. He was a nice-looking man, but I had doubts. Aunt Grazyna's letter said that he was a Protestant, and I was Catholic. I said, 'Mama, I can't marry this man. I can't marry outside the faith. What would happen to our children?'

" 'What children?' Mama said. 'You have no children, Matylda, and if you stay here, you never will. No one here will have you. Go to America, where you'll at least have a chance at some kind of life.' "

Mrs. Ludwig stopped and sighed. She reached across the table to the teapot and poured herself a fresh cup. By this time I was completely drawn into her story, amazed to learn that this old woman had been sent away from her family, just like I had. "So you went to America?"

Mrs. Ludwig rolled her eyes as she took a slurp of tea. "I'm here, aren't I?" I blushed a bit at her reproach. She put down her cup and continued the story.

"I sent him my picture and a letter. I told him everything about me, even that I had been married before and had been unable to have children. It was important to me that we be honest with each other. Even so, he wrote back and asked me to marry him. I sold the bakery to one of my brothers and used the money to buy a passage to America. That was in eighteen eighty-five. When my ship arrived in New York, Joe was there to meet me, and we got married that same day."

"And you loved him?" I asked anxiously.

Mrs. Ludwig gave a short laugh, and her eyes twinkled. Her already wrinkled forehead wrinkled even more as she paused to consider my question. "We built this farm together," she said. "I gave him eleven sons. One day he was out in the barn stacking hay, and a pile of bales fell on him. He was nearly crushed under the weight of it, but he lingered on for almost a month, though he never regained consciousness. Stayed by his bedside every moment until he died. We were married forty years." She paused, and her eyes looked past me, focusing on some image visible only to her.

"Yes." She nodded. "I loved him. We loved each other."

I couldn't help but sigh, pleased that the story had reached such a satisfying conclusion, which seemed to irritate Mrs. Ludwig all over again.

"But that's not the point," she said shortly. "The point is that I've lived longer than you, and I know a few things about the world, including the fact that Poles are not now and never have been sitting around praying for some damned fool to come along and attack their country so they can be 'reunited' with Germany. In the Great War, they played both sides against the middle, fighting and dying alongside everyone, be they German, Russian, or Austrian, in hopes of eventually gaining independence. Which they did in nineteen-eighteen, but not until over two million Polish soldiers died. You can't believe everything people tell you, Elise—not your teachers or even your father. Or even me. Someone once said that the pure and simple truth is seldom pure and rarely simple. You've got to think for yourself. Keep an open mind."

"Is that why you wanted me to come here today?" I asked.

"No!" the old lady said with a snort. "I wanted you to come here for exactly the reason I gave you at the supper last night—I never saw a girl as old as you be as helpless around the house as you are. It's a disgrace!"

My cheeks reddened with shame. My hands twisted in my lap, and I began examining my fingernails with great interest.

"Don't be embarrassed. It's not your fault. You can't be expected to know what nobody taught you. Of course," she mused, shaking her head as though trying to solve an unsolvable riddle, "I would have thought you'd picked up something after living five months in Sophia Muller's house."

After considering this puzzle for a moment and finding no answer, she gave both her knees a decisive slap as though to bring herself back to the business at hand.

"Still, you're never too old to learn. That's why I wanted you to come over, so I could start teaching you your way around a kitchen. You've already mastered the art of tea-making," she joked, displaying a grin that was minus a few teeth. Grunting with the effort, she heaved herself out of her chair, took an apron off the hook on the wall, and handed another to me, indicating that I should put it on.

"Now you need to know how to bake something to go with it. We'll start with *paczki,* a kind of polish donut. My own daughter-in-laws would kill for this recipe, but I have never shared it with anyone. Once you've got that down, we'll move on to pies, breads, and if you are good and work hard, even my special cheesecake, called *sernik babci.* It's my mother's secret recipe." Her voice lowered to a whisper, and she looked around the room as though someone might be listening.

Clearly Mrs. Ludwig intended to confer some great honor on me by sharing her family baking secrets with me, but it was an honor I felt I could do without. The idea of spending Saturdays with the demanding, blunt old woman was not exactly appealing.

"But, Mrs. Ludwig," I questioned, "why would you want to give me your secret recipes? You said it yourself, I am hopeless in the kitchen."

She gave the apron strings a final and definite tug before looking up, her face sober, her gaze even and honest. "There are several reasons—three, to be precise. First, I feel sorry for you. I know what it's like, coming to a new country and feeling out of place and out of step with everything around you.

"Second, you are going to need someone to talk to, someone who can help you with more than baking. This war is going to make things difficult for you around here, especially if America gets involved like it did in the Great War."

"And the third reason?"

"Because I am lonely," she said and tipped her chin up toward me in an expression that was simultaneously proud and touching. "I am eighty years old. My sons respect me, and their wives fear me. They come to see me out of duty. 'Most everyone in this town is afraid of me, except Sophia Muller. I blame no one but myself for that, so don't go feeling sorry for me. I am a stubborn old woman who seems to have lived out her usefulness. Maybe I can be of some use to you and you to me. I need a purpose. You need a friend. Or at least someone who understands what you are feeling and can help you understand these people and this place. I know I'm not the most pleasant person to pass an afternoon with, and I can't promise I'll change. In fact, I can guarantee you that I won't. I'm too old for that. So I don't blame you if you decide to leave, and I won't complain to Sophia. But I hope you'll stay."

Her speech was delivered without a trace of sentimentality. She was both dignified and vulnerable. I thought for a moment, then put on the apron I was still holding, crossing the strings around the back and tying them in front, just like Mrs. Ludwig did.

* * *

When I returned home from my morning at Mrs. Ludwig's, Mama and Papa were waiting for me. The house was completely silent, and I wondered where the other children were. It was the first time I could remember ever seeing Mama just sitting without doing anything. Even when we listened to the radio in the evenings, Mama always had her knitting or mending to keep her hands occupied. But at this moment, she and Papa sat at the kitchen table with the morning paper between them, the words *Germany Invades Poland!* emblazoned on the front page like a scream.

War. My father was a warrior, and he was at war. I was in Brightfield, Massachusetts, USA—where I was bringing a plate of freshly made Polish donuts to my adopted family. It seemed ironic and not quite real. It shamed me to realize that while I had been in Mrs. Ludwig's kitchen, measuring flour, taking orders, and actually enjoying myself a little, I had forgotten all about the war that my own father was fighting half a world away. My pride over a morning of successful, or at least not disastrous, baking seemed suddenly trivial and a little embarrassing. I put the plate on the countertop without telling the Mullers what was on it. As I took off my coat, Papa sat up a bit straighter in his chair and squared his shoulders, the way I'd seen him do just before starting his sermons.

"I already saw it," I said dully before he could speak. "Mrs. Ludwig told me. I suppose Father must be there."

Papa Muller nodded his head. "Probably."

Mama pulled a letter out of her apron pocket and held it out to me. "This came for you today."

I took the envelope and held it in my hands, examining the stamps pasted in the upper right-hand corner. *Ein Volk, Ein Reich, Ein Fuhrer,* the stamps said. "One People, One Nation, One Fuhrer." A date of April 10, 1938, was printed on the right edge of the stamp. It was meant to commemorate the Austrian Anschluss. I had seen such stamps many times before I came to America, but how odd it was that this particular stamp suddenly seemed strange, so foreign.

Not once in all the times I had opened a letter or glued a stamp to an envelope had I ever questioned such slogans. Mrs. Ludwig's speech made me wonder how I would have felt about the Anschluss if I had been an Austrian girl. And if I lived in Poland, what would I be feeling right now as I watched German tanks roll down the streets of my town? The hair stood up on the back of my neck, as though even thinking such things was disloyal. I shook myself, as if to rid my body of an unwelcome chill and chided myself for asking such questions when my own father was at war and possibly in danger. I was angry with Father, it was true, but I could not doubt that his decisions had been made with my welfare in mind. I felt I must not doubt that any side he fought on was the side of right.

Who was I going to trust on questions of such importance—an elderly, cantankerous Polish peasant or my own father, a distinguished graduate of the German War College, an officer, an aristocrat, a Braun? There was no contest. I dismissed all the uncomfortable questions from my mind and looked up to see the Mullers watching me, a mixture of curiosity and concern evident on their faces.

"Excuse me," I said quietly. "If you don't mind, I would like to go and read this now."

"Of course," Mama said getting up from the table and crossing the room. She stood next to me with her arm across my shoulder, patting my arm reassuringly. "You can go into the parlor, or up to your room if you'd like some privacy. We gave Junior the keys to the truck and asked him to take the other children into town for some ice cream."

"You didn't have to send them away on my account," I said, hearing an unintended twinge of irritation creep into my voice. I didn't like the idea of the Mullers discussing me behind my back.

"Well, we thought it would be best." Papa smiled understandingly, glancing first at me and then at his wife. "We thought you just might need some peace and quiet for a little while. It must come as quite a surprise."

"Not really," I lied coldly. "We all knew this was coming. Father did, certainly. After all, that's why I am here, isn't it?"

The smile faded from Papa's face, and I felt a momentary prick of guilt. Mama patted my arm again and spoke with a forced cheerfulness, "The fighting doesn't seem to be very heavy, at least not according to the newspaper reports. I'm sure your father is fine."

"Yes," Papa added, "I'm sure he is, but we'll make sure to pray for his safety at supper tonight."

"Thank you," I replied formally, "but I am sure that will not be necessary. My father is a fifth-generation officer. He has trained for battle all his life. If experience and skill have anything to do with it, then I am sure he is safe. If not, and he has been unlucky, then there is nothing that God can do about it."

Even as the words left my lips, I hated myself for speaking that way, in a manner calculated to wound the Mullers most, but I could not stop myself. I mumbled an excuse and ran upstairs to my room. Sitting uneasily on the edge of the bed, I found a loose corner on the envelope flap and ran my finger carefully under the edge that had kept Father's letter sealed and secret during a long journey across the ocean. As I slid the letter out, bringing with it that faint aroma of dust and cigar smoke that always hung in the air of his study, I could see him as he sat at his desk writing—his two extra pens laid out at the ready on the left side of the desk, reinforcements ready to be called into action, a sheet of ivory stationery in front of him at precisely the correct angle, his posture immovable and ramrod straight as his right hand moved at an even pace across the paper, the point of the pen scratching ever so lightly as he wrote.

The entry in the upper right-hand corner of the page told me he had written it three weeks previously while still in Berlin, so I knew before I began that the letter couldn't tell me if he was safe. The push into Poland had taken place only the day before, but, still, in my heart I had hoped that by some magical trick of will or time the letter would reveal that he was, at this very moment, unhurt and far from the fire of guns and the dangers of war. No matter what I'd said to the Mullers, I was worried for my father. Worried for his safety. Worried that we would be robbed of one another, and I would be truly alone. I began to read.

Dear Daughter,

I hope that this letter finds you well and safe. I suppose it must be nearing time for school to begin. There is no doubt in my mind that you will pour yourself into your studies with diligence and discipline and that, by doing so, you will achieve excellent marks in all your subjects. Though you may, at first, find it challenging to complete all of your work in English, you must not use that as an excuse to accept anything less than top marks in every class. I expect no less of you and you should expect no less of yourself.

I found your last letter disturbing and disappointing. Frankly, I resent your assertions that I have somehow "abandoned" you in America. Whether you understand it or not, I am making the best decisions for you and at some considerable personal cost. It hurts me more than you know to have you so far away from me.

You aren't a child anymore. You are a young woman, only a few years younger than your mother when we married. I suppose it is natural that you have begun to question authority. So I have decided to address your concerns because you are reach-

ing an age at which, I hope, you are mature enough to understand and accept both my reasoning and my decision.

I have only had two loves in my life, you and your mother. Now that I have lost one, I cannot risk losing the other. You are the only person on earth who means anything to me. It is not easy for me to speak of such things. It never has been, even to your mother, but you must understand that it is because I care for you that I have sent you away. In America you may not be happy, but you will be safe. That is more important than your happiness. It is my responsibility, as well as my desire, to make certain that you continue to live and grow into the young woman your mother would have wanted you to become.

As the daughter of an officer, you should understand the nature of duty and should not presume to question the decisions I make on your behalf. We all have our duty to perform; whether we like it or understand the orders given us is of no importance.

As I write this letter to you, I am preparing to embark upon a duty about which I have doubts and misgivings, regarding both the necessity of the action I have been ordered to perform and the wisdom and integrity of those who have ordered it done. However, I have pushed aside these doubts because years of experience have taught me that, in order to accomplish anything of importance as a nation, people must put aside their own petty concerns and concentrate on the common good, even to the point of ultimate sacrifice. Imagine what would happen if everyone questioned everything? It would result in nothing but endless and unresolved debates and argument! No! A society that hopes to advance must put its trust in their leaders, in spite of their private misgivings and you must put the same trust in my leadership.

By the time this letter reaches you, you will probably

understand more about the action to which I allude above. I am certain that all will turn out well, but the moment we had spoken of, the reason that I sent you to be with the Mullers, is at hand. There is no way of knowing how long this business will take to conclude or what the outcome will be, whether you and I shall be reunited soon or ever. No matter what the result, know that I care for you deeply and trust that you will continue to make me proud.

I will write as often as time and conditions permit. You must not worry about me.

Your Affectionate Father,
Herman Braun

Chapter 8

That letter marked the first time that Father had spoken to me not as a child who should be seen and not heard, but as an adult with ideas and opinions of her own. In an odd way, his attitude made me want to be that mature young woman he saw me as. Father's letters continued to arrive, but irregularly, and they were never as frank again. They contained little real news about his whereabouts or what he was doing. Somehow I sensed that the doubts he had spoken of in his earlier letter had grown, though he never said so directly.

I do recall that in one of his letters he said, "It is hard here. If I had not seen it for myself, I would not have believed that human beings were capable of such things." I read that letter over and over, looking for something I couldn't quite define.

It was strange, too, that his letters said almost nothing about how the campaign was going, though I knew that the German victory in Poland had been decisive and quick. Of course, he couldn't have divulged any detailed information or secrets, even in a private letter being mailed to an as yet noncombatant nation, but it seemed odd that he gave no reports or even vague allusions as to the performance of his troops.

The county newspaper, which only came out twice a week, wasn't much help, either. It was devoted more to farm prices, obituaries, and announcements for used tractors and pig nipplers for sale than to international news. Every now and again, I would hear a few scraps of news on the Mullers' radio, but these tended to be more in the way of speeches by politicians promising to keep America out of the fighting than actual reports on battles. The Mullers preferred radio dramas and music to news programs.

It seemed so odd to me that while much of the world was at war, life in Brightfield went on pretty much as it always had. Americans and America seemed determined to ignore the war for as long as possible. I couldn't blame them; life was so pleasant in Brightfield. Why would anyone want to complicate it by getting involved in a war across the sea?

Shortly after the beginning of the hostilities, President Roosevelt reaffirmed U.S. neutrality in the war. I was glad of that. Things were already awkward enough for me. I couldn't imagine how awful it would be if Americans, people I saw every day and had come to feel some affection for, were suddenly to don military uniforms and go off to fight against my home country, perhaps even coming face to face with Father on some distant battlefield. It was confusing and uncomfortable to think of that, so whenever possible I chose not to think of it at all.

School and the coming of Christmas made my forced mental neutrality a bit easier. The challenge of doing all my schoolwork in English was a welcome distraction. I threw myself into my studies, partly in an attempt to live up to Father's expectations, and partly because I liked my new teacher, Miss Gleason, and wanted to please her—but mostly just because it provided me with an escape.

The other students in my class treated me with a kind of aloof diffidence, which Cookie's hostility toward me did nothing to alleviate. One or two were purposely mean to me, but those were the boys who were openly mean to everyone, so I didn't feel especially picked on.

I studied hard, and my English improved rapidly, but as the days passed I grew tired of the routine. At home, Father and I hadn't really celebrated the holidays other than to exchange a gift at breakfast on Christmas morning. Christmas with the Mullers was a very different kind of celebration.

"It's b-b-bad enough I gotta sing in the stupid choir, without wearing this!" he had moaned as he stood on a kitchen chair while Mama marked the hem in his robe.

"Curt, shush up and hold still!" Mama muttered through a mouthful of pins. "I've told you ten times. Everyone in the church has to serve in some way, and this is yours. You've got a beautiful voice. Mrs. Karlsberg asked for you especially. You should be honored."

"That's right," said Chip with a teasing grin. "Mrs. Karlsberg said you've got the sweetest voice she ever heard! You can even sing higher than Cheryl Post! Bet she's mad you got her solo."

"You sure look the part," Chuck chimed in. "Positively angelic! Much, much prettier than Cheryl would have." With this Chuck pursed his lips and squeezed out a slurpy kissing noise. The twins laughed, and Curt called for his mother to make them stop.

"Knock it off," said Junior, who was putting more wood into the stove. "I remember when you were in choir, Chuck. Remember? They did a manger scene that year, and you were such a bad singer Mrs. Karlsberg made you wear the donkey outfit so no one could hear you inside the mask." Chuck grinned sheepishly, but Chip enjoyed a good laugh at his twin's expense.

"Don't know what *you* think is so funny," Junior said blandly, addressing Chip. "You sing so bad they made you be the back half!" The twins laughed in spite of themselves, and Curt joined in.

Although I generally had no use for Junior and his cutting sense of humor, especially when it was aimed at me, I appreciated the way he stood up for his youngest sibling.

It was snowing again, and the wind blew so hard it made the house shudder. The door blew open with a bang when Papa came in, shivering and stamping the snow off his boots. He closed the door. Mama pulled the pins from her mouth, laid them on the table, and came over to unwrap Papa's muffler from his face.

"Carl, you're frozen through!"

"Heater's broken in the truck." His teeth chattered, but he smiled and gave Mama a hello kiss. "Brrr! What say we start looking for a nice pulpit in Florida?"

Mama smiled back and hung up the wet muffler, hat, and coat near the stove to dry.

"Say! There's the girl I was looking for," Papa said to me. "Mrs. Karlsberg showed up in my office in a panic this afternoon. Seems her son, Otto, broke his arm sledding and won't be able to play for the children's choir on Christmas."

Curt shouted, "Hooray! Does that mean I don't have to sing?"

"Nope. In spite of Mrs. Karlsberg's conviction that the whole Christmas Eve service and perhaps Christmas itself might have to be cancelled, I thought we might be able to come up with a solution. What do you say, Elise?" He held out a piece of sheet music. "Would you be willing to give it a try?

"You don't have to do it if you feel there isn't enough time," he added as he handed me the music. "I don't know much about music, but Mrs. Karlsberg says it is a very complicated piece. It took Otto three months to learn it, so if there isn't enough time, just say so. The children can always sing without accompaniment if they have to."

I glanced at the music, thinking Otto Karlsberg must be a musical moron if it had taken him three months to master it, but I didn't say that to Papa. Instead I just said that I would be willing to try. It would be my first time playing in front of a real audience, but the piece was so simple that I wasn't really worried. Even so, I spent a few hours practicing just to make sure. Finding time to practice was easier since the Schollers had given us their old spinet piano. They had said we might as well have it since Mrs. Scholler's arthritis was too bad to allow her to play anymore, but I thought it was awfully nice of them to give it to us, anyway. The much used upright was a bit scarred, and the piano stool was a bit wobbly, but a little tuning brought out a tone that was surprisingly rich considering its size and age. Of course, I still loved playing the shining, ebony church piano whenever I could, but having a piano in the house was awfully convenient.

We had a two-hour rehearsal with the choir just the day before the service. The children were much more interested in shoving one another and comparing lists of hoped-for Christmas gifts than they were in singing. Curt did well enough, though his solo was tentative and his voice too weak to fill the empty room. The best that could be said about the rest of the children was that they were cute and sang on-key, most of the time. Mrs. Karlsberg was frazzled. She kept tapping her music stand impatiently with her baton in order to bring the group to attention, which didn't really do any good.

Mrs. Karlsberg finally dismissed the children with a forced smile and an encouraging "Well done," but I could see she was convinced that the whole thing was going to be a disaster. Frankly, I thought so, too. However, none of that seemed to matter on Christmas Eve.

The church glowed with the light of dozens of candles that had been placed on the altar and, as welcoming beacons, at the base of every window. A fresh, resiny scent of newly cut pine boughs filled the air, released by the heat of the candle flames and the warmth of human bodies packed tightly together.

Every pew was filled. The ushers had come around three times asking people to squeeze in just a bit more toward the middle so they could make room for a few more congregants. I recognized many of the faces in the crowd. Oddly, even the people I didn't know seemed somehow familiar. They were farming folk; their faces were lined, tanned, and a little weary. Life was hard for them, and they never expected it to be any different, yet it was Christmas, and most of them were in good spirits. When the ushers asked them to move, they obliged willingly. Only a few of the older people were disgruntled at the idea of being forced to abandon their usual seats to accommodate the crowd.

From my seat at the piano, I could hear one of the old ladies sitting in the second pew grumble that she didn't know "why we have to be shoved in like sardines to make room for a bunch of people who only show up for Easter and Christmas. Where are these people when it comes time to fill up the collection plate every week, that's what I'd like to know!" She muttered on to herself like this for some time, but she slid over to make room for a mother and son who'd arrived late just the same, and returned their "Merry Christmas" with a smile, though it wasn't a broad one.

On the other side of the church I spotted Mrs. Ludwig in her usual spot, third pew from the front on the right and directly on the aisle. Christmas or no, she clearly had no intention of yielding her territory to a lot of interlopers. Each time an usher approached with yet another churchgoer in search of a seat, Mrs. Ludwig would glare at them and then pull her knees over to the side so the person could squeeze past her, but it was clear she simply would not be moved out of her accustomed place.

At five minutes after eight, Papa Muller stepped up to the podium and in his warmest and loudest voice welcomed the worshippers. "Members, families, friends, and visitors! We are glad you have joined us on this very special night. Let us pray."

When the prayer was finished, he turned and gave a slight nod to Mrs. Karlsberg. She opened the door that led from Papa's office to the altar and began shepherding her young charges into the sanctuary, arranging them into the correct groupings because, even though Mrs. Karlsberg had warned them not to, they'd gotten out of order while waiting to go on.

There were about twenty children in all, dressed as angels with white robes, tinsel halos, and wings fashioned from pasteboard and glitter. Some of the little angels smiled and waved at parents and grandparents who sat in the pews. Others had wide eyes and frightened expressions.

Curt, however, was the most irritated-looking angel I'd ever seen. He tried sneaking into the back row where people would be less likely to see him, but Mrs. Karlsberg spotted him and pulled him up front and center, right in front of Cheryl Post, who looked almost as annoyed as Curt did. When the angels had been rearranged to her satisfaction, Mrs. Karlsberg took her place in front of the choir, gave the children a nervous smile, looked over to see if I was ready, and then raised her baton. I gave Curt an encouraging wink as I positioned my hands over the keyboard and waited for Mrs. Karlsberg to give me the downbeat.

Something magical happened as I touched the keys and played the first notes. The children opened their mouths in perfect, matching, round o's, and their voices blended together in a sound so innocent and sweet that, had I believed in angels, I would have sworn they were standing there in front of me. At the proper moment, Curt took one step forward and sang alone in a high, pure soprano.

A thrill of hope, the weary world rejoices!
For yonder beams a new and glorious morn,
Fall on your knees! O, hear the angel voices!
O, night divine! O, night! O, holy night!

He stepped back into line, and the rest of the children joined in to repeat the chorus. Every child was perfectly attentive, eyes fixed on Mrs. Karlsberg's baton as she led them into the final chorus, bringing them note by note though a perfectly timed and triumphant crescendo. A thrill of hope. A weary world rejoicing. For one moment it seemed possible.

The choir hung on to the last note for as long as it could. Mrs. Karlsberg, now beaming, lowered her baton, and for a split second the crowd sat in stunned silence. Then it broke into a thunderous wave of spontaneous applause. I was shocked! Musical performances in the Brightfield church were normally acknowledged by a reverent "Amen." Mrs. Ludwig herself had told me that clapping in church was for Baptists, Pentecostals, and other overly demonstrative types. I looked over to the third-row aisle to see her reaction. She was applauding with the rest.

The noise died down as the children trooped away from the altar to join their families. I sat down next to Mama, and she gave my hand an approving squeeze.

Papa stepped up to the pulpit and paused for a long moment, inclining his head as he looked down at the open Bible in front of him as though considering what he should say. The sanctuary was perfectly quiet, pricked with anticipation. Even the babies ceased their fussing and seemed to be waiting to hear what their minister would say. Finally, he looked up and slowly scanned the room as if trying to make direct eye contact with every person in the crowd.

"If you've read your bulletin, you know that the title of my sermon is supposed to be 'The Star That Leads to Bethlehem' and my text is taken from the second chapter of the book of Matthew. Until about five minutes ago," he said in a voice that sounded surprised, "I thought that was the message I would be preaching, but I believe God wants me to speak of other things, and so I will."

Out of the corner of my eye I could see Junior and Cookie exchange questioning glances. Papa had been practicing his Christmas sermon for at least three weeks. At this point any one of us could have delivered that sermon word for word. It was amazing to think that now, at the last minute and after so many hours of preparation, Papa had abandoned his prepared text and was going speak without notes. This was an intriguing development. I leaned forward to hear what he had to say.

"Instead, I'd like to speak about the Christmas story as it is presented in the second chapter of Luke, but perhaps not in the way you are used to hearing it. You know that story well, how the angel of God appeared to shepherds abiding in the fields who were watching their flocks by night and told them that Christ had been born. In fact, many of you know that story so well that you can probably recite it verse for verse.

"It is a marvelous story, the story of God's coming to earth as a man that he might bring salvation to an undeserving world, but I am afraid we may have heard it so often that it is beginning to be sound like just that, a story—something that happened once upon a time in a faraway land. We'd like to believe it but can't quite bring ourselves to the point of credulity.

"Can it really be true? Does it make sense to think that God would come down on earth as a baby born in a manger? If God the king is coming, then why doesn't he appear as a king, entering His dominions with power and wrath? And then there is this whole business of angels making announcements to shepherds. If God wanted to announce His arrival on earth, why not send angelic messengers directly to Herod himself? Why not surround Herod with a great company of the heavenly host and make him sore afraid instead of the shepherds? Does it make sense to think that the first people to be told of His coming would be a band of poor, dirty, seminomadic shepherds who were sitting around a fire at night, telling stories and trying to keep warm?"

Papa considered his own question for a moment before continuing in the same straightforward manner, as though he were just having a conversation with a friend.

"I think it does. You see, these shepherds were simple men, men of the earth who worked close to the land to make their living, like most of you. Being people of the land, like you, the shepherds already knew something about miracles. They were daily witnesses to the miracles of life and birth, the regularity of seasonal cycles, the mysteries of seeds and harvests. They were surrounded by miracles every day. They were dependent on them.

"Kings and princes aren't too good at being dependent. They are used to relying on their own riches and power and armies to make things happen according to their own will and to satisfy their own lust for more power, more armies, more riches—often with nightmarish results." Papa's voice became more hushed as he said this last part, and I knew, as everyone else did, that he was thinking not of infants murdered by Herodic decree but of the war raging across the sea that seemed to draw closer every day.

"Then, as now, simple people of the land must depend on God's grace as shown through the miracle and provision of creation to survive. Shepherds are familiar with miracles. Just like you. So when this greatest of miracles was announced to them, they were prepared to believe. They did believe.

"The second the angels left, these shepherds ran, literally ran, to Bethlehem to see this miraculous thing they'd been told about. And something about that sight, something about that child, must have been truly miraculous, because the shepherds told everyone they knew about what they'd seen, and those who heard their story were amazed. Their lives were forever changed in ways they could never have anticipated. If you already believe the truth of this story—if you've already stood by the manger in amazement and gratitude to look on the face of God come to earth out of love for you, then you understand what I'm talking about."

Papa smiled and looked around the church to acknowledge the nodded agreement of many listeners. Their faces glowed with an emotion I could not quite name, but their eyes held the same quiet peace I'd seen so often in Papa and Mama's gaze. I suddenly felt very lonely.

Papa paused and inclined his head slightly toward me. "Yet, some of you are not yet able to believe, though you may truly wish to. That's all right. All right for now. But in the meantime, prepare for belief. Prepare yourself for belief now so that when the moment comes, when the angel announces the arrival of the king, you will be able to respond and run into His presence. Draw closer to God by acknowledging the simple and the wonderful in the miracle of creation—the stars in the night sky that seem to hang like so many diamonds in the heavens. The transformation of the fields from fallow, to seed sown, to providential harvest and back. The river that gives life to the valley and whose streams make glad the city of God. Acknowledge these miracles of creation, believe in them for what they are, and, in time, you will acknowledge and believe in the presence of God Himself. "

I swallowed hard in an effort to dislodge the lump in my throat, and I could feel my eyes sting with tears that I refused to release. He was speaking to me. I wanted to believe in whatever it was he was describing, this presence that seemed real to everyone except me, but I could not believe it was as simple as Papa said. If he would just tell me what to do, I would do it, but there had to be more to it than what he was saying.

"Be patient," he said gently, as if he knew what I was thinking. "This is not a test you can study for, or a task you can master through your own strength or power of intellect. God reveals himself in His own way, in His own time, to those who least expect it and least deserve it. Prepare yourself to believe, and belief will come."

That night I lay in bed with my eyes closed and said a prayer to the God I did not believe in. "If You are there," I said, "I am willing to believe, if You will show me how. I can't do it myself. It will have to be up to You."

I kept my eyes shut tight. Waited for something to happen. Nothing did. I opened my eyes, and the dark room looked just like it had a moment before.

Silly, I thought and pulled the covers up tight under my chin and went to sleep. For a long time, I forgot about the whole thing.

Chapter 9

"Cookie! Elise!" called Mama from the bottom of the staircase. "This is the third time I've called you. Your eggs are getting cold."

She stood silently, waiting to hear some sort of movement from our room, and when none was forthcoming she tossed out her most effective threat. "Girls! Don't make me come up there!"

At this last, Cookie leapt out of bed and promised she'd be downstairs in five minutes. I lingered under the covers a minute more, dreading the moment when I'd have to put my feet on the chilly floorboards. How could it be so cold this late in May? Here it was the last day of school. . . . The last day of school! I suddenly remembered that the spelling bee was today. I threw back the covers and got out of bed.

Cookie was nearly dressed by now. She didn't speak to me or wait for me. That was nothing new. Cookie scurried out of the cold room with her shoes and clean stockings in hand so she could finish dressing in front of the stove in the kitchen. Fine with me. I stayed where I was. Better to dress in the cold bedroom than spend any more time than I had to with Cookie. We'd be together again soon enough. Our desks were right next to each other, and with each passing day our proximity increased our mutual dislike.

I looked out the window as I dressed. There was a silvery glazing of frost on the grass, but the sun was shining, throwing a gleaming reflection onto each blade of grass. It would not take long for those bright rays to melt the frost and warm the fields. In the distance I could hear the rattle of a tractor starting up. Someone was thinking about planting.

Spring had finally come to New England, but—cold floorboards notwithstanding—I wished it were still winter. During the winter there had been little talk about the war. Every once in a while someone would shake their head and "tut tut" a bit about the poor Poles or the poor Finns, but winter is a quiet time for battles. After a while it seemed like people forgot there was a war. Father's letters regained their vague and impersonal nature, only rarely giving a hint of what might be going on in his life. That made it easy to imagine he simply was a businessman away on some extended journey involving details of commerce and economics that were too dull to write about rather than a warrior. When youth and an ocean separate you from the harsh realities of life, it is easy to ignore all sorts of realities.

But whereas spring came late to Massachusetts, it arrived right on schedule in Europe. As the pages on the calendar turned from March to April to May, German tanks began rolling again. Day after day, the newspaper headlines screamed *Invasion!* The list was long: Norway, Denmark, Holland, Belgium, Luxembourg, France. Suddenly the talk around the Muller table was all about war and rumors of war. Would America fight? Should she fight?

But no matter the state of world affairs, farmers are always farmers, and as the weeks passed, the main topic of conversation in Brightfield shifted from worries about war to worries about when planting could begin. Even Mrs. Ludwig said she couldn't remember a spring as cold and wet as this one, and she had seen more springs than anyone in town.

Today the sun was shining. It wouldn't be long before the barren fields would be transformed into verdant, humid tobacco jungles and people would be too busy to think about the war.

From the window I could see Curt playing next to the big oak. He called to me and waved a greeting. I waved back. He was such a sweet boy, I thought, as I did up my braids. It was a shame the rest of his siblings weren't more like him.

I didn't feel the twins truly disliked me; they just followed Junior's lead because he was their big brother. They ignored me rather than going out of their way to truly hurt me. Actually, in a way they kind of ignored everyone. They were so complete in their own relationship and usually so absorbed in their latest project or invention that they didn't seem to need anyone else.

Junior was another matter. Almost from the moment he'd met me, he disliked me, and the situation had not improved as the months passed. It was too bad, I reflected, because in many ways we were a lot alike. We were both proud, and we both liked to be right. He ordered his brothers and sister around like the captain of his own private army. Yet, in spite of his clear position as the commander of his siblings and his habit of taking them down a notch when he felt they got out of line, he was intensely and fiercely protective of his family. I respected him for it. Why couldn't he do the same for me? The pastor's son and the officer's daughter, we both carried the unwanted weight of family expectations. I wished we could have been friends. Had we been, I would have told him I understood how it felt to have everyone expecting so much of you just because you'd been born into a particular family. As it was, I couldn't remember the last time he'd spoken directly to me.

Cookie was just as skilled as her brother when it came to enforcing the silent treatment; however, when it came to her, I almost never entertained a kindly thought. For that one brief moment before harvest supper she had seemed to thaw toward me, but the minute she saw me dancing with Papa the chill was back in the air. My success in playing at the Christmas service and the ensuing admiration I received made everything worse. It made me mad every time I thought about it. It wasn't as though I had asked to be dropped into the middle of the Muller family!

The jealousy between us had reached glacial proportions. If we'd been boys somebody probably would have thrown a punch and we could have worked the whole thing out with one good fistfight, but girls' means of proving themselves are slower and leave more scars. Cookie and I were both good students and both driven to excel in our studies, so the classroom became our boxing ring.

As Father had predicted in his letter, I struggled a bit with reading and writing in English initially. However, considering that English was not my native language, I did quite well. Soon Cookie and I were jockeying for position at the head of the class, and, in the previous few weeks I had actually pulled ahead of her. The other children in the class began teasing me by calling me "teacher's pet." Cookie joined in their catcalls with vigor, though she herself had been the victim of such taunting only weeks before and had seemed bothered by it. Now it appeared as if she would prefer nothing more than to regain her former status as the object of schoolyard derision and jealousy. Not if I could help it.

At the beginning of the year I had understood Cookie's irritation with me, at least in part, just as I understood her drive to be first in her class. But the more I excelled in the schoolroom, the more Cookie made fun of me in areas where I was less adept, especially when it came to schoolyard games and domestic chores.

My Saturday lessons with Mrs. Ludwig were slowly improving my cooking skills, but I was still nervous and afraid of making a mistake when I was in the Muller kitchen. Hearing Cookie's sighs or seeing her roll her eyes whenever I did make an error did not improve my confidence. Once, I was absolutely certain that she deliberately tripped me as I was putting away a stack of coffee cups and caused me to drop and break one, though I could not prove it. I wanted to get back at her, and I knew how to do it.

The eighth-grade spelling bee was the last event of our last day in grammar school. First prize was a beautiful illustrated dictionary bound in blue leather with page after page of color drawings and photographs. Mr. Flanders, president of the school board and owner of the five-and-dime, donated the dictionary and would personally present it to the champion speller. It was as fine as any book in Papa Muller's study and I was determined to win it.

So was Cookie, and that made me want it all the more.

The good-natured joking and smiling carelessness of the spellers who had gone down in the early rounds had been replaced by a sense of mounting tension and suspense as the students still standing dwindled down to the final few who actually had a chance to win and desperately wanted to do so. John Harkness, the class bully who was known as Hark, had been the first to be eliminated when he spelled *paragraph* with an *f*. I had been next in line after him. When I spelled my word correctly, he gave me a glare and coughed a derisive "Kraut!" into his fist, but the teacher hadn't heard the insult, so I pretended I hadn't, either.

Miss Gleason stood at the front of the room calling out the words. Mr. Flanders, a man of considerable bulk, was wedged into a desk in the front row, observing the scene with folded arms. I was surprised to see how many students had been confounded by even relatively simple words, words we had gone over time and time again in class and which had made up the previous weeks' spelling tests. I noticed that Miss Gleason's jaw clenched every time a student missed one of these words. However, her spirits appeared to lift as the words became harder and the competition between the remaining spellers became more intense. Her encouraging exclamations of "Excellent!" and "Well done!" seemed genuine and more enthusiastic as we progressed to more and more challenging words like *mellifluous, financier,* and *abhorrent.*

Finally it was down to Cookie, Betsy Semple, and myself, but Betsy went down on *pellucid.* I was relieved that Cookie was after her, because I had never heard the word before. Cookie rattled it off without a moment's hesitation, and we went on.

The pressure mounted. The room was perfectly quiet, and in the silence I could hear my own heart beating harder and louder as Miss Gleason announced every new word. I can't remember how many rounds we went through before the clock finally struck two. Miss Gleason got up from her desk, closed her spelling book, and said, "Well, we certainly have two very talented spellers here, but I'm afraid we have run out of time." She smiled apologetically.

There was an audible groan from the students. I was surprised by their reaction, thinking they'd all be impatient to leave and start their summer holidays, but they'd become wrapped up in the drama and were anxious to see the conclusion.

The noise of a male throat being cleared sounded from the front row. Mr. Flanders pried himself loose from the grip of the desk and got to his feet. He took a step up to the front of the room and stood next to the petite and pretty Miss Gleason, utterly dwarfing her with his bulk and imperious presence. He grabbed one of his lapels with his left hand and addressed the class in a booming bass voice. "I think these two young ladies have done a wonderful job. They are clearly both excellent scholars and a credit to our school and"—he nodded toward Miss Gleason—"to the skills and dedication of their teacher. She deserves a round of applause!"

The students clapped enthusiastically, and Cookie and I joined in. Some of the boys whistled enthusiastically. Just about everyone in the class liked Miss Gleason. She was blond and pretty, with big blue, laughing eyes. The girls tried their best to ape her breathless way of speaking and her hairstyles, and most of the boys were a little in love with her.

When the applause died down, Mr. Flanders continued in his best oratorical style. "And I also think we need to congratulate our two champion spellers!" The students began clapping again, and I couldn't help but notice that Betsy Semple, whose eyes were still a bit red from the tears that she'd unsuccessfully tried to suppress when she'd been eliminated, was applauding harder than anyone else and smiling at me and Cookie. I felt ashamed of myself. The whole competition seemed suddenly childish and stupid. I was glad it was done with.

"You girls have done a great job," Mr. Flanders said as he turned to us with a beaming smile. "I think I'd have been hard-pressed to spell quite a few of the words you two were given." He chuckled warmly at his own joke, and a few of the students joined in, some more vigorously than was proper. Mr. Flanders was right in his assessment; more than once I'd noticed spelling errors in the hand-lettered signs posted in the window of the five-and-dime advertising specials on everything from *Burma-Shave* to *knockwurst.*

Miss Gleason quieted the class before the laughter got out of hand, and Mr. Flanders, who suddenly realized that he had become the butt of a joke but wasn't quite sure how, continued in a voice even louder and more pompous than before.

"As I said, both of these girls are champions, so I think the only fair thing to do is to declare the spelling bee a draw and congratulate our two winners!"

The class broke out into applause again, but Ernest Rohleder, who clearly found this to be an unsatisfactory solution to the problem, interrupted. "You can't do that," he protested. "There's only one dictionary. Which one of them is going to get the prize?"

"I will donate another dictionary," Mr. Flanders hissed through clenched teeth, obviously irritated that he would have to spring for another prize.

This seemed like a perfectly fair and reasonable solution to me, especially after my earlier observation about the difference between Betsy's attitude and my own. I was more than ready to declare the contest a draw. But before I could speak, Cookie surprised everyone and said, "That's not fair. It's not what we agreed to. You can't just go changing the rules in the middle of the competition."

The room went dead silent. No one could quite believe that Cookie, who was known as one of the most polite members of the eighth-grade class and a special favorite of every teacher in the school, was standing there contradicting the president of the school board and practically accusing him of being a cheater! Mr. Flanders sputtered and looked at Cookie as if she'd lost her mind. Miss Gleason, who could not have been ignorant of the increasingly heated rivalry between her two best students and probably guessed that a showdown was inevitable, came to the rescue.

"Mr. Flanders," she said soothingly, her voice soft and rich with admiration that just skirted the edge of flattery, "you have already been more than generous. You not only donated this truly magnificent prize"—she smiled as she patted the dictionary that was sitting on her desk—"you've honored us with your time and presence here today. We simply couldn't ask you to do more." Miss Gleason smiled her broadest and most sincere smile. Mr. Flanders was, of course, completely enchanted and ducked his head and shuffled his shoes with pleasure.

"However," she continued pleasantly, "it is time for school to be dismissed, so I suggest that the rest of you children go home, and Cookie, Elise, and I will stay here and finish the spelling bee."

There was a rumble of protest among the students. Ernest waved his hand above his head and said, "Miss Gleason, can't I stay and watch? I don't need to be home at any special time, and I want to see who wins. I just can't go home! It would be like leaving a ball game with the bases loaded in the middle of the ninth inning!"

Miss Gleason's eyes twinkled, and she laughed at Ernest's intensity. "All right, Ernest. We'll take a break and begin again in ten minutes. You may stay if you wish, and that goes for the rest of the class." Her eyes scanned the faces of her students. "But you certainly don't have to if you don't want to. I'm sure some of you are expected at home."

At this announcement most of the students scurried to retake their seats, although a few of them headed for the cloakroom. Cookie went out into the hall to get a drink, and I went back to my desk to take a last-minute look at my spelling book. I turned to the back of the book, where the really hard words were, because I reasoned that, in an attempt to finally bring the contest to an end, Miss Gleason would look for the most difficult words she could find.

Jerry Brandt and Homer Miles, John Harkness's flunkies, gathered up their things. Noticing that their leader hadn't moved, Jerry yelled, "Hey, Hark! You're not gonna stay and watch this, are you? I'd just as soon watch paint dry." He guffawed at his own joke, and Homer joined in.

Hark froze them with a withering look, and they snapped their mouths closed. "Yeah, I'm staying," he reported and then, looking around and seeing that Miss Gleason had left the room, he got up from his desk. In a voice just loud enough so I could hear, he snarled, "I want to stay to see Miss Smart Nazi here get her tail waxed. She thinks she's really something, coming in here, making up to the teacher, and trying to make everybody look bad. She's nothing! She's going to lose, and I'm gonna stay and see it happen." He glared at me with a look so full of hatred that for a moment I was truly frightened. The hair stood up on the back of my neck. I knew that answering him would just make things worse, so I lowered my head and tried harder to concentrate on the word list in front of me.

He walked up behind me and bent over me so close I could feel his breath. "You hear what I said?"

I ignored him.

"Hey!" he spat, and tugged on my braid to get my attention, but I didn't move. He pulled on my hair again, hard enough to hurt, and raised his voice to a shout. "Hey! Did you hear me? Huh?" He jerked my braid so hard that my scalp hurt. "Hey, Fraulein! Hey, Kraut-Eater! Hey, you Nazi! You deaf or something?"

"John Harkness! That will be enough of that! Sit down this instant!" Miss Gleason shouted with a volume and energy that was astounding. Who knew our gentle, petite, maiden teacher with the breathless voice could yell like that? Her high heels clicked irritation as she came into the room. Cookie was right behind her. Miss Gleason's usually blue eyes flashed violet thunder, and even Hark seemed a bit afraid of her. In any case, he obeyed and sat down in his desk, cowed but still scowling.

Miss Gleason stared at him for a moment. Her breast heaved with poorly suppressed anger. "I will not tolerate that kind of talk in my classroom. Do I make myself perfectly clear, or shall we go to Principal Harney's office and discuss it with him?"

Hark shifted in his seat and mumbled something inaudible.

"I'm sorry?" Miss Gleason barked. "Did you say something, Mr. Harkness? I didn't hear you."

"Yes ma'am," Hark said softly but sharply, his voice still tight with anger.

"Yes ma'am what?" asked Miss Gleason with a warning stare.

"Yes ma'am. You make yourself perfectly clear," he replied flatly.

"Good," said Miss Gleason. Then, turning to Jerry and Homer, she said, "You boys may go now. Good luck in high school next year," she said distractedly. "Have a nice summer."

Jerry and Homer left. Miss Gleason took a deep breath and looked around the classroom at the remaining students, whose eyes were still wide from surprise and seemed to hold a new respect for their teacher. "Cookie? Elise? Are you ready? Good. Everyone else—take your seats. Let's get started."

I followed Cookie to the front of the room, but I was so unnerved by what had happened that I would have preferred to just withdraw from the contest and let Cookie have the prize and the title of Best Eighth-Grade Speller. In fact, I considered saying exactly that, but every eye in the classroom was now fixed on us, and it seemed too late to do anything but go ahead and finish what we had started. As Miss Gleason was taking her seat at her desk and opening her book, it did occur to me that I could go a couple more rounds, then purposely misspell a word, throwing the contest. Maybe if I did, Cookie and I could finally put this stupid jealousy behind us. The more I thought about it, the more it seemed like the best solution. The idea cheered me, and I stood up a little straighter, waiting to hear the first word.

"Cookie," Miss Gleason said evenly. "You will go first. Your word is *soiree*."

Cookie blinked, and I could see a look of panic spread across her face. It was the first time I'd ever seen her look like that. I knew she had no idea of how to spell it. But I did.

Only minutes before, I had been sitting at my desk pretending to study the "For an Extra Challenge!" section at the back of the spelling book, and one of the words on the list was *soiree!* I could scarcely believe it! If you had asked me at the time if I had been able to recall any of the words on that page I would have said no, but now the list was clear in my mind. I could see that one word perfectly as though it was printed on my memory. The room was absolutely silent as everyone waited for Cookie to begin spelling. I could hear the clock evenly ticking off the seconds.

Cookie took a deep breath, closed her eyes and began. "Soiree. S . . ." She hesitated and wrinkled her brow. "O-I-R-" I thought that she had it. The first syllable was the most difficult.

"Wait," she said opening her eyes and looking at Miss Gleason. "May I start again?" Miss Gleason nodded. Cookie closed her eyes and began to spell again with more confidence.

"Soiree. S-O-I-R-E . . ." She hesitated again. "Y?" she asked and looked to Miss Gleason for confirmation.

"I am sorry," Miss Gleason said, and the students exhaled a collective sigh of disappointment. "That is incorrect. Elise, if you can spell the word correctly, you will be our new champion. If not, we will continue with the next word."

In my mind I had already worked out that I was going to spell it *soiray* and then purposely misspell the next word, no matter how easy it might be, but just at that moment I heard Hark sneer from his seat in the back of the room. "She can't do it! She's a stinkin' Nazi! Her father is a—"

"That's enough!" Miss Gleason barked. "Mr. Harkness, I have lost my patience with you!" She reached for a pad of paper on her desk, scribbled out a note and held it out. "Here. John, take this note and go wait outside Mr. Harney's office. I'll be down later to make sure you are there."

Hark sat in his chair for a moment, as though daring Miss Gleason to make him get up. She didn't say a word but just continued to hold out the slip of paper, her arm as straight and unwavering as an iron rod and her eyes like steel. Finally, Hark slowly got up, walked to Miss Gleason's desk and took the note, crumpling it in his hand as he did. Miss Gleason whispered in a steely voice. "Go, John. Now!"

He did, but he took his time going to the door. Miss Gleason, her nostrils still flared with anger, composed her voice and turned her attention to me. "Elise? Are you ready? The word is *soiree.*"

I squared my shoulders and bit my lip in mock concentration, fully prepared to make my error look convincing. As I was about to begin, I heard a short, hacking sound. Hark approached the door and pretended to cough again, barking an unspeakable insult into his fist. Then he clicked his heels and raised his hand in a mocking German salute before opening the door.

It happened so quickly that Miss Gleason didn't really have a chance to respond. He shot me a final look of utter hatred, and I hated him back. I would show him! Without thinking I opened my mouth and fairly shouted, "Soiree! S-O-I-R-E-E!"

Chapter 10

Miss Gleason's heels clicked urgently behind me as I trudged down the hallway of the empty school building toward the main doors. The wood floors shone shiny and slick between the scuff marks left by the shoes of children anxious to begin an entire summer of vacation. The halls were empty. Cookie had run out of the building as soon as Miss Gleason had presented the dictionary to me, her eyes filled with tears. The other children were gone just as quickly. I lingered behind as long as I could, not really wanting to go home.

Rays of afternoon sun spilled in through the high, transomed windows. The corridor smelled pleasantly of beeswax and pencil shavings, ink and rubber balls. It was the schoolhouse smell, the same the world over—in America or in Germany, there is no difference. Normally I found the aroma comforting, but not today. Nothing had turned out as I had hoped, even though I'd gotten everything I'd hoped for. The beautiful blue dictionary, still wrapped with ribbons, was heavy in my arms. For weeks it had sat on the edge of Miss Gleason's desk, and I had admired it, imagining how wonderful it would feel to carry it home, solid and sure with the weight of victory. Now that the prize was mine, I felt no pride in my accomplishment or satisfaction in the settling of scores, just the weight of a guilty conscience.

When I opened the door and walked down the steps into the playground I saw little Curt lying facedown on his stomach over the hard seat of a wooden swing, swaying idly back and forth, and looking at the ground as though deep in thought.

"Curt? What are you doing here?"

At the sound of my voice, his head lifted and he grinned at me, showing a row of shiny baby teeth and a space in front where one was missing.

"Waiting for you," he replied happily. "Cookie ran out and didn't even see me. Can I walk home with you?"

Curt always walked home with Cookie, but she must have been so wrapped up in the results of the contest that she had forgotten all about him. So had I. The poor little thing must have been waiting for at least an hour.

"I'm sorry, Curt. You must be so tired of waiting!"

"Naw," he said dismissively. "I been playing." Noticing the prize dictionary tucked under my arm, his eyes grew wide with admiration.

"Is that it?" he asked with a touch of awe in his voice. "Did you win?"

"Yes."

"It's beautiful! Can I hold it?"

I handed him the book, slipping the ribbon off the binding so he could see the pictures. He turned the pages reverently, admiring the illustrations and pointing to some of the longer words and asking me how to pronounce them. After a few minutes he looked up from the pages and beamed at me again, but something in my face must have concerned him, and his smile faded.

"Don't you like it?" he asked.

I thought for a moment. "Not as much as I thought I would."

"Well, you should," he said practically. "It's the best book I ever saw."

"Would you like to have it?" I asked. "I'll give it to you." It seemed like a wonderful idea to me. The elegance and symbolism of the prize had been spoiled for me, but maybe by giving it to Curt I could redeem something of its value.

Rather than looking pleased by the offer, Curt seemed bothered. His cheeks flushed bright red, and his eyes darted away from mine as he answered. "No . . . no thanks."

"Why not? Really, Curt. Go ahead and take it. It's all right," I assured him, wondering if he doubted my sincerity.

"I can't."

"Yes, you can! It's just a book. Of course, it is a very nice volume, and you must take good care of it, but you are always so careful with your things that I'm sure—"

"I can't read it!" he blurted out. "I can't read anything!"

I was confused. "Of course you can't read all those big words yet. You're only in the second grade, after all. You'll see—before long you'll be able to read every word in this dictionary! In the meantime, you can always ask me to tell you any of the words you don't know."

Curt's eyes welled up with tears, and he tried to blink them back as he spoke. "You don't understand. I c . . . ca-can't read any of the words. Not any of them!"

"What are you talking about? I've seen you read many times. Just last week I was listening to you as you were reading 'The Three Bears' out of the big fairy-tale book we have at home."

"No. I know all the words. I can t-t-tell the story, but I can't read the words," he explained.

Suddenly I understood. He had memorized the stories, word for word, but he didn't recognize the arrangement of letters that made up the individual words. Night after night of listening to the same twenty or thirty children's stories had allowed him to remember them perfectly, and by acting like he was reading the words and turning the pages in the proper places, he had convinced all of us that he could read.

I simply didn't know what to say. Curt hung his head low, and I heard him sniff. "Oh, Curt," I murmured inadequately, putting my hand on his shoulder. He mumbled something unintelligible, and I had to ask him to repeat himself.

He lifted his head, his eyes full of tears. "I said, I'm the only one in my class who can't read. I'm stupid," he said softly.

" Curt! You mustn't say that! You're a very, very smart boy." It was true. He was bright. He was able to build complex and detailed model cities out of old cardboard boxes, cans, bottles, empty spools of thread, or anything else he could find. His creations were truly ingenious. He had fashioned a hand-cranked elevator for his model skyscraper, and he had painted and carefully joined tiny bits of cellophane to create a stained-glass window for his church. Any seven-year-old who could think up and actually construct such complicated designs was obviously very clever. So why couldn't he read?

Curt wiped his nose on the sleeve of his coat. "Mrs. Halvorsen says I have to give this note to Papa and Mama," he said, dejectedly holding out a folded piece of notepaper. "I guess I'm in trouble."

I took the paper from him and read it. "You're not in trouble, Curt." The teacher's note said that she wanted to meet with the Mullers to discuss having Curt repeat the second grade, but I couldn't bring myself to tell him that. "It just says here that you're having some trouble in class and that Mrs. Halvorsen wants to see Mama and Papa."

"Then I'll be in trouble," he said gloomily.

"Don't be silly! Are you trying your best in class?" Curt nodded his head.

"Do you behave yourself in school?" He nodded again.

"Then there's nothing to worry about. It just sounds like you need some extra help. Once you get it, I'm sure you'll be able to read."

He wasn't convinced.

"It's true. Look at me," I reasoned. "I am good at schoolwork, but cooking is very hard for me. Now that I am getting some extra help from Mrs. Ludwig, I'm improving."

Curt's eyes grew wide with fright. "I won't have to go to Mrs. Ludwig's house for help with reading, will I?"

"Of course not," I said, smiling. "But she really isn't that scary once you get to know her. I go to see Mrs. Ludwig for extra help with cooking because she is a good cook. You'll need to get help with your reading from someone who is good at reading."

Curt paused for a moment as he considered this line of reasoning. "Well, then, why don't you help me? You're good at reading."

"I'm not a proper teacher," I demurred. "I'm sure Mrs. Halvorsen will have some kind of plan to help you. Maybe by spending some extra time after school."

"Well, Mrs. Halvorsen is a proper teacher, and she hasn't been able to teach me to read no matter how hard she tries," Curt replied logically. "Maybe it's time to try something else. You couldn't do any worse than her."

He had a point. Mrs. Halvorsen hadn't been able to help him. Maybe someone else could. Maybe me. I still had my doubts, but one look at Curt's pleading blue eyes convinced me that I at least owed it to him to try. "All right. I don't know if it will do any good, but if you really want me to, we can work on your reading together."

"That's great, Elise! When can we start?"

"Soon," I said. "Give me a day or two to think about what we should do. All right?"

"All right," he agreed. "I really do want to read, Elise."

"You will," I said, hoping that I wasn't lying to him. "Now let's go home. It's late."

"You know, I'm really good at math," he said earnestly as we trudged along.

"I know you are. I've seen your math papers. You can do very hard problems."

"Ask me what five times five is, Elise. Go ahead! Ask me," he urged.

I obliged, and he gave me the answer. We walked on for some time playing this game, with Curt supplying both the questions and the answers while I served as narrator. Occasionally, I posed a couple of my own problems, and he was able to answer those just as quickly and accurately as the others. He had a good memory for figures, and, of course, he'd memorized all the stories he'd convinced us he was able to read. He really was a bright little thing. I wondered if it wouldn't be possible to take advantage of his remarkable memory in helping him learn how to read.

I considered all this as we plodded down the hill toward the house. Curt jabbered on, happily tossing out more equations, and I repeated them automatically, my mind so absorbed by my thoughts that when Hark stepped out from a big oak tree, it took me completely by surprise.

"Look at what we got here," he sneered, planting himself firmly in the center of the path, dropping his satchel of books by his side. "H . . . h . . . h-how y . . . y . . . you doin', C . . . C . . . Curt? What's the matter, Shrimp? Cat got your tongue?"

Curt was frozen with fear. His big eyes silently begged me to do something, but I was frightened, too. When we were in the safety of the schoolroom, I found Hark merely irritating, because I knew that Miss Gleason would intervene if necessary. Now, caught here, still a good half a mile from home and with no other houses nearby, I was scared. He saw the dictionary tucked under my arm. His eyes narrowed. I looked away, not wanting to provoke him. The important thing was to get Curt home as safely and quickly as possible.

"Come on, Curt." I whispered out the side of my mouth with studied calm, as though Hark were an agitated animal that I was trying to back away from. I took Curt's hand and stepped off the path, trying to break a new trail around Hark, who seemed suddenly enormous in comparison to myself and Curt. Hark barked out a short, quick laugh and moved directly in front of us, even closer than before.

"Hey! I asked you a question, Shrimp. Answer me!" he demanded, ignoring me completely and turning the full weight of his ire on Curt.

Clutching Curt's hand even more tightly, I tried once more to dodge past the bullying Hark, but he blocked us again.

"Huh? Did you hear me, dummy?" he screamed at the terrified Curt, who began to cry. "Are you deaf as well as stupid? *Answer me!"*

He shoved Curt as hard as he could. Curt collapsed onto the ground, sobbing. I was furious! Without a thought for what I was actually doing, I pulled my arm back, doubled up my fist, and threw a punch that landed squarely on Hark's nose, which began to bleed.

"Ow!" he cried. His hand flew up to his nose. He pulled it away, and inspected the blood on his fingers. For a moment he seemed surprised, but his expression of shock was quickly replaced by one of anger.

"Nobody hits me and gets away with it," he growled menacingly. "Not my dad. Not any stupid 'teacher's pet.' I don't care if you are a girl." He took a step toward me and grabbed my shoulder, pinching his fingers into my flesh. I winced with pain, and reached back with my fist preparing to throw another blow at his face. He grabbed my wrist before I could land the punch, then quickly wrenched my arm behind my back and twisted it hard, making me cry out.

Curt was still crying but, seeing how Hark was hurting me, climbed to his feet and jumped on Hark's back and started throwing punches of his own, pounding the big bully on his shoulder and yelling for him to leave me alone. Another voice joined in with his.

"John!" Papa shouted. *"John Harkness, stop it! Right now! Let her go!"*

I felt Hark's grip on me loosen and looked up to see Papa pulling him back and shaking him. Cookie came running up a few steps behind him and leaned against the oak tree, puffing from the effort of running.

Papa's eyes were full of fire. He spoke in a voice thick with anger, one I'd never heard him use, not even during his most fervent preaching. "What the hell do you think you're doing?" he shouted. "What are you doing? Hurting a girl? Pushing down a little kid half your size? What's the matter with you?"

Now it was Hark's turn to be frightened. Hark was a big boy, but next to Papa's towering six foot three, he seemed small. Papa had a tight grip on the boy's shoulders by now and shook him hard with every question. Hark tried to open his mouth to answer, but each time he tried, Papa shook him again and Hark just flopped back and forth with his mouth gaping and closing stupidly. Finally, Papa gave him one final shake, let go his grip on Hark's shoulder, and pushed him away.

"Go home, John," Papa spoke through a set jaw with a quiet intensity that was more menacing than his shouting had been. "Go home and stay there. I don't ever want to see you near any of my children, ever again. Do you hear me? Never again."

Hark mumbled something and backed a few steps away from Papa, who was still breathing hard. With his eyes still on Papa, he reached down to pick up the satchel of books he'd dropped on the ground, then turned around and ran east across the field in the direction of his own farm.

Papa stood with his arms down by his sides but his fists clenched and watched the boy go before speaking to me and to Curt. "Are you all right? Did he hurt you?" He turned his eyes on each of us in turn.

"No," I answered. "He pushed Curt and twisted my arm, but we're all right now."

"You're sure?" he questioned again. Curt and I nodded. Seeing that we meant it, he took a deep breath, and I could see his hands relax and his fists open a bit. "Good," he said. "That's all that matters."

Cookie, who had not said a word or moved a muscle since her arrival on the scene, suddenly exploded with excitement. "Papa! I thought you were going to kill him! I never even knew you knew how to fight! And I never heard you swear!" she exclaimed.

Papa rubbed his eye with his hand. He looked suddenly tired. "Well, I don't think you need to be quite so pleased. I'm sure it's nothing to be proud of."

"Yeah, but Papa! I just never saw you like that before!" Cookie continued in amazement. "You were like Tom Mix, riding in to rescue the women and children from a band of evil outlaws!"

Papa chuckled and turned to me. "Elise was the real hero of the day. That was quite a punch you threw. I think you may have broken his nose!"

"Elise broke his nose?" Cookie squeaked with surprise. "She punched him? I don't believe it!"

"She did, indeed," Papa replied, and Cookie laughed aloud at his confirmation. "I saw her do it. That's why I started running so fast to get over here. I figured if I didn't pull her off, she might kill the boy."

Cookie grinned. "I guess the properly brought up German young lady is turning into a real American girl." Papa smiled at me, and Cookie was obviously delighted, but I found the situation somewhat embarrassing.

"You don't really think I broke his nose, do you?" I asked, hoping that it wasn't true. "I didn't mean to hit him. He pushed Curt and then . . . I don't know what happened to me. I wasn't thinking. I was just so mad."

"It's all right," Papa said. "You were protecting someone you care about, and that was the right thing to do. But it's a bit frightening to realize how easily our protective instincts can get out of hand, isn't it?" I nodded in agreement.

"Yeah, Papa!" Cookie exclaimed in admiration. "For a second I thought you were going to kill him!"

"For a second I probably could have. I should have shown more control." Papa's face darkened.

I took his hand, squeezed it, and smiled up at him. "I'm glad you came when you did. But how did you know we needed you?"

"Cookie came home with red eyes and ran up to her room. Curt wasn't with her, and neither were you. It was getting late, and I was worried. Then Cookie came downstairs and told us the whole story. We decided we'd better come look for you."

"Papa, can we go home now?" Curt asked. "I'm starving!"

"Good idea!" Papa said. "Mama has some beef stew simmering on the stove. She even baked a pie in honor of the fact that we have the two best spellers in Brightfield in our family!"

"Is Elise a member of our family now?" Curt asked Papa eagerly, but it was Cookie who answered his question.

"Of course she is. Any girl who can land a punch like that is obviously a Muller!" Cookie and I exchanged grins.

Papa reached down and picked up the heavy dictionary from where it had fallen in the dirt. Then he invited Curt to climb up for a piggyback ride, and when he was securely on board with his arms wrapped tight around Papa's neck, Papa turned to Cookie and myself. "Come on, you two. Let's race to see who can get home fastest. Boys against girls. Ready, Curt?"

"Ready, Papa!" Curt answered, and we all took off at a clumsy lope through the uneven fields.

As we came closer to the house, Papa pretended to stumble, so we all arrived at the same time. The race was declared a tie. Mama opened the door to greet us. A wonderful aroma spilled out into the open air, a rich mixture of simmering meat, newly baked bread, and welcome. It smelled like belonging.

The last time I'd smelled that smell was when my mother was alive, when she'd still been well enough to smile and tell me what she liked to have me play and to remind me to keep the tempo even.

On Alexander Platz, the aroma of belonging was lavender, menthol, and strong tea. In Brightfield, the recipe was different, but the result was the same. I breathed in deeply, and a peace settled in and around my heart, the same way it did when I stood on the hillocks just above the river. At those times I simply knew there was no place else I needed to be, and I was able to rest and breathe easier, not waiting for anything else to happen.

That night someone accidentally left the light on and the door open in the garden shed. The glow from the bare bulb pushed out onto the grass and drove a wedge of illumination into the black night sky, dividing dark from light.

In the silent bedroom, I lay warm and safe under the comfortable weight of sheets and blankets. Outside the wind was blowing, carrying the blossoms off the ornamental plum tree that grew near our bedroom. The tiny flowers drifted lazily through the night like snowflakes, taking their time, as if they knew this was their singular dance, their moment of glory, and that once they hit the ground they would become just another bit of fluff in a carpet of flowers, destined to be trod on by careless feet.

"Elise? Elise, are you asleep?" Cookie whispered in the darkness.

"No. I'm watching the plum blossoms fall."

"Elise, I . . . I forgot to tell you something. Congratulations on winning the spelling bee. You deserved to win."

I rolled over so it would be easier to see her, but in the darkness it was difficult to make out her features. Probably that was best. Something about the anonymity of a dark room makes it easier to speak the truth, as though your thoughts are detached from your body and actions and all the troubles they have caused you in the past.

"Cookie, we both deserved to win. Betsy Semple probably deserved it too, but today I was lucky. The words I was asked happened to be words I had studied. I was so relieved I didn't have to spell *pellucid* after Betsy missed it! I didn't even know what it meant, let alone how to spell it!"

"Really? You're not just saying that to make me feel better?"

"No. It's the truth."

"Elise, there's something else." Cookie paused for a moment before going on, as though trying to compose her words carefully. "Ever since that day when we were playing baseball, I haven't been very nice to you. I'm sorry."

"Well, I'm sorry, too. I shouldn't have made the spelling bee into such a big contest between us. I'm too competitive."

"Me too. And I was so mean to you about doing things around the house! You just seemed so smart and pretty. You can play the piano and everything. . . . I just felt like I had to be best at something, even if it was something as silly as spelling. You may be too competitive, but I'm much worse!"

"No! I am!" I was smiling, but in the darkness Cookie couldn't see me and only heard my insistent whisper. "I am much, much worse than you could ever think of being! I am the most competitive, and that is that!"

Cookie was silent for a moment, thinking. Then she said flatly, "That's a joke. Isn't it?"

I burst out laughing, and Cookie joined in. After so many months of tension between us, it was wonderful to let it all out. We couldn't stop ourselves. We giggled uncontrollably. After a while I heard footsteps on the stairs. Mama tapped on our door, telling us to settle down so we wouldn't wake up the boys, but she didn't sound annoyed; she sounded relieved.

We pulled the blankets up over our noses to muffle our giggles, but it wasn't easy. I finally had to close my eyes and breathe deeply to calm myself down. After a few minutes Cookie said, "Do you know something? That is the first time I've ever heard you make a joke. In fact, it's the first time I've heard you really laugh."

"Hmmm. You're probably right. I don't laugh very much. I should do it more often. It feels good."

Cookie shifted under the covers, as though she were getting ready to sleep, but I could feel her hesitation in the moment of silence that followed, as she considered the boundaries of our newfound intimacy and whether our shared laughter gave her the right to ask questions. I wondered the same thing. How far would I let her come into the hidden places and sad memories of my life?

Cookie rolled onto her side to face me and drew in a long breath before speaking.

"Elise? I saw you crying—that day when we went to see *The Wizard of Oz*. Are you homesick?"

"Sometimes," I admitted.

Cookie rolled onto her back and looked at the ceiling for a moment. "Do you miss your father?"

"Yes."

"And your mother."

I felt a lump rising in my throat as I answered that yes, I missed her, too.

"Do you want to tell me about her?"

"No," I whispered. "Not tonight. Maybe someday."

Cookie was quiet for a moment before bidding me good night. I said good night back and rolled onto my side, facing the window. The screen door creaked, and I heard the thump of Papa's boots on the porch. He shut the door to the shed, and the wedge of light disappeared. I closed my eyes and tried to sleep.

Chapter 11

1941

"Elise! Aren't you done in there yet? I gotta go!" Chip pounded on the bathroom door, and I jumped, startled by the noise.

How long had I been standing there staring at myself in the mirror? My cheeks colored at the thought of my own vanity, but it was just so hard to believe that the girl in the mirror was me. "Sorry!" I called through the door. I gave my hair one last stroke of the brush, blotted my lipstick, and sopped up the water from the edge of the sink with my used facecloth before tossing it into the clothes hamper. A final, disbelieving glance into the glass, and then I opened the door to face Chip, who had continued to hammer on the door in spite of my apologies.

"Sorry," I repeated sincerely. Sharing one bathroom among eight people wasn't easy. Primping had to be kept down to the bare minimum. This was an unwritten but well understood rule in the Muller household. "It's all yours."

Chip looked at me. His expression changed from irritation to incredulity, and he let out a low whistle. "Wow! What happened to you? You're gorgeous!"

His reaction surprised and embarrassed me and I felt my cheeks flush with heat. Cookie heard the commotion in the hallway and emerged from the bedroom still fussing with the tricky clasp of the Eisenglass crystal bracelet she'd borrowed from Mama for the occasion. "What's all the noise out here, Chip? Can't you wait five minutes and give Elise a chance to . . ."

Her eyes grew wide as they shifted from the successfully fastened bracelet to the shimmering cascade of real silk that was the skirt of my dress.

"Oh," she breathed. "Oh, Elise. You look beautiful!"

I blushed again, this time from pleasure instead of embarrassment. "Do you really think so?"

"Are you kidding? You're a knockout!" Chip shouted. He grabbed my hand and started pulling me down the hall toward the stairway. A smiling Cookie followed right behind.

"Where are we going?" I asked, laughing. "I thought you had to use the bathroom."

"Forget about it," he said. "I can't wait until everybody sees you!"

We must have sounded like a herd of elephants clomping down the stairs, what with Chip pulling from the front and Cookie pushing from behind. I nearly tripped and fell. "Hold on a second!" I protested. "I can barely walk in these heels, let alone run down stairs."

"Wait here," Cookie whispered excitedly as she hatched a plan of action. "We'll go on ahead and announce your grand entrance. Take your time coming down the stairs, Elise. Remember what Miss Runyan says." Cookie transformed her face into a pinched-lipped impression of our maiden history teacher, Miss Runyan. "Don't thump down the stairs like a hired hand, girls. A lady *descends* the staircase as delicately as a butterfly alighting on the petal of a rose and is an adornment to every room she enters." Cookie spread her skirts, dipped a little curtsey, and fluttered her eyelashes in a perfect imitation of the prudish Miss Runyan, whose annual job it was to give the sophomore girls a vague and wholly uninformative presentation on the facts of life and rules for ladylike behavior. As far as I could tell, three decades of these informative talks had yet to make any lasting impression on Brightfield's female population. While there was much I had come to admire about these strong, stoic, and capable Yankee women, I had yet to see one of them descend delicately onto anything.

Thinking of Miss Runyan started me giggling, which made the job of navigating in high heels simply impossible. Cookie was an accomplished mimic. Chip couldn't help but smile at the accuracy of her impersonation, but he was anxious to get on with the show.

"All right, you two. That's enough. Cookie, are you going down to announce her or should I?"

In the end, they both decided to go, and I could hear them scurrying around the lower floor of the house, gathering up the family and ushering them into the kitchen for a surprise. Quietly, I took a couple of practice steps down the stairs and back up again. How in the world was I supposed to keep my balance and keep my heels from thumping on the steps all at the same time? Like the rest of her talk, Miss Runyan's advice in the area of ladylike descending had been long on theory and short on practical information.

Down below Chuck was complaining loudly and wondering what was so important that it warranted interrupting *The Shadow*. Cookie shushed him, and Chip told him to just sit down and wait a minute.

After everyone was seated, Chip took up a post on one side of the banister, and Cookie stationed herself at the other, standing tall like liveried footmen in one of those movies where the heroine casts off her peasant disguise, reveals her noble bearing, and wins the heart of the hero.

Cookie looked upstairs to make sure I was ready, then nodded to Chip, who cleared his throat theatrically before announcing in a very loud, very bad imitation of an uppercrust English accent, "Ladies and Gentlemen, may I present . . ." Chip nodded to Cookie, who took over as herald.

"Miss Elise Braun of Brightfield, Massachusetts!"

I took a deep breath. Then, holding the railing for balance with what I hoped appeared to be a relaxed grip, and curling my toes in the bottom of my shoes to prevent the heels from clacking, I descended the stairs.

For a split second the room was quiet. Everyone sat with wide eyes and delighted expressions, except for Junior, who looked momentarily confused, as though he had just been presented to someone whom he ought to know but whose face and name he couldn't quite recall. It was the first time in months and maybe in years that I could remember him looking at me square on, as if he really was seeing me.

Yesterday, as I'd sat on a folding chair in the Brightfield Bulldogs gymnasium and applauded with the rest of the family as Junior had crossed the stage to receive his diploma, I couldn't help but think he was the best-looking boy in the class, despite the fact that he did look a little uncomfortable in his cap and gown. Now, dressed in the fashionable blue pinstripe suit and red tie that had been his graduation present, he was suddenly a man instead of a boy. I wondered if a similar transformation had happened to me.

His eyes met mine and locked. My voice cracked a bit with nervousness, but I spoke loudly enough so that everyone in the room might assume I was speaking to them, though in truth the question was meant for him alone. "Do you like it?"

The family erupted into a chorus of approval and admiration. Only Junior was silent. Nothing unusual there. The incident with John Harkness marked the moment I'd finally been accepted by the younger Mullers. But it was obvious that my actions had not completely redeemed me with Junior. He stopped being openly hostile to me; he didn't wound me with cutting words anymore. However, he didn't say anything at all to me. Sometimes I wondered if I was simply invisible to him.

But that night, for just an instant, his eyes flickered with recognition. He opened his mouth as if to speak, then closed it again and drew his lips into a flat, judging line as though he'd suddenly remembered what he didn't like about me. His eyes became steely and darted away from mine, focusing on their former target, a remote spot where he could observe me from a safe distance. He became a clinical observer who could dissect me into a collection of disembodied parts so he would never have to know me as a whole person.

I felt a short, sharp twinge in my breast. For a moment I thought that my brooch had come unpinned and was sticking me, but when I looked down I saw that the clasp was secure and tight, right where it was supposed to be. I blinked, a little surprised by the intensity of the pain, but recovered quickly, smiling and giving my attention to the rest of the Mullers, who were on their feet, encircling me with a wreath of affection.

Even Chuck, who, like his twin, at age thirteen was still more interested in internal combustion engines than girls, seemed genuinely admiring. "You look fabulous! The dress, shoes, hair—everything!"

Curt piped up, "You look like a movie star, Elise!"

"Thank you," I said sincerely. "Cookie deserves the most credit. She showed me how to put on my makeup and curl my hair. I didn't know where to start. If it wasn't for her I'd be standing here wearing my first grown-up dress with two braids trailing down my back!"

Everyone laughed, and Cookie shrugged off the compliment, but it was the truth. Since turning sixteen, Cookie had become an avid reader of movie magazines. Her transformation from tomboy to expert in all things female was nothing short of miraculous. It had all started in the spring of our freshman year when Mark Woodward, the catcher on the Brightfield Bulldogs High School baseball team, had smiled and winked at her as we walked home past the field where the team was practicing. That very day she'd traded in dungarees and baseball mitts for skirts and curling irons. Now she knew how all the stars fixed their hair and had modeled my style on a picture she'd seen of Joan Fontaine in *Photo Play.* It had taken her most of the afternoon to get it right.

"Well, I think you both look beautiful," Papa said, beaming at me and putting his arm around Cookie, whose own party dress was very becoming. It was made of rayon instead of silk, but the midnight blue color complemented her eyes and light complexion, making her look as pale and delicate as a china doll. Her tiny waist appeared even tinier encircled by the wide belt embellished with silver embroidery. The borrowed crystal earrings and bracelet sparkled on her ears and wrist and added to the simple elegance of the gown.

"I just feel bad for the other girls. Who will want to dance with them when we've got the prettiest two girls in town standing right here?" Papa asked and shook his head in pretended sympathy for the wallflowers of the world.

"Oh, I think the other girls might end up taking a turn or two around the floor," Mama said with a gentle smile. "But you are both beautiful young ladies. Your dance cards will be full before you know it."

"Mama!" exclaimed Cookie. "Nobody uses dance cards anymore."

"No? That's too bad," said Mama. "They always made nice souvenirs. I still have one from the first time I danced with your Papa."

"Really?" Cookie asked in wonder. "That is so romantic! Can I see it?"

"Later," said Papa. "You'd all better get a move on unless you want to be late."

The younger boys went back into the parlor to finish listening to *The Shadow.* Junior said he wanted a glass of milk before we left and started rummaging around in the icebox. Papa went outside to warm up the car for him. The old Ford truck had finally given up the ghost the previous month and had been replaced with a not quite as old Pontiac sedan complete with a Motorola push-button radio. I was glad. I would have felt odd arriving at the dance dressed in an elegant party dress only to climb down from the cab of the truck.

Cookie scurried upstairs to get her wrap. Mine was already waiting downstairs—a beautiful, soft cape of black Persian lamb. It was a sixteenth-birthday gift from Uncle Wilhelm. Father had sent it in a package, along with his own gifts: the beautiful silk dress, the shoes and stockings, and, most importantly, my mother's pearl choker—the one he had been saving for me all those years. The gifts had come months before, and I had been thrilled with them, but until now, the night of the prom, I hadn't had occasion to wear them.

Mama helped me put on my wrap and fasten the hook and eye at the throat. "Turn around once more so I can look at you," she said, and I obliged, enjoying the way the skirt swirled as I moved. I felt as if I were dancing already.

Mama clasped her hands together, then drew them up under her chin. She bit her lips and nodded with approval. "I want you to know that if your own mother were here she would be very, very proud of you. That is a simply beautiful dress, but more importantly, you are beautiful in it—inside and out."

"Thank you." I whispered because my voice was too tight with emotion to allow me to speak properly. I thought how lucky I was to know Mama and how much she and Mother would have liked each other. Mama and I hugged, and I think I would have started to cry if Junior's voice had not interrupted the moment, slicing through it with a sarcastic edge.

"Yeah, it's a beautiful dress all right. Real silk. I wonder where it could have come from? Paris, do you suppose? And the shoes, what do they call them . . . French heels, isn't that right? How much do you think he paid for them—or did he just commandeer them at gunpoint from some cowering French shopkeeper?"

Mama spun around and froze her eldest son with a furious look. "Junior! Stop that!" she snapped. Her eyebrows drew together. "What's got into you? Why do you have to be so mean?"

Junior ducked his head, and I thought I saw the barest blush of shame rise in his cheek. He glanced at me and then at Mama. I could see a hint of bewilderment in his eyes, as though he didn't quite know himself. His shoulders twitched in a sort of half shrug.

Mama sighed wearily. "Go on," she said. "Go and help Papa with the car." Junior turned to leave but not before giving me a look that lay somewhere between contrition and accusation—I couldn't tell which. He hesitated before opening the door, and for a moment I thought he was going to say something. Instead he followed Mama's orders and went outside to warm up the car.

Mama followed his exit with a disappointed look before turning to me and smiling again. "Don't pay any attention to that, Elise," she said and gave me another quick squeeze. "You are going to be the belle of the ball tonight. Just enjoy yourself."

"Yes, Mama. I will," I replied dutifully, but somehow the shine had gone out of the evening.

Junior drove. Cookie was graciously going to let me ride in the front seat, but I declined, saying that she needed more room because her legs were longer—which was not true; I was a good two inches taller than Cookie. She hopped into the front seat next to

Junior, being careful to arrange her skirts around her so they wouldn't look wrinkled when we arrived at the dance.

Cookie chattered away like a magpie about the evening ahead, wondering what the decorations would look like, asking questions without waiting for answers, now and then urging Junior to drive a bit faster, but not too fast. She didn't want to be late to meet up with Mark in front of the main door of the gymnasium, but she didn't want to be too early, either, and risk standing around looking awkward while waiting for her date to arrive.

"Do you think he'll bring me a corsage? It would be awful if I were the only girl there without . . ." She stopped in midsentence, remembering that I didn't have a corsage and that there would be no one waiting at the door with a flower for me. She paused awkwardly and then spoke again, more slowly this time.

"You'll have lots of dances, Elise. You'll be the prettiest girl there. And you'll certainly be the best dressed."

I murmured my thanks, knowing in my heart that she was right, at least the part about being the best dressed. I knew that when I walked into the room, all the girls would be talking about my dress and wondering where it had come from. Would they all reach the same conclusion that Junior had? Was he right?

I stroked the miraculously silky fabric with the tip of my forefinger and thought about its origins. The ice blue hue of the skirt read as flat gray in the diminishing light of the summer evening. It didn't shine as it had in the warm light of the Muller kitchen.

I looked out the window and began counting telephone poles, trying to calculate how many poles and miles of wire it would take to stretch from Brightfield to Paris.

I walked into the gymnasium and knew it had been a mistake to come.

In my mind this occasion, the graduation prom, had become

something much more elegant and glamorous than a high school dance. My imagination had conjured up a scene that was a cross between a Viennese ball, with swirling couples waltzing through gilded banquet halls, and a ritzy New York supper club, where the men all wore tuxedos and the women dressed in evening gowns every night and I was Norma Shearer, the most stunning woman in the room, wearing a dress of gold cloth and smoking cigarettes in a slender ebony cigarette holder.

The real setting was much more humble, despite a wonderful job by the decorations committee. The dance floor was ringed with tables covered by white cloths. Each table had a floral arrangement with three small white candles, which looked a lot like the candles we used to decorate the church at Christmas, and white roses interspersed with willow branches dipped in silver paint. Longer tables with bigger versions of the same floral bouquets, flanked by tall silver candelabras, which I was also sure had been borrowed from the church storeroom, stood on either side of the gym. Each one had a silver punch bowl in the center and trays of cookies and tea sandwiches and bowls of nuts.

It really was quite pretty and yet . . . the scent of rose petals couldn't quite mask the odor of floor wax and damp towels that seems to permeate the pores of every high school gymnasium. Instead of the dance orchestra I'd invented in my imagination, there was a simple combo consisting of a pianist, bassist, saxophone player, drummer, and combination lead singer/clarinetist who tried his best to mimic a Benny Goodman grin. And while my classmates did look nice in their party dresses and suits and ties, they were still my classmates, as giggly, gangly, and acne-scarred as they had been when I'd left them on Friday afternoon. No amount of perfume and Brylcreem could transform them into sophisticated socialites.

It is not vanity on my part to say that my dress was the prettiest in the room; it was simply a fact. When I came in, all the girls ooohed and ahhhed over it and asked me where in the world I got it. I brushed off their questions and their compliments. I was in the Bulldogs gym, not the Rainbow Room; I felt embarrassed. I was clearly overdressed, and I knew that no matter how fawning their admiration to my face, when the girls gathered in the powder room they would criticize me behind my back.

I decided that I would not allow myself to think about that. The evening might not live up to the mental fantasy I'd embroidered, but it was a lovely party. For the first few minutes everyone seemed a little tentative, as though not quite sure how to behave in such fancy, unfamiliar surroundings. It was as if they were all dressed up in their parent's clothes and playing at being grown up. The band started to play, but for the first three or four tunes, couples just milled around nervously, not wanting to make themselves conspicuous by being the first pair to take the floor. Cookie and Mark finally worked up the courage to dance, and it wasn't long before other couples—those who, like Cookie and Mark, were "going steady"—followed suit and took the floor. Soon dancers were packed together like sardines, swaying in time to the musical stylings of George Kaplan and the Hep Cats.

There was a row of folding chairs arranged along one wall. This was where a line of dateless girls sat, perched primly on the edge of their seats with their gloved hands folded neatly in their laps, trying to appear interested in the music but completely disinterested in the clumps of boys who had come stag and might, or might not, rescue them from the indignity of wallflowerdom.

The girls seemed determined to ignore the presence of the other young women seated next to them; possibly they felt it would be easier for a boy to ask a lone girl to dance than it would be for him to interrupt a conversation between chatting females. The boys, however, hung about the corners of the room in groups, eyeing girls, guffawing, and, when the chaperones' backs were turned, sneaking a pull from a flask stored in a pocket. Every now and again, the boys would start elbowing one another and laughing more vigorously, obviously daring one of their gang to ask one of the girls for a dance until finally the gauntlet was thrown and their buddy took the dare. The brave youth would then cross the room and ask the girl of his choice if she wanted to dance while the lucky female would try to look as if the suggestion took her completely by surprise. This elaborate ritual was repeated every few minutes. Each time it was, and their numbers were reduced, the unclaimed girls would sit up a bit straighter and try harder than ever to look as though they were just happy to listen to the music.

In all the weeks that Cookie and I had talked about the prom and discussed what we would wear and practiced our dance steps, taking turns leading, I hadn't considered the possibility that I wouldn't have a dance partner. It wasn't that I was pining to dance with one particular boy—I just had a vision of myself swirling around the floor, guided by a pair of sure feet and strong arms, my hand resting lightly on one of his broad shoulders. There was no special masculine face involved in my fantasy. No, that wasn't quite true.

The previous night I had awoken from a dream. I was waltzing to the music of a full orchestra, the dance floor was ringed by sparkling lights, and the air smelled of gardenias. My partner and I moved like one person, gliding easily together in long, flowing arcs, and I realized that the dance floor had turned into a shining sheet of ice and our shoes were really silver skates. It was exhilarating! I laughed aloud, pushed myself lightly off my partner's shoulder into a spin. I saw Junior's face smiling back at me, momentarily coming into my field of vision, then disappearing again as I spun around and around until I finally awoke with a start and found myself sitting upright in bed, the music and lights all gone. The room was silent except for the sound of my heart beating steadily in my ear and Cookie's heavy, slow breathing. My cheeks were hot, as though still flushed from the dance, but the heat faded from my face even as the dream faded from my memory. I pushed the picture of Junior as my dance partner from my mind, dismissing it as nothing more than one of the absurdities of the world of dreams, as inconsequential and improbable as a dance floor made of ice.

Now, seeing myself through the eyes of my classmates, in my too-fine finery, and feeling the weight of my German accent heavy on my tongue, I knew that I would not dance that night. I would not take a chair among the chain of unclaimed hopefuls. There was no point. If I did, that was where I would spend the rest of the night, sitting taller and taller, my eyes more and more determinedly glued to the dance floor as the numbers of unmatched girls around me dwindled and only I was left without a partner.

I would not subject myself to the humiliation. At the same time, I couldn't spend the rest of the evening loitering by the punch bowl, feigning an unquenchable thirst. I considered hiding out in the ladies' room, but I knew that it would be filled with giggling girls who had briefly and coyly abandoned their dates on the pretense of needing to powder their noses while their real aim was to retire to a female sanctuary to compare notes and boast about the attributes and devotion of their escorts. The idea of joining them was too depressing for serious consideration.

I glanced around the room as I considered my options and saw Junior standing alone in the opposite corner of the room, staring at me. My face colored, not from any embarrassment but from irritation at the thought that he could somehow read my mind and was enjoying my predicament. His lips curled in a smug smile as he saw me looking at him.

Furious, I turned away and held out my empty punch glass to Mr. Simmons, the ancient bachelor science teacher and assistant principal who manned the refreshment table.

"My! You must be awfully thirsty tonight, Miss Braun. That's your third glass of punch."

I fumbled in my mind for some explanation but was rescued by the arrival of Cookie and Mark, who, having danced to five or six tunes in a row, truly were thirsty. Mr. Simmons handed them each a glass of punch and asked if they'd mind keeping an eye on the table while he went to refill the sandwich trays.

"I'll be right back, Mr. Woodward. Make sure no one touches that punch. If I come back and there is the slightest trace of alcohol in that bowl, I will know exactly who is to blame. Understood?"

"Understood," replied Mark. We all smiled as Mr. Simmons walked in the direction of the cafeteria with the empty tray in his hand, but under his breath I could hear Mark mumble something that sounded like "sanctimonious old goat."

"Hey, Cookie," I said. "Do you have a cigarette? I think I'll go outside for a smoke."

Cookie's carefully penciled eyebrows raised in surprise. "Of course I don't have a cigarette! I don't smoke. Neither do you. What are you talking about?"

Mark reached into the pocket of his jacket and, after checking about him to see that no adults were watching, retrieved a crumpled pack of cigarettes. "Here," he said surreptitiously pulling a smoke from the pack. "Take one of mine."

"I never knew you smoked," Cookie said doubtfully.

"Why shouldn't I?" he asked, without a trace of defensiveness in his voice. "My old man grows the stuff. Three quarters of the kids in this room live on tobacco farms. I think it's stupid that the school won't allow me to smoke when it's tobacco money that pays the taxes to run the place."

"Still, I don't think it can be very good for you."

I ignored Cookie's objections and took the cigarette, concealing it in my palm so none of the chaperones would see. "Thanks."

The air outside was clear and cool. I was grateful to be out of the stuffy gymnasium and away from the crowds. Retreating to a quiet corner on the back wall of the gym, I leaned back against the bricks and tilted my head up to see the stars. Suddenly a star shot across the sky, expending itself in a last burst of brilliance before dying, determined to leave some kind of impression so that after it flamed out and disappeared, someone might look up and notice an empty place where a small light had once lived. I squinted up at the heavens, trying hard to pinpoint the spot where the star had been only a moment before.

Loneliness threatened to overwhelm me. I moved away from the dark part of the wall and into a tight, distinct circle of light under a spotlight where it was harder to see the night sky and easier to ignore sad thoughts. Inside, the band was playing "I'll Never Smile Again." I closed my eyes and hummed along.

The air felt colder than it had at first. I wished I'd thought to bring my wrap with me but didn't want to go back inside to get it. Having successfully made my escape without being noticed by chaperones or nosy classmates, what was I going to do out here? The cigarette was just an excuse to get outside, but now that I was standing around with nothing to do, I supposed I might as well go ahead and give smoking a try. I fished the cigarette out of my evening clutch and put it to my lips but then remembered I had no matches.

"Need a light?"

His voice made the hair stand up on the back of my neck. Without waiting for my answer, he scraped the match head against the rough brick. I caught a faint, acrid scent of sulphur as the match flared and glowed to reveal the leering grin of John Harkness, who took a step toward me with the lit match in his right hand, cupping the flame with his left.

We had not spoken directly since that day after the spelling bee, nearly two years before. Of course, it was a small school, so we shared some classes and we frequently passed in the halls, but I was careful to ignore him, pretending not to hear him snickering with his friends when I walked past.

My eyes darted about to see if there was anyone else nearby, but we were alone. The door leading to the safety of the gym was on the far side of the building. John was taller and much more muscular than he had been when we were in grammar school. His legs were longer than mine, and I knew I had no hope of outrunning him, especially in my wretched French heels.

Telling myself I mustn't let him see my fear, I leaned toward his outstretched hands, positioned the tip of the cigarette in the midst of the flame and drew in my breath and a mouthful of smoke with it. The taste was awful, and I couldn't imagine actually pulling the noxious vapors down into my lungs. Instead, I held the smoke in my mouth for a long moment, pretending to inhale, before blowing a thin column out steadily through my lips, trying to adopt the careless, world-weary expression of a practiced smoker.

"Thanks."

Still grinning, Hark pulled a pack of Luckies from out of his coat pocket and lit one up. "Funny. I never figured you as a girl who smokes."

I didn't say anything but nodded my head and took another shallow puff. From around the corner, I thought I heard the squeak of a door opening. I cast a glance in that direction, hoping that someone would appear on the scene. John heard it too, and I could feel him tense up as he stood next to me. A minute passed and then another, but everything around us was silent. John gave a short sigh of relief.

"Thought for a minute that it might be old busybody Simmons. He caught me having a smoke last month and gave me detention. Said if it happened again he'd suspend me. Jackass." Hark took another deep drag on his Lucky and leaned back into the wall, seeming to relax for the moment.

I tried to appear relaxed, too, hoping that if I just stood there, listening to him, sharing the feigned camaraderie of fellow smokers and rule breakers, in a few minutes I could finish the cigarette, casually grind the butt out against the wall, and even more casually say "Thanks for the light," then walk steadily toward the door and the security of the well-chaperoned gymnasium.

"Yeah," he said, continuing his soliloquy, "never figured you for a girl who'd smoke. Always thought you were too goody-goody—too pure for such nasty habits."

He turned and looked at me. The leering grin returned to his face as his eyes moved from my face and traveled slowly down my body to my shoes and then back up, stopping at the place where the blue silk stretched tight over the swell of my breasts. His eyes were fixed there and refused to stray from that spot. His stare beamed through the fabric with the intensity of red coals burning through tissue paper. I was unable to move, frozen to that spot in fear, like a trapped, small animal whose only defense lies in staying very, very still and praying that danger will pass it by.

I could see Hark's chest move up and down as he breathed heavily. Slowly, he took the cigarette from between his lips and tossed it to the ground with a flicking movement of his fingers. He leaned his body toward me.

"Are you?" he whispered. "Are you as pure as you look? Or have you been faking that, too?"

He took a final step to close the last distance between us. A small, panicked cry escaped my lips. Unable to stop myself, I instinctively pulled away, making a bolt for the door, but he grabbed my wrist and stepped in front of me, blocking my escape with his body. Finally his eyes sought out mine, and he laughed at the fear he saw there. He was enjoying it, I knew. The more afraid I was, the more powerful he felt, and he liked power. I told myself to calm down, to make my face a mask, but I couldn't do it.

"You have been faking it, haven't you? Trying to make me think you're tough," he snorted. "You've never smoked before, have you? Have you?" He tightened his grip on my wrist. "Answer me!"

"Let me go!" I cried in a voice I hoped sounded angry rather than frightened. "I've got to go inside now. My date will be looking for me."

"I don't think so," he said. "You don't have a date. Nobody in Brightfield would ask you to the dance. Not you, Fraulein. That's why you're out here, isn't it? You know they're all in there laughing at you, so you came out here to get away from them. Yeah, I know what that is all about. You had a good time making everybody laugh at me that day when you threw a punch at me. Bet it seemed funny at the time. Not so funny now, is it?"

He moved closer, pressing his body into mine, his shoulders looming at the level of my eyes, blocking out the light and the stars.

"Nobody in there is missing you. Even if they were, nobody'd come out here looking for you, because this isn't a place where a nice girl would be. And you are a nice girl, aren't you?" he asked hoarsely. "That's all right. I can change that."

He reached up and grabbed the back of my head with his free hand, pulling my hair and tilting my head back as he leaned down to try and kiss me.

"Stop it!" I cried. I tried to break away from him, but he had me pinned to the wall. I could feel the sharp grit of the brick wall scraping at my back. I wrenched my head away at the moment before his lips touched mine.

His eyes flashed in bright anger, and I saw something terrible there. "Don't want me to kiss you? Fine. Don't matter to me if I kiss you or not. I was just trying to be nice, but I don't have to be nice. Not to get what I want from you, I don't."

He pulled me close to him and squeezed my wrist again, twisting my arm up behind my back just as he had done that day two years before when Papa came to rescue me, but this time Papa didn't come. He jerked my arm tight, and a sharp pain seared the socket of my shoulder. He started pulling and pushing me over toward the dark corner, where he had been hiding before, out of the circle of light and into the deep shadows where no one could see us. When I cried out in pain and fear, he clapped his other hand over my mouth to block out the noise.

He shoved me into the corner and planted his tree-trunk legs wide on either side of me, imprisoning me between them. With his hand still across my mouth he lowered his head to the bodice of my dress. I could feel his other hand fumbling at the hem of my skirt, reaching under the fabric and moving along my leg to the top of my stocking.

Panic ran through me like an electric current. I pushed against him with all my might, but it only increased the ferocity of his attack. I shoved my shoulders upward and jerked my head hard to the left to loosen it from the clamp of his hand.

I screamed as loud as I could. His hand was in front of my face, trying to recapture his grip on me. Instinctively, my mouth sought out his groping hand, and I bit down on it as hard as I could. Hark's body jerked back from the surprise of the pain, and a string of expletives poured from him as he fought to pry his fingers from between my teeth.

For a moment we struggled like animals snarling over a fresh kill. Hark was so much bigger than I; ultimately it would be impossible for me to prevail over him, but terror and rage boiled up inside me and spilled over into every part of my body, making me far stronger than I actually was. I shoved my shoulder into his chest, succeeding in pushing him back from the corner and giving myself just enough room to pull my right arm free. My fist swung free and landed powerfully and squarely on the orbit of Hark's left eye.

"You little . . . !" He howled in fury and called me a name that I'd never heard before but whose meaning was very clear to me. "You're gonna pay for that!" He lunged at me, his rage now matching my own and grabbed me by the shoulders, trying to force me to the ground. I fought as hard as I could, but I wasn't strong enough. If he succeeded in pushing me down, there would be no way I could fight him off.

Then, just as my knees began to buckle under the force of his weight, he suddenly froze, turned sharply to his left, and let go of me completely. Unfortunately, his body still blocked my route of escape. Without thinking, I started pummeling him with both my fists, raining down blows on his head and shoulders as hard and fast as I could. He flinched under the attack, but his attention was elsewhere.

Turning his back to me, he started throwing punches of his own, his hamlike fists connecting with the jaw of his assailant and making a flat, sickening crack as they found their target. I couldn't see the face of my rescuer, but, still trapped in the corner behind Hark's hulking frame, I silently cheered him on even as I continued my own assault on Hark's back and shoulders.

Hark made a ferocious charge toward his opponent, leaving a wide opening between himself and the imprisoning brick wall. Over the sound of bare knuckles smacking against bone and skin, I heard Junior's voice ring out. "Elise! Get out of here! Run!"

I bolted out of the corner and instinctively started running as fast as I could toward the safe haven of the school building. The noise of the fight, the sound of men grunting in effort, of feet scuffling in the dirt and landed blows, echoed in my ears. I wanted to keep running but only got a few yards before my feet slowed. Something inside me wouldn't let me just leave Junior alone. He was strong, but I knew he would be no match for Hark.

I turned around and saw the two of them with their arms wrapped viselike around each other, looking for all the world like a pair of pythons determined to squeeze the life out of a foe. I ran back toward them. Without thinking, I wrenched off one of my shoes and started pounding the heel against the back of Hark's head.

His head jerked back. When he turned to see what had struck him, he gave me a look of such hatred that it was clear to me that he'd kill me if he could. Hark let go of his death grip on Junior and swung his arm wide and free through the air, striking my face with full force and throwing me back against the wall. Junior charged him and threw three quick, punishing blows into Hark's midsection.

Hark doubled over for an instant, and Junior, his nose streaming blood, turned toward me and shouted, "Quick! Go get help!"

For an instant I was torn; I didn't want to leave Junior alone, but it was clear that even with my help, Junior wouldn't be able to defeat this giant. I pulled off my other shoe, and in my stocking feet, ran as fast as I could toward the gymnasium door. Just as I rounded the corner I met a group of boys led by Mark, who was shoving a pint bottle of whiskey into his jacket pocket. His eyes grew wide when he saw me, and I was suddenly aware of how disheveled I appeared—barefoot, breathless, and with a jagged tear in the bodice of my dress. Instinctively, I wrapped my arms around my chest.

"Junior and Hark . . ." I didn't have time to gasp out the rest of my explanation before Mark and several of the others started running full speed toward the sound of the fight.

I followed on their heels. Mark tried to wedge himself between Junior and Hark to break up the fight, but when he did, Hark struck him on the jaw with a hard right cross. With that, Mark abandoned his role of peacekeeper and joined in the battle. The boys stood in a ring around the combatants and cheered them on, offering encouragement, advice, and warnings to Junior and Mark.

Word of the fight must have quickly made its way back into the school building. Soon a stream of boys and girls left the dance floor to watch the fracas. With two opponents to face, Hark was definitely getting the worst of it. He didn't back down, and his blows were still powerful, but he was definitely slowing, and his nose was bleeding profusely. Though Hark was outnumbered, it was clear that the crowd was on the side of his adversaries. The boys cheered loudly each time Junior or Mark landed a punch and groaned in disappointment when they received one. The girls gasped and squealed in excited horror at every blow, no matter who the recipient was. I looked on in horrified silence, wincing every time Junior took a hit.

The battle couldn't have gone on for more than a few minutes, but it seemed much longer. I heard a murmur of voices behind and one that rose above the rest, shouting, "What's going on here? Move!"

The crowd parted, and Mr. Simmons stepped into the ring, his eyes flashing, suddenly transformed from a fussy, elderly biology teacher to a man of authority with a booming voice. "Boys! Break it up! Right now, do you hear me? Break it up!" He waded fearlessly into the combat zone and stood solidly amongst the three boys, who were panting with effort. Seeming almost relieved by his interference, they quickly obeyed. Mark was certainly winded, but not as badly as the other boys. Junior bent down and put his hands on his knees as though to support himself and pulled deep, labored breaths into his lungs. Hark was no better off as he gasped for breath and wiped the blood from his nose with his sleeve, staring in exhausted surprise at the red gore that stained his white shirtsleeve.

"What in the world is going on here? Mr. Harkness? Mr. Muller? Mr. Woodward? Who started all this?"

"I don't know, Mr. Simmons," Mark answered. "Elise came running up to me with her dress all torn and said Junior and Hark was fighting." The eyes of the other students turned to me and, seeing the rip in my gown, started whispering amongst themselves. I blushed in embarrassment and wrapped my arms more tightly around myself.

"I tried to break up the fight, but Hark slammed his fist into my jaw, so I punched him back." As Mark spoke, the teacher's gaze darted from Mark, to me, to the still breathless Junior and Hark, then back to me, looking for all the world like a human adding machine, quickly tallying up the personalities and facts and coming to an accurate summation of the events. His eyes bored into mine, his questioning concern obvious. For the first time that awful night, my eyes began to fill with tears, and I fought hard to blink them back, not wanting anyone to see me crying.

Mr. Simmons turned his attention from me to the gaggle of students and clapped his hands officiously. "All right, boys and girls! There's nothing to see here. It's all over. Go back inside, everyone." The students grumbled and began to disperse reluctantly. Mr. Simmons threw me a quick look that I knew meant I should stay where I was.

The crowd began breaking up and shuffling back in the direction of the gym. I could hear snippets of murmured conversation and whispered speculation.

"What was she doing alone out here with him, anyway?"

"Did you see her dress? I mean, really!"

"I don't know," someone else said. "She doesn't seem fast, and everyone knows Hark is wild. My mother said he's a juvenile delinquent and I should steer clear of him."

"That's my point. Everyone knows about him, so what was she doing with him? Dressed like that. She wanted everybody to notice her, and they certainly did. She was asking for it, that's what I think."

My face flamed with anger. Part of me wanted to turn around and slap the girl who was so liberally dishing out her opinion, and another part of me was sick with shame.

Mr. Simmons threw a steely gaze at the boys. "Gentlemen, I'd like you all to join me in my office, and we'll see if we can't get to the bottom of this. Here, Mr. Harkness," he said, pulling a handkerchief out of his pocket and holding it out to Hark, "wipe the blood off your face."

Then Mr. Simmons looked at the retreating crowd and spotted Miss Gaffney, one of the dance chaperones, who taught home economics and was now herding a clucking group of girls back to the building. He silently summoned her from her task with a bend of his forefinger. "Miss Gaffney, would you please take Miss Braun somewhere and help her get cleaned up?" He lowered his voice and added confidentially, "Let me know if we need to call a doctor."

Seeing my disheveled state and torn gown, Miss Gaffney's eyes registered a moment of shock, but she quickly regained her usual demeanor of motherly efficiency. "Come along, Elise." She draped her arm sympathetically around my shoulder and began shepherding me back into the school, but toward a different door, away from the swarm of gossiping students. "We'll go to my classroom. I've got a first-aid kit there. You can wash your face while I make you a nice cup of hot tea. Then we'll take a look at that dress; I might be able to repair it for you."

I mumbled my thanks and let Miss Gaffney lead me away. There was a sound of running feet behind us, and I turned to see Cookie jogging toward me, carrying a coat and my discarded heels in her hands.

"Elise! Are you all right?"

I couldn't answer her. I knew that if I did, it would be impossible to keep from crying. There was just no way to explain all my feelings without bursting into sobs. I nodded a mute reassurance.

Miss Gaffney reached out and laid her hand on my shoulder. Her eyes grew dark and serious, and she ducked her head down toward mine, insistent on establishing an unbroken line of communication. "Elise," she said with gentle firmness. "You mustn't keep any secrets from me. You can trust me. If you were"—she searched for a soft word—"If you were hurt, you must tell me."

"I'm fine," I assured her, sniffing back my tears. "There's no need to call the doctor. Truly, there's not."

The teacher eyed me questioningly, but after a moment's hesitation she seemed convinced of my veracity. Her expression of doubt was replaced by one of relief.

"Here," Cookie said, "you forgot your shoes." She held them out to me one at a time while, leaning on Miss Gaffney for support, I slipped them back on my feet. They were scuffed and muddy. One heel was loose, and I knew that even if they were repaired, they'd never be the same.

Cookie draped her own coat around my shoulders. I pulled it closed in front of me so it would cover my exposed bosom. "I couldn't find your wrap, so I just grabbed mine instead." I smiled gratefully at my friend. Leave it to motherly Cookie, upon hearing such shocking news, to have the presence of mind to think I would need a coat. She was never dearer to me than she was at that moment.

"Thank you, Cookie," said Miss Gaffney. "That was very thoughtful of you. You run along now. I'll see to Elise. She'll be just fine."

"Can't Cookie come, too?" I asked. "Please? She's my best friend."

Miss Gaffney looked first at my pleading face and then at Cookie's. She smiled understandingly. "Of course she may."

Chapter 12

I slept late the next day. Mama had come into my room after I'd fallen asleep and closed the curtains tight to block out the light. When I finally opened my eyes, I rolled over and groaned; every muscle in my body ached. For a moment I was confused by the onslaught of pain, but then I remembered the dance and everything that had happened.

The clock on the bedside table said it was nearly eleven o'clock. How could I have slept so late? It was Saturday, and I was supposed to be at Mrs. Ludwig's. Over the objections of my aching body, I pulled myself upright and sat on the edge of the bed. My neck hurt. I got up and walked across the room to look at myself in the mirror that hung over the bureau I shared with Cookie. There was a raw, red cut around my neck, thin and cruel, as if carved by a knife blade.

I couldn't imagine how I'd gotten such a nasty cut. Hark hadn't had a weapon, and he hadn't scratched me; his punishments had been inflicted entirely with his closed fists. Then I remembered my mother's pearls, the necklace Father had sent along with the note explaining that she had been saving them to give me when I turned sixteen. They were gone! Hark must have reached up and jerked them loose from my neck during the scuffle. They were probably scattered all over the ground—unless—of course, someone had already found them and taken them for themselves.

I was heartbroken. My eyes welled up and threatened to rain down tears, but I forced myself not to cry. There were so many awful things to regret about the night before, but dwelling on them would do no good. The best thing was to get up and go on with my day.

I took a plaid skirt and cotton blouse from out of the armoire and put them on, then sat back down on the edge of the bed to put on my shoes, pointedly ignoring the broken-heeled pumps that were lying under the chair where I'd draped my dress the night before. My gown had come apart at the seam, so Miss Gaffney had been able to fix the tear, but, as I'd suspected, the shoes were ruined. Later that day I threw them in the garbage. Then I hung the dress up in the back corner of the armoire and left it there.

At least the prom was the last event of the school year, I thought. I wouldn't have to face the inquisitive stares of my classmates anytime soon. In spite of the ache in my muscles, I was looking forward to going to Mrs. Ludwig's. Once I got to her house and put on the fresh, clean apron she always had waiting for me on a peg by the door, I would be able to forget everything and lose myself in some mindless, mechanical task like kneading bread or chopping onions. Yes, chopping onions would be perfect. Then I could cry to my heart's content and no one would ask why.

But when I came downstairs Mama informed me that one of Mrs. Ludwig's sons had called to say that she had a cold and I shouldn't come that day.

"Is she all right?" I asked Mama. "Maybe I should go over and look after her. I could make her some soup."

"There's no need. Harold said he was going to spend the afternoon with her and that his wife was already on the way over to make

Milda's lunch. I'm sure everything will be fine, and it wouldn't hurt you to just stay home and get some rest today."

"But Mrs. Ludwig can't stand Betty," I protested. "She says she can't even fry an egg without burning it and that she's got the personality of a field mouse. Betty will never be able to manage her, and it will be just awful for both of them."

Mama smiled at my assessment of the relationship between Mrs. Ludwig and her youngest son's wife. "I am sure they'll get on just fine without you. Besides, it's time Milda realized you can't pick your relatives, so she might as well learn to get along with them. Betty Ludwig is a perfectly nice young woman, even if she is a little on the mousey side. Though it isn't very nice of Milda to say so, and"—Mama raised her eyebrows and scolded me gently—"it isn't very nice of you to say that Milda said so."

"Sorry."

Mama smiled to show I was forgiven, then turned to a shelf and began pulling down mixing bowls. "Now, what can I make you for breakfast?" she asked brightly before launching into an artificially cheery monologue. "Everyone else ate hours ago. Curt and the twins are out in the barn. Said they were working on building a human glider kite, so if you look out the window and see one of them up on the roof, let me know so I can stop them before they crash. Mark came by in his father's car to pick Cookie up about an hour ago. They said they were going to the library, but seeing as the school year is out, I kind of doubt that. Probably they're just off for a joyride." She paused for a moment. "I hope that's all they're doing." Her brow wrinkled with momentary doubt before continuing.

She shrugged. "Well, Mark seems like a nice boy, and Cookie is relatively sensible for being sixteen, so I'm sure they're fine. Papa asked Junior to drop him off at church so he could work on his sermon for tomorrow. I thought he'd be back by now, but maybe he's out joyriding, too. It's a nice day for it. The sun is shining, and it must be about sixty-five degrees outside. Anyway, I can make you some pancakes or scrambled eggs and ham. Miss Gaffney came by to check on you this morning and left a coffee cake, so you can have a slice of that, too."

"That was nice of her. Too bad I missed her," I lied and drew my lips up in what I hoped would pass as an appreciative smile. I didn't want to be reminded of last night.

Mama murmured in absentminded agreement as she opened a drawer and rattled through a collection of utensils until she finally located the object she'd been searching for. Pulling a wire whisk out of the drawer, she brandished it triumphantly, and said, "There it is! Now, what would you like for breakfast?"

"I'm not really hungry."

The smile faded from Mama's face and was replaced by a look of searching concern. I could see that she'd been working as hard as I had at pretending everything was normal. "Elise, are you sure you're all right? You can tell me anything."

The tears I'd been working so hard to suppress came rushing out in a convulsion of sobs. The wire whisk dropped from Mama's hand and fell to the floor with a metallic crash. Mama ignored it, rushed across the room, and wrapped me in her arms.

"Elise. It's going to be all right." She rocked me in her arms, stroking my hair and shushing me as if I were five years old. I let myself melt into her comforting embrace, releasing all my pent-up anguish until I was spent from the effort. Gradually, my tears subsided, and I rested in Mama's arms, hiccupping and out of breath.

Mama looked at me soberly and asked, "Elise, I know you were hurt last night. You're bruised, and have that cut on your neck, and I'll bet you feel as sore as if you'd run ten miles, and simply wrung out with exhaustion. But is that all? If something else happened, you need to tell me. It's important that I know."

I shook my head mutely and wiped my wet cheeks with the back of my hand before speaking. "Honestly, Mama, nothing else happened. I just feel so ashamed. Some of the girls said it was my own fault, being out there alone and wearing that dress. They said I was asking for it, that I was trying to get the boys to notice me. I'll admit I did want to be noticed, but not by Hark! I swear not!"

Mama pulled a chair out from the kitchen table and sat down. "Of course not. I know that," she said sincerely.

I pulled out another chair and sat down next to her. "When we got to the dance, I could feel everybody looking at me, and I knew I was overdressed. All the girls were talking about me. I felt like a fool, and I knew no one would ask me to dance, so I went outside and pretended to smoke cigarettes. It was silly, I know, but I just had to get out of there. I never thought about anyone else being outside.

"Then, when I heard those girls talking, I suddenly felt like it was all my fault. I shouldn't have been outside alone. I shouldn't have worn that awful dress," I reprimanded myself.

"Nonsense!" Mama retorted. "Elise, that is a perfectly beautiful dress. There is nothing awful or immodest about it! Do you think I'd let you leave this house if I thought you were improperly dressed?"

I eyed Mama and shook my head doubtfully, surprised by the vehemence of her reaction.

"Maybe it wasn't the wisest thing for you to be outside alone, but that doesn't make any of this your fault!" she snapped. "It's just beyond me how people can be so ignorant and stupid! Those girls are just a clutch of jealous, gossiping, little . . ." She let out a frustrated, undecipherable word in a huff of exasperation, leapt to her feet, and began striding back and forth in front of the table. She had recovered the wire whisk from where she'd dropped it and held it in her hand, stabbing the air with it emphatically, underscoring the certainty of her convictions, as she continued.

"If it were true that wearing a particularly pretty dress turned men into animals, then every man who saw the dress would react the same way, but they don't! Some men act like animals because they *are* animals! Those girls were just jealous. There's nothing at all wrong with wanting to be noticed. You looked absolutely stunning, but that doesn't mean you were asking for some brute to beat you and try to . . ."

She stopped her pacing and spun around to look at me, her eyes still popping sparks of righteous rage. She pointed her finger squarely at me, and she raised her voice to the edge of shouting. "None of this was your fault! Do you believe me?"

I paused to think for a moment before quietly answering. "Yes, Mama," I said, not to appease her, but because it was true. What she said made sense. If my dress had somehow possessed the power to inflame men to fits of violent lust, then all the men would have had the same reaction. Hark had been inflamed to violence because he was a violent person. He had proven it before.

Mama chest was heaving with emotion. She stared at me evenly, as if she didn't quite believe me.

I answered again, louder and with more conviction, "Yes, Mama. I believe you."

Mama took a long breath and gave her chin a quick jerk, as though doing so would help unclench her tightly locked jaw. "Good," she said. "Now, how would you like your eggs?"

"Over medium, please."

After breakfast, I sat down to play the piano, letting the last lingering traces of humiliation and self-doubt pour out through my fingertips onto the keyboard. As my hands moved up and down the keys, my mind wandered again over all the things Mama had said, and the more it did, the more I came to understand why she had been so indignant. I became indignant, too, and before long my indignation blossomed into anger.

Not just at Hark but also at the gaggle of girls who had whispered such terrible things about me. They'd meant for me to hear them talking about me; they'd wanted to embarrass and humiliate me! It wouldn't work. I wouldn't let it!

My fury reached a crescendo, and I played faster and more furiously, banging out Beethoven with an intensity that expressed my rage in a manner that could never be matched by words. The last livid bars were an indictment against my enemies, and I slammed out the chords with such tremendous force that the whole instrument vibrated from keyboard to pedal. When the last notes faded and the piano was finally quiet and still, I felt spent, but somehow relieved and absolved. I sat still on the piano bench, my chest heaving with the effort of my exertions, for several long silent minutes before my breathing settled into its regular, even pattern.

Rather than feeling worn out by my cathartic playing, I felt oddly refreshed. I got up from the bench and went into the kitchen to find Mama.

"I bet that got it all out. Feel better?" she asked. I said yes, and she smiled her approval. "Good. It's important for a woman to have some productive way to let off steam. That piano seems to be your pressure valve. Now that you're finished, why don't you go for a nice, long walk? With everyone out of the house, this is the perfect opportunity to start my spring cleaning. It'll be easier to wax the floors without having to dodge eight pairs of feet."

"Oh no, Mama" I protested. "Let me stay and help you. It's too big a job to tackle by yourself."

"No," she insisted. "You'll be doing me a favor, letting me clean by myself. It's not too often that I get to have the house to myself. That's how *I* let off steam," she confided, "and I'm so mad at those thoughtless, stupid girls with their thoughtless, stupid comments, by the time I'm finished, these old wooden planks should have quite a shine!"

I understood what she was talking about. Usually, when I felt upset, I worked out my frustration by baking. I loved pounding and kneading the dough and by the time the fresh loaves of hot bread stood lined up on the counter and the whole house was permeated by that sweet, yeasty smell, I always felt much better.

When I stopped to think about it, it was amazing how much I had learned about housekeeping, farming, and other kinds of work in the three years I had lived with the Mullers. It was even more amazing to realize that I really enjoyed doing my share of the simple, humble tasks which were required in the day-to-day business of living. It made me feel as though I had something of worth to offer this dear family who had taken me in and treated me as one of their own.

During my childhood I had been taught that working with your hands, especially menial tasks such as cleaning and cooking, were beneath me and that the performance of such jobs required no real intelligence or skill. A few weeks previously, Papa had given a sermon on the value and dignity of doing one's work, no matter how unimportant it might seem, with dedication and joy.

Papa called it "working as though unto the Lord." A year or two before, I wouldn't have understood what he was talking about. Now I understood just what he meant and found my head bobbing up and down along with the other members in the congregation as we expressed our silent agreement with his declaration. What a remarkable change, I reflected. Perhaps I was finally growing up.

My walk took me down past the Schoellers' farm. Mr. Schoeller was out in the field, hoeing weeds from between his precious, newly sprouted tobacco plants. Though he was a good distance from me, he paused in his work for a moment and waved to me. "Hey there, girlie! How're ya? Where ya' off to today?"

"I'm fine!" I shouted back. "I'm going down for a walk by the river. Your crop is looking good, Mr. Schoeller. Should be a good harvest this year!"

"God willin' and the creek don't rise!" he shouted back jovially, his lips split into a wide grin, revealing all this teeth, yellowed and stained from smoking. Mr. Schoeller liked to sample his own product.

"You gonna come lend a hand to bring in the crop this fall? Could sure use the help. Still say I never saw anybody take to the tobacco quick as you!"

"I'll be there!" I promised. Mr. Scholler was always kind to me, and I'd spent many an afternoon at his place, sometimes working, but often just following him around. As a consequence, I'd learned quite a bit about tobacco farming and what it took to get a crop from seed to leaf to dried and cured tobacco. It was much more of an exact science than I would ever have imagined, and, for some reason, I found the process fascinating.

Since that first year, when he had been so complimentary of my work, I had helped bring in every one of Mr. Schoeller's crops. I truly enjoyed the work, and now that I reflected upon why, it all seemed to make sense. Spearing those tobacco leaves on lathes was the first work that I'd actually been able to perform with anything approaching skill. That initial success had given me the confidence to go out and try other new things.

"Have a nice walk!" the old man shouted as he waved good-bye.

Though it was only late May, the day was warm, yet not too warm, for there was a cool, playful breeze coming out of the southwest. I passed through the Schoellers' property and onto the edge of the Jorgensen place, one of the largest and most profitable farms in the county, as evidenced by acres and acres of shade-tent frames—

expensive, ambitious investments that, if they paid off, could make a man wealthy or, if they didn't, could ruin him.

The Jorgenson fields had yet to be sown, but the unplowed furrows were well outlined by a series of unclothed tent frames. The empty tent poles stood tall, straight, and expectant—waiting patiently for that day when tender tobacco seedlings would be set out between their rows, when their naked frames would be draped with mile upon mile of billowing linen, and they would be dressed in redeeming white and new purpose, their cracked, sun-silvered skins covered by folds of fabric.

It wouldn't be long before this field would be planted and truckloads of workers would come to roll the shades out over the tops of the frames. The whole field would become alive with the buzzing activity of dozens of hands, moving among the tents, pouring all their sweat and knowledge into the land in hopes that their sacrifice would yield a richer harvest. It might. Or it might not.

After the laborers left there was nothing to do but wait and see, because in spite of all the hard work and knowledge of men, the success of the crop was determined in the dark, secret depths of the earth, in a process that humans could observe and explain but never replicate. The farmers would do their best to coax the sprouted seed to come out of hiding by creating an inviting, tropical environment in the midst of the sharp New England climate—an incubator-world that would encourage the sprouts to grow tall and unfurl lavish, showy leaves as a sign they took pleasure in their transplanted surroundings. But no matter how well the farmers did their work, there was no guarantee of success. The growth of seeds is a mystery—a miracle that takes place in silence and darkness.

I discarded my shoes and socks and walked barefoot through a field of soft, newly turned earth. My toes sunk deep into the luscious soil, and I breathed in the rich, loamy scent that was a mixture of things rotting and things sprouting, the smell of both death and rebirth. It was a hopeful smell; I filled my lungs with it and let it seep into every part of my being.

Reaching the crest of the hill, I paused at the spot where the land began its downward slope to the edge of the river. The sight of the waters flowing smooth and flat, gently but insistently cutting through soil and rock to form a valley, as they had been patiently doing since the beginning of time, filled me with the same sense of belonging that I'd felt when I first set eyes on them. Although I hadn't been born in this place, I was of this place, because something about this vista and the life of the river reflected my own life and journey and spoke to hidden places inside me.

I loved everything about the valley and the trees and river—for example, how they were never the same from one day to the next. Depending on the time of year, the river might be flat, low, and placid or high, swirling, and impatient, even to the point of spilling over its banks and flooding the valley.

The valley was always new to me. Even if I came to this exact same spot every day, it was possible to see tiny differences that had not been there the day before. If I waited a week or two between visits, those tiny differences added up to complete transformations and a whole turn of seasons. I was certain there was no place on earth as alive as this. In spite of everything, I was happy living here.

I still carried my shoes and socks, but now I stuffed the socks inside the empty shoes, tied the laces together, and draped them over my shoulder so I could run down the trail that led to the river's edge. As I jogged down the hill, wincing now and then as my bare feet found a sharp stone, I kept on, knowing that as the days of summer passed, the soles of my feet would become tougher and tougher, until they were impervious to all but the deepest of cuts.

When I reached the riverbank, I stopped for a moment to admire the way the sun glinted and bounced off the water and to notice how different the river was when seen close up—not at all the patient, silver ribbon it appeared to be from the edge of the valley, but an impetuous, swollen, selfish child of a river, made wild by the spring thaw and eager to get to some unknowable destination.

I picked up a fallen tree branch, submerged the tip of it in the river, and walked along the riverbank humming to myself. Then I sang out loud, one of the first songs Mother had taught me when I was a little girl and we took walks through the park on the banks of the Spree.

Ich weiss nicht was soll es bedeuten, dass ich so traurig bin, Ein Marchen aus alten Zeiten, das kommt mir nicht aus dem Sinn Die Ludt ist kuhl und es dunkelt, und ruhig fliesst der Rhein, Der Gipfel des Bergest funkelt im Abendsonnenschein—

"That's nice," said a voice from behind me, "but what does it mean?"

I turned around and saw Junior standing there, a slight smile playing at the edge of his lips, or was it a sneer? I couldn't tell.

"I didn't know you were there," I answered, blushing.

"I'm sorry if I startled you. Really, what does that song mean? It reminds me of one I learned in grade school."

For a moment, I thought he was making fun of me, but his interest seemed genuine, and his voice held no trace of the sarcastic tone that I had come to recognize only too well in the years I had known him.

"It's called 'The Lorelei.' It's about a mermaid. My mother taught it to me when I was little. There is a beautiful mermaid sitting on a cliff by the sea, and when the sailor spots her he sings,

I know not the cause of my sorrow or why I should be so tormented.

An ancient story I never knew has come out of nowhere to me.
The breeze is cool as the day fades. Serenely flows the Rhine.
The crest of the mountaintop sparkles in the last rays of the evening sun.

I spoke the words rather than sang them. When I finished, Junior just stood staring at me. "It doesn't translate so well into English," I continued apologetically, "but that is more or less the idea. The mermaid's beautiful song enchants the sailor so that he doesn't see the dangers of the reef. His boat crashes against the rocks and he drowns. It really quite a sad song."

"And very beautiful," Junior said quietly.

I nodded and stood silent, not sure what I should say. I wanted to thank him for coming to my defense last night, but I felt terribly awkward. Junior and I had rarely been alone together, and I couldn't ever remember us having a conversation. Finally, I mustered up the courage to speak.

"Last night, you were . . . well . . . I just wanted to say that I'm glad you came when you did. Thank you."

"You're welcome."

Again the awkward silence separated us. Without really stopping to consider how ungracious I would sound, I opened my mouth and said exactly what was on my mind.

"What are you doing here? I mean . . . is there something you want?"

"I came down here looking for you. I know this is your special place."

"Oh," I replied feebly.

He took a step closer, and a smile spread across his face. For a second I wondered if he found my discomfort amusing, but then he reached into the pocket of his dungarees and fished out a string of pearls. Mother's pearls.

"You found them!" I stretched my hand out to his but didn't actually touch the necklace, not quite able to believe they were truly there.

"I found them," he confirmed with a self-satisfied bob of his head. "They were spread all over the place! I spent an hour crawling around making sure I had them all. You can have them restrung later but for now I just put them on some fishing line. I didn't have anything else. Hope that's okay."

"Of course!" I exclaimed. My eyes moved from the pearls to his face. I've always had a good imagination, but I simply couldn't conjure an image of Junior crawling on his hands and knees, searching through blades of grass and weeds to find something for me. I was stunned into immobility.

A shadow of concern crossed his face, and he thrust his hand forward. "Here. Take them. Is there something wrong with them?"

"No!" I answered, shaking myself from my reverie and taking the pearls from his outstretched hand. I ran a finger across the necklace, touching each ivory sphere. I shrugged helplessly. "I simply don't know what to say."

"Well," Junior said with a laugh, " 'thanks' would be fine."

"I do thank you," I said earnestly. "For so many things. I know you've never really liked me, and yet you came to my rescue last night. I don't want to think what would have happened if you hadn't come when you did, and after all that, you go to all this trouble for me!"

"It was no trouble," he insisted.

"These were my mother's—one of the only things I have to remember her by. When I woke up this morning and realized they were gone, I felt terrible, as though I had forgotten her or dishonored her memory by not taking better care. Last night was so . . . so terrible. If I'd lost Mother's pearls, I don't think I would ever be able to forgive myself." Impulsively, I kissed him on the cheek. A veil of color rose in his cheeks. I smiled inwardly at his discomfiture. I had never made a man blush, and, in spite of his embarrassed reaction to my kiss, Junior was a man now.

Last night, when we were getting ready to leave for the dance, I had thought his transformation might be only an illusion of maturity, that his new suit and tie were a mere disguise of manhood. Now, as he stood before me, dressed in nothing more elegant than dungarees, a blue-striped shirt, and a cardigan, he seemed more a man to me than he'd ever been. His actions and thoughtfulness had proved it.

"You're welcome," he said. His hand moved up to his face, and his fingers briefly touched the spot where I'd kissed him. He didn't seem to know what to say next.

"I wanted to thank you last night, but I didn't see you anywhere. Miss Gaffney brought me home in her car, but when we got there you still weren't home. I guess I fell asleep before you arrived."

"Yeah," he said wryly, "I got to hang out awhile in Mr. Simmons' office while he 'sorted things out,' as he calls it and handed out our punishments."

This information left me aghast. "Punishments? You were a hero last night! You didn't get in trouble, did you?"

"Yup. Mark and I both got a month's detention for fighting."

"You must be joking. That's awful! I can't believe it! That just isn't fair!" I was indignant. "I'm going to school and see Mr. Simmons first thing Monday morning and explain exactly what happened. It isn't right that you should get detention for helping me!"

Junior interrupted me with a stream of hearty laughter. "Elise! Calm down—it's all right! Mr. Simmons gave Mark and me detention and then he suspended our sentence."

"He did? Why?" It was all too confusing, and I couldn't understand why Junior seemed so lighthearted about the whole thing. My English had become very good in the last years, but every now and again I'd come across phrases or ideas that were unfamiliar to me. Perhaps this was one of those times, I thought.

"We graduated yesterday! We are no longer students at Brightfield High, so the punishment can't apply to us."

Suddenly I understood the joke and the cleverness behind Mr. Simmons's brand of justice. Junior smiled as he saw comprehension break across my face. For a moment we just stood there grinning at each other.

"You want to go for a walk?" Junior asked. "We could go up by those shallows at the bend—see if the fish are biting."

"All right," I agreed. "If they are, we can put the pearls in my pocket and use the fishing line you strung them on. But we don't have a hook or a worm. Do you think pearls would make good bait?"

"Absolutely! We've got very refined fish here in Brightfield."

We strolled upriver toward the shallows, walking side by side, keeping an arm's length between us. Though we had been joking only a moment before, I was suddenly overcome by a wave of timidity. I moved closer to the riverbank and started dragging my stick through the water again. Junior cleared his throat as though he was going to say something, but when I turned to look at him, he just shoved his hands deep into his pockets and scuffed a rock with the tip of his shoe.

"Yeah," Junior said evenly, as though we had been talking steadily and he was just picking up the thread of the conversation where it had left off, "Yeah, Ol' Hark didn't get off quite so easy, though."

The mention of John Harkness made my stomach lurch. Here, walking with Junior in my favorite spot on earth, it had been easy to forget about him. Hark was in my grade, so I knew that there could be no "suspended sentence" for him, but a few weeks' detention wasn't going to chasten him. If anything, it would only anger him, and he would blame his troubles on me, just as he had before. Every time he saw me at school or on the street, his hatred of me would grow; I could never feel completely safe again.

Something in my expression must have betrayed my thoughts. Junior reached out and touched me lightly on the shoulder. "Hey, Elise. Don't look so worried," he soothed. "Mr. Simmons was too smart to try and saddle Hark with detention and think that would be the end of it. He called the police station, and then they called John's dad. Officer Fuller didn't exactly come out and say it, but he suggested to Mr. Harkness that it could get pretty uncomfortable for Hark if he stuck around Brightfield. Something to the effect that the next time John got caught littering or jaywalking, he might be looking at doing some hard time.

"Mr. Harkness got the message," Junior continued. "They went home, packed John's bags, and headed to Hartford first thing this morning. Even as we speak, John Harkness is enlisting in the U.S. Marine Corps. You won't see him around here anymore."

"He's joining the Marines?" Junior nodded in confirmation, but I still found it hard to believe him. "But, isn't he too young? We're in the same grade, so he can't be more than sixteen."

"Nope. He's seventeen, and that's old enough. Hark had to repeat the third grade."

I felt as if I'd just had a terrific burden lifted from my back. "Junior! Really? That is great! I simply can't—"

Without waiting for an invitation or permission, Junior leaned across the space that divided us, placed a hand on either side of my face, and kissed me softly but certainly on the mouth.

I didn't pull away. I let him kiss me. Then I kissed him back. This was what I had wanted ever since I'd turned around to see him standing on the riverbank. No. Before that. Long before.

Without bothering to worry about how it looked or what he

would think of me, I pressed my body into his, letting him wrap his arms around me while I placed my two hands on his back, one resting comfortably on each of the strong, muscled blades of his shoulders. We stood that way a long time, enveloping one another, letting our mouths discover this new world of kisses. Our lips touched lightly at first, then again, more boldly. I could not have imagined that his kiss would be so sweet.

Finally Junior lifted his head up, momentarily breaking the connection between us. I looked in his eyes and saw they were filled with pain. Somehow I knew he was thinking about all the cruel things he'd said to me in the past, all the barbs and intentional slights he had subjected me to in the past and regretting every one.

"Elise," he began.

"No," I whispered. "You don't need to say it. It doesn't matter anymore. This is our first day, and I am so glad, Junior. So glad."

Chapter 13

Mama was sitting on the porch, snapping the ends off a bowl of bush beans, when Junior and I came home. By the time we returned, the sun was streaming its last rays over the edge of the horizon before yielding its territory to the moon and the night. Mama was alone, but I could hear the sound of machine gunfire and squealing sirens floating through the open parlor window. The younger Mullers were inside, gathered around the Philco, listening to *Gangbusters*.

"Hi, Mama," Junior said when we came inside. I echoed his greeting, and I closed the door behind us.

There shouldn't have been any noticeable way to mark the change in our relationship. Junior and I had let go of each other's hands when we'd gotten within sight of the house and had been careful to pat our tousled hair back into place, but when we spoke Mama glanced up and paused in her work, clutching a bean in her left hand and its stem in her right. Her mouth had been set in a thin, flat line as though she was annoyed and prepared to give someone a talking-to, but upon seeing us together, her irritated expression gave way to one of questioning appraisal. She didn't ask us anything directly, but I think we both knew that she knew, and for a moment I felt a bit guilty, though I wasn't exactly sure why.

Mama broke the tension. "Dinner is a little late tonight. Doing the floors left me behind schedule." She got up from the rocker and opened the screen door that led into the kitchen. We followed her inside.

"The floors look great, Mama," Junior said, and he was right.

"Don't they, though," she agreed, the satisfaction evident in her voice. "I feel like a new woman." She sighed contentedly and then continued speaking, directing her words to either or both of us. I wasn't quite sure. "You've got to take your pleasures where you find them. As long as they are wholesome ones and don't cause others pain. There are little joys in every day, if we have the good sense to look for them."

Junior and I looked at one another, neither of us quite grasping the full meaning of Mama's speech, but we got the idea that, indirectly at least, she was giving us her blessing.

"Well said!" Papa's voice boomed as he entered the room. "Whatever did I do to deserve such a wife? Not only beautiful, but wise!" He bounded across the room and leaned down to plant an appreciative kiss on the nape of Mama's neck. Once again I was struck by the wonderful intimacy between them, something that I was only just beginning to understand, but recognized as rare to have lasted across so many decades and the hardships of life.

Mama tapped Papa mildly with her hand to remind him that they weren't alone. Papa asked when dinner would be ready, stating that he was hungry enough to eat a bear, which was how hungry he claimed to be at about this same time every evening.

"Soon," Mama answered, and Papa wrinkled his forehead, obviously dissatisfied with the indefinite nature of her response.

Junior opened the Frigidaire and rummaged around inside,

searching for the glass milk jug with studied casualness. I stood there awkwardly, trying to decide whether it would look more natural to go up to my room or to sit down and start helping Mama with the beans.

Papa heard the sound of milk being poured into a glass and said, "Junior, pour me a glass, too, would you?" Then his brow furrowed again as if he had suddenly remembered something. "Hey, come to think of it—where have you been? I haven't seen you all day long. Or Elise, either for that matter. What have you two been up to?"

I knew a moment's panic as I racked my brain for a response. I glanced at Junior. He stopped drinking his milk in mid-gulp and looked a bit pale. Neither of us were accomplished liars, but Mama came to our rescue.

"Elise has been down at the river taking a long walk. I thought it would do her good."

"Oh," Papa said vaguely, and I sensed he was a little reluctant to speak of the events of the previous night. "That was a good idea. I always feel better when I go there myself. Good place to think things through."

"Yes," I agreed quickly. "I saw Mr. Schoeller when I went by. He was doing a little hoeing. I thought I might go over tomorrow afternoon after church and give him a hand." I spoke confidently, knowing that everything I uttered was the truth. "That is, if it is all right with you. I know it is Sunday and all."

"That's all right," Papa replied. "I don't think it counts as breaking the Sabbath if you are helping someone else. Of course, I don't know what Mr. Schoeller's excuse would be, but that's his business."

Papa turned to Junior, who had finished his milk and was staring intently into the bottom of the empty glass as if there were something interesting written there. Papa eyed him suspiciously.

"And what about you? Where have you been all day? You were

supposed to come back to the church at three to pick me up. I waited for you for a half hour, then I finally walked over to the café and got Joe Klein to give me a ride."

Junior gulped hard and opened his mouth to answer, but again Mama came to our defense. However, this time she wasn't as careful with the stick-to-at-least-some-semblance-of-truth principle as she had been before. Maybe she felt her lie was justified by the same logic Papa was using to justify letting me break the Sabbath—it didn't count if you were doing it to benefit someone other than yourself.

"That was my fault, Carl. I had him bring a jar of hot soup to Milda Ludwig's," Mama lied. "She's got that cold, you know, and at her age she can't be too careful. Then I sent him over to Lester's Market in Harmon to see if they had a bag of boiling onions. I know how you like them, and I wanted to have some to go with that roast chicken in the oven."

She turned her attention to Junior and gave him a questioning look. "Did you get the onions?"

"No, Mama. They were all out."

Papa stood listening to this exchange with an expression of confusion on his face. "I thought you'd said that Betty and Harold were over taking care of Milda. And what are you doing sending the boy all the way to Harmon for boiling onions? Parker's has them on hand every week—for that matter, so do we! There's a ten-pound bag sitting in the cellar as we speak."

"Really?" Mama questioned innocently as she snapped the last bean and walked to the sink to rinse them before dropping them into a pot of boiling water that was waiting on the stove. "I guess I just didn't see them down there. These beans will be good, though."

"Well, what did you do when you got back from Harmon, Junior? When Joe dropped me off, I saw the car sitting in the drive, but you weren't anywhere to be found."

Mama opened the oven door and exclaimed, "Just smell that

chicken! It looks wonderful, too—the skin is nice and crispy, just the way you like it, Carl." Papa, who was a big man with a big appetite, though never overweight, peered into the oven, momentarily distracted by Mama's diversion.

"Junior," she continued cheerfully, "go and call the children. Tell them it's time to eat." Donning oven mitts, she pulled the two huge roasters out of the oven. Papa pulled himself upright and breathed in the delicious aroma of baked chicken.

"Sophia, I swear I don't understand you. One moment you are imbued with sagelike wisdom and the next moment you are jabbering nonsense about hot soup and invisible onions." Papa shook his head as he picked up a bowl of mashed potatoes and placed them in the middle of the table. "I still love you, though."

"I love you too, Carl."

I turned away to open the drawer where the silverware was kept, and as I did, I heard two pairs of lips meet in a smacking kiss.

The dinner table was abuzz with conversation, everyone talking at once and no one really listening, but that was all right. Everyone in the family had enjoyed a productive Saturday. When I'd first come to live with the Mullers I had been appalled by these chaotic mealtimes, but now I was used to them. I had come to realize that the louder and more disorganized the dinner-table talk, the more the Mullers were enjoying each other. And while it wouldn't have bothered me if Chuck and Chip would have outgrown their childish habit of throwing bits of food across the table when they thought no one was looking, I would never want to go back to the quiet, overly regulated meals of my childhood. Nothing about growing up in the orderly, regimented atmosphere of my home had prepared me for the jovial frenzy that reigned around the Muller family board, but slowly I had come to appreciate and even enjoy their warm, disorderedly, loving ambiance.

This was never truer than tonight. Every eye was closed and every head bowed in silent prayer as Papa gave thanks for the food, the day, and the family, but the moment he finished the blessing, it was pandemonium. Everyone was so busy talking and eating and talking and asking for more potatoes and talking that no one seemed to notice how silent Junior and I were. Of course, this was not so unusual for me; I was naturally reserved. But not Junior. He waded into family arguments with ease and voiced his opinions freely—sometimes too freely, I thought. Reverend Muller's affection for his firstborn was obvious, but it was also obvious that he had great expectations for him. I think Junior felt pressured by his father's hopes for him. It seemed that, especially as Junior was teetering on the brink of adulthood, he and Papa argued more and more, often about the silliest things. No matter what Papa's opinion, Junior took the opposite view, and not always from any real conviction, or so it seemed to me, but just for the sake of being contrary.

As the platters were passed around the table, Papa tried to go over his sermon outline with Mama, who tried to listen to him while at the same time telling the twins that, no, they could not use any of her bedsheets as sails for the human glider, no matter how safe it was. I thoughtfully chewed a mouthful of green beans and nodded appropriate encouragement while Curt, who, thanks to a summer of intensive tutoring from Cookie and myself, and a new pair of eyeglasses, was now an avid reader and writer, described in detail a play he was writing about the three little pigs. In his story, the wolf would actually succeed in bringing home the bacon, though he would eventually be killed by a mob of angry townspeople, who in turn would be killed in a terrible flood.

"It's a morality play," Curt said soberly and without a trace of his former stutter. "Everybody dies."

"I see." I was about to ask him where he'd learned about morality plays, but before I could, Curt jumped in his seat and let out a howl.

"Knock it off, Chuck! Mama, make him stop it! He keeps kicking me under the table!" Mama raised her eyebrows and threw Chuck a glare that made her displeasure clear.

"What?" Chuck asked innocently as he cut into his chicken with a shrug. "Tattletale!" he snarled out the side of his mouth. "Mama's boy!"

"Chuck, that will be enough of that," Papa said firmly without really looking to see what the fuss was about. He continued speaking to Mama. "Where was I?"

"Made in God's image," she prodded him.

"Right! Genesis makes clear that being made in God's image gives us incredible dignity and honor. Though we cannot be God, we were created to be God's ambassadors on the earth, reflecting his character to the world. However, we weren't satisfied with that. We wanted every fruit in the garden. Therefore, the fall of man was as much about the sin of dissatisfaction as disobedience . . ."

This was about the third time Papa had made the same point, because he kept losing his train of thought. Cookie kept interrupting him with repeated requests and justifications as to why she should learn to drive and why Mark Woodward should be the one to teach her.

"He's a very good driver, Papa, and very experienced. Mr. Woodward has a tractor, and Mark's been driving it since he was twelve years old. Twelve years old, Papa! And he's never had an accident or even a ticket. Well, only that one . . . but it was hard to see that stop sign, it was just about overgrown by sumac. Papa! Papa, you're not listening!"

"No, Coral, I am not." Papa only used the children's Christian names when he was completely exasperated. He dropped his fork onto his plate with a clatter and glared at his only daughter. "I am trying to get your mother's assessment of the sermon I am giving tomorrow. I don't care how long Mark has been driving his father's tractor, I am not letting him take charge of my new sedan. Especially not with you behind the wheel!"

At this last, Cookie started to blink very fast, and her eyes threatened to brim with tears, a ploy that never failed to make her tenderhearted father feel awful.

"I'm sorry." He sighed, but his voice was firm. "I didn't mean that to hurt your feelings. I'm sure you'll make as good a driver as anyone once you get some practice. It's just that right now you have no driving experience. Mark is a perfectly fine young man, but he's only been driving a couple of years himself. What if you were in an accident? Mark would feel terrible if something happened to my new car while he was in charge. If either of you got hurt, I'd feel terrible. How could I explain that to Mr. and Mrs. Woodward?"

"But, Papa," Cookie whined. "I've got to learn to drive someday!"

"I know that, Cookie. I'll teach you myself. I'll do it this summer."

Cookie rolled her eyes and mumbled glumly. "That's what you said last summer."

This was true. Papa couldn't deny it, so instead he growled something unintelligible. Cookie saw her opening.

"Papa," she said sweetly, "it's not your fault. You have a whole church to manage. You're just so busy, and Junior can't teach me because he's going to work at the Jorgensens' all summer. Mark is only going to work part time this summer, so he'll have his afternoons free." Papa was silent. He took another piece of bread from the platter in front of him and buttered it thoroughly, giving himself time to think. Cookie, sensing his weakening resolve, plowed eagerly on.

"Think what a help it would be to have another driver in the family! What with Junior headed off to college in the fall and everything, it would be nice to have someone else who could run errands and—"

"I'm not going to college."

At Junior's announcement, all of the several separate conversations going on around the table came to an abrupt halt. Everyone in the room was perfectly silent and stared at Junior in stunned disbelief.

"What was that?" Papa asked.

"I've decided not to go to college," Junior repeated more quietly than the first time.

Mama let out a slow breath and glanced around the table at the younger of the children, whose eyes were darting expectantly from Junior to Papa and back to Junior. "Boys, you can be excused," she said, nodding her head in the direction of the staircase to indicate they should go to their rooms.

Chip complained. "I'm still hungry." This was probably true. When I'd first come to Brightfield, Chip had been very finicky, and Mama had to coax him to eat. But now he'd grown six inches taller in as many months, and his appetite was constant and ravenous.

"I've got a plate of cookies on the counter. You can take them upstairs with you."

"Yeah, but I wanna stay and hear Junior get bawled out," protested Chuck. "Usually, Chip and me are the only ones that get hollered at. It'd be nice to see somebody else get it for a change."

Mama's voice took on an impatient edge. "Go!" she commanded. "Both of you. You too, Curt."

They hesitated for just a moment. Mama gave Chip her no-nonsense glare. Chip sighed resignedly. "C'mon, Runt," he said to Curt. "Bring the cookies."

All three boys did as they were bid but with much grumbling

and shuffling. They thumped up the staircase even more loudly than usual, signaling their displeasure at being sent into exile just when things were getting interesting, and slammed the door at the top of the stairs as a final protest.

Papa's voice was even, but I could see that the tips of his ears were turning red. Papa was sometimes irritated by his children, but only rarely did he show true anger. On the rare occasions when that did happen, red ears were the first signs of his rising ire, and, once unleashed, Papa's fury was an awesome thing to witness.

"Junior, you've already been admitted. We discussed it," he said through slightly clenched teeth. "You're going to get your undergraduate degree at State, then you're going on to seminary. We talked about it."

"No sir," Junior corrected his father with quiet intensity. "We didn't talk about it. You talked about it. You never asked my opinion."

"That's not so, Junior! We discussed the whole thing. Nobody is going to give you a pulpit if you don't get a college education. You can't enter the ministry without—"

"Papa! I don't want to enter the ministry!" Junior shouted.

Papa tolerated this interruption, but I could see it was an effort for him to remain silent in the wake of his son's outburst. His jaw tightened as he waited for Junior to continue.

Junior lowered his voice and continued in a tone that was contrite but determined. "I'm sorry I shouted, Papa, but I don't want to be a pastor. You're a wonderful pastor. I mean that. I admire you so much, Papa, but I'm not like you. It wouldn't work. I wouldn't be any good at it."

Papa's jaw relaxed a little. "I understand, son. I do. It's an awe-inspiring and sometimes frightening responsibility to respond to God's call to ministry. But you're absolutely up to it," he said reassuringly. "You're young yet. It will be a long time before you come face to face with a congregation. When you finally do, you'll have years of education and training behind you. You'll be ready."

"No, Papa," Junior said firmly, "I won't. I'll never be ready.

"Papa, do you remember a few weeks ago when Bob Klein, Joe's son, was home from college for the weekend and came over to get your advice on him going on to seminary instead of taking over his dad's farm?"

Papa nodded affirmatively.

"Well, I was listening outside your study door when you were talking to him. You told him that it wasn't enough just to believe in God and become a pastor just because you thought it would make God happy or other people happy. You told him that a pastor had to have a calling, and that meant ministry wasn't a choice you made—ministry was what you did because you had no other choice, because you simply had to serve God in the church and your soul wouldn't rest unless you did."

Junior looked intently at his father across the broad expanse of that table. For a moment, it was as if he and Papa were the only people in the room.

"I'm not called, Papa."

Papa took a deep breath and closed his eyes. It was impossible to know if he was thinking, praying, or both. Every pair of eyes was glued to his face, wondering what he would say next. When his eyelids finally opened, his response was simple and direct.

"All right."

Junior's face broke into a relieved, grateful, and somewhat astonished smile, as if it had all been so much easier than he'd imagined. "Thank you for understanding, Papa! You see my point, don't you?"

"I do," Papa said somewhat irritably and raised his hand up to keep Junior from going on, "but don't belabor it." There was a palpable sense of relief in the room. Everyone relaxed a bit and began eating again, though much more quietly than before. They were still listening for Papa to say something more.

"My own words come back to haunt me. A man mustn't enter the ministry if he's not called. If you aren't, there is nothing I can do about it, though, who knows? Your feelings may change when you're older. Many men don't get a call until late in life. My grandfather didn't get a pulpit until he was well past forty."

Junior bobbed his head in appeasing acknowledgement, reaching across the table to get the bowl of mashed potatoes.

"However," Papa continued, "Just because you don't see yourself in the pastorate doesn't mean you shouldn't go to college. You're a smart boy, and you've got to do something with your life. You'll go to State in the fall, just like we'd planned."

Junior groaned, and the balloon of tension quickly reinflated in the kitchen. "What's the point of going to college now? We're going to get into the war any second! I'm planning on working at Mr. Jorgensen's all summer so I can put some money away for the future." He threw a quick, furtive glance in my direction as he said this last word, and I knew it was for my benefit. Only hours before we had shared our first kiss. And though we hadn't discussed it, and wouldn't do so openly for some time, we knew that our futures lay together. How amazing! I lowered my eyes to my scarcely touched plate, but I could feel my mouth draw up in a small, shy smile.

"I'm going to work all summer," Junior continued with conviction, "and unless the war starts before the crop is in, I'm going to join up. If I sign up early as a volunteer, I'll have more choice about my duty than I would if I waited for a draft."

Mama lifted her eyes from her plate and looked at Papa, then at Junior. "It sounds as if you've thought it out and made up your mind," she said gently.

"I have."

Papa's eyes darted from Junior to Mama and back to Junior. He was quiet for a moment, but I could see a glimmer of acquiescence in his face. He took his napkin from his lap and wiped his mouth.

"Well," he said slowly, "I think you're wrong about the war starting any day. President Roosevelt said he'd keep us out of it, and I believe he'll keep his word."

No one wanted that to be true more than I did, but by this time no one really believed America could sit out the war, not even Papa, not really. War talk had been going on around Brightfield for years. Almost from the day I'd arrived I'd heard people discussing it, and although the conversations had tended to become more subdued if people noticed me in the room, my presence didn't stop them from giving their opinion about the war and the probability and wisdom of U.S. involvement in the European conflict. At first, the preponderance of opinion had been that America should keep out of the war, that it was too far away from her shores and had too little to do with her national interests to be worth risking the lives of American boys. But lately the sentiment had changed.

The younger generation, boys like Junior, tended to be more gung-ho when it came to the subject of American intervention in the war than older people. Initially, men who had lived through the first war, and remembered too many friends who had not, had been firm and vocal in their insistence that America must stay out of the war at all costs. But as time had gone on, and especially after the German occupation of Paris and the sudden very real possibility of the occupation of England, their rhetoric softened. Poland and the Ukraine were one thing, but Paris! London! These were places that many of them had visited and grown to love as young, eager privates and second lieutenants. These were the cities in which they'd had their first drink of liquor and their first romance. It had been impossible for them to believe that the German army would ever get so far, and yet it had! If the Nazis could occupy Paris, then why not New York, Boston, or Washington?

The war was raging "over there," but suddenly it seemed very close indeed. And yet, in spite of the seeming inevitability of war, many of those old soldiers, men like Papa, hoped that if they could just stay out of it for as long as possible that somehow the war would end and their idealistic sons would be spared the knowledge of what their fathers had learned: there is no such thing as the glory of war.

"No," Papa said, with less conviction in his tone than in his words, "I don't believe that America is going to enter this war."

"Papa," Junior broke in derisively, "you can't mean that! We've *got* to get into it. It's our duty, for cryin' out loud!"

"What do you know about it?" Papa shouted, pounding his fist on the table so hard that the silverware next to his plate jumped in response to the force of his blow. We all froze in surprise at this unexpected outburst of emotion. "I have been to war, Junior! I know what war is!

"In 1917 someone said it was our duty to go to war because this would be the war to end all wars. I believed them. So did my kid brother, Gordy, and most of our friends. I was in my second year at seminary, but I quit as soon as the war was declared. I came home to see my folks and say good-bye before I enlisted. My dad was furious. He said, 'Why don't you wait another year and a half and finish your degree? If you want to join up after that, I won't object; at least then you'd be able to do those poor boys some good instead of just becoming one more wasted piece of cannon fodder!' We argued for three days, but I wouldn't listen. Neither would Gordy.

"We went to the recruiting office together, and we shipped out together. By late October we were in the trenches of France, some of the first Americans in the fight. We were so young . . ."

Papa's voice trailed off, and his eyes clouded with memories. He stared at a blank wall on the far side of the room, as if the shadow of his younger self were standing there and only he could see it. Then he went on with his story.

"Just three days after we got there, the sergeant said to get ready—we were going out over the top. We were so nervous. We already realized that the war was nothing like we'd imagined it. So many dead men. I knew Gordy was as scared as I was, but we didn't talk about it. We just smoked a few cigarettes and joked around while waiting for the order to go. It turned out to be our one and only day in combat.

"When the order finally came, Gordy and I charged out with the rest of our unit. I was surrounded by shouting soldiers and smoke. I lost sight of Gordy, but I kept going. I made it twenty or thirty yards before an explosion knocked me off my feet and unconscious. I woke up in the field hospital pretty torn up and completely deaf. The force of the explosion had burst my eardrum.

"Bud McCandless, a guy from our unit, came to visit me. I couldn't hear anything, so he wrote out the news on a piece of paper. Gordy was dead. He had gotten up pretty close to the German line before he got hit by some mustard gas. The gas blinded him, and he stumbled into a tangle of barbed wire. He was caught there like a spider in a web, and the Germans riddled him through with bullets. Dozens and dozens of bullets. He was almost unrecognizable." Papa choked with the pain of the memory. His eyes filled with tears.

I felt my own throat tighten. How could they not hate me, I wondered. It was Germans who had killed Papa's brother, German bullets tearing his flesh until he was disfigured beyond recognition. My people had done this. Why didn't Papa hate me?

My father had spoken with pride about the glorious history of Germany in battle, of the beauty of sacrifice and the honor of duty.

And though he was always distant, though he had sent me to live far from him, a part of me had always idolized my father. When I pictured him in battle, I imagined him in full dress uniform, riding a white stallion and leading his cheering men into battle, wading bravely into a sea of enemy soldiers, only to make them scatter and retreat in terror without him ever having to fire a shot. Father had never mentioned bullets, or barbed wire, or blood. Father had fought opposite Papa and his little brother, Gordy. He was assigned to a U-boat at the time, so they had not shared the same battlefield, but they had been enemies, just the same. And now he was fighting again. If America entered the war and Junior enlisted, he would be Junior's enemy, and they would be in the business of trying to kill each other. The thought was almost too terrible to bear.

Papa pulled his handkerchief out of his pocket and blew his nose before going on. "I wrote my mother a letter about Gordy, but I didn't tell her the whole story. There's a lot of things about the war I never told anyone before now."

The room was silent as we waited for Papa to continue. He reached out and picked up his water glass and put it to his lips, but put it back down without taking a drink, as if he'd suddenly realized he had yet to finish the story.

"I was transferred to a hospital behind the line to see if I might regain my hearing so they could send me back into combat. I was there a long time and was on good terms with the hospital staff. Most of the patients were too badly injured to respond much, but my wounds healed quickly. Other than my hearing loss, I was pretty healthy. I felt ashamed and guilty just because I was alive. Sometimes I'd try to give the orderlies a hand just so I could feel useful.

"Over time, I became very friendly with one of the doctors, Dr. Markowski, a nice man from New York who was about twenty years older than me. He loved to play chess. So he'd stop by my room for a game almost every night. After he learned that I'd been preparing for the ministry before I'd enlisted, he took to calling me 'Rabbi.' " For the first time since he'd begun relating his story, Papa smiled.

"He was a lovely man," Papa remembered, "and an outstanding chess player. I never won a game against him, not one. Eventually my hearing improved, though it was never as good as it had been before. I'm still partially deaf on the left side. Almost everyone in my unit had been killed by the time I could hear again, but still I wanted to be sent back to the front.

"I begged Dr. Markowski to clear me and send me back up, but he wouldn't do it. 'Rabbi,' he'd say, 'it's crazy to go back up there just to get yourself killed—and for no reason! Nobody is winning this war, and nobody ever will! There is no point in you dying over something so stupid! Go home, finish your studies, get married to a pretty girl' "—Papa glanced at Mama—" 'get yourself one of those black shirts with the round white collars, and make speeches telling people they should be nice to each other. That is a noble and important calling. God already saved you once, Carl—don't test His patience!' "

Papa smiled a little at the memory.

"I was determined not to follow his advice. I just couldn't imagine coming home to Brightfield on account of a little deafness after my brother and so many of my friends had died. I couldn't imagine facing those dead boys' parents, knowing that every time they looked at me they would wonder why their son was lying in his coffin and I was still alive. Every day Dr. Markowski and I would play chess, and every day I would hound him to clear me for battle.

"One day he came into my room and handed me some papers. I was very excited because I was sure these were my orders to go back to the front, but I was wrong. Dr. Markowski had cleared me for duty, but not for combat. He had tried to get me a chaplaincy, but they wouldn't take me because I wasn't ordained. He did the best he could, but the only duty I was qualified for was working in the morgue."

I gave a little gasp of horror. I couldn't help myself, it was such an awful thought. Mama reached across the table and squeezed Papa's hand while he stared hard into Junior's eyes and went on with his tale.

"It was my job to prepare the bodies of dead soldiers for burial, dress them in clean uniforms, put them into caskets, and nail the lids closed. Hundreds and hundreds of bodies, probably even thousands. Just before I would close the lid on the coffins, I would say a prayer over the dead man, even though I knew my prayers were too late. I wished I'd listened to my dad and finished seminary before enlisting. If I had, I might have been in a position to help the living instead of praying over those who were beyond help."

Papa sniffed and looked kindly at Junior, who was sitting at the opposite end of the table, listening to his father's story with an expression of rapt attention and, I thought, a hint of respect that had been missing before.

"Politicians and blowhards speak of duty with such frequency and ease, just as they say that every war is the war to end all wars, but now we're fighting again."

Junior shifted in his chair. "So, you're saying it is always wrong to go to war? That you shouldn't have fought?"

"No. Sometimes war is inevitable, and you've got to defend yourself and your friends, but not as often as we think. As pointless as that war was, and even knowing its outcome, I do believe it was my duty as a citizen to serve. But I missed my opportunity to be of any true value in the war because I was in too much of a hurry to think through what my highest duty was. If I had gone to the front as a minister, I might have put those years to good account. I might have died trying, but at least it would have been for a reason. Think of it, Junior! All those men, thousands of them, standing on the threshold of eternity! I wasn't able to offer the least word of comfort to them—not even my own brother."

"Papa," Junior said gently, "I understand what you are saying, I really do, but I'm not called to the ministry. It's different for me."

Papa tipped his head slightly to the side, acknowledging that there was some truth in Junior's point. "Yes, but in other ways the choices you face are similar to the ones I faced when I was your age. Our duty in life lies in using our lives for their highest purpose. I'm not saying this just because I want to see you safe, though, of course, I do.

"But, it seems to me that God may be giving you some new ideas about where your destiny lies, and you ought to give that some careful consideration before you make any rash decisions." Here Junior's eyes narrowed, and his brow furrowed, exactly the way Papa's did when he was searching for a response.

"Junior, have you thought this whole thing through? Have you really thought about what it would mean if you charged into a German battle line? You'd be fighting Elise's people—maybe even her own father. Think what that would mean for the two of you!"

My eyes opened wider, and I stared at Papa, my jaw slack with surprise. What was he saying? How could he know? I looked at Junior and saw him swallow hard; the Adam's apple bobbed up and down in his throat.

"I can't pretend to know where your duty lies, son. It would be arrogant of me to pretend I did. But take some time to figure it out." Papa's voice had an almost pleading edge to it. He took a deep breath and continued in a tone that was much more detached and businesslike, as though he and Junior were a merchant and middleman negotiating a price. "Son, I am asking you to wait one year before you make any decisions about enlisting. If you decide to join up after that, so be it. I've yielded on the idea of you entering the ministry and won't even insist that you go to college, though I'd prefer it if you did. I am willing to concede all that ground without another word if you will just do this one thing. I'm not asking you to do this for me. I'm asking you to do it for Elise, because if you care for her, this is a decision that you must make carefully. Think of how difficult this could be for her."

His businesslike demeanor softened, and he smiled knowingly at his son. "And you do care for her, don't you?"

My heart warmed within me as Junior slid his hand evenly across the table and opened it to hold mine. He turned his face to me and repeated with that same honest certainty. "I love her. I think maybe I have for a long time, but I didn't know it until today."

Even I was a bit surprised at his declaration, but I knew without a doubt that he was speaking the truth. Although we hadn't actually spoken about our feelings, I'd known from the moment I'd felt his fingertips, cool and soft on my cheeks as he'd drawn my lips toward his, that Junior loved me and I loved him; in some way, I had always loved him.

Papa opened his mouth to speak. For a moment I thought he was going to say we were too young and this was all happening too fast, but he couldn't seem to find the right words. He searched Mama's face. She smiled at him, and her brows lifted, as if to remind him of something that had happened between them along ago, something impetuous and unstoppable. Papa's echoing smile said, yes, I remember.

He turned back to Junior and tried to speak again, but his voice caught, and he had to clear his throat. "Well, son . . . that's fine." Up until now Papa had only looked at Junior, but now he shifted in his chair and fixed his eyes on me. "Because you'd be a fool not to."

My cheeks grew warm, and I knew I was blushing deeply, partly from pleasure and partly from embarrassment. Papa was so dear to me. I knew he cared for me almost as if I were his own. His approval meant the world to me.

"Thank you, Papa," I said sincerely. Papa smiled at me before turning to address Junior again.

"And so you'll do as I ask? You'll wait a year before you make any decisions about going into the service?"

Junior hesitated, and I could read the turmoil that was going on inside him. *Please,* I pleaded silently, *please listen to him.* My eyes begged him to think of how much our future depended on the next word he would utter.

"All right. I'll wait," he promised.

The anxiety that had permeated the room gave way to relief. Papa gave a quick, approving nod of his head and said, "Good."

Mama smiled and started clearing dishes from the table, despite the plates still being piled with food. Everyone had been so mesmerized by Papa's amazing tale and the drama playing out between father and son, we'd forgotten to eat.

I squeezed Junior's hand and smiled reassuringly at him. He smiled back, though his lips were tightly pressed and resolute. His promise had been given haltingly, but he would keep it. I hoped he would.

Cookie was still frozen to her chair. She bit her lips and blinked a few times, the same way she did when she was trying to solve a particularly challenging math problem.

Mama said she had a cake back in the pantry and asked if anyone would like some coffee to go with it. She put the kettle on to boil when Papa and Junior said they would.

I started to get up from my place to give Mama a hand when Cookie shouted, "Wait a minute! Am I missing something? Junior and Elise in love? But they've always hated each other!"

"I never hated Elise!" Junior retorted, seeming genuinely surprised by the accusation.

"Ha!" Cookie barked. "Then you did an awful good imitation of it."

Papa laughed one of his big, booming laughs, and Cookie stared at him incredulously. Clearly, none of this was making sense to her.

"Cookie, haven't you heard the old saying that hatred is one step removed from love? Of course, they're in love. Anyone can see that. You'd be a fool not to!" Papa narrowed his eyes in a mockingly accusing expression and then trained them on Mama.

"Almost as much of a fool as your mother must think I am not to have noticed that something unusual has been going on around here today. Sophia," he scolded lovingly, "did you think I'm a man so ruled by his appetites as to be distracted by a chicken? For shame! Trying to put one over on your own husband." He clucked his tongue and sighed in feigned disappointment.

Mama put a slice of chocolate cake on a plate and brought it to him. "I wasn't exactly trying to fool you. I just wanted to wait to talk about it when we were alone." She leaned down to put the cake plate in front of him. At the same moment a tremendous, heavy thump sounded from the floor above, followed by the glittery sound of shattering glass and a chorus of howling, accusing boy voices.

"What's going on up there?" Papa bellowed as he took three bounding steps across the kitchen floor and started to mount the stairs. "Boys! What happened? Are you all right?"

Above us, a stampede of feet galloped across the floor. Chuck opened the door and called out, "It wasn't our fault, Papa. Honest! If Curt had just stayed put like we'd told him!"

"What are you talking about?" Papa scowled in exasperation.

Chuck came halfway down the stairs and tried to explain. "It was a game, Papa. Well, it was kind of a game. Curt was telling us all about his new play, and we decided to act some of it out. See if we couldn't come up with a better ending. You know, something really flashy!"

Papa looked bewildered. "Curt wrote a play? What play?"

"Curt is working on an adaption of 'The Three Little Pigs,' " I explained. "It's a morality play."

"A morality . . ." Papa stammered. "Never mind," he muttered with the worn resignation of a judge who has already heard it all and wishes he hadn't. "Go on."

By this time Chip had joined his twin on the stairway to aid in his defense. "Yeah, so we were working on the last part where the angry mob of villagers kills the evil wolf, and we thought that it would be neat if, instead of just clubbing the wolf to death, they hog-tied him, hung him from a pole, and carried him back to the village, where they'd burn him at the stake."

Mama turned deathly white, and her hand flew to her mouth. "Oh my Lord! Boys! You didn't!"

"Well, of course not!" retorted Chip as though insulted that Mama could even think they would do such a thing. I couldn't blame her, though. There were precedents. "You can't burn somebody at the stake inside the house. You'd have to do it at a bonfire outside."

"Right!" affirmed Chuck. "We were just looking for a pole to sling him from," he said brightly, as if this were the most innocent and reasonable thing in the world.

Mama just shook her head and put her hand up to her forehead.

Curt arrived on the scene. He pushed past his brothers and came stomping down the stairs, furious. His nose was streaming blood, but he was so angry and intent on seeking justice that I'm not sure he noticed. "They tied me up with Papa's neckties, stuffed a handkerchief in my mouth and left me there for fifteen minutes!" he howled. "I finally worked myself loose enough so I could hop out to look for them, but my feet and hands were tied up, so when my feet got accidentally tangled up in the lamp cord, I fell down, bashed my head on the floor, and took the lamp with me!"

"Well," Chuck said a little hesitantly, as it had finally dawned on him that he was really in trouble, "we were looking for something that would work for a pole."

"They were not! They were eating the candy I had hidden in the secret box under my bed!" Curt stabbed his finger accusingly at his torturers and yelled louder, which made the blood stream from his nose even faster.

"Oh Good Lord . . ." Papa muttered, throwing up his hands in defeat.

Mama sighed and took over. "Curt, honey, come here. Put your head back so the blood stops running. Elise, take some ice out of the tray in the freezer. Cookie, get a towel from the linen closet, but not one of my good ones."

"Hey!" Chip piped happily as he spied plates on the kitchen table. "Why didn't you tell us there was cake?"

Chapter 14

The murmurs, rumors, and conversations about the possibility or inevitability of war became more intense as the summer wore on, but I didn't seem to hear or notice them. I was much too much in love to think about anything but Junior and myself.

As I write this, I am mortified to recall my self-absorbtion in those days. I was young and in love, and there is no combination that is quite as selfish, but that is no excuse. There is no use in denying my behavior or trying to explain it; I'll just report it. I have given up the habit of refusing to see things for what they truly are.

Father's letters came only rarely now. When they did, I opened them with some dread, but not because I was worried about him. He had been safe for so long that I supposed he always would be. He had been physically removed from my life for so long that I had almost ceased to think of him as real. Father had become something like a character from a book of mythology or fairy tales in the life that I might or might not have lived many lives before, interesting but unreal, a product of my imagination or someone else's. It was easier to think of him so.

But all that would change when one of his increasingly rare letters arrived and I held in my hand a palpable reminder of him—and of the specter of war that threatened to break the charmed circle I had drawn to protect myself. My hands would tremble as I took the letter from the envelope, unfolded sheets of white stationery, and saw the words written in Father's neat, orderly handwriting with its even script and nonexistent slant; each of the letters stood up straight and tall like little soldiers at attention—like Father himself.

I could see myself a little girl again, standing perfectly still next to his desk in his dark, silent study, watching him write letters in his saluting-soldier script. I wanted him to notice me, but I was afraid that if he did, he would send me away so I wouldn't bother him. He finished a sentence with a perfect, pointed stab of a period and, without lifting his eyes from the paper but with a small smile on his lips, he reached out his hand and patted me awkwardly on the head before going on with his work. A painful stab of love would pierce my heart.

His letters confronted me with the truth. I had not imagined him; Father was real, part of me, and fighting for the nation that had given me birth. Soon he might be fighting against the nation I had come to love. Sometimes I would put the letters back in their envelopes without reading them, saying to myself, *It can't touch us. Not for a year. It will be over by then. Junior promised. Not for a year.*

Like the rest of America, the Muller family was glued to the radio whenever President Roosevelt delivered one of his fireside chats. I never paid much attention to the content of the broadcasts, but I loved them because they gave me an opportunity to sit near Junior on the parlor sofa.

Junior and I had decided that it would be disrespectful to be affectionate when we were in the presence of the family. We thought this a very mature resolve on our part, but I suspect we also realized that to do so would leave us open to unrelenting teasing from the twins. With these incentives in mind, we were fairly circumspect in our behavior when others were in the room. However, during the president's addresses we sat close together on the tufted sofa near the radio—Junior sitting up straight and listening with rapt attention, his head inclined just slightly toward the glowing dials of the Philco, while I snuggled as close to him as possible, reaching out to hold his hand in mine when I thought no one was looking. I was so happy to be near him.

Of course, whenever we could steal away from the family and our work, we went down to the river, to the spot that was now our special place instead of mine alone. In our safe, private world, we spent hours walking at the water's edge, holding hands, exchanging confidences and kisses while the waters swirled over the stones, murmuring its approval of our presence. We were passionate about each other, and the moment we were out the sight of prying eyes, it was impossible not to touch one another, though we kept our contact chaste. And yet, we were joined in the astonishing intimacy that comes from completely opening your mind to the one you love and the indescribable joy that comes from realizing that finally, finally there is someone on the earth with whom you can be utterly yourself. There is no need for cover, or calculation, or dissembling, because your lover knows you already, virtues and vices, and celebrates them all without judgment or disillusionment, because the weakness of each joins seamless with the strength of the other—together you are whole.

It was a happy time, the happiest summer I had known, and the busiest. Given the chance, Junior and I would never have spent a moment apart, but we were both working and so had only our evenings together. Still, even the hours we spent apart at our jobs seemed to join us closer in spirit. Our labors were more than just work to us—they were testaments of faith in the future we meant to build together. Each dime we saved became an imaginary brick in the home and future we were building in our minds. We felt very grown up and serious, and each payday gave us confidence that we were more than prepared to face whatever the world could throw our way.

I got a job working for Mrs. Ludwig. She was getting on in years, and she hadn't recovered fully from the cold she caught that spring. She needed someone to look after her. Betty had tried to manage it on her own for a few days, but when Mrs. Ludwig got mad and threw a mustard plaster at her, Harold had called and asked if I would like a job taking care of his mother every day from nine to four. Although Mrs. Ludwig tired easily and spent a good part of the day sleeping, she was still the same crusty, demanding, lovely old woman I had come to think of as the grandmother I had never had. I fixed her meals and read to her, and sometimes we talked, but not as often as before. The effort of long conversations wore her out. I did the housework when she was sleeping, and often, as I was scrubbing the floor, I would imagine that the old yellow farmhouse was mine—mine and Junior's—and I would scrub harder, making old pine floorboards glow with cleanliness and hope.

But that was only one of my jobs. One of the mothers from the children's choir had asked Mrs. Karlsberg if she knew a good piano teacher, and Mrs. Karlsberg suggested me. Next thing I knew I had three beginning piano students coming to the house for weekly lessons. Emmaline, Jean, and Rose were dear girls, all around nine years old and good students, eager to please. I enjoyed teaching them.

Junior was working full time, and then some, at the huge Jorgenson place. They always needed extra hands in the summer. It was hot, hard, backbreaking work. "But it does have its advantages," Junior would joke as he flexed his arms to show off muscles. He did such a good job that Mr. Jorgenson asked him to stay on after the harvest.

In the fall, I went back to high school, though I still worked at

Mrs. Ludwig's every Saturday. Mark Woodward left for his freshman year of college, but Junior stayed in Brightfield, spending his days checking drying tobacco leaves for signs of mold, baling cured leaves for market, and doing odd carpentry jobs around the farm. I knew Papa was disappointed that Junior had not changed his mind and decided to go to college, but he never said another word about it. Papa was not a man to go back on his word.

The pay at Mr. Jorgenson's was good, and Junior's bank account was growing. During one of our walks, Junior told me he was thinking of becoming a tobacco farmer himself. "I'm turning out to be pretty good at it. It's kind of interesting, and if you can get a couple of good crops in, it sure pays. Mr. Jorgenson's rolling in it," he said with obvious admiration. "He's bought two trucks this year—both brand-new!"

"That would be wonderful! And I could help you!" I began excitedly. "There is something almost poetic about it—the way the plants grow so high and so fast is miraculous! When you walk though the middle of the rows it's like being lost in a jungle of green. Have you noticed how the tobacco sheds look when they pull the slats out to let the air circulate? It's like a cathedral! Shafts of light beam through the open spaces and leave patterns of dark and light like the sun shining through stained glass, and the roof is so steep and high, it just disappears behind the shadows of the leaves, row upon row of them. And the way the drying tobacco smells! Musty and mysterious, like the pages in a very old book. Oh, I think we would be wonderful tobacco farmers!"

"Whoa!" Junior raised his hand up like a stop sign, and his face broke into a wide grin. "What do you mean, *we* would be tobacco farmers? Women don't farm."

I was indignant. "Why not? Mr. Schoeller says I've got a real feel for it."

"Well, sure, you helped him some, but that's not the same as farming." Junior raised his eyebrows doubtfully. "He was just being nice to you because he likes you. I mean, you don't see Mrs. Schoeller out there working in the field, do you? She takes care of the house, and Mr. Schoeller takes care of the farm. Women don't farm."

"Maybe they don't, but that doesn't mean I can't."

"Come on, Elise! Helping out by spearing a few piles of tobacco, or doing a little hoeing when you feel like it isn't the same as bringing in a whole crop. It's hard work! You've got to be strong, and you've got to know what you're doing. Why, even men who've worked in it their whole lives can go broke quick if they make a couple of bad bets. Look at Mr. Schoeller—he would have gone under for sure if Papa hadn't pressured the bank to give him a break."

I knew there was some truth in what he said. Tobacco farming was hard work, and it took skill. There were a million things that could go wrong, and lots of them were things a farmer had no control over, like weather, insects, and disease. It definitely came under the heading of those things which were labeled "man's work," but still . . .

"I could do it."

"Boy! You're stubborn." He puffed with exasperation.

"You say that like it was news to you," I said bluntly. "Besides, you're just as stubborn as I am."

Junior grinned and put his arm around me. "That's true," he conceded.

"I still don't see why I couldn't—"

He laughed. "You just don't give up, do you? Let's talk about something else."

"Like what?"

"Like what kind of car we'd like to have someday. I saw this beautiful roadster. Red with a convertible top . . ."

* * *

And so the days sped by like bright water rushing over the rocks in the river while we talked about something else, something easier, spinning out bright threads of optimistic dreams with all the assurance and thoughtlessness of youth, blissfully ignoring the tides of history that were beginning to lap at our feet, refusing to think of what they might mean for us.

No. That's not quite true.

We were not ignorant of what was going on in the world—we simply chose not to talk about it.

There weren't any real restaurants in Brightfield—just the café, and that was only open for breakfast and lunch. So to celebrate our six-month anniversary, Junior and I drove to Harmon and ate at the Greek diner. It wasn't fancy or anything, but we were all dressed up because it was a very special occasion; we could count the times we'd eaten in a restaurant on one hand. Junior ordered lamb because he was determined to try something he'd never had before, but it was fatty and he didn't care for it much. I ordered a hamburger, and Junior teased me for doing it.

"You could have had that at home," he said, laughing. "Where's your spirit of adventure?"

I shrugged my shoulders. "I know I like hamburgers, so I ordered one. I'm adventurous—just as long as I know everything will turn out all right." Junior thought this was hilarious.

"Don't make fun of me." I tapped his shoulder in a playful slap. "At least I'm enjoying my dinner. You ordered lamb, but you don't like it, and there it is, sitting on your plate getting cold. And it was expensive, too! I don't think I'm the one who should be getting laughed at," I said coyly.

"Yeah, but at least now I know I don't like lamb. How would I know if I never tried it?"

"You lived eighteen years without ever tasting lamb and it never bothered you. You could probably have lived happily the rest of your life and never touched a bite of lamb." I smiled, took a big bite of my hamburger, and made sounds of exaggerated enjoyment while I chewed. Of course, I was just teasing, but Junior didn't laugh, just smiled half-heartedly. His mind was somewhere else. I held my partially eaten burger out to him.

"Do you want some? I can't eat it all."

"Huh?" He shook himself as though suddenly waking. His eyes refocused. "Oh. No thanks. Well, maybe." He bent his head down and took a bite.

He murmured appreciatively through a mouthful of hamburger. "Mmm. Good."

"I told you," I said, pushing my plate toward him. "Here, have some more."

He waved away my offering. "No, that's okay. You finish it."

I cut the remaining burger in half and laid a piece on his plate next to the partially eaten lamb. I gave him half my French fries as well. He picked one up and swirled it around in a pool of catsup, but then put it down without taking a bite. After a minute he pushed the plate aside and looked out the window toward the street. His eyes were fixed on some point in the distance, staring but not seeing.

I snaked my hand across the table and tapped his arm with my fingertips. "You're so far away. What are you thinking about?"

I smiled when he said, "You and me." But my smile faded as he went on. His eyes were earnest and suddenly seemed to turn a deeper, more serious shade of brown. "We've got to talk about it, Elise."

"About what?" I asked, though in my heart I already knew what he would say next.

"The war. It's going to happen, and soon. We'll have to get in the fight."

"You don't know that," I argued. "America is still neutral—"

"A German U-boat sank an American destroyer yesterday, the *Rueben James.* One hundred and fifteen men died on that ship, Elise. These were people's sons and brothers and fathers. They were sailors just doing their jobs. They weren't at war with anyone, and a U-boat saw them, fired a torpedo at them, and killed them."

He looked at me hard and pressed his lips together a moment before speaking. "It is inevitable, Elise."

I was silent. There was nothing I could say to contradict him.

"So many men lost, and they weren't even armed to defend themselves. The paper said President Roosevelt is going to send a bill to the Congress authorizing American vessels to be armed for defense. Just a few months ago, I think it would have been voted down, but now . . . The bill will pass, Elise. The ships will be armed, and the next time they are fired upon, they will fire back, and that will be that. We'll be at war. Nothing can stop it now."

"Junior," I pleaded hopelessly, "you promised to wait a year. You promised."

"One hundred and fifteen men," he repeated slowly. His brown eyes were somber and angry. "They were unarmed. You can't be neutral about that, Elise. I can't be neutral about that."

I ducked my head to avoid the accusation I read in his eyes—that I knew him too well to think he was the kind of man who could stand on the sidelines if his country had to defend itself against an aggressor, no matter who that aggressor was. I, of all people, should have known that.

I did know. He was stubborn and brave and honorable. This was who he was and what made him mine. I took a deep breath, lifted my head, and looked into the eyes that were searching out mine, wanting to know if I really knew him.

"I love you." That was all I said. It was all I had to say.

He reached out and covered both my hands with his—four

palms clasped and closed as if in prayer. He bent his head down and brushed my fingertips with his lips.

The next day was Saturday, the day I worked at Mrs. Ludwig's. When the summer ended, and I had to go back to school, Mrs. Ludwig's daughters-in-laws started taking turns coming in to take care of the old woman for a couple of hours each day, but they just made a little food and tidied up. I took care of the heavy cleaning when I came on Saturday.

I don't think any of the daughters-in-law were too keen about the prospect of caring for Mrs. Ludwig, and, really, who could blame them? They'd all heard Betty's tale of woe about how she'd been beaned by a mustard plaster her mother-in-law thought was too hot. Everyone in town knew the story, because Betty told it over and over again in that whiny, simpering voice of hers. It was probably the most interesting story she'd had to tell in her life—not that having nothing interesting to say had ever stopped Betty from talking in the past. She did have a habit of going on and on about nothing at all.

Anyway, in spite of their trepidation, the daughters-in-law all survived their sickroom rotations without incident. Even if she had wanted to, Mrs. Ludwig was too weak these days to throw mustard plasters or anything else. It had been ages since she'd had the energy to teach me a new recipe; however, thanks to her, I was really pretty proficient in the kitchen now. I could cook just about anything unaided, but I missed our talks and the cranky, impatient, affectionate way she had of telling me I was overbeating the egg whites or underboiling the potatoes, even when it wasn't true. Now, whenever I brought her lunch into her room on a tray, she nibbled at whatever I'd made and told me it was good, with no criticism at all. That worried me.

I arrived early that day and found her completely dressed and sitting at the kitchen table waiting for me.

"You're late," she croaked as she stirred some sugar into her coffee.

"I am not," I returned jovially as I put on a clean apron. "I am twenty minutes early." You couldn't let Mrs. L. push you around or you were a goner. She was like a horse that way; she could smell fear. That's what her daughters-in-law had never understood about her.

"You're looking better today. It's good to see you up and around," I said.

She nodded. "I still have that cough, but it's not too bad. The day is warm for November. My joints don't hurt much at all. Look," she said, opening and closing her hands to demonstrate her flexibility, "they feel strong. I think I could even knead some bread dough. Thought I'd show you how to make those special rolls I always do for Thanksgiving."

My eyes narrowed for a moment as I tried to remember what rolls she was talking about. "Oh, I know! Those nice chewy ones that have the orange-colored dough."

"Those are the ones," she confirmed. "What do you suppose goes in 'em to make 'em that color? I've never told anyone the secret. Go on. Guess."

I thought for a moment but nothing came to mind. Admitting defeat, I shrugged.

"Pumpkin!" she proclaimed with a triumphant flourish of her index finger.

"Pumpkin? Why would you put pumpkin into bread?"

Mrs. Ludwig sighed and mumbled something inaudible before answering me very slowly, as though speaking to a not very bright child. "Because pumpkin is what gives them that chewy texture and that nice orange color—pretty for fall. Also, this time of year there's always more pumpkin around than a person can possibly use. How much boiled pumpkin and pie can you really eat? You don't want to waste it, so I had an idea to try them in rolls, and it worked fine."

"I would never have thought of that."

"That's the problem with you young people," she grumbled. "You're wasteful. Never been hungry. Always had everything handed to you on a silver platter, so you just throw out perfectly good food without giving it a second thought. There's an old Yankee saying, 'Use it up, make it do, wear it out—' "

" '—or do without!' " I finished for her.

"Are you trying to be saucy?"

I just grinned as I took the coffeepot from the stove and poured her a refill.

She grunted. "Told you that one before, have I?"

"Uh huh."

"How many times?" she asked, drawing her eyebrows together, making the deep wrinkles on her forehead even deeper.

The answer was at least ten. Probably closer to fifteen, but why bother her with numbers. "I don't remember. It doesn't matter."

She picked up her coffee cup and took a drink from it. "I guess I'm getting old," she commented, more to herself than me. "Well, what of it? Not like I got a whole lot of other alternatives."

She took another sip from her cup. "Coffee tastes good. Good work."

"You made it," I reminded her.

"Hmm. That explains why it tastes so good."

I pushed my lips together to keep from smiling. I would have laughed, but I knew she wasn't joking. It was nice to see her feeling like her old self again.

"Don't just stand there with your teeth in your mouth!" Mrs. Ludwig barked. "Get out the mixing bowls!"

* * *

Mrs. Ludwig talked me through the recipe, telling me how much flour, pumpkin, salt, and sugar I needed to add to the proofed yeast. I commented that a little cinnamon might be a nice addition, and, to my great surprise, Mrs. L. agreed. When I asked if she was sure, she told me that I was as good a cook as she was now, or almost anyway, and that I should trust my instincts.

"There's nothing in this world so good that it can't stand a little improvement. Except my mother's recipe for *sernik babci,*" she said. "That's perfect."

I cleaned the kitchen and the rest of the house and chatted with Mrs. Ludwig while the dough went through its first rise. Sitting side by side at the scarred wooden kitchen table, we kneaded the dough, then divided it into egg-sized lumps and shaped the lumps into rolls. While they were baking the whole house smelled wonderful. When they came out of the oven, I made a pot of fresh coffee, and we ate them hot, slathered with butter and peach preserves.

"You remember the day we put up these preserves?" Mrs. Ludwig asked, continuing without bothering to wait for an answer. "About a month after you got here. You still had your German accent and wore dirndls and braids. Couldn't find one nice thing to say about Brightfield. You sat right on that stool and told me that Junior Muller was the most brutish, ill-mannered boy on the face of the earth."

Her eyes narrowed as she looked at me, wondering if I was going to try to deny it. Instead I just said, "I was pretty awful, wasn't I? Everything was so new and confusing to me, and now Brightfield seems more like home to me than Berlin ever did. It feels like such a long time ago."

"Not to me it don't, but time moves quickly when you're running out of it. It wasn't that long ago, really. Not even three years. Now you talk, act, and look like any other American girl." She looked me up and down but frowned when she came to my feet.

"I see you're even wearing those ridiculous bobby sox. I suppose Cookie started you on 'em. For a smart girl from a good family, she sure does follow the fads. Silly things make your legs look too long."

I didn't respond. I had spent too many afternoons with Mrs. Ludwig to get into an argument about fashion with her. That was a battle you simply couldn't win.

Mrs. Ludwig shook her head over the stupidity of young girls. Then she paused and thought for a moment. "What was I talking about, anyway? Oh yes! Fresh off the boat not three years ago, and now you're a bobby-soxer. And I hear tell that the brutish, ill-mannered Junior has been suddenly transformed into Prince Charming."

I was surprised. Mrs. Ludwig had been ill and homebound for so long that I didn't suppose she knew anything about Junior and me.

"Ha!" she laughed when I stared at her.

"How did you know?"

"Oh, I've got my sources," she said slyly, and I remembered that Mama dropped by to visit her at least once a week. "It was bound to happen. Junior is stubborn and pigheaded. Just like you. You're perfect for each other!"

Now it was my turn to laugh. "It's true! We're both always sure we're right, and even if we know we're wrong, we'd rather die than admit it. But I do care for him. Very much." Mrs. Ludwig nodded at this last comment and took another bite of pumpkin roll.

"Do you write your father much these days?" she asked, abruptly changing the subject.

I reached for another roll and buttered it carefully, keeping my eyes on the bread.

"Whenever he writes me, I write back. Not too many letters are getting through these days."

There was nothing untrue in what I had said, but it wasn't the whole truth. As summer turned to fall, the correspondence between

Father and me had taken a strange twist. His missives were becoming longer, more open and honest, and for the first time in his life he seemed beset by doubts. In his last letter he had even said that he now felt it had been a mistake to send me away and that, while he still believed it was safer for me outside of Germany, it would have been better if he had sent me to school somewhere in Europe. Or—and this was most shocking of all—that we should have left Germany together! I could not imagine my father—my strict, patriotic, thoroughly Prussian father—even considering the possibility of living anywhere but Germany. Why, even when he had been to Paris, that legendary "City of Lights," he had written to me that, while he did enjoy French wines, he didn't care for their so called gourmet cooking nearly as much as good German fare and that he considered the French themselves to be "slack in body and mind, lax in moral character, and utterly lacking in national will." And now he was saying that we should have come to America together! If I had not known his orderly handwriting so well, I might have thought that someone else was writing these letters.

By contrast, my letters to him had become more like the terse, obligatory "field reports" he had sent during my first months and years in America. I always thanked him for his letter, gave him a few facts about my progress in school, the weather, my general health and that of the Mullers, and then closed with my wishes for his continued good health and the required "Your affectionate daughter, Elise." It seemed that as the war drew closer and my feeling for Junior grew stronger, I wanted to draw back from my past, not wanting my heart to be caught in a tug-of-war between Father and Junior.

"Elise! Elise!"

"What?" I asked with a start and turned toward Mrs. Ludwig, who was glaring at me impatiently.

"I was asking you a question," she growled irritably.

"Sorry. I didn't hear you."

"Have you written your father about you and Junior."

"No," I admitted.

She sighed. "You should, Elise. I know he is a long way away and that you've been angry with him for a long time, but he is your father."

"I'm not angry with Father!" I countered, and Mrs. Ludwig gave me a piercing look.

"I'm not," I insisted weakly.

"Maybe, and maybe not, but you should write him about Junior. When the war comes . . ." Mrs. Ludwig began with surety.

Oh, why did everyone always use the words "when" and "war"? I asked myself. Only a few months before, the word had been "if," and my life had been so much simpler.

"When the war comes you probably won't be able to send or receive any letters from your father. You need to tell him what you are feeling while there is still time, if there is still time."

"Yes," I conceded in a soft voice. "I know you are right."

"Have you thought about what it will be like for you when Junior goes to fight? He will be fighting against your own country and people, perhaps your own father. How will you feel about that?"

"I haven't wanted to think about it, but, of course, I have. I don't know how I'll feel," I said honestly. "I love this country. I love the people here. I love the Mullers, and I love Father. I don't know . . ."

"Well, as difficult as that will be for you, it will be nothing compared to what you are going to have to deal with every day right here in Brightfield."

"What do you mean? I love Brightfield. This is my home now."

She bobbed her head in understanding and reached over to pat my hand reassuringly. "I know. I know. This is your home, and everyone in town likes you. You are a nice young woman. Polite, cheerful, hard-working, and abounding in charity to the elderly and infirm," she said with a wrinkly grin.

"But the minute the war starts they are going to remember that you are German and that your father is an officer in the Nazi army—the army that will be pointing rifles at their sons and husbands. You won't be considered a nice young woman anymore. You will be the enemy, and a lot of people—not everyone, but most of them—are going to start treating you differently."

"But," I protested, "I'm not a soldier. I'm not fighting anyone. Why should they look at me as an enemy? No one wants this war less than I do."

"Because it is human nature. When we are attacked and hurting, when our loved ones are in danger, we look for someone to blame our problems on. It doesn't have to be someone culpable, just available. In Brightfield, that will be you. It is called being a scapegoat."

I could not accept her assertion. "But I know all of these people. They are good people. They wouldn't act like that."

Mrs. Ludwig sighed again, and her eyes looked suddenly weary. "Maybe I'm wrong, Elise, but I don't think so. By the time this war is ended, you may feel very differently about Brightfield and the people here. You may even feel differently about yourself."

The old woman's voice trailed off. She paused, bowed her head, and closed her eyes. She stayed that way for a long, long moment. I began to worry that something might be wrong with her and was just about to ask if she was all right when she suddenly took a deep breath and lifted her head to train her bright, beady eyes on me as though she had reached some important conclusion,

"What is it?" I asked.

"War is always terrible. Always. I have lived through enough of them to know. But there are things about this war, things you could not possibly know about, that make it horrible beyond imagining.

Not many people know about it. Not yet. I didn't want to tell you, but I think I must."

"I don't understand."

"Elise," she said evenly, "do you remember that day, a few months after you'd been coming to see me on Saturdays, when you came to my door and you knocked and you knocked, but I wouldn't answer?"

"Yes," I replied slowly, remembering. "I think I'd been here about a year. Maybe a little longer. When you didn't come to the door I was worried that you were sick or had fallen."

"That's right. You started calling my name, shouting through the door and jiggling the knob until I finally came and said that I wasn't feeling well and you should come back another time."

"I remember that you wouldn't open the door even a crack. You said you didn't want me to catch anything from you."

Mrs. Ludwig nodded as I spoke, indicating that my recollections were accurate. "That was a lie. I wasn't sick."

I tipped my head to one side, trying to understand why she would have lied to me. Her eyes shimmered liquid, but her voice was flat and unemotional, like someone reading a newspaper story aloud. "I didn't want to see you because I had received a letter that day. It was from one of my relatives in Poland, my great-nephew Dodek, one of my brother's grandsons. He wrote to tell me that in April of 1940 a troop of Nazi soldiers came to his village. They made everyone come out into the street and . . ." She paused. A single tear seeped out the corner of her ancient eye and down her crinkled cheek. She covered her face with her hands, unable to go on.

A sharp taste of bile rose unbidden in my throat, and I swallowed hard to keep it down. I waited for her to finish the story, but a part of me wished she wouldn't.

Mrs. Ludwig dropped her hand and looked at me with eyes full of tears and sympathy. "Oh, Elise. Dodek told me about many things . . ."

"Like what?" I pressed.

The old woman wiped her eyes. "Things I won't burden you with, but there are such terrible things happening in Europe. Such terrible, terrible things."

The bitter, punishing taste rose in my throat again. It tasted like shame. I understood what she was trying to tell me.

She took a handkerchief from the pocket of her blue-checkered workdress and blew her nose. "When I first met you, I felt sorry for you—a poor, motherless child. But since the first day you came to see me, that day when you yelled at me and spilled tea on my lap, I have loved you. If God had ever given me a daughter instead of all those boys, I think she would have been a lot like you. Hardheaded. Strong. Kind. Like you.

"You are so dear to me, but on the day the letter came though, all I could remember was that you were German and the daughter of a Nazi officer." Mrs. Ludwig reached up and gently pushed a stray lock of hair off my face.

"Elise, I didn't tell you this to hurt you but only to make you understand, to prepare you. Things are going to be very difficult for you when the war comes. You need to be prepared for what is coming and how you will feel—caught in the crossfire of a battle between the places and people you love. I cannot tell you how you are to survive this; I only wanted you to know that you can. You will. You are strong. No matter what happens, you must stay strong."

When I got ready to leave, Mrs. Ludwig did a thing she had never done before. She hugged me. I had put on my jacket and thanked her for the basket of rolls. Then, just as I was about to say good-bye and that I would see her next week, she put her arms around me and squeezed me as hard as she could, and I realized that she knew something I didn't. That she was saying good-bye.

I squeezed back. "I don't know what I would do without you!" I cried. "You are so good to me, and I don't know why. You have taught me so much! I can't think what I would do if I didn't have you to talk to!"

"No, no," she said, patting me on the back and shushing me. "You don't need me anymore. Remember what I said, Elise—you are strong. It's important that you remember."

I wiped my eyes on my sleeve and promised I would.

As I walked down the lane toward the Mullers', I turned around to see Mrs. Ludwig standing on the porch of the farmhouse with cracked yellow paint, watching me go. I waved good-bye, and she waved back.

She died on Wednesday. Papa said her funeral service.

When Harold was cleaning out her kitchen, he found a manila envelope that said *Give to Elise.* Inside was Mrs. Ludwig's handwritten cookery book, all the recipes she had taught me. On the inside cover there was a note scrawled in her big, impatient writing. It said,

Dear Elise,

You don't really need this because I know you know all my recipes by heart. You have learned everything I can teach you, but I wanted you to have them to remember me by. Besides, I have to give them to someone I trust, if only to keep them out of the hands of my daughters-in-law. They would only make a mess of things.

With love, Matylda Ludwiczak

Harold and Betty moved into the old farmhouse. They put in a new bathroom and radiators and gave the clapboard a new coat of paint. They left it the same sunny yellow, though, and I was happy about that. Somehow it made me think Milda was somewhere nearby, doing what she'd always done, baking *sernick babci* and bossing people around, but she was doing it in a better place, where the paint was fresh and the sun shone warm all day.

Chapter 15

I continued to hope that somehow American involvement in the war would be avoided, but I wasn't surprised when it finally came. Neither was anyone else, though the way we entered the fight was a shock. It was as if the whole country had been standing in a field watching a thunderstorm move in from the west, certain that at any moment they were going to hear the boom of thunder and see the crack of lighting, only to find themselves pelted by an unexpected tempest of hailstones that fell without warning from the east. Pearl Harbor caught us unaware, and when Germany declared war on the United States almost immediately after, we found ourselves suddenly and surprisingly forced to engage two separate enemies on two separate fronts. In the space of a few hours, everything had changed. We went from peacetime to wartime with hardly a breath in between.

Almost as shocking was Papa's announcement that he would be joining the army. He declared his intention five days after the attack on Pearl Harbor, right after saying a particularly long dinnertime grace in which he thanked God for each and every member of the family. We were astonished by the news.

Only Mama seemed calm. She kept her eyes on her plate and cut her pork chop into tiny pieces without commenting. Obviously, she and Papa had discussed his decision, but I couldn't tell from her demeanor if she was supportive of his plan or not.

The twins were the first to speak. Chuck, tactful as always, asked the question that the rest of us were too polite to voice. "Aren't you kind of old to join the army?"

Papa smiled. "I want to be a chaplain. That is kind of like an army minister. I'm too old to fight, but not too old to bring spiritual comfort and guidance to the men who will be doing the fighting. They'll be needing a lot of that."

Curt asked the next question. "You'll have to go away? To Japan or Germany or somewhere far away like that?" His eyes were sober, and his expression was concerned.

"Maybe," Papa responded gently. "I probably won't get to decide where I will be sent. It is always possible I could get a posting somewhere in America, but if I can, I would like to be sent closer to where the battle will be taking place. I think that is where I will be most needed."

"But," Curt countered in a voice so soft and forlorn it was almost a whisper, "I need you here."

Mama suddenly got up from the table to refill the water pitcher. Her back was to us as she ran the water from the faucet. I didn't see the slightest tremor in her shoulders, or any other sign that she was crying, but I knew that at that moment she didn't want anyone to see her face.

"Curt, it will be hard for you, I know. It will be hard for me, too, but I can't think only about what I want right now or even what you want. In the next few weeks you are going to find that a lot of papas are going to be leaving to help in the war."

Papa lifted his head slightly and looked around the table. "I won't lie to you. This war is not going to be easy. We've got to fight on two fronts on two opposite sides of the globe. It won't be over in a few weeks or months, and there is no guarantee that we'll win. In the whole history of our country, we've never faced a situation like this. If we are going to have a hope of winning, every single one of us is going to have to make sacrifices. My sacrifice will be in leaving my family behind. Yours will be in letting me go and holding together as a family while I am gone. I know you'll do the right thing. No matter what happens, I know we are going to make each other proud."

Cookie's lip had been trembling the whole time Papa had been speaking. When he finished she could hold herself together no longer. "Oh, Papa!" she wailed.

Chip rolled his eyes, obviously disgusted by his sister's emotional outburst. "Cookie, knock it off. You're makin' everybody feel bad. Women!" he complained. "Papa, are you going to get a uniform and a gun and everything?"

Papa gave his son an amused smile and said, "I don't think so, Chip. The waging of spiritual warfare doesn't require quite the same kind of artillery as physical combat."

"But you might get to fire a few shots?" Chip inquired hopefully.

"Well"—Papa shrugged—"I suppose it is possible, though highly unlikely."

Chip practically leaped from his chair for joy. "Whoo-whee! My dad might become an actual war hero! Just wait'll Roy and Gary Gilbert hear this! After all these years having to listen to them brag about their old man just 'cause he's a railroad engineer and razzin' me because you got such a sissy job!"

Realizing what he had just said, Chip suddenly turned a mortified shade of pink. "Gee . . . sorry. No offense, Papa."

"None taken, Chip," said Papa and broke into that wonderful booming laugh of his. It seemed to break the tension in the room. I think we all felt that if Papa could laugh like that, it must mean everything would turn out all right. Mama returned to the table with a full water pitcher and a composed smile. The children all started talking at once and passing the platters of food. Everyone except Junior, who sat at the end of the table with his head lowered, silently spooning applesauce onto his plate.

It was a school night, so Mama shooed the younger children off to bed as soon as the dishes were cleared, but I lingered in the kitchen after supper. Cookie wanted to spend time studying for the geometry test that was scheduled for the next day. I offered to do the washing up. Papa wanted to talk with Junior. They were in his study with the door closed. After getting the younger boys tucked in, Mama came back downstairs to help me clean up. I washed and she dried.

I really didn't mind doing dishes; I liked working in the cozy kitchen, the feel of the warm, soapy water on my hands, and the way the lamplight cast tiny rainbows on the surface of the sink full of soap bubbles. It was always such a quiet, reflective activity for me, and when the work was done and the shelves were full of sparkling glasses, the countertops still slick and shiny from washing, I felt a sense of accomplishment, even though I knew that in a few hours the job would need doing again.

I was trying, somewhat feebly, to explain this to Mama, but she seemed distracted. She nodded in all the right places and murmured agreeably, but she didn't seem to really hear me. I wanted very much to say something wise and comforting to her, the way she always did to me when I was worried, but I couldn't think of anything. Instead I jabbered on nonsensically about how good the dinner had been and how it had been a good idea to add walnuts in with the green beans.

I turned my back for a moment to scrape the congealed grease from the roasting pan into the empty coffee can that was reserved for this purpose, and heard the sharp ring of breaking glass. The sound startled me, but not as much as the sound of Mama's angry "Damn it!"

I turned around and saw her squatting on the floor picking up pieces of the cut-glass pickle dish that had slipped from her hands as she was drying it. "Damn it!" she repeated.

"Let me help," I said and got down on my knees beside her. The shards of glass were still slippery from the rinse water and some of the pieces were so small that the only way to find them was to move your head from side to side and look for the telltale glint of light on crystal. Mama squinted as she carefully searched the floor for broken glass and muttered in frustration as she did. "So stupid of me. So careless. How could I be so careless?"

"Was it expensive?" I asked tentatively. I was having a hard time understanding the vehemence of Mama's reaction. It wasn't like this was the first time something had broken in her kitchen, but I'd never heard her swear over a broken dish or anything else.

"No," she said irritably. "Not expensive, but valuable. To me, I mean. When we got married my Aunt Rose sent me ten dollars as a present, and I used the money to order an iron and some laundry baskets from the Sears, Roebuck catalog. We needed just everything, practical things, but I saw this pickle dish, and I ordered it instead of an ironing board to go with the iron. It came in the mail the morning after our wedding, and I thought it was beautiful. It was the first pretty thing on our table. So stupid of me!" she repeated through clenched teeth and reached out to pick up another tiny glass sliver of the ruined dish. She was so focused on that tiny shard that she didn't notice a larger piece of the dish lying next to it. As she reached out the heel of her hand accidentally brushed over the sharp glass edge of the other piece, cutting her and drawing a thin line of blood that stretched from the base of her pinky finger almost to her wrist.

"Damn! Damn! Damn!" she practically yelled, grabbing her cut hand with her whole one. She sat down hard on the floor and started to cry, not from the pain, I could tell, but from frustration at her inability to keep the things she cared for intact.

I got quickly to my feet and found a clean kitchen towel and the box of bandages Mama kept on a lower shelf in the pantry. I kneeled down next to her and wrapped her bleeding hand in the dishtowel. It was an old one, soft from use and covered with a pattern of fading white daisies which were suddenly transformed into a field of brilliant red ones as Mama's blood soaked through the fabric.

Mama sniffed and shook her head. For a moment I thought she was going to argue with me that she could do it herself and that I shouldn't fuss, but I interrupted before she could utter anything more than a weakly protesting "Elise . . ."

"It's all right. This won't take a minute." I spoke soothingly as I pressed the towel down to stop the flow of blood, put iodine on the cut, and covered it with a clean gauze bandage. "There!" I said as I surveyed my handiwork with satisfaction. "All better."

Mama sniffed again and used the clean end of the bloodstained towel to dry her eyes. "Thanks, nurse." She smiled weakly. "I'm sorry I fell apart like that. I don't know what's got into me. It's just that . . ."

"Papa . . ." I hesitated before going on. I felt a little presumptuous, talking to Mama about her and Papa as though I were grown up and entitled to comment, but I sensed that it was all right for me to speak to her as a friend right now. She needed a friend. She needed to talk.

I sat down next to her on the floor with my legs crossed. I'm sure if anyone had come into the kitchen they would have thought it was awfully strange to see us sitting on the floor next to a puddle of water and broken glass, but we didn't even think about that, and no one disturbed us.

"Is it all right with you—his joining up? Did you talk about it first?"

"Yes, we discussed it. Even before the Japanese attack, we'd been talking it over. For weeks and weeks. Since that night when he told you about the first war and his brother. He feels like he should go, and as much as a part of me wants to keep him here, I think he might be right," she said softly. "There will be so many young men, hurt and afraid and alone, teetering on the very threshold of heaven. We need him, but I believe they will need him more. I said he could go."

"But now you've changed your mind?"

"No. I haven't changed my mind. It is just that, well, it's real now. I don't know how I'll manage without him and . . . I'm afraid."

Mama dropped her head and stared at her bandaged hand while the silence grew. Someone had to say it. I took a deep breath. "You're afraid he won't come back."

"Yes," she whispered.

"Well, why don't you just tell him that? Tell him you've thought it over and you've changed your mind, that you need him here. He's not so young, Mama. He's nearly fifty." Mama's lips turned up just slightly as I reported this information. "Surely there are other men, younger men, who can go. The army doesn't need him as much as we do!" These last words left my lips a bit more urgently than I'd intended. I couldn't help it. Why should I risk losing two fathers to this war?

A gentle understanding replaced the vacant expression in Mama's eyes. "I know," she said. "It doesn't seem that anyone could need him more than we do, but that's not true. We have to let him go." She spread her hands apart, palms up, as though she were releasing an injured bird into the air.

"Elise," she continued, "do you remember when we were talking that night, when Papa told us about the first war?"

I nodded.

"Junior reminded Papa what he'd said to that young man who was considering entering the ministry."

"About not doing it unless he was called?"

"Yes. A calling to the ministry is more than a decision. It is God's irresistible pull toward the things He has planned since the beginning of time. Sometimes those things are hard. Sometimes they will cost you everything, but if you are truly called it doesn't matter. It is what you must do, and if you resist it, you deny your whole reason for being. You lose yourself."

"But that doesn't seem fair," I protested. "It doesn't just affect Papa. What about you?"

Mama smiled bemusedly. "Let me ask you something. You and Junior have butted heads from almost the moment you laid eyes upon each other, and now, inexplicably, you say you are in love. How did that happen?"

I blushed a little. "I don't know exactly. He was always so mean to me, and I wasn't any nicer to him, but one day, that day down by the river, everything changed. He kissed me. I didn't try to stop him. I kissed him back—"

"Why?" Mama asked flatly.

"Because I . . . I couldn't help it. I loved him. Until that moment I hadn't known it, but then it seemed like I'd always known it."

"Like it was meant to be?" Mama asked confidentially, and I was amazed at her ability to read my mind. Mama laughed. "Those old clichés sound so silly because we've heard them so often, but maybe the reason we have heard them so often is because they're true.

"Elise, in a way, love is a calling. You may not have been looking for it—maybe it didn't arrive at a convenient time, but when it does appear there is nothing else to be done. You love. It is part of who you are and what you are meant to do, even when it hurts," she said a little sadly, "as it very often does."

I knew what she meant. She loved Papa. That was her calling, and because she loved him, she had to let him follow his calling. To ask him not to would be to ask him to be someone different, and less than the man she loved. Oh, yes, I understood.

From behind Papa's closed study door we could hear the sound of male voices raised in conflict. I was pretty sure I knew what they were arguing about, and so did Mama.

"Papa is going to try to hold him to his promise to wait until summer to enlist," Mama said. "He's worried about Junior and about how I will handle all the work when he leaves. Papa has already made arrangements for John Holbrook, a retired minister who lives in the next county, to come and preach on Sundays. I'll take over the pastoral duties as best I can—sick visitations and such. Then, of course, there is the house to run. It won't be easy, but I'll manage. Lots of women will be in the same boat, and we'll all manage. But Carl would feel better about going if he knew that Junior was here. He's trying to make him feel guilty about leaving, but I think it is mostly because he feels so guilty himself." She sighed and shook her head.

"It won't work," I said with resignation, wishing I were wrong. "Junior won't be able to stand back and let everyone else do the fighting."

"I know," Mama replied. "I told Carl that."

We sat quietly on the floor for a minute, picking up the last bits of broken glass and listening to the muffled sounds of an argument going on between father and son. When the job was done, Mama made a soft, grumbling noise of frustration and started to get up. "They are too much alike, those two, and they don't even know it."

I jumped up and held my hand out to Mama. She smiled gratefully as I pulled her to her feet.

Suddenly I was filled with a great sense of confidence and purpose. "We'll manage," I said with certainty as I grabbed a mop and started cleaning the spilled water from the floor. "Don't worry about a thing, Mama. I'll help you. Together we'll manage."

Chapter 16

March 1942

I was setting the table for supper when Curt came running into the kitchen, having slammed the door so hard that I nearly dropped the tray of glasses I was carrying.

"Knock it off, Curt! Mama's trying to nap, and you're running around making enough noise to wake the dead," Cookie hissed as she pushed a stray piece of hair off her forehead with the back of her hand.

Her face was sweaty with steam from the bowl of boiled potatoes she was mashing, and her eyes were ringed with fatigue. When Mama took over all Papa's visitation duties, Cookie and I volunteered to prepare all the evening meals. We were both proficient cooks, but I think we were both surprised by just how much work was involved in feeding a family of seven day after day. Mama had made it look so easy.

Curt's shoulders drooped at her rebuke, and his eyes began to well with tears.

Cookie immediately softened her tone. "Curt, I'm sorry. I didn't mean to snap at you. Just try to be a little quieter, all right? Mrs.

Taylor has pneumonia, and Mama was up half the night nursing her."

"I'm sorry," Curt mumbled guiltily. "I was just excited, that's all. I'll be quieter, Cookie."

"It's okay. I'm not mad at you. Here," she said, holding a basket out to him. "You want a pumpkin roll? Elise just this minute pulled them out of the oven, and they're still hot."

Curt rubbed the cuff of his shirt across his eyes to sop up any remaining dampness, took a roll from the basket, and bit into it. "Mmmm," he murmured. "These are good, Elise."

"You can have another if you want," I said. "So what were you so excited about?" Curt already had a second roll in his hand, but his mouth was stuffed so full from the first one that he had to chew for a long moment and swallow hard before answering me.

He got up from the stool and pulled an envelope from his back pocket. "Look!" he said, waving it at us with a delighted smile, "A letter from Papa!"

"A letter?" Cookie wiped her hands eagerly on her apron and snatched the envelope from Curt's outstretched hand. "Why in the world didn't you say so? I'll go tell Mama!" She trotted up the stairs happily, her fatigue momentarily forgotten.

"But I tried to tell you . . ." Curt replied helplessly to his sister's retreating form.

I opened the oven door, letting the delicious smell of onions and roasted pork fill the kitchen. "This is just about done. Why don't you go outside and let the other boys know it's time to wash up for supper." Curt grabbed another roll from the basket and headed outside to call his brothers, letting the door slam just as hard as he had when he came in.

Junior and the twins had been outside all afternoon staking out a large plot of ground on the south side of the house. It would be our victory garden. Cookie and I had bought seeds the previous Saturday, and now the gaily colored packets of carrots, squash, beans, and radishes were lying on the kitchen counter near the stove, looking like a pile of cheery greeting cards.

The night before, I sat next to Junior while he drew a plan for the garden. As he measured and penciled in lines to mark the spacing and placement of various crops, I fanned out the seed packets like a deck of cards, arranging them into graduated color suits, starting with the yellow wax beans and orange carrots, moving on through crimson strawberries and rhubarb, to varieties of lettuces in graduated shades of green, and finally ending with the deep blue-green of stalks of broccoli. Junior was amused by the intensity of my concentration on this task.

"What are you doing, Elise? We're raising vegetables, not painting a picture."

"I know, but they're much prettier this way. Don't you think? There's something so wonderful about planting a garden. . . ."

Junior raised his eyebrows. "You mean the hoeing and sweating and hauling water?"

"No," I protested. "I just think the whole process is so magical. You put one of these tiny seeds in the ground, and you wait, and one day you walk outside and all these tiny little shoots have appeared out of nowhere! It's breathtaking!"

Junior leaned over and kissed me—just a quick peck, but my heart glowed warm inside me, as it did whenever we touched. "Only you could find romance in digging hills of potatoes. I just like the fact that you get something to eat at the end of the process." We laughed, but then his face became serious. "The tire rationing is just the first step, you know. Food rationing won't be far behind. Come fall you're going to be happy to have a good crop. You make the twins help you with this," he instructed. "They've got to water every day and keep the weeds down. It's important."

"I don't mind doing the gardening myself."

"I know you don't, but you can't do everything. You and Cookie and Mama already have your hands full, and after . . ."

He didn't finish the sentence. He didn't have to. I knew how it ended; after he left we would be even busier. He was doing everything he could now to make sure that we could shoulder the load in his absence. He wouldn't be with us much longer.

I leaned my head into his shoulder, wanting to be as close to him as possible, wanting him to realize how much he was going to miss me. "I read where the government has declared tobacco an essential crop," I whispered. "Vital for the war effort. Farm workers on essential crops can get a deferment. You don't have to go."

Junior sat up straighter, shrugged his shoulders as if he were shrugging off an annoying insect. His voice was cold and firm. "I'm staying until June. That's what I agreed to. That's what I promised Papa. But come June I'm leaving."

I was instantly ashamed of myself. "I know, but I can't help wanting you to stay. I just can't."

We made up, but the fun had gone out of the evening. I gathered up the seed packets and left them in a haphazard pile on the counter. Junior finished drawing the garden plan in silence, and I went into the parlor and played slow, lonely ballads.

Now the packets of seeds lay in a confused pile where I'd left them. I pushed them aside to make room for the roast to rest. The door burst open, and the kitchen was instantly full to bursting with Mullers all talking and laughing at once. The voices I had come to love blended in familial harmony: Cookie's flutey laughter with Mama's alto tones, as soothing and sure as sounding brass, the boys bickering cheerfully in the middle register, while Junior's manly timbre intoned in gentle, fatherly reminders to wipe their feet. My chest choked with a painful joy. They were so wonderful, this family—my family. The world was raging with war, but just at this moment it was hard to quite believe it. I felt so safe. I found myself not quite praying, but, rather, questioning God. *Surely You won't change this? Surely we'll always be as happy as we are right now?*

Mama came over and put her hand on my shoulder. "Everything smells delicious!"

"The letter!" Curt shouted, "Mama! Read it right now!"

Mama smiled, looking more relaxed and refreshed than she had in days, and bent down slightly to speak to Curt. "We'll read it, but let's get ready for dinner first. Go on," she said and patted him on the cheek. "Get washed."

Cookie, Mama, and I brought the food to the table while the boys washed their hands. Then we all sat down in our usual places, Mama at the foot nearest the stove; Curt and the twins on one side; Cookie, Junior, and I on the other. Papa had been gone two weeks, but no one had thought to fill his vacant spot at the head of the table. We bowed our heads as Mama said grace. When she was finished, we passed platters and bowls while Mama slit the envelope open with her butter knife and read.

Dear Ones,

Forgive me for not writing a longer letter last time, but there really wasn't much to write beyond informing you that I had passed my physical examination and had arrived safely at chaplain school. If all goes well, in three more weeks I will be given the rank of first lieutenant and a posting.

I was hoping to be given an assignment in the Pacific, but I have been informed that because of my age, I will be sent to a base in the states. Boy! They sure know how to hurt a guy! All kidding aside, I am a bit disappointed. I had always pictured myself as ministering to our soldiers on the battlefield, which I feel will be their time of greatest need. Well, God knows best and I will go where I am called and serve anyone who has a need.

Junior and Cookie, I forgot to mention in my last letter that I saw Mark Woodward in line at the induction center. He said to send you all his greetings. Cookie, I think he wanted to send more than just a greeting to you, but he was smart enough to realize that there are some salutations that can't be sent via messenger, especially if that messenger is a father.

I felt pretty odd when I got to the induction center and found myself surrounded by all those strapping young warriors but they looked just as uncomfortable having an old preacher in their midst. I noticed that one or two of them who seemed given to somewhat colorful language clammed up when they caught sight of my collar. There was another one, kind of a joker, who got halfway through a story, spotted me in the crowd, and was suddenly struck mute. He didn't say a word after that. I guess he'd gotten so accustomed to using expletives to express himself that not using them seriously depleted his store of adjectives.

"What's 'expletives' mean?" Curt inquired. The twins guffawed, and Cookie shushed them. Junior said he'd explain it to him later. Mama just continued reading the letter as though she hadn't heard the question.

Well, it was all pretty uncomfortable, but that didn't last long. Standing in long lines wearing nothing but your jockey shorts is a great equalizer among men. Before we were through, the boys were joking with me and calling me 'padre.' They were all fine young men. I hope that at least a few of them might be stationed at whatever base I am eventually sent to, but I sup-

pose most of them will be sent into combat. May God bless them.

By the way, sorry to disappoint you, Chip, but as I had thought, chaplains do not carry weapons.

Chip clicked his tongue in disgust, and Chuck drawled a nasal groan of disappointment.

I'll be assigned a chaplain's assistant whose job it would be to protect me in combat situations, but since, at least for now, it seems that I will be far away from the fighting, I imagine my assistant will do more typing and filing than shooting.

Except for missing you all so much, I am enjoying my time at chaplains' school more than I could have imagined. The best part of the experience is the camaraderie that has developed between me and my fellow chaplains-in-training.

Everywhere you look there are rabbis, priests, and ministers huddled together in groups, living opening lines to a hundred jokes, talking and debating and enjoying themselves immensely. There is no denominational bickering here, only deep theological discussion and shared devotion to God. I have not taken part in such profound conversations since seminary, and if my purpose for being here were not so solemn, I could say I was truly happy here. However, my separation from all of you, and the knowledge that in just a few weeks I and my fellow chaplains will be personally involved in the hellishly real business of war casts a shadow over this brief, heavenly sojourn.

I miss you all very much and pray for you daily. Children, make sure you keep your noses to the grindstone at school. Junior, keep helping your Mama. I know I don't have to remind you about your promise. . . .

"Funny," Junior grumbled under his breath. "You just did." I reached my hand under the table and squeezed his sympathetically.

"He asks us to write when we can," Mama continued, pointedly ignoring Junior's comment. Then she stopped reading, though her eyes continued to scan down the page. She raised her hand to her breast and laid it flat at the base of her throat. Her eyes shimmered wet as they moved higher on the page so she could read it again. Papa's private message brought a smile to her lips. She looked up and, for just an instant, seemed a bit surprised to see six intent pairs of eyes watching her.

"And he closes with 'my very dearest love to you all, Papa,' " she finished with determined brightness.

Everyone was silent for a moment, our previously festive mood now as flat and useless as a deflated balloon. Mama took in a deep breath and let it out. "Well," she said, looking down at her untouched plate, "this looks good." She took a bite of the pork roast and nodded approvingly in my direction, but I bet she didn't taste a thing.

We all dutifully picked up our forks and started picking at our food. Only Junior didn't move. I shot him a nudging glance, but he just kept glaring darkly into space. Mama took a drink of water and cleared her throat.

"Junior, you haven't eaten anything. Are you feeling all right?"

Junior dropped my hand and stood up abruptly. His chair made a scraping sound across the wooden floor planks, and his napkin dropped from his lap.

"Mama!" he began, his voice suddenly sharp and impatient. Then he stopped himself from going on, and his face crumpled into a grimace, as if the effort of forcing himself to hold back the words caused him physical pain. He closed his eyes for a moment and shook his head. In a quieter, almost apologetic tone, he said, "I'm just not hungry tonight, Mama. I'm going out for a while." Before

Mama could respond, he took five long strides toward the door, grabbed his coat off the hook, and was gone.

We sat in silence, listening to the sound of the slamming sedan door, the angry clatter of flinging gravel from under spinning tires, and the roar of the motor that faded as the miles separating Junior from the farm steadily increased.

Chuck, who was normally the least talkative and least sentimental member of the family, sadly voiced what we were all thinking. "He's going to leave too, isn't he?" He looked to Mama for an answer. She said nothing, but the way she pressed her lips together and the renewed look of fatigue on her face signaled her concurrence.

"I wish Papa were here," Chuck said. "Seems like we're coming apart at the seams since he left."

"That's not so," Mama answered quickly. Her tone was hard. "We're a family, and we always will be, even if we can't all be together. Even if . . ." She wouldn't let herself finish the rest of the sentence, wouldn't let herself voice the possibility that before the war ended some of the empty chairs around the table might never be filled again.

Sitting up taller in her chair, she started piling mashed potatoes onto her plate. The serving spoon clanked against its edge with metallic resolve, and then she started heaping some onto Chuck's plate as well, even though he hadn't asked for any. "We're not coming apart—we've just got to figure out how to come together better than we are now. We're not going to be helpless, Chuck. I won't allow it. Do you understand me? I simply won't allow it."

She tilted her chin in the direction of Chuck's plate, now piled high with potatoes, silently indicating that he should start eating, which he did. She held out her hand to each of us in turn, taking our plates, filling them until they could hold no more, and then watching eagle-eyed to make sure we ate. She was a mother bear preparing for the ravages of a long winter, urging her cubs to build up their strength and reserves for whatever might lie ahead, filled with a furious, instinctive determination to ensure the survival of her line.

"None of us are going to be helpless."

Junior stayed out all night and returned the next day, tired, hungover, and enlisted. After he'd torn out of the driveway, flinging gravel and promises off his tires, he'd found some friends and a case of beer—his first—and consumed enough alcohol to induce a plausible amnesia. Then he and the last of Brightfield's unenlisted barreled into the recruiting office high on liquor and valor. The recruiting officer put the pen in Junior's hand, showed him where to sign, and that was that.

I wasn't surprised, but that didn't stop me from being angry. Now that I look back on it, it seems so silly, so pointless the way I punished him for reneging on a promise I knew he couldn't keep, but punish him I did. We only had ten days until he was scheduled to report for duty, days we could have spent walking by the river, savoring the minutes, laughing and crying and making plans together, but as it was, we barely spoke to one another. Such a waste.

Mama was supposed to take Junior to the depot where he would catch the bus to boot camp on Saturday, but early that morning she said she had a headache and asked if I wouldn't mind driving him. At the time I took her excuse at face value. She didn't look well at all. Her eyes were red and swollen, but if I'd stopped to think about it, I would have realized this was caused by tears. It must have been agony for her to let him go, and harder still to give up that last hour with him, but she yielded her time to me so Junior and I wouldn't part in anger. It was an act of stunning selflessness.

The twins insisted on carrying Junior's bags downstairs for him. If it hadn't been for the scarred brown suitcase sitting next to the back door, it would have been easy to believe that it was just another Saturday at the Mullers'. Everything seemed so normal, the clock tick-ticked just as cheerfully as it always did, the scent of bacon lingered comfortingly in the air, and the sun glinted off the row of newly washed glasses sitting in the drainer. As I looked around the room, it all seemed so solid and unchangeable.

Cookie's eyes were a bit shiny, but she kept her emotions in check. The younger boys took turns manfully exchanging handshakes with Junior as he doled out last-minute reminders along with playful chucks on the chin before picking up his suitcase and heading out the door. Curt started to follow him, but Mama put a hand gently on his shoulder. "You go run up and get your bed made, Curt. I want to talk with Junior alone for a moment."

Curt hesitated and frowned at her, but Junior stepped in with, "Go on now, Squirt. Do as Mama says. I'll write as soon as I get to the camp, and you can be the one to read the letter to the family. I'll write every week," he promised.

Curt dragged his feet unwillingly up the stairs, and Junior gave him an encouraging grin when he turned his head for a last look at his big brother.

Mama and Junior walked out onto the porch. I brushed quickly past them so they could have some privacy, mumbling an excuse about needing to warm up the car, though the air was springlike and temperate.

I climbed into the driver's seat and started the engine. The car was parked a fair distance from the house, but I could still see what was happening on the porch. Junior's back was turned to me. Over his shoulder, I could see Mama speaking to him earnestly but with a calm expression, as if they were discussing a list of things that needed doing around the house or what he could pick up at the store for her rather than saying good-bye for who knew how long. They stood a good two paces apart from each other, and in spite of the warm weather Mama kept her arms wrapped around herself. For a moment I wondered if she was afraid that touching him might cause her to lose her composure, but then the smile left her face for just a moment, and she said something, nodding and serious, before taking one step toward him and wrapping him in her arms, reaching her hand up to stroke his hair. When she stepped back, she lay her hand on his cheek, letting it linger for just a moment before lifting it off again, quickly, gracefully, the way a butterfly lights on a blossom to bestow a fluttering blessing before rising, hovering, and moving on. Mama smiled, but even from so far away, I could see a shiny film of tears in her eyes. She tilted her chin in the direction of the car, signaling that I was waiting.

Junior stepped across the expanse of space that lay between them and scooped Mama up in his arms, lifting her so that her feet dangled helplessly a good foot above the painted porch planks. She wrapped her arms around his neck and shut her eyes tight, and they were locked in an embrace that seemed like it would last for always. Before I could take a breath or wipe my own eyes, I heard the heavy thunk of the suitcase landing on the backseat and the solid slam of the back passenger door. Junior slid onto the bench seat of the sedan, his jaw tight with resolve and regret.

"Let's go," he said hoarsely.

Driving away, I could see Mama in my rearview mirror, smiling and standing tall, with one arm wrapped around the front of her waist and the other raised high over her head in a sweeping wave of farewell. She kept waving bravely as we made our way down the long drive, but as I moved the steering wheel slightly to the left to guide the car around the bend in the road, I glanced in the mirror one last time and saw her hand drop weakly to her side and her face crumple like discarded wrapping paper.

Junior and I drove in silence through the center of Brightfield. It would have been faster to take the state route, but I went through town because I thought Junior might want to have one more look. As we drove down Main Street and past the green, his eyes scanned each building and tree as if trying to memorize a poem. In Brightfield, where everyone knew everybody else's business, the people who were walking on the sidewalks and the merchants who were lounging in front of their stores gave Junior big smiles, thumbs-up, and waves of farewell as we drove past. One or two called their good wishes to him, and Mr. Flanders, who was standing in front of his store washing his latest sale ad off the glass in preparation for painting a new one, turned, stood at attention, and threw Junior a stiff-armed salute. Junior nodded in acknowledgment. He rolled up the car window as we turned onto the state road and picked up speed.

"It's cold in here," he commented. I glanced at him for a moment; his eyes were on the road ahead. Suddenly I realized what a great fool I was, but now, having been stupidly silent for so long, there seemed to be no dignified way to open my mouth and say how wrong I'd been. I turned my eyes back to the front as we drove south toward the bus stop.

We passed fields already clothed in linen tents, hiding tobacco seedlings under their shade, groves of birches budding out in full green that only days before had stood naked and bleached like valleys of dry bones waiting for a word to bring them back to life. Now and then, as we ascended and descended the hills, between the green world and the expanses of heaven, we could catch a glimpse of the silver ribbon of river that divided and connected the world above from the one below, fed by the sky, and feeding the earth in turn, and making sense of everything.

I didn't know how to say I was sorry, but something in the green gift of the land and the certainty of the passing of spring told me I didn't have to. There would never be another day exactly like this, and if I wasted it, there would be no second chance. All I had to do was open the door by saying something, anything. A word would be enough.

"What did Mama say to you?" I asked.

"She said she expected to hear only good news. She said she was proud of me. She lied," he said flatly.

I was a bit taken aback and looked over to see if he was teasing, but there wasn't a trace of irony on his face. I was genuinely confused by his reaction. "What are you talking about?" I asked.

"It's not what she says that's a lie," he answered. "It's what she doesn't say—what our whole family doesn't say. No matter what is happening, we smile, we put a good face on things, we don't talk about things that are too dangerous or too emotional or too anything. Avoid extremes. That should be the Muller family motto. We're such cowards," he puffed derisively.

I had heard enough. "Junior, sometimes you're really an idiot, do you know that? Mama didn't lie, and she's not a coward. Don't you dare say that about her! She's probably the bravest woman I know. What did you want her to do? Cry and howl and beg you not to go? I'm sure that's what she felt like doing, but she didn't, because she didn't want you to feel bad about leaving."

"Yeah," he mumbled. "Well, I do feel bad."

"She *is* proud of you. We all are." He rolled his eyes. I took a deep breath. "I am proud of you, too."

His eyes darted towards mine, and the barest trace of a smile twitched on the edge of his lips. "You've got a funny way of showing it, not speaking to me for days on end." His words were scolding, but his tone told me I was already forgiven.

"I know," I confessed. "But I was so mad at you. It wasn't that I thought my not speaking to you would make you stay. I guess I just wanted you to feel bad, or at least guilty."

"It worked," he said with a half-smile.

"Sorry." I was.

"Naw," Junior said, waving off my apology. "I knew what you were doing and why you were doing it. I like your honesty, Elise. It sounds kind of strange, I know, but I like the fact that you were so clear about how angry you were. In some ways I'm angry with myself, but having you give me the cold shoulder kind of freed me up from thinking about what I was doing. Does that make any sense?"

I thought about it for a moment. "No," I answered plainly. I looked at him, and we both burst out into loud, sincere laughter.

"Boy, we are a mess," Junior said, grinning, and I nodded in agreement.

"Stubborn. Both of us. Why did I go and waste these last ten days? So stupid," I berated myself. "What did I think I'd gain? I always knew you were going—April, May, June. What was the difference? It wasn't like you had picked June as the magical date, anyway." I shrugged.

Junior let out a short, irritated laugh. "No. It was Papa who did that, and then he pushed me into a promise I never wanted to make. Now I'm the one that feels like a heel. All that rattletrap about someone needing to stay behind to protect the family." He laughed again, but his voice dripped bitterness. "The thing is, he was right. Somebody should stay here and take care of the family. He's the one who should be doing it instead of running off and jousting with windmills at his age. So how come I'm the one that feels like a deserter?" He slumped back against the seat and turned his head to look out the window, not really expecting an answer to his question.

"Nobody thinks you're a deserter. But I don't think Papa is, either. You're doing what you think you need to do, and so is Papa. We are going to be fine. Really. I'll watch out for everyone. I'm tougher than you think I am—look how far I can hit a baseball now," I said, trying to make a joke of it, but Junior wasn't in the mood for joking. He just shook his head and kept watching the world outside the window.

"Junior, don't be mad at Papa," I begged. I took my right hand off the steering wheel and reached out to hold his. "You've got to realize he did that out of love. Maybe it was unfair, but he was trying to protect you. In his heart, he knew that the war wouldn't be over by June, but he picked June because he figured that was as long as he could get you to hold off. Maybe he was hoping for a miracle. Maybe he thought that every day he could keep you home was one more day he could keep you from danger."

"Well, that's ridiculous!" he cried. "What is going to happen is going to happen! There is nothing he can do to prevent it. It's a war, Elise, and somebody's son is going to die! If I'm one of them, then there is nothing Papa can do about it."

His words made my blood run cold, and I could feel the color drain from my face. *He's not having a premonition,* I silently reassured myself. *He's just frustrated and upset. He's not thinking about how his words sound.* I swallowed hard and willed myself not to give into fear.

"I know that, Junior," I said softly. "Papa does, too, but when you're talking about someone you love . . . Well, I don't think logic enters into it. You'll do anything to protect them. Anything to . . ." My voice dropped, and Junior turned to look at me as I concentrated on trying to steer the car, blinking back the film of tears that made the road markings blur.

"Elise, pull over. On the shoulder, there by that big elm." He pointed to a wide turnout on the side of the road. I veered from the road, let my foot off the gas, and shifted into park.

We were still miles from the nearest town or farm, and with the engine shut off there wasn't a sound in the whole world except for birdsong from somewhere in the branches of the elm tree. What were they? Robins? Starlings? I don't remember, but I do remember Junior sliding across the seat and reaching out to pull me toward him. I remember how his arms felt holding me, how easy and right it felt to tilt my chin up to him, and how soft, how very soft his lips were when they met mine. We kissed and clung and there was no time anymore, no bus to catch or war to win. That was our time. It would always be there. No matter what happened tomorrow or in the days after that, I knew we would always be able to go back to that moment, and it would be more real to both of us than all the moments before and after. It was a gift.

Kiss by kiss, the fear that had frozen me for days and weeks and years, before Father had turned his back to me on the dock in Hamburg, since Papa had announced his intention to enlist as a chaplain, since I had turned the key in the ignition to take Junior to the bus depot, began to thaw in the heat that was love and gave me the courage to let love go, knowing it exists eternally in a place unbound by the physical world.

I pulled my head back, releasing Junior's lips from mine. My breath was coming in short gasps, and Junior's chest was rising and falling fast, as if he'd run for miles and miles. His eyes searched mine, asking silent permissions, permissions I wanted to grant with all my heart. At that moment, I knew I could have asked him anything in the world and he would have said yes. I knew that if we held on to each other one moment more we would never be able to let go, never be able to stop ourselves, and that the bus would pull away empty, and we would be left with no options but to flee in the other direction. With one more kiss, I could have kept him by my side, but I didn't need to. No matter what might happen in the future, he would never be more mine than he was at that moment. I wanted him close, but knowing who he was, I could not say yes to his unspoken desires or my own. To do so would have been to reshape him into someone neither of us recognized.

He leaned toward me, lowering his head to mine. I stretched out my finger and touched the perfect, full curve of his lips. "You have to go," I reminded him, and I knew they were the most loving words I could have spoken.

Junior closed his eyes, nodded, and drew back from me a rational inch, with his mouth opened ever so slightly as he forced his breathing to steady. Resting sideways against the upholstered back of the seat, he slowly traced the curve of my cheekbone with his index finger.

"We still have a few minutes," he said as he reached into his shirt pocket. "I want you to know that I am planning on coming back. I'm not having any premonitions or nightmares or even vague ideas about heroic sacrifice. But I won't make any promises I can't keep. I don't know what will happen, but I want you to understand that I am planning on coming home. That's why I wanted to get you this."

He opened his hand, and lying in his palm I saw a tiny circlet of gold mounted with a crimson-colored stone. "It's a garnet—your birthstone. I bought it months ago," he said. He didn't move to put it on my finger but let it lie still in his open hand, as if to say the gift was mine to take, but he would not require me to accept it. Without hesitation, I picked up the ring and slipped it on my finger.

"It's lovely," I breathed as I turned my hand to see how the stone glinted with the sun. "Thank you."

He smiled. "It looks nice on your finger. It's a promise ring. I thought about getting an engagement ring, a diamond, but I didn't think it would be fair. We can't know how long the war will last or if I'll—"

"Shh," I hushed him, reaching my hand up to cover his lips. "We don't have to talk about that now."

He pulled my hand gently away from his face. His lips flattened into a stalwart line. "Yes, we do," he said firmly and took my left hand and held it between his as gently and carefully as if he were holding some delicate blossom in his hands.

"This ring is my promise to you," he vowed. His eyes focused on mine and held them fast. "This is a pledge I'm making to you with all my heart. But I want you to know that I'm not holding you to anything. I'm not asking you for anything. I just want you to wear this so that no matter what happens, you'll remember my promise—as far as it is possible with me, I intend to come home to you and spend the rest of my days with you. So even if something should prevent that from happening, you'll know that I love you. Even if someday you decide that your feelings for me have changed and you don't want me anymore—"

"That would never happen."

"Even if it did," he insisted. "No matter what comes next, no matter who I meet, or what I do, or where I go, or who my enemy is in battle, I love you. Nothing will ever change that. I will love you always."

"Always," I echoed.

There was so much more to say, but no time left in which to say it. We shared one more kiss, a hurried, urgent one, before driving the last miles to the depot, arriving just as the driver was helping the last of the passengers aboard and getting ready to close the doors. There was no more time for good-byes or kisses or promises or scenes. Junior grabbed his suitcase from the back seat and disappeared inside the bus. I got out of the car and stood in the road, watching as the gray monster swallowed him up, shuddered, and roared to a start, then pulled slowly away, kicking up a little dust as it heaved its way onto the road.

I waved broadly, not knowing exactly where Junior was seated inside the coach. As I waved, he opened a window near the back and leaned out, pointing to his hand and shouting a word I couldn't hear above the noise of the bus engine but whose meaning was all too clear to me as I saw his lips move.

Always.

Chapter 17

It sounds odd, but during those first months of the war there was a certain kind of excitement in the air. It reminded me of that kind of purposeful tension that happens when a big snowstorm is brewing and everybody pulls together to beat it, everyone knowing their task, giving encouragement and confirmation to each other as they scurry about making sure there is enough wood in the shed and food in the cupboard, that the window sashes are tight and the animals are in the barn. It feels like a grand adventure; arguments, rivalries, and slights are forgotten when the clouds of tempest begin to form on the horizon. Everyone is on the same side. With the preparation completed and the first flakes beginning to fall, the family gathers in the warmest room in the house. Jockeying for spots close to the fire but with a clear view of the window, they marvel as the winds howl and flurries turn to a blizzard. They sip hot drinks, feeling awed and proud to know that they are seeing the worst that nature can send and yet they are safe inside the tight cocoon of warmth and provision they wove with their own effort and good sense.

That was the mood in Brightfield during 1942, an excited sense of preparation to survive a gathering storm that was serious but would pass before too long. Of course, we reasoned, there would be losses but not among our personal circle. So we cheerfully planted victory gardens, collected rubber, bought bonds, and presented our ration books without complaint, proud and eager to do our part. After months of worrying about getting into the war, it was almost a relief to actually be in it. In many ways life wasn't all that different than it had been before, at least not for me—not for a little while.

It seemed I'd lived half my life in the shadow of war, near it but not in it. Father had gone to a place called war, and I had missed him, but he wrote and life went on as it always had. As a little girl, I knew the stories of all the great German battles and warriors, and that was what they were—stories told at bedtime just before I drifted off to the world of dreams where all the soldiers rode white horses and uniforms dripping with gold braid, where the enemy was ugly and formless and scattered unwounded at the first artillery thunder. That was war to me, a bedtime fairy tale, something not quite real. I did not associate it with bullets and blood, cannon fire and corpses. When Papa and Junior left, I tried to mentally remove them to the fantasy world that was "war" in my mind, but I couldn't manage it for long. I wasn't a child anymore but a young woman of seventeen. I couldn't keep dreaming forever.

It was a Sunday when I finally understood the truth. I wasn't the only one.

That day the aged Reverend Holbrook, who filled in for Papa on Sundays, was preaching one of his wandering, somewhat vague messages just as he did every week. Reverend Holbrook only seemed to have seven or eight sermons in his repertoire, which he rotated every couple of months. His subject that Sunday was purity, which he somehow tried to link to fasting. I'd heard it at least twice before and still didn't understand it. I shifted in my seat, crossing and uncrossing my legs and turning my head to look at the rest of the congregation. Mama looked fixedly at the reverend, determined, I supposed, to give the old man her support. Cookie noticed my restlessness and gave me a curious look. "What's wrong?" she mouthed silently.

"Nothing," I whispered, but it wasn't true. Something was different, and it bothered me, but I couldn't quite put a name to it. I did my best to sit still for the rest of the sermon.

When the sermon was finally finished it was a relief to get to my feet for the closing hymn, "Like a River Glorious." It was my favorite, because it reminded me of the river and the peace and certainty that flooded my soul when I walked along its banks. However, that day the music did nothing to lift my spirits. Even as I sang the words "perfect yet it floweth fuller every day, perfect yet it groweth deeper all the way," I was pricked by anxiety, although I couldn't pinpoint its source.

The sticky F sharp on the piano and the way that Mrs. Karlsberg pounded at the keys without ever feeling the necessity to use or even acknowledge the existence of foot pedals was irritating, but that wasn't any different than any other Sunday. I wasn't the only one plagued by this terrible disquiet. Normally the singing of the final hymn was robust and enthusiastic, and it had been even more so since the beginning of the war—as if the singers were determined to demonstrate their optimism and intimidate the enemy by a fierce display of assurance. But not today. Today the voices sounded thin and reedy even though the church was full, as full as I'd ever seen it. Attendance had picked up every week since the war began, so the lack of vocal strength couldn't be blamed on low numbers. Suddenly I understood.

There are no men here, I thought, *only old men, young boys, and women. Hundreds of women.*

It was true. The pews were packed nearly as tightly as if it had been an Easter or Christmas service instead of an ordinary Sunday in summer. Scores of mothers dressed in Sabbath hats and gloves held pew hymnals bravely in their hands and gathered their brood close to them for protection. They were the heads of the family now, a position they filled by default.

Until now the women's courage had not failed them, but for some reason on that day they suddenly saw what I saw and knew what I knew. They were all thinking the same thing: *we've all been left alone here and no matter how determined we are or how many bonds we buy, some of the men who used to sit in this pew, men who sat by their wives and held the hymnals and hushed the children and whose shoulders were strong and tall enough to support the weight of a wife's head, aren't coming back. Maybe mine. And there is nothing I can do about it.*

That's when I knew for certain that it was a war, not a dream, and a war has casualties, on both sides. Papa. Junior. Father. Mama. Cookie. The boys. Myself.

Whoever won, I was going to lose.

The next day a package wrapped in brown paper and covered with foreign stamps arrived for me. The postmark showed it was from Switzerland. Everyone gathered around to watch me open the exotic-looking parcel.

"Switzerland?" Curt asked. "Who do you know in Switzerland, Elise?"

I shrugged. "No one." Of course I thought of Father but could not imagine him being given leave to cross the neutral Swiss border in the midst of battle just to send me a package. I tore away the brown paper to reveal another layer of gaily colored blue birthday wrap tied with a white ribbon. Beneath that I found a large box of Swiss chocolates—a treasure unheard of since the war began!

I was astounded by the generosity of the giver, whoever it was. I looked and looked, but there was no card enclosed. "I can't think who would have sent them," I said.

"Who cares who sent them? Jeepers!" Chip exclaimed. "There must be a pound of chocolate in there! Elise, can I have one?"

"Chip," Mama admonished him, "those are for Elise."

"Mama, it's all right. I couldn't possibly eat them all. Here," I said, passing the box to Mama, "take some. Everyone, take as many as you want! There's plenty here for us all." And that is what we did. The whole family sat down and gorged ourselves on the best, darkest, most delicious chocolate any of us had ever tasted. The six of us ate the entire box at one sitting and sat around the table afterwards groaning with pleasure. Mama mentioned something about it being late and we should start making dinner, but no one wanted to eat. We were all too full of chocolate.

I rose from the table and started to clean up, gathering up the pink frills of paper that had housed each individual sweet and tossing them into the trash basket. When I picked up the candy box, the pink cushion of tissue paper that the chocolates had rested on during their long journey fell out, and an envelope fell with it.

The room was suddenly quiet and all eyes were on me as I slit open the edge of the envelope to reveal a greeting card with a drawing of white daisies and pink roses on the front. Inside the card, an unfamiliar hand had written,

Dear Elise,

Your father and I send special greetings on your special day! Your father apologizes for not responding to your last letter personally, but wants you to know he is fine, his work goes well, and you would be very pleased with the progress he is making and that, even if he is unable to see you in the future, he thinks of you fondly and often.

Best wishes for a very Happy Birthday!

Your affectionate Cousin,
Rev. Dietrich Bonhoeffer

"I didn't know you had a cousin who was a pastor," Curt commented with surprise, his face still smeared with chocolate.

"I don't," I replied and scanned the note again, trying to make sense of it. "I don't have any cousins, except for my cousin Peter, and this isn't his handwriting."

Cookie stood up and read the card over my shoulder, laying her hand on my arm and squeezing me encouragingly. "No, but you do have a father, and whoever sent you this candy was trying to let you know that he is alive and well."

"You're right! Father is safe!" For a moment my heart flooded with a profound relief. I read the card a third time and noticed the date—May 31, 1942. On that day Father had been safe, but it was already late June. Who knew if he was still safe? The words on the card seemed suddenly ominous: ". . . even if he is unable to see you in the future, he thinks of you fondly and often." What did it mean? Was he trying to say good-bye, knowing he would not survive the war? What was the work he spoke of, and was it dangerous? Being a soldier was always dangerous, I knew that, but Father had never felt compelled to express any doubts about his survival before. What could be so hazardous that he would take the risk of sending me such a message?

That night and for many nights after, I lay awake, trying to sort out the answers, but the note was a puzzle to me, and try as I might, I couldn't fit the pieces together. I didn't hear of Father again for a long, long time.

It was August. The thermometer read over ninety degrees, as it had every day that week, but however hot it was outside, inside the tobacco tents it was ten degrees hotter and twice as humid, like a man-made jungle, which is just what it was supposed to be. Mr. Jorgenson bragged that tobacco grown under his shade tents was as fine as any on earth.

"Sumatra, Cuba—my wrappers are every bit as good as theirs," he'd say, his words clear as a bell despite the cigar wedged firmly between his teeth. "Probably better. If you build the tents right, tend the plants proper, the leaf don't know if it's in New England or New Guinea. We needed ourselves a tropical climate, so somebody thought about the problem and went and built himself one, but ours is better 'cause we can control the environment." He nodded sagely, took a long pull on his cigar and exhaled a plume of self-satisfied smoke. "That's Yankee ingenuity for you."

He was right. It was ingenious. If I hadn't been able to spot glimpses of linen roof and walls through the emerald forest of tobacco leaves, it would have been easy to believe I was lost in the jungles of Darkest Africa—a place I felt well-acquainted with due to Curt's fascination with Tarzan movies and his insistence that the entire family troop off to the matinee every time a new picture came to town. The only thing that was missing was the sound of hooting monkeys and cawing parrots, but if you had a good imagination, the cries of blackbirds roosting in the nearby maple trees sounded pretty close to the real thing.

I don't know if it was the jungle atmosphere or that mysterious chord that had sounded in me upon my first sight of a tobacco field dressed in miles of white linen, but in spite of the heat, I loved working inside the tents.

After Junior and the other young men left for the service, Mr. Jorgensen had no choice but to hire women to work on his tobacco farm, and I was one of his best hands. Many of the women Mr. J. hired were unable to stand working in the heat of the tents without fainting, but I moved through the verdant rows of tobacco leaf with a grace and speed that eluded me during the rest of the day, pausing only to take deep draughts of water from the jugs that were kept filled at the end of every third row. I knew instinctively how to handle the leaves, working quickly and fluidly to clear out the weeds without bruising the plants. Under the incubating humidity of the shade tents it was easy to forget the world outside with all its worries.

Even if it hadn't paid as well as it did, I would have liked the work. But it did pay well, and with the family having to live on Papa's reduced military salary, the job was a godsend. When my first payday came, Mama didn't want to accept the money I offered her.

"I can't take that," she protested. "You worked hard for that money. You keep it."

I was insistent and shoved the pay packet into her hands. "It's yours." Mama started to speak, but I cut her off before she could say anything else. "How many years have I lived with you? You've fed me and clothed me and never been given a dime towards my upkeep. Father never sent you anything in all those years, did he?" I asked accusingly.

"Elise, you mustn't speak of your father that way," Mama admonished me gently. "When he first wrote and asked if you could come to live with us, he sent a very generous check, but we sent it back. Later he even tried to have money wired into our bank account, but we simply wouldn't accept it."

I was struck dumb by this revelation. All these years I'd been secretly ashamed to think that Father had foisted me off on the Mullers without paying my way. Learning the truth filled me with an even deeper affection for Papa and Mama and a twinge of guilt for believing my own father could have been so ungenerous.

"You're family, Elise. We wanted you to come. We didn't need money for taking care of you. We still don't," she said, and I knew she meant it. We were cousins so many times removed it was hardly worth counting, but as far as Mama was concerned we were family. Before I'd come to live under this roof it wouldn't have made sense to me, but now I understood perfectly. We were family, bound together by love. The volume of shared blood flowing through our veins mattered very little.

Mama held the money out to me, but I wouldn't take it back. "Mama, just let me do this for you. Let me do this one thing, not because I feel I owe you, but for the same reason you took me in. Because we're family."

Mama lowered her head and thought for a moment. "All right," she said hesitantly. Then she opened the envelope and pulled out a five-dollar bill. "Here. At least take some for yourself. You should get something out of all your hard work."

"I already took some," I lied. "I don't need any more."

"Well, thank you," Mama replied with genuine gratitude. "I have to admit, this really does come in handy right now. I was wondering where I'd come up with the money for school clothes next month. I can alter some of Junior's old things for the twins, and, of course, Curt gets their hand-me-downs, but you and Cookie need new skirts and sweaters, and we all need shoes. I can't patch them well enough to get through the winter."

"What about you?" I asked. "You need some new things too, don't you? When is the last time you had a new pair of shoes?"

Mama dismissed my questions with a wave of her hand. "I'm fine. It's the children I was worried about."

"Well, there's more where that came from," I said proudly and tilted my chin toward the money in Mama's hand. "Today Mr. Jorgenson said I was his best worker and that he's going to raise my pay a dime an hour from now on."

"That's wonderful, Elise! You must be very pleased, but I won't be taking any more of your money. This is more than generous. Next payday you should go down and open a savings account."

I didn't argue with her, but by the time the next payday rolled around, Mama had gotten a bill for restocking the woodpile and reluctantly accepted my offer to pay for it. However, this time she really insisted that I keep five for myself, so I did, and Cookie helped me look through the catalog and pick out a new pair of shoes in Mama's size.

It gave me a lot of joy to be able to help the family. I could never repay Mama for all her kindness to me, but I wasn't trying to. I just wanted to help in a time of need because it was the right thing to do, and I wanted to show Mama a little of the love and care she'd always shown for me.

Saturday was payday at Mr. Jorgenson's. As the sun began to dip slowly toward the edge of the horizon, I started humming to myself as I worked, anticipating the pleasure of bringing my pay envelope to Mama and wondering if there might be a letter from Junior waiting for me when I got home. He wrote two letters every week, one to the whole family and a second, private one that was just for me. Normally his missives arrived on Monday, but occasionally they were delivered on Saturday. It would be wonderful if that happened today, I thought as I carefully reached under the lower leaves of a tobacco plant to pull the weeds that were crowded around the stalk.

A few minutes before quitting time, I heard Mr. Jorgenson calling out, "Elise! Elise, where are you?"

I got up off my knees and saw him inside the tent, rising up on his toes and scanning the field, trying to spot me through the forest of leaves. He couldn't see me, so I raised my arms high over my head and waved. "Here I am, Mr. J!"

His eyes sparked with recognition as he caught sight of my fingers waggling over the tops of the plants. "Oh. Good. Elise, could you come out here for a minute? I need to talk with you."

I threaded my way through the stalks to the end of the row where Mr. Jorgenson was waiting for me, being careful not to break any of the tender leaves as I walked. The plants rustled overhead as I moved slowly through them, and when I looked up it was like passing under a canopy made from twenty different shades of green sun-kissed silk. So lovely and so tall; it wouldn't be long until the harvest, I thought. I hoped I could work in the drying sheds. I'd always thought it would be fun to climb up into the highest reaches of the sheds to hang the full lathes, dangerous and exhilarating, working your way across the rafters with nothing below you, like a monkey swinging from branch to branch in the jungle, a trapeze artist working without a net. I decided to ask Mr. Jorgenson about it.

I wasn't surprised by his summons. We'd gotten along well since my first day of work. Sometimes he liked me to brief him on the day's progress or give me instructions about where to begin the next day. Sometimes he just liked to compliment me on my work, and, of course, that first week he'd even given me a raise. That had only been a month before, so it seemed unlikely that he'd be giving me another pay increase so soon, but who knew? I was the fastest worker on the place.

I smiled to myself and thought, *If he does give me a raise, I'm going to take the whole family to the diner for dinner. Maybe we can even go to the movies after that. It's been so long since Mama had a night out.* But as I emerged from the row of tobacco stalks, the serious look on the farmer's face told me that he hadn't called me out to offer me a raise.

His forehead was furrowed, and a cigar he seemed to have forgotten to light drooped from his lips. His eyes avoided mine. "C'mon out here where it's cooler," he said and held open a slit in one of the white fabric walls so I could pass.

When we were outside the shade tent, he cleared his throat a couple of times and then, like someone who has decided the best way to swim across a cold river is to simply plunge in, he took a deep breath and blurted out, "Elise, I gotta let you go."

For a moment I really didn't understand what he was saying. I was just about to ask him where he was going to let me go to, but then his big brown eyes rested sorrowfully on mine, and I understood.

"You're firing me?" I asked, still not quite believing it. He nodded mutely while chewing nervously on the bedraggled end of his cigar. "But why? Did I do something wrong?"

"It's nothing like that, Elise. You're a good girl and a hard worker. Never saw a woman who could work like you can, especially in this heat." He took off his straw hat and mopped his brow with a bandana.

"Tell you the truth, I never wanted to hire women on the place. When the war came and all my hands joined up, I didn't have much choice. I didn't really think women could do the work, but I had to give it a try. More than half of 'em don't last out the first week, but I've been pleased with the ones that have stayed on, you more than anybody. You should be real proud of yourself, Elise. Real proud." He reached out and patted me apologetically on the arm.

I was completely confused. "I don't understand. If what you're saying is true, then why are you letting me go?"

"I don't want to," he said with sincerity, "but I got no choice. You heard about Jerry Samuelson?"

"Yes," I answered. "Janice's husband. He died in Guadalcanal from a burst appendix. Cookie and I made up a basket of food for Mama to take when she went to visit Janice." Even though he hadn't died in combat, Jerry was Brightfield's first casualty of the war. Everyone had known it was bound to happen eventually, but the news had come as a shock. Jerry was only twenty-two. He and Janice had a little boy who had just started walking.

"It's terrible," I added, and Mr. J. nodded in agreement. "But I don't understand what Jerry's death has to do with you firing me."

He pushed his hat back on his head and rubbed his eyes like he had a headache. "It's just that now, with Jerry dying, and the war and all . . ." He stumbled and paused a moment, looking at me as if hoping I would somehow be able to finish his sentence for him. He waited a moment, but when I said nothing he continued.

"Elise, the other girls say that if you keep working here, they won't. If I don't let you go, they're all gonna quit. Good as you are, you can't do the work alone."

My head was pounding as I finally realized what Mr. Jorgenson was saying, but I still couldn't quite bring myself to believe it. "You're telling me that because Jerry Samuelson died in the Pacific, thousands of miles from here, thousands of miles from Germany, and that because he died from a ruptured appendix that could have killed him here just as easily as it could have overseas"—my voice began to rise in volume and incredulity as I watched the farmer's grizzled head bobbing up and down while I spoke, confirming my words—"the other women want you to fire me? They want you to fire me because . . ."

"Because you're German," Mr. Jorgenson finished in a tone that was both disgusted and resigned. He raised his hands to block out my protestations. "I know. I know it's ridiculous, Elise, but I got no choice. The crop will be ready for harvest in a few weeks. I can't afford to have them all walk out. Not now." A soft flush of embarrassment rose on his suntanned cheeks. He was ashamed of himself. If I hadn't been so angry, I might have felt sorry for him.

"I'm sorry, Elise." He eyes looked mournfully up at mine. "I really am." Just as he spoke, the bell marking the end of the workday sounded and other women started coming in from the tents and fields, walking wearily toward Mr. Jorgenson to collect their pay. He stood up a little straighter, pressed his lips together, and held my pay packet out stiffly in front of him, signaling his resolve. Out of the corner of my eye, I could see a group of women approaching. One of them smirked and elbowed her girlfriend as Mr. J. handed me the envelope.

For a minute, I felt like taking the money and throwing it on the ground at his feet or tearing it up in little pieces and flinging the bits in his face. I almost did, but then I remembered something Mama had read to us over breakfast just the day before, something about not casting your pearls before swine. Normally I didn't pay too much attention during Mama's morning devotional readings, but that particular phrase had stuck in my head because it sounded so odd and I couldn't quite imagine what it meant. I still didn't know what it meant, not really, but I somehow felt that throwing down my hard-earned money and letting Mr. Jorgenson and the growing circle of women who were watching see my fury and shame would be doing just that, throwing my pearls before swine.

Besides, I needed the money. The family needed the money. No matter how much it might salve my wounded pride to refuse it, or to turn around and tell that gallery of hateful females just what I thought of them, I couldn't sacrifice the interests of the family on the altar of self-gratification. I was backed into a corner, and it made me furious.

I squared my shoulders and took the packet from his outstretched hand, pleased to notice that it was trembling a little. I looked at him evenly and said, "I forgive you." Not because I did, but because I knew that the thought of my forgiveness would pile even more guilt onto his already guilty conscience. It was the most hurtful thing I could think of to say.

Pain flashed in his eyes as quickly and neatly as if I'd stuck him with a knife.

I turned slowly around, gave the watching women a cold stare, and walked away.

The house was empty when I came in, but there was a letter from Junior waiting for me on the kitchen table. I tore open the envelope and read it standing up in middle of the kitchen.

Camp Conrad,
August 10, 1942

Best Girl,

I was so happy to get your last letter. Hearing my name at mail call, especially when the letter is from you, is the highlight of my day!

Don't get me wrong, I'm not complaining, but boot camp is hard and I get pretty lonely here sometimes. Hearing from you always lifts my spirits. You shouldn't apologize for writing about everyday things that happen in Brightfield. You can't imagine how hungry I am for every little detail of what is going on at home. Your letters always make me feel like I was right there. I'm so lucky to get so much mail from all of you.

You'd be surprised at the number of fellows who never get so much as a postcard! I feel sorry for them. One of my bunkmates, Jim Harrison, a nice country kid from New Hampshire, was watching me one day when I had three letters, one from you, one from Papa, and one from Mama—and the look on his face just about broke my heart. He wasn't jealous, just kind of sad and wistful. We got to talking and he told me that he doesn't have much family; no brothers or sisters and his father is dead. Only his mother is alive and she can't read or write and is too ashamed to ask anyone to do it for her, so he never gets any mail. I wish there was something I could do to help, but I can't exactly share my letters with him. The cookies were a different matter though! I passed those around to Jim and some of the guys and they disappeared pretty quick, let me tell you! Wouldn't mind having some more—hint, hint! I showed them your picture and they all said what a lucky guy I am. Don't I know it!

I sure miss you, Elise. I know I've told you a hundred times, but you're just the best thing that's ever happened to me. You're the last thing I think about when I fall asleep and the first thing I think about in the morning. The thought of you makes even the hardest, loneliest days bearable. I love you so much, Elise.

I'm so proud to hear that you're doing so well at Mr. Jorgenson's place. Nobody knows more than I do that Jorgenson is a hard man to please. He's fair, but he's tough, so if he gave you a raise, that really says something about you! Maybe I'll have to take back what I said about women not being able to grow tobacco. Who knows? You might be the first female grower in the valley. Of course, I don't know what that would leave for me to do. Can't see me taking up cooking or sewing, but I sure am proud of you, sweetheart, especially to know that you're helping the family out with your earnings. You didn't say much about it, but in her last letter Mama said what a blessing that money has been. I'm sending her most of my pay, but it doesn't add up to much. It sure sets my mind at ease to know you are there and doing everything you can to help her.

Here's something that'll make you laugh. The base chaplain called me into his office yesterday and said he'd been reading my file. He asked if I might consider applying to be a chaplain's assistant! He said they really needed men for those spots and thought with my "family background and experiences" as he called it, I might be a good candidate. Boy! I just can't get away from it! Once a preacher's kid always a preacher's kid, I guess. Anyway, I told him I really wasn't interested, that I was hoping to score high enough at the firing range to become a sharpshooter and even if I didn't make it, I really wanted a combat position. He said he could pretty much guarantee I could be assigned to a combat chaplain if that's what I wanted, but I don't know. It sure is the last place I ever thought about serving. I think I'm going to say "thanks but no thanks", but I did promise him I'd think and pray about it so I will even though I'm sure what my answer will be.

Well, the bell is about to ring for chow, so I'd better close for now. The food is pretty awful here, but after a day of running and marching with a full pack, I'll eat anything! Write me soon. I love, love, love you!

Junior

The door opened just as I finished reading. Mama, Cookie and the boys tumbled in talking and laughing and dripping wet. Everyone was smiling, and Mama shouted orders in a cheery voice as she walked in behind her brood.

"Boys, go on upstairs and get dried off! Comb your hair, and don't leave any wet towels on the floor. Hang them up in the bathroom to dry." The boys complied, greeting me noisily as they raced up the stairs. "Cookie, you can help me put away the picnic things and get supper ready."

"Yes, Mama. Hi, Elise!" exclaimed Cookie. "It was so hot we all went down to the river for a swim. You should have come!"

"Cookie, you know Elise was at work," Mama reminded her daughter as she scurried happily about the kitchen putting away the remnants of a picnic lunch she was carrying in a basket and rinsing off the dirty picnic plates. "I tried to get them to wait, Elise, but the boys were all complaining so about the heat that I finally gave in. I hope you don't mind, dear. You must be exhausted after working all day in the tents. Why don't you let me run you a nice, cool bath before supper?"

Cookie interrupted before I could answer, not that I was making any attempt to do so. "Mama?" Cookie said and looked at me with concern. "Mama, I think Elise is crying."

"What?" she asked, looking up. "Elise? What's the matter?"

She glanced from my face to the sheets of stationery covered with Junior's handwriting that were clasped in my hand, and she turned pale. "Is it Junior? Is something wrong?"

"No!" I assured her quickly, wiping my face with the back of my hand. "Nothing like that. It's just that, I was reading Junior's letter and he was praising me for my work at Mr. Jorgenson's—"

"As well he should!" Mama interrupted. She walked across the kitchen to lay her arm comfortingly around my shoulder. "We're all so proud of you, Elise. You're such a help to me, both of you are. Cookie is doing a wonderful job taking care of the house and freeing me up to take over Papa's pastoral duties, and the money you've given me has been an absolute answer to a prayer. I don't know what I'd do without you girls—that's a fact." She beamed a smile at us both.

I was trying hard to control my emotions, but Mama's words launched me into a fresh wave of tears. "I got fired today!"

"What?" Cookie exclaimed.

"Mr. Jorgenson fired you? I can't believe it! Why?" Mama asked.

I told them the whole story. When I finished, Cookie was fuming. "That's not fair! You're his best worker, and he fired you just because you're German? It's not like you are over there firing guns or anything! How can people be so stupid?" she cried indignantly.

"Mr. Jorgenson didn't fire Elise because she's German," Mama corrected her quietly, though I sensed that in spite of her calm reaction she was just as mad at the old farmer as Cookie was. "He did it because if he hadn't, his whole workforce would have walked out on him and his crop would have rotted in the fields. He must have felt like they had him over a barrel, but that doesn't make it right."

She furrowed her brow and shook her head, wearing an expression that was half disbelief, half disappointment.

"I feel like such a fool," I muttered. "Mrs. Ludwig warned me that people would blame me when the war came, but I didn't really believe her. It just didn't seem possible that people in Brightfield could act like that. Not when they've known me for so long.

"When I think about how happy I was when he called to me this afternoon," I spat in disgust, marveling at my own naïveté, "how I was thinking he might give me another raise! I was making plans for how to spend the extra money. I wanted to take you all to dinner and a movie. The other girls watched me leave the tent all happy and smiling, and they knew! They knew he was going to fire me. They told him to do it, and they were standing there laughing at me. I hate them!"

"Oh, Elise," Mama said mournfully and reached up to push my hair tenderly back from my forehead. "You mustn't. They were just as wrong as they could be, but you mustn't hate them. Hate doesn't change anything, and if you give into it, you'll end up saying and doing things you'll regret."

I thought about Mr. Jorgenson and how I'd wounded him with my words. Mama was right, but I didn't tell her so, and I couldn't bring myself to forgive the other women or forget their mocking expressions. "I can't help it, Mama. They made me feel so . . . so ashamed," I whispered.

"Ashamed!" Cookie retorted hotly. "What in the world do you have to be ashamed about? You didn't do anything."

I shrugged my shoulders helplessly. "I don't know exactly, but it was just like when I was new at school, when I first came here. The kids made fun of my clothes and my accent, and even though they were the ones who were being mean, I felt like it was my fault. Like I must be doing something wrong."

"Working at Mr. Jorgenson's made me feel like I really belonged here," I went on, "like I was finally of some use. You've all been so good to me, Mama. From the first day I came, you treated me like one of the family."

"You *are* one of the family," Mama interrupted.

"But I didn't feel that way, not really. When you accepted the money from me, I finally felt like I belonged here, because for the first time, I was actually helping the family."

"Elise, you've always been a great help to me," Mama corrected.

"Well," said Cookie wryly with a half-grin on her face. " 'Always' might be stretching the truth. You may recall she broke about ten dozen glasses in the first year or so." Cookie raised her eyebrows and bit her bottom lip, and her expression was so comical that I couldn't help but laugh through my tears. Mama and Cookie joined in, and I felt a little better.

I took my handkerchief from my pocket and blew my nose. "I guess there's no point in standing here feeling sorry for myself. What are we going to make for supper?" I walked over to where the aprons were hanging and took a clean one off a hook. "I'll give you a hand."

Mama followed me and took the apron out of my hand. "What are you talking about?" she asked. "I thought you said you were taking us all out for a night on the town."

"Yes," I answered slowly, "but that was before I was fired."

"What does that matter?" Mama asked, her eyes sparkling playfully. "You got paid, didn't you? I say we all go out and enjoy ourselves." She hung the apron back on the hook and called up the stairs, "Boys! Put on some clean shirts and slacks I had ironed for Sunday! We're going out!"

Cookie ran over and gave Mama a squeeze. "Good idea! I'm going to run upstairs and fix my hair and change. C'mon, Elise!" Her feet tripped lightly up the stairs as she called to the boys, informing them she wanted the bathroom next.

All this gaiety in the face of our sudden poverty was confusing to me. "Mama," I protested, "don't you think it would be better to save our money for a rainy day? There's nowhere for me to work around here except Mr. Jorgenson's."

Mama smiled, and the peaceful expression on her face was more than a display of mere bravado in the face of adversity. She radiated a genuine confidence. "Elise, do you remember what I said when Papa left?"

"You said we weren't going to be helpless."

"That's right, and we haven't been. You especially. We've all pulled together, and through hard work and the grace of God, we've had everything we needed at just the moment we needed it. It's been a pretty good plan so far, wouldn't you agree?"

I nodded an affirmation, but my agreement was tentative. "But, Mama. It's going to be a long war. Everyone says so. It could be months and months before Papa is home and making his old salary." I didn't mention what would happen if Papa didn't come back at all. "Don't you think it would be wise to keep something in reserve?"

"Elise, it is because it will be a long war that we need to budget for a few pleasures now and then, to keep up our morale so we can stand up to the days ahead, even the dark days. Don't worry so much," Mama said, as she observed the doubt that was still written on my face.

"Before you got that job, we didn't know how we were going to be ready for winter, but we didn't despair. We prayed and worked, and God provided. It's been a pretty good plan, and it's worked for us so far. Let's not toy with success." Mama grinned and jerked her chin in the direction of the staircase. "Now, go on up with the others and get changed," she said. "If we don't get a move on, we'll be late for the movie. I don't want to miss the newsreel."

Wanting so much to believe she was right, I mirrored Mama's

encouraging smile, but I couldn't quite bring myself to embrace her faith in happy endings. As I climbed the stairs, I remembered the circle of women standing by and drinking in my humiliation with ill-concealed pleasure. The war had barely started. Not a single American soldier's boot had taken a step on German soil, and yet those women who hardly knew me were more than willing to label me the enemy. Mr. Jorgenson, who did know me and seemed to like me, let them do it. Helped them do it. Mrs. Ludwig had warned me about it; now I knew why.

Once the real fighting was underway, when the battle reports and casualty lists started coming on thick and fast, when the sons of Brightfield and the sons of Berlin stared down their gun barrels at one another, who would be willing to make me play the scapegoat then? Who would be willing to believe that I was just an innocent bystander? Would I even believe that myself?

Chapter 18

Christmas 1943

"Cookie! Where do you want us to set it up?"

I turned away from the ladder I was holding to see who was speaking. For a moment I thought the voice was coming from an enormous four-legged shrubbery that seemed to be walking up the aisle toward the altar. Two red heads emerged from under the greenery and shouted at Cookie, who was perched on the highest rung of the ladder, her mouth full of nails and her hands full with the hammer and the large, prickly Christmas wreath she was trying to hang at exactly the same height as the wreath we'd placed on the other side of the sanctuary.

"Cookie, c'mon already!" Chip demanded. "It's heavy!"

Cookie looped the wreath over her arm and spit the nails out of her mouth into her free hand. "My gosh! That tree is huge!"

"Fifteen feet," Chuck reported proudly. "And it weighs a ton and is dripping melted snow on me, so where do you want it?"

"Over there," she said. "In the corner next to the piano. Be careful not to drop needles all over the floor."

Ignoring her admonition about dropping needles, the boys hauled the tree over to the corner. Cookie hooked the wreath on the nail she'd just hammered, then climbed down from the ladder, bringing the tools with her. Her face was smudged with dirt and evergreen pitch. "We should have measured the other one before we tried to hang this one," she admitted wearily as she looked up at the unevenly hung wreath.

"Let's help the boys with the tree and try again after we've had a break," I suggested.

Cookie nodded. Her gaze shifted to the aisle, and she sighed as she noticed the trail of pine needles on the carpet runner. "I'll get out the sweeper and clean them up later. They sure make a mess, but I have to admit, they picked out a beautiful tree."

By this time, the boys had pushed the evergreen into an upright position. Cookie and I walked over to admire it. The whole church was filled with the fresh, sharp, resin smell of newly cut pine. "Boys, you did a great job, but it's so big! Are you sure you'll be able to keep it upright?" Cookie asked doubtfully. "If it falls on the choir in the middle of a song, I'll never forgive you!"

"Not to worry, Little Lady," Chip said in an artificially low, theatrically officious voice. Now fifteen, the twins towered over all the women in the house and had taken to calling all of us—Cookie, Mama and myself—"Little Lady" at every possible opportunity.

"We have that all figured out. My brilliant brother," Chip continued pompously, in his best carnival-barker imitation, "Chuck Muller, Esquire, is going to climb to the top of the ladder and, working without a net, drill a large eye-screw directly into the spot above the dead center of the tree. I will then—again without use of nets, mirrors, or protective devices—tie several pieces of high-test, nearly invisible fishing line to strategic tree branches and run them up to the ceiling and through the eye screw, thus insuring the tree will continue to remain secure and upright during the entire performance." Chip grinned and took a bow as his brother applauded enthusiastically.

"Besides," Chuck piped in cheerily, "if it did fall, it'd probably only hit Elise, anyway. She's the one who'll be closest to it."

"Oh well! If it's only going to hit Elise," Chip joked, "then I say we leave it as is. Save ourselves some work."

"Ha. Ha. You're hilarious," I said flatly and rolled my eyes at the grinning twins. "What I want to know is how you were able to afford such an enormous tree? I thought Cookie said we only had a couple of dollars to spend on a tree."

"Yeah," Cookie said, "how much was this one? Mr. Collier must have given you a great break on the price."

"Well"—Chip scratched his nose and sniffed—"we didn't quite go to Collier's. That is, we went, but the only trees we could afford there were so scrawny that we decided on an alternate plan."

"Chip?" Cookie questioned, a tone of warning creeping into her voice. I tried to suppress a smile. The twins really were incorrigible, always into some kind of trouble or another, but they were so funny that it was impossible to stay mad at them for long. Besides, their hearts were in the right place. "Chip," Cookie continued, "where did you get that tree?"

"Back of Hazelton's place," Chip reported unapologetically.

"You didn't take it from the yard!" Cookie was aghast, but the twins just grinned at each other. "Did you at least ask Mr. Hazelton if it was all right to cut it?" Cookie asked weakly, but I was sure she already knew the answer.

"Sheesh, Cookie! Don't get so worked up. It was way on the back corner of the property, and he's got at least six or seven others bigger'n this. I did knock on the door to ask if it was okay to cut it," Chip said.

"Not very loud, you didn't!" Chuck reported gleefully. "Mr. Hazelton's so deaf you'd have to knock with a sledgehammer to rouse him."

"That may be true, but at least I tried. Mr. Hazelton was unavailable for consultation, so I took matters into my own hands."

Cookie groaned, and Chip sighed impatiently before continuing, "Oh, come on, Cookie. He's about ninety years old! He never goes out in the yard anymore. He won't even know it's gone. Besides, if we had been able to ask him, I'm sure he would've agreed. Two of his great-grandsons are in the navy. Heck! He should be proud to have his tree as the star of the show at our benefit"—Chip's hands spread wide toward the towering evergreen, and the theatrical timbre returned to his voice as it raised to a stirring crescendo—"shining goodwill down on the audience, filling them with that warm, glowing spirit of giving and a patriotic fervor that'll inspire them to toss wads of paper money into the collection plate and buy war bonds in large denominations!"

"Makes me proud just to think of it!" affirmed Chuck, pretending to wipe a tear from his eye.

Cookie shook her head in defeat. "If anybody finds out . . ."

"They won't!" the twins promised in unison.

I agreed. "They're right, Cookie. I'm sure Mr. Hazelton won't even realize it's gone, and it does look awfully nice there." Cookie murmured doubtfully, and I put my arm around her. "It'll be even prettier when we decorate it. Come on. Let's go get the ornaments down from the attic."

Chip winked at me as I led his sister away in search of Christmas decorations. "It *is* pretty," she admitted in a hushed voice, then, biting her lip thoughtfully, she asked, "Do you think we'll have enough ornaments?"

* * *

The Brightfield Battlefield Benefit Christmas Concert had been Cookie's idea originally, but it didn't take long for the whole family and quite a few folks from the congregation to get behind it.

Tickets were one dollar each, fifty cents for children under twelve, which, together with any extra donations people gave during the collection and proceeds from concessions, promised to raise $500 for the USO, maybe more. Additionally, Mr. Loomis, one of the church deacons who also sat on the local draft board and had contacts in the state government, had arranged for a special appearance by Shirley Calloway to come and sell war bonds at intermission and sign an autograph for everyone who bought a bond. Miss Calloway wasn't exactly what you'd call a shining star in the Hollywood firmament, but she'd had speaking parts in a couple of Westerns. Everybody was excited about having a real, live actress in Brightfield.

Tickets sold out in the first couple of days, so we'd decided to put extra folding chairs in the balcony and aisles to accommodate as many people as possible. Suddenly what had seemed like a nice, patriotic means to make a few dollars for a worthy cause took on a life of much bigger proportions than Cookie had ever imagined. With the concert less than two days away, she was understandably nervous.

I was nervous, too, and had been from almost the first moment Cookie told me about the concert and asked me to play for it.

"You've just got to help me, Elise! People are going to be paying good money to attend. We need some real musicians!"

"No, Cookie. Look at all the names on your list. You don't need me."

She glanced at the clipboard she was carrying and scanned the list of acts. "I've got numbers, but no talent. Albert Grimes is going to do a violin solo, but he's more fiddle player than violinist, and Mrs. Soames volunteered to sing an aria from *Carmen.*"

Cookie's forehead creased with worry as she mentioned Mrs. Soames. "She was so excited about it that I couldn't really tell her no, but she's pushing sixty, and sometimes she kind of slips off the note. Come on, Elise! You've got to help me!" she pleaded. "I don't want this to turn into some amateur-hour talent show. You're the only one in town who can play or sing well enough to make it a real concert. I want you to play something really impressive. Something grand!" Her eyes and face lit up as a new idea popped into her mind. "A concerto or something like that!"

"Cookie, that's crazy!" I said, trying to help her see reason. "You need an orchestra for a concerto, and all we've got is Chester Grimes and some kids who play drum and bugle for Boy Scout jamborees. We can't pull off something like that."

"Fine," she replied efficiently. "What could we pull off? What about that thing I heard you practicing the other day? The really hard one?"

I knew exactly what piece she talking about, but I hesitated before answering. "The Sonata in C Minor?" It was the composition I had attempted, unsuccessfully, to learn so many years before. The one piece of music that I'd thought could save my mother's life and heal the hurts of the world. I hadn't touched it since she died until I'd found it a few weeks previously when I'd been going through my old music folders. Looking at the complex tangle of notes graphed on the staff, I knew that it was just as complicated as it had always been and that my earlier struggle to master it had not been for want of talent or technical expertise. The music was as challenging as any I had played, but the difficulty lay not just in musical technique but in something that couldn't quite be expressed in mere musical notation. No, this music required honesty and maturity, a willingness to be vulnerable and emotionally bare in order to play the music and not just the notes. I wasn't sure I was ready for that, but something compelled me to try to master it—not as a performance piece but for myself alone. I had not intended that Cookie or anyone else would ever hear me play it. "The Mozart Sonata in C Minor?"

"Yeah! That one! I heard you working on it. It's perfect!"

I paused a moment before answering. "Oh, Cookie. I don't know . . ."

"Great! Piano solo by Elise Braun!" She seized upon my indecision and her pencil, and scribbled my name on her list. "Thanks, Elise!"

"Now, wait a minute!" I protested. "I just started working on it, and I'm miles from ready. I'm not sure this is a good idea. I don't know how I'll find time to practice." That wasn't an excuse, just the simple truth. We were all working to the point of exhaustion. After graduation that spring, Cookie had taken a job as a seamstress at a plant in Harmon that made military uniforms, backpacks, and tents. Mama had been busier than ever, seeing to the spiritual needs of Brightfield's growing population of widows and orphans. In addition, she had volunteered to roll bandages and assemble packages for the Red Cross whenever she had a spare moment. This left me as the logical person to take care of the house and children. We never really discussed it, but after my experiences working at Mr. Jorgenson's, I think we all sensed it wouldn't be good for me to make myself conspicuous by taking a job in one of the myriad industrial plants that had sprung up as part of the war economy.

The pre-storm calm of two years before had definitely passed. The war was in full, bloody flower, and the citizens of Brightfield were gripped by patriotic fervor and righteous hatred of their enemies. I read the newspaper accounts of battles taking place abroad. I added up the numbers killed in battle, and I saw the pain written on the faces of the waiting wives and parents who opened Defense Department telegrams with trembling hands, knowing the worst even before they read the dreaded phrase, "We regret to inform you." I could not blame them for despising their German and Japanese foes.

At the same time, I envied their position inside the loop of information. Every major battle brought with it a new wave of anxiety. We were all on pins and needles, praying that the Western Union man would pass us by, knowing only a moment's peace—immediately after the letters arrived and we knew that our loved ones were safe, or at least that they had been when they wrote the letter. Every envelope from Junior was a reason to rejoice, but my worries could never be completely assuaged.

More than a year had passed since Reverend Bonhoeffer's letter had arrived, telling me that Father was safe, though it seemed he was involved in something very dangerous. There was no way for me to know what had happened in the months since then. When the papers reported the numbers of enemy casualties, there was no corresponding list of names, no way to know if one of those reported killed had shared my last name and deep-set eyes. If the worst had happened, no telegram conveying condolences and explanations would arrive for me. Ten times a day I thought, *Father could be lying cold and dead on a battlefield right now. He could be wounded, or captured, or buried long ago. There is no way of knowing.*

When I read the casualty reports, I mourned every lost soldier on both sides of the battlefield, but I didn't say this to anyone, not even Mama. In fact, I didn't say much these days. My accent had faded over the years, but to my own ears it sounded thicker than ever before. When I went out to buy groceries, I could see the eyes of clerks narrow when they heard me ask for flour or oleo or potatoes. I started sending Curt to do the shopping on his bicycle.

Now a big, strong boy of ten, he was happy to take on the responsibility of doing the shopping, making sure we had the proper ration stamps for each purchase. It made me smile to see him carting the bags of food manfully from his bicycle basket into the kitchen. It was good for him to know he was shouldering his share of the responsibilities; besides, it spared me the shame of having to see the recruiting posters that lined Main Street, caricatures of leering, cruel-eyed, knife-wielding German soldiers, and feeling the boring stares of passers-by in my back as I walked past. No, it was better for everyone if I stayed at home, out of sight.

In my heart, I wondered about the wisdom of making myself conspicuous by playing for the benefit, but Cookie interrupted my train of thought, and the look of desperation on her face fought against my better judgment.

"Please! Think what it will mean to the war effort! Think what that money will mean to all the soldiers far from home, to Junior and all the rest of them. Come on, Elise! I really, really need you!"

My resolve began to soften. I thought of Junior, now a chaplain's assistant in Italy with the Fifth Army, and Papa stationed at a training camp in Tennessee, trying to comfort scores of frightened boys far from home at Christmas, both of them probably in need of comfort themselves. How could I refuse to help?

Besides, Cookie really did need me. Her concert was definitely short on musical talent. I couldn't stand idly by and let it fail. This was the first time she'd shown any enthusiasm for anything since we'd learned of Mark Woodward's death at the Battle of Kasserine Pass, the first large-scale American engagement of the war. Junior had survived Kasserine, but at least five families from the valley had lost sons there. Cookie had been inconsolable when she'd heard the news, and listless in the months since. Planning this concert seemed to bring her back to life.

There was no way out of it. Looking at those pleading eyes, how could I tell her no?

"All right. I'll try." What was I agreeing to? It was only weeks until the concert, not nearly enough time to prepare. Where would I find the time to practice?

She took up her pencil again and asked for confirmation before writing it down. "The Mozart Sonata in C Minor?"

"I'll try."

"Have you ever seen so many people?" I asked.

"Not even on Christmas Eve," Mama answered as we peeked through the door off the altar that led to Papa's private study. The church was already full to bursting, and more people were filing in every minute. "I don't recognize half of them. Look! The boys are trying to squeeze some more chairs into the aisles." I peeped through the crack in the door and saw Curt and the twins carrying folding chairs from the basement and setting them up anywhere they could find a spot.

Cookie strode purposefully up the center aisle toward us, wearing her best dress and a panicked smile as she returned greetings from well-wishing members of the audience. Her pasted-on smile faded as she entered the study and closed the door.

"Mama! What am I going to do! A whole bus just drove up full of people who came over from Cheshire. We're out of chairs. I don't want to turn them away, but where am I to put them?"

"Charge them seventy-five cents instead of a dollar and tell them they can stand in the back," I suggested.

"Good thinking," Mama said.

But Cookie was doubtful. "Do you think they'll really want to stand for the whole thing?"

"If it's a choice between standing or missing the show, I'm sure they'll be happy to stand. At least offer it to them. They can stand or they can leave." I shrugged. "It's their choice."

Mama chuckled. "Elise. Always so practical. She's right, Cookie. There isn't anything else you can do. Go on. Run up there and offer them standing room. I'll go out and see if I can get everyone else to squeeze in toward the center of the pews. I'm sure we can wedge in another twenty or so if we try. I'll ask some of the mothers to hold their children on their laps."

Cookie scurried back to the lobby. Mama was right on her heels but turned and spoke to me just before she left. "Nervous?" she asked. I nodded mutely.

"You'll be fine. You'll be wonderful. You're the last one on the program—you've got at least an hour before you go on. Just sit down and try to relax." She gave me a quick hug and disappeared.

Easier said than done, I thought.

The show was going well. The audience was enthusiastic and forgiving. They cheered for Albert Grimes and Mrs. Soames. They cheered for the kindergarten class singing "God Bless America" accompanied by three Boy Scout buglers who couldn't quite hit the high notes. They whistled and stomped so hard for "Don't Sit Under the Apple Tree" that you'd have thought it was the Andrews Sisters themselves performing instead of Mrs. Gorman and her two daughters, Daphne and Daisy. When sixteen-year old Betty Hauser fell during her tap dance number and got up from the floor red-faced with embarrassment and nearly in tears, they cheered louder than ever before. When she finished, the entire audience jumped to their feet.

Having the chance to buy a war bond from Shirley Calloway may have helped swell the crowd, but as the show went on, I got the feeling that they would have showed up even if a real, live actress wasn't signing autographs after the concert. These were the ones left behind. They'd come to show their support for their husbands, brothers, sons, and friends in any way they could. Cookie didn't need me. She could have put a gaggle of performing geese on the stage and the audience would have applauded, because they were all in this together.

Most of the audience wouldn't know if I made a mistake or not, but I was still gripped by nerves. I wanted to do well. To prove I was one of them.

Mama had agreed to serve as the mistress of ceremonies for the evening. I stood waiting for her introduction; my heart felt tight and suddenly much too big for my chest. Mama said my name and led the audience in a round of encouraging applause. For a moment, I was simply paralyzed with fear.

A memory flashed in my mind, of Father and myself at the skating rink. I was little, perhaps three or four years old, content to go round and round, holding onto the railing for balance. Father led me out into the ice, holding both my hands so I wouldn't fall. When we got to the center, he let go of my hands, skated back to the rail, and called out, "Now, skate to me, Elise!" But I couldn't move. I stood frozen and rooted to the ice, afraid of falling, afraid that Father would see I was afraid.

"Come on! Skate to me!" he demanded.

"Yes, Father," I responded dutifully but didn't move.

He watched me, his face clouding over with impatience. For a moment, I thought he was going to shout at me, but his expression softened and he held out his arms to me. "You're in the middle of the ice. You don't really have a choice, you know. Be reasonable. What's the worst that could happen?" And though his words weren't quite a reassurance, I knew that was how he intended them and that if I should start to fall, he would catch me before I hit the ground.

I pictured Father standing across the stage, next to the waiting piano, holding out his arms to me. Mama cleared her throat and introduced me again, louder this time. *What's the worst that could happen? Be reasonable,* I thought and took a step forward.

A lovely, warm wave of applause met me, and I found the courage to smile as I walked to the piano and settled myself onto the bench, shifting it forward so my feet could comfortably reach the pedals. I positioned my hands over the keyboard, arched and ready to strike.

A female voice rang out, "Hey, Fraulein! What're you gonna play? 'Deutschland Über Alles?' "

A questioning murmur rippled through the crowd.

Janice Samuelson stood up and shouted again. "Maybe a little Wagner? That's Adolf's favorite, ain't it?" The confused murmur rose to an indignant buzz. Janice shouted, "Her dad's a Nazi! Fighting against our boys! You left that part out of the introduction, didn't you, Mrs. Muller!"

Janice stabbed the air with her fist, pointing it at Mama. Members of the audience started leaning into one another, asking if it was true. Some gasped in shock as they learned the truth. Some booed. Some yelled, "Get off the stage!" and things worse than that.

For a moment, Mama seemed rattled, but she gained her composure quickly. "Mr. Paulus! Mr. Raeder!" She motioned to two of the deacons who were standing near the back of the room, and they started trying to move through the crowd to where Janice was standing, but the aisles were blocked with bodies and folding chairs.

Janice's eyes were shot through with hatred. She pointed at me and started screaming. "My husband is dead, and I want to know who is to blame! My husband is dead! Someone is to blame!" The deacons finally reached her, and as they came around each side of her to remove her from the church, she collapsed into their arms sobbing hysterically and crying over and over, "Someone is to blame!"

The crowd parted as the men half led, half carried her toward the door. The shouts of anger subsided to whispered rumbles of sympathy and concern as she passed by. The lobby doors closed behind her, and the crowd was silent, listening to the echo of Janice's keening sobs.

Mama waited a long moment, until the cries faded into the distant night, and then gave me a questioning glance. I shook my head violently, no! She couldn't possibly expect me to go on, but she responded to my refusal with an insistent, proud, almost angry glare. She cleared her throat. "Ladies and gentlemen, in our final performance of the evening, Miss Elise Braun will play Mozart's Piano Sonata in C Minor."

As she finished, someone in the back of the balcony split the silence with "Get off the stage, you Nazi pig!"

The crowd exploded. I covered my head with my hands, trying to shut out the cacophony of insults and outrage that battered me. I sprang up from the bench, desperate to get out of sight before the eruption of sobbing that boiled inside me broke through the surface. The piano bench fell and struck the floor with a crack; one of the legs had broken completely off. I didn't care. I left it lying on the floor and turned, ready to fly to the safety of Papa's study, to hide behind closed doors.

Suddenly a voice, Papa's voice, boomed over the din and stopped me in my tracks. "Who said that?" he demanded.

Papa shoved his way through the mob, parting the mass of bodies as if they were nothing more than a sea of swaying reeds. He mounted the altar steps two at a time and turned to glare at the swarm of stunned faces in the pews. He tilted his face upward and shouted to the balcony, "Come on! Who said it?"

No one answered. His eyes scanned the crowd, glaring a defiant challenge to every face in the room. The veins in his neck stood out, threatening to burst the seams of his white clerical collar. His nostrils flared as he tried to bring his fury and breath under control.

"This is my daughter!" he declared, raising his arm and stretching it toward me. "She was born in Germany eighteen years ago." At this admission, a few members of the audience whispered to one another, but Papa went on. "Like the ancestors of everyone in this room, she came here seeking refuge. Seeking safety. Just like you, or your parents, or your grandparents. She came as a child, knowing nothing of wars, or politics, or battle lines. We welcomed her into our home, and she has grown into a woman here, working alongside my own children, sweating in the fields like a man to earn extra money to feed our family when my pay wasn't enough to do the job, hoeing and harvesting tobacco for GI cigarettes. That is, until she got fired for being German, an ancestry she shares with about half the people in this room." His eyes moved smoothly across the room. A couple of people shifted uncomfortably in their seats, and someone in the back row coughed.

"When she was fired from that job, she took over the running of our home and the care of my sons, freeing up my oldest daughter to work making uniforms for our troops and my wife to tend to the spiritual needs of nearly every family in this town by visiting sickbeds and mourning with bereaved wives and mothers. This beautiful young woman is the most gifted musician I've ever known. She came here tonight after hours and hours of practice, to share her gift with you, as an offering and support to our sons in uniform, including my own." He paused for a moment before continuing, his tone quieter and more intense than before.

"Elise wasn't born into our family, but she is as much my child as any born of my body. If anyone is going to call her a name, he'd better come down here and say it to me first." The room was dead silent.

"No takers?" he asked in a loud voice. "Good. Now, let's get on with the concert." Papa clapped his broad hands together, and Mama, beaming at him from the far side of the platform, echoed him as the crowd took up the signal and scattered applause rang though the sanctuary and grew in strength.

Papa turned and walked toward the door where I was standing.

He held his arms out and enfolded me in a tight embrace. I leaned my head into his chest and whispered, "I can't do it, Papa. They hate me! I can't do it."

He kissed the top of my head and pushed me back, taking my chin in his hand and looking me in the eye. "Elise, you must. You need to. *You* need to," he repeated. I understood.

I had to play. Not for them and not to prove I was one of them, but for myself alone. If I didn't, I would be afraid from that day forward.

Papa smiled. His words and countenance were gentle, but he was as firm in his resolve as my own father would have been. He waited on the sidelines, ready to catch me if I fell, but I was standing alone in the middle of the ice. There was no other choice.

I walked to the piano. Papa brought up a chair to replace the broken bench. I sat down at the keyboard, closed my eyes, and played.

It was like that first time again, like the day when Mother had perched me atop a pile of books, told me to play, and showed me a part of myself I'd never known before. I felt her presence in the room, in the keys and pedals and hammers that shuddered and pulsed under my touch, taking everyone within hearing to the place of my choosing. The journey was mine alone, but they could come along if they liked, and if they didn't, it didn't matter. I knew the path without opening my eyes. I had no fear of losing my way. My hands and mind and soul were sure.

My fingers stretched apart as I neared the destination, spreading wide, reaching beyond myself to sound the last chord. Pain like penance surged through my fingertips, turned liquid, a river flooding the secret caverns, soothing and salving the raw, hidden places. I was a little girl again—powerful and magical, curing all diseases, erasing all scars, binding the wounds of the past with healing music.

I was a woman—mature enough, survivor enough, brave enough to pour my past into each note and phrase, releasing them into the air for everyone to see and understand, or judge, or not. It didn't matter. For the moment I was whole again.

Chapter 19

That night, I slept deeply and awoke refreshed before the sun was up. I put on my robe and slippers and crept down the stairs, careful to avoid the creaky spot in the next-to-last step. My plan was to make a special breakfast to celebrate Papa's homecoming. The chickens were laying well, so there were plenty of eggs. I would scramble them with a little chopped ham and onion. The Christmas ham that was allowed in this week's ration would stretch far enough to allow that, I was sure. With some fresh-baked popovers, cinnamon apples, and chicory coffee, it would be a real feast. There was so much to celebrate—Papa's arrival, the first morning of his surprise Christmas leave, and Christmas Eve. Tonight Papa would preach the candlelight service, and everything would be like before. Almost. I thought of Junior. Was it already Christmas in Italy? Had he gotten the package with the dozens of rum balls I'd baked, using a whole month's sugar ration so he'd have enough to share? Cookie and I had made him a pair of gloves, she the left and I the right, and, miraculously, they'd come out exactly the same size. Our stitches were perfectly matched. Would the gloves fit? After I finished the breakfast dishes, I'd write him a letter and ask.

As I reached the bottom of the stairs, I heard low, urgent voices,

Mama's and Papa's voices. I turned around, not wanting to disturb them, but this time I forgot about the step, and when it creaked under my foot, Papa asked, "Who's there?"

I opened the door. "It's me."

Mama and Papa looked up and tried to smile, but there was something false in their faces. Mama's eyes were red and swollen, and Papa had lines around his eyes that hadn't been there the night before.

"I was coming down to start breakfast. I didn't know you were down here. Sorry," I apologized as I turned to go.

Mama urged me to stay. "It's fine, Elise." She sniffed and got up from her chair. "Let me give you a hand with breakfast."

I should have minded my own business, I know, but I had never seen Mama like this. Without stopping to think, I blurted out, "What's the matter with you two? What's going on?"

An image of Junior flashed into my mind. My mouth was suddenly dry and my tongue fat with fear. "Is it bad news?" I whispered.

"No!" Mama and Papa assured me in unison. Papa went on.

"Nothing like that," Papa insisted. "It's good news. I finally got the transfer I've been asking for. With a combat battalion in Europe—where I can do some good." He cleared his throat and looked at Mama, waiting for her to speak.

She nodded silently, drew in a deep breath of air, and let it out again. She looked pale and small. Her eyes were focused on the ticking wall clock, but I didn't think she really saw it.

"Mama?" I inquired, reminding her we were still there.

"Yes," she said and bit her lip. "We've decided." She walked to the window and peered out into the blackness. "It's dark as night outside. Winter can fool you that way. Makes you think morning will never come, but it's not true." Papa came up behind her and wrapped his arms around her shoulders. She leaned into him and stayed very still for a moment, as though resting herself for what would come next. Then she lifted her arm and laid one hand on top of his.

When she turned around to look at Papa, her eyes were smiling again. "Nearly seven o'clock," she observed. "Help me with the breakfast. Let's not waste time."

The Christmas Eve sermon was Papa's best ever, but I can't tell you exactly why. In some ways it was similar to many other messages I'd heard him preach over the years, but there was something different about that night. Everyone there thought the message was just for them, and in some ways they were right. It was a message for me, too. But only I knew that Papa had prepared it with Mama in mind. It was his love letter to her, a renewal of the vows they'd made to each other and to God many years ago, a promise and reminder that no matter what happened, their future was sure.

Papa stood tall, his big hands gripping each side of the pulpit confidently. The light from the candles warmed the sanctuary and smoothed out the lines of worry on the faces of the congregation as Papa issued the proclamation: "And there were in the same country shepherds abiding in the fields, keeping watch over their flock by night. And, lo, the angel of the Lord came upon them, and the glory of the Lord shone round them, and they were sore afraid. And the angel said unto them, 'Fear Not.' "

Papa took off his reading glasses, closed his Bible thoughtfully, and looked up at the congregation, as though he'd just noticed them sitting there. "Why were the shepherds so afraid?" he asked as he looked around the room to see if anyone might be willing to venture a guess.

"I think it was because they were people not so different from you and me, and like you and me, they had a natural fear of the unknown. In other words, the shepherds were startled by the unexpected appearance of something they did not understand and they were not prepared for, because, like us, they possessed a natural human fear of the unknown and uncertain."

Papa paused a moment and looked out over the people he knew so well, whose weddings and births he had celebrated, whose loved ones he had buried, whose deepest secrets he had kept. He turned his head toward Mama and looked straight at her, for just one moment not sharing himself with anyone but her.

"I know," he said tenderly, and then, lifting his head, said to the congregants, "I know that there are unknowns and uncertainties in your life now. On the verge of a new year, in a world at war, with loved ones far from your touch and protection, there are uncertainties in your future. But for all these unknowns, God has a message for you: 'Fear Not!'

"Whatever fear you have tonight, God wants to rescue you from its control. And that is the nature of fear—it controls you. But it doesn't have to be that way. We have a choice in life, and it is this: we can be controlled by God's peace, or we can be controlled by fear. You will be controlled by one or the other, but the choice is yours.

"God understands your fear. He does." Papa gripped the pulpit tighter and leaned forward, wanting to convince us of this truth.

"He doesn't promise that none of the things you fear will come to pass. In fact, He knows that some of them will. This time next year, some of us will be gone. Some of our loved ones will have left us. In time of war or in time of peace, it has always been that way. God understands that you are afraid of the unknown, but nothing is hidden from Him—the unknown is known to God. He will be with you through your worst fears. He won't abandon you or those you love." In these last two statements, Papa for a moment dropped every trace of oratorical grandeur and looked directly at Mama, as though the two of them were having a private conversation. He smiled at her widely, reassuringly, and, I saw Mama out of the corner of my eye, smiling back.

Her smile seemed to give him new energy. He spoke with such wholehearted conviction and passion that I began to listen in a new way. I'd heard Papa speak similar words in sermons before, but now something inside me finally began to really understand what he was saying—as though I'd been trying for years to read in a dark room and suddenly someone turned on the light, making sense of words and phrases that had been blurry, indecipherable typeface only a moment before.

"God sent His only son to earth as a sign of His love," Papa proclaimed, "because He wants to make peace between you and Him. As He declared through Isaiah, God says to you, 'Fear not, for I have redeemed thee. I have called thee by thy name and thou art mine. When thou passest through the waters, I will be with thee; and through the rivers, they shall not overflow thee. When thou walkest through the fire, thou shalt not be burned; neither shall the flame kindle upon thee. For I am the Lord, thy God.' "

He stopped for a long moment to examine the faces that examined his. He turned his eyes directly to mine and said solemnly, almost pleadingly, "Dearly loved of God, be at peace tonight. Invite God to dwell with you, to walk with you through the waters, rivers, and fires that will come, and, no matter what happens, He will be with you. Believe, and fear not.

"Amen," he said.

"Amen," I echoed, and believed.

Chapter 20

November 20, 1944
Luxembourg

Dear Ones,

Thanksgiving will have passed by the time this letter reaches you, and I only have time for a short letter today, but I want you to know that I have a special reason to be thankful this year! At long last my request for a new assistant has been approved. He seems to be an efficient and dedicated young man and has a good sense of humor, though at times he can be a little sassy, as all of you know so well! Still, I am overjoyed and so grateful to have Lt. Carl Muller III assigned as my official Chaplain Assistant!

You may be wondering how I managed to secure Junior's transfer to our outfit. Well, all I can say is it involved an unnamed General, some cards, and an amazing string of good luck. Don't scold, Sophia! God works in marvelous ways His wonders to perform—and maybe that good officer will learn something about the evils of gambling.

He's just been here a few days, but Junior has already been a real help to me, getting me caught up on my correspondence and helping organize a new mid-week prayer service. I know he says he isn't called to the pastorate, but he would make an awfully good minister. The men love him. Well, we'll see. In addition to his office duties, Junior serves as my bodyguard. Not too much need for that right now, thank Heaven. Winter has arrived in full force, so I don't imagine we'll see much action until things warm up again. I'm happy for the sake of the troops. They've barely had a chance to catch their breath since D-day. It'll be nice to winter in someplace and let the boys get some rest. Junior and I are making big plans for our Christmas services. I am looking forward to receiving the Christmas stockings you spoke of in your last letter. Cookie and Elise, thank you so much for organizing the women at church to fill all those stockings. They will be a wonderful treat for the men.

You needn't send anything for me; I have already received the second greatest gift I could hope for, being reunited with my son at Christmas. The greatest gift would be to be together with all of you at home again. Pray God it will be so next year.

With All My Love,

Papa

"Papa won Junior in a card game!" Cookie's disbelieving eyebrows were pasted high on her forehead, and she laughed out loud and everyone joined in. "I hope word of this doesn't get out to the deacons!"

Mama held the letter to her chest and smiled. "They'll be together for Christmas!" She picked up the open envelope and looked at the postmark.

"He mailed it the very next day. But it took a month to get here," she mused. "He didn't know they were going back into action."

"Well, Mama, nobody did," said Chuck, our resident expert on troop movements and frontline positions. He read the papers and listened to the radio reports every day to make certain we were up to date on the war news. The twins had put up an enormous map of Europe on their bedroom wall and filled it with various colored pins and flags to indicate the placement and progress of the army. It was such an intricate display that you'd have almost thought they were planning the battles themselves.

"Papa couldn't have known the Germans would attack, especially not during the winter. Everybody thought they were done for," Chuck informed us.

"Goes to show how desperate they are," Chip sneered. "They've had it." He lolled out his tongue and pretended to hang from an imaginary noose.

Cookie glared at her brother, shooting him an admonishing look as he jerked his head in my direction. "Chip! For gosh sakes!" His siblings echoed their disgust, and Mama looked irritated, too.

Chip's neck and face turned red. "Gee. Sorry, Elise. I . . . I didn't mean it the way it came out," he stammered.

"It's okay, Chip," I shrugged. "Don't worry about it." I got up from the sofa and started collecting empty coffee mugs. We'd all gathered in the parlor to enjoy the warmth of the fireplace and cups of warm milk while Mama read Papa's letter. "I'm just going to take these into the kitchen and rinse them off."

"Here," Mama said, rising from her chair. "Let me help you."

"No, no!" I motioned her back into her seat. "I'm fine. It won't take me five minutes to clear this up."

"Sorry, Elise," Chip said again and paused awkwardly. "Have you heard from your father yet?" Cookie's eyes bulged, and she practically hissed at him, but I gave Chip what I hoped was an encouraging smile. After all, not talking about it didn't make things any better.

"No, I haven't, but thanks for asking."

"The war can't last much longer, Elise. You're bound to hear from him then," he said sincerely.

"I'm sure you're right," I replied and carried the dishes out to the kitchen, leaving Chip to deal with the trail of hissed reprisals left in my wake. They were more worried about me than I was about myself, more worried about Father than I was myself. I ran hot water over a cup as I stood stupidly and watched a milky pool rise from the ceramic bottom and spill over the edge and into the sink, like watercolor washing from a canvas and running down the drain. I was so ashamed.

I hardly thought about Father anymore. When the letter had come from Bonhoeffer, frightening, unsolvable clues concealed in a candy box, I had worried. I worried that he was hurt and that I'd have no way of knowing it. I worried that he was already dead and that I was such a bad daughter, who knew him so little, that I wouldn't even sense his absence in the world. Sometimes I would wake up in the night and lie very still, waiting to see if a premonition would grip me in the darkness, almost hoping one would, just to prove I wasn't as heartless as I feared. And then one day, I wasn't sure when or why, I stopped worrying. I didn't have the energy for it anymore.

No. That's not true. I decided to stop. One day in August of 1944, I decided to stop worrying. I decided he was already dead. I decided it was better that way.

* * *

I had worked outside all that morning, hoeing weeds in the victory garden and harvesting carrots. The boys were at the movies, and Cookie was at work. Mama got up early to drop Cookie off at the factory so she could use the car to visit Betsy Semple in the hospital. Betsy Semple was now Betsy Rohleder. She and Ernest were married right after high school graduation. They'd only had a three-day honeymoon before Ernest shipped out, but it had been enough. Betsy had delivered a seven-pound boy a few days previously.

After seeing Betsy, Mama planned on going to clean the church so it would be ready for Jim Flanders's funeral the next day. Actually, it was a memorial service, because they'd buried Jim in France. Jim was the son of Mr. Flanders, who owned the five-and-dime. He'd been killed at Normandy on D-day, along with three others from Brightfield, including John Harkness. No one had known what happened to Jim until almost two months later. Mr. and Mrs. Flanders received a telegram saying Jim was missing in action. It turned out he'd been shot and crawled under an embankment, probably trying to shield himself from more gunfire, but he'd died there, and no one had found his body for several weeks.

It was a grisly picture to imagine—terrible to think of him bleeding and dying alone thousands of miles from home, waiting for help that came too late. Everybody said it was too bad, but that it must have been a relief for the Flanderses to know the truth at last. Maybe it was. I wasn't so sure. Better to imagine the best than know the worst. That's how I felt, anyway.

I finished pulling the carrots, got up off my knees, clapped my hands together to shake off the chalky dust, and told myself to think about something besides Jim Flanders. There had already been so many funerals.

I went inside and lay down on the sofa in the parlor to rest. It was cooler in there than in the rest of the house. I'd intended just to rest my eyes for a minute before getting up to run a bath, but I fell asleep on the sofa.

I heard the door between the parlor and the kitchen creak open and heard Mama calling my name, but I was too groggy to answer right away. The sun sat low in the sky, shining directly into the parlor window and my eyes. How long had I slept? I lifted my hand to my face, blocking the light to give myself a chance to adjust to the glare.

Yawning, I blinked myself awake and was about to answer Mama's call when I heard her say, "Hmm. I guess she went to the movies with the boys. Well, Carolyn, it looks like we've got the house to ourselves. Sit down." A kitchen chair scraped the floor as it was pulled out from the table. "We don't have any tea. Would you like a glass of ice water?"

"That'd be nice." It was Mrs. Scholler.

"Thanks for helping me with the cleaning. It sure goes faster with two." I could hear Mama moving around the kitchen, taking down glasses from the shelves, opening and closing drawers.

"Don't mention it. Least I can do. I made a pound cake for tomorrow. What time is the service again?"

"Two," Mama replied. "That's the only time Dr. Holbrook could do it. It's such a long drive from Harmon."

Mrs. Scholler grumped disapprovingly. "Well, I guess he's better than nothing, but I'll sure be glad when that husband of yours comes home and we can hear some real preaching."

A cool sound of water being poured, ice cracking, another chair being pulled out as Mama sat down. "Carolyn," Mama reproved gently, "Dr. Holbrook is a fine preacher. It's awfully good of him to interrupt his retirement and fill in for Carl like this, driving all this way every Sunday. And for funerals, too." A brief silence and ice clinking as Mama took a drink. "That being said, I'll be glad when Carl is home, too." The two women shared a moment's laughter.

"I can't stay long, Sophia. Want to get home and check on Vince. I keep tellin' him he's too darned old to be working tobacco in this heat, but he don't listen to me. Says it's his patriotic duty. Bah! He just don't wanna be cooped up in the house with me." She chuckled. "Well, I don't much relish the idea of having him underfoot, either, but you'd think he could take up a hobby. I told him he oughta try horseshoes or boat building—something proper for a man his age."

"What did he say to that?" Mama asked, but it sounded like she already knew the answer.

"Something I can't be repeating to the minister's wife, that's what," Mrs. Scholler cackled. "Naw, he'll keep working till it kills him. Nothing I can do about it. Did you know that after Milda Ludwig died, God rest her soul, he was actually thinking about making an offer on her place."

"Really?"

"Can you believe it? At his age! Thinking of taking on sixty more acres! Breaking up new fields! Old fool," she grumbled admiringly. "Say, speaking of Milda. Did I tell you about that day I went to see her, not too long before she died? About that letter she got?"

"No," Mama said. "I don't think so."

"Well," she said eagerly, and I heard the chair scrape again. I pictured Mrs. Scholler leaning in for a good gossip. "This is what happened—I brought her some soup that day because I heard she'd caught a cold. I knocked, but there was no answer. I was worried, so I started pounding on the door and calling her. Finally, I hear her yellin'. She said, 'Elise! Go away! I said I don't want to see you today! Come back tomorrow!'

"So I hollered back it was me, and she finally opened the door. I could see her eyes were all red and puffy, like she'd been crying. I knew Milda for forty years and I'd never seen the trace of a tear on her, not even when Joe died. But that day she was awful broke up. I asked her what was wrong, and she invited me in and fed me coffee and cake. She made a fresh pot—like I was company or something."

"Milda?" Mama asked wonderingly.

"I know! She never was much for hospitality, but I think she just needed to talk to someone. Awful upset, she was. She told me she got a letter that day from one of her great-grandnephews back in Poland. One of her brother's grandsons."

"Poland? Are you sure you heard right? There's no mail coming out of Poland. It's occupied."

"The boy wasn't in Poland anymore. He escaped. Don't ask me how, but he did. Walked all the way to the Swedish border and snuck across. Must have taken him weeks. Months probably. Anyway, soon as he got to Sweden he sent Milda a letter, and she'd got it that day. The letter said her whole family in Poland was dead!"

"Oh no!" Mama breathed, horrified. "Dear Lord, no! The whole family? What happened? A bomb?"

"No. The nephew said that a troop of Nazi soldiers came to town and called everyone out into the street. They searched all the houses and barns, everything. Made everybody come outside and line up. They gathered up everyone in the village—the women and children, too—marched them into the woods outside of town, and shot them. Just shot them all—two hundred and twenty people. They didn't say why. They just killed them like they were a herd of cattle."

"Oh, dear God," Mama said. *Or was it me? Oh, dear God.*

Mrs. Scholler went on, an excited horror in her voice, the voice of a witness to a terrible accident that had been seen but not quite believed. "The boy survived only because he got hit in the shoulder and had the presence of mind to lay there and pretend he was dead. Bodies piled on top of him, but he lay still until it was all over and the Nazis drove off. When the coast was clear, he got up and decided he had better run in case the Nazis came back. He ran all the way to Sweden, and he wrote Milda. She was the only person left to tell. The whole family was wiped out."

An acrid taste of bile rose in my throat, the same flavor of suspicion and shame that had surfaced on the day Mrs. Ludwig started to tell me about the letter. She had stopped short of telling me the whole story. Mrs. Scholler had held back nothing. I swallowed hard and fought to stay silent, to hold back the cries and questions backed up inside me. It was like choking on knots of rope.

No! I thought. *That can't be right. Not a whole village. It's a lie. Or a mistake. The commanding officer went mad, or . . . This would never happen!* I thought about Father's letter, back at the beginning of the war, when he was in Poland. He'd said he couldn't believe that people were capable of such things.

What things, Father? What people? Was this *what you meant in your letter?*

My head pounded with a vision of the boy—Dodek, Mrs. Ludwig had called him. His shouder searing with pain and burning lead, fighting to keep silent and still in spite of his agony, his ears filled with the nightmare rhythm of war:

CRACK—thump, CRACK—thump, CRACK—thump, as bullet after bullet found its target, and body after body fell on top of his, covering him like so many clods of fleshly dirt. I tried to force myself to think of something else, the way I'd forced the vision of the perishing Jim Flanders from my mind, but this time it didn't work. The vision wouldn't stop. I rolled onto my side and quietly retched into one of the sofa pillows.

Mrs. Scholler heard something. She asked, "What was that?" Mama didn't answer; she was distracted.

"Oh, Carolyn! Are you sure? It can't be. It had to be an isolated incident. Some kind of mistake."

"That's what I said, but Milda said no. She was crying, Sophia!

Milda Ludwig was out-and-out crying! She said it was no mistake. Said her nephew wrote about many things, things she didn't want to talk about, but it wasn't a mistake. She said things like that were happening all over Poland."

I lay on the sofa, soaked with my own vomit, still as death, and waited for Mrs. Scholler to leave. Mama walked her to the door to say good-bye. Asked her not to repeat the story to anyone else.

"Please, Carolyn, don't. I wouldn't want Elise to hear this. Think how it would upset her. She's a good girl."

Mrs. Scholler was embarrassed. "Oh no," she said. "Of course not! I didn't think of it that way. I'm sorry, Sophia. I shouldn't have said anything. I wouldn't want to see her hurt. I'll never forget how she helped us that day when the hail came. Hadn't been for all of you, we'd have lost our place for sure. I won't say anything to anyone else."

"Thank you, Carolyn. If these kinds of stories got out . . . Things have been hard enough for her."

"But you know," Mrs. Scholler said soberly, "if these stories are true, it'll all come out when the war is over. You can't protect her forever."

"We'll just cross that bridge when we come to it."

After Mrs. Scholler left, Mama climbed the stairs. Her feet sounded tired and heavy on the treads, and after a minute I heard the bath water running.

I rolled quietly off the sofa and crept out the kitchen door, clutching the soiled cushion against my breast. I took off my shoes and walked on the dirt-and-gravel road toward the river. The stones hurt my feet, but not enough. I stomped on them. I ran as hard and heavy as I could until the rocks cut my feet and made them bleed and left a trail of foot-shaped bloodstains behind me, painting the stones and soaking into the dry, thirsty dirt. I ran over the crest of the hill and down the hard slope to the edge of the river.

I plunged into water up to my waist with all my clothes on, still holding the pillow. It was cold, but not cold enough. I wanted it icy, freezing and bitter and painful, so cold you can't breathe or cry out, but it wasn't that cold. I did cry out. I screamed and blubbered. Tears and saliva ran down my face and neck, onto the front of my dress and the pillow, washing the vomit into the river and downstream. Standing in the river, I threw up again and again. Everything inside came choking out in spasms of splashing liquid and bile, and the current took it all away. Blood from my feet seeped into the water, turning it pink.

Finally, when I had nothing left inside, no screams, or tears, or stomach, or blood, I let go. I lifted my feet from the sandy bottom, ducked my head beneath the surface of the water, hidden from sight, complete immersion. The current pushed against me, tugging at the folds of my dress, billowing the fabric out in front of my body, pulling at my hair and skin, washing me, removing everything that wasn't Elise alone. It would be so easy to let go and let the current take me with it, through the valley, past the tobacco fields, to Connecticut, past Hartford, past Saybrook, to the sea. I floated for a moment, submerged, and thought about taking a deep breath to make sure that every part of me was truly cleansed inside and out. I opened my mouth, felt the water cool and fresh on my tongue, but as I was getting ready to inhale, one of my feet brushed against the riverbed and held on. There was nothing left in my lungs. It was time to decide. Both feet found the bottom, gripped the sand, and pushed hard against the riverbed. I exploded into the air and gasped, found my footing, and stood in the water again, panting, sucking oxygen and reprisal into my body.

Disappointment and self-loathing surged though me. *I'll never be clean,* I thought. *Not completely. I am too much of a coward.*

But somewhere in my mind I heard voices. My mother's—breathless and loving. Mrs. Ludwig's—scolding and caring. And other voices I did not yet recognize.

No, they said. *None of us is ever completely clean, but we stand our ground. That is courage. Standing up. Staying still. Facing your destiny with unclean hands. That is the best we can do on this side of the river. Just to stay standing.*

I hid the wet pillow behind a bush, well out of sight of the house. The sun would dry it there, and I'd put it back on the sofa in the morning. No one would know.

Mama came out onto the porch, fresh and clean from her bath, rubbing her shampooed hair with a towel. Her eyes flew open at the sight of me walking toward her, dripping a trail across the grass. "Elise! What happened to you?"

"I went for a swim."

"With your clothes on?"

I didn't answer. Mama's forehead puckered with worry. "Is something wrong? Elise? Tell me." She reached out and picked up a lock of my wet hair, took her own towel and started drying me with it. "Tell me."

"I think my father is dead."

Mama's face was blank for a moment. "I don't understand. Why would you say that? Did you get a letter? A telegram?"

"No," I said evenly. "I just believe he is dead." I didn't know how to explain it; I had drowned him in the river and would not think of him again.

Mama frowned and took my hands in hers. "Come on. Sit here on the porch with me, and we'll talk."

I shook my head. "No. I'd rather not. Maybe later," I lied. "I'm going to go upstairs and dry off, change into something clean."

"Elise?"

"I'm fine. Really. I love you, Mama." I kissed her on the cheek and went inside.

It was better to imagine the best than to know the worst. Right then that was the best I could imagine, that Father was dead. If it was worse than that, I didn't want to know, I had decided.

It was impossible to explain to Mama, not then. Later she understood. Christmas came, and we all went to service and thanked God that Junior and Papa were together. We imagined them singing carols to the soldiers, passing out the Christmas stockings we'd sewn and sent to share with the troops.

It was better, that day, not to know the truth. Not on Christmas. We didn't know until afterward that Papa had been killed in the Battle of the Bulge. He'd been shot while giving last rites to a soldier. Junior had been shot, too, trying to protect Papa, and was in a field hospital. The telegram said his condition was grave.

Chapter 21

1945

"I can do it, Mama. I'm sure I can," I said earnestly. "I'm not saying it wouldn't be a lot of work, but the twins will be graduating in a few weeks—"

"But they could be drafted at any moment, Elise," Mama said soberly. "Then what would you do?"

"Curt could help, too, when school lets out," I reasoned. "He's strong for his age."

We stood at the edge of the yard, where the close-mowed grass gave way to the untended fields. Mama stood with one hand wrapped around her waist and the other covering her mouth, her eyes darting back and forth across the landscape, considering. "I don't know."

I opened my mouth to begin restating my arguments, but the sound of Cookie screaming from inside the house stopped me cold.

"Mama!"

"Out here, Cookie! Why does she have to yell like that?" Mama looked irritated, but as the screaming continued, her expression changed to one of concern; Cookie shouldn't have been home from work for hours. Mama started walking quickly toward the house and I went with her.

As we approached the porch, the screen door flew open with a bang, and Cookie came out onto the porch with tears pouring down her face. *"Mama!"*

"Come on!" Mama said to me as she broke into a run.

I followed, a knot forming in my stomach. How many tragedies could one family bear, I thought? What had we left to lose? The boys? Oh, dear God. Please don't let anything have happened to the boys!

"Cookie!" Mama cried as we came near. "What happened?"

Cookie threw her arms around Mama, sobbing. "It's over! It's over! The war in Europe is over!"

Mama's chest was heaving from the effort of running. Her hand flew to her mouth.

"Are you sure?" I asked. I didn't want to believe it if it wasn't true. "Cookie, are you absolutely sure?"

"It was on the radio," she confirmed, bobbing her head urgently. "They played the announcement over the loudspeaker at work. I came home as fast as I could to tell you. It's over! It really is over!" she exclaimed as the tears streamed down her face.

By now we were all crying. We put our arms around each other's shoulders and cried together, forming a circle of tears and loss, relief and thanksgiving. We just stood there, leaning on each other, heads bowed, sobbing and laughing and sobbing again. We let flow all the tears we'd swallowed over the years of war, so many tears that at times it had felt like we'd drown in them. We'd had to be brave then. Not anymore.

The screen door opened again. Mama lifted her head from the circle and turned to the porch. "Did you hear, Junior? The war is over in Europe! Isn't it wonderful?"

I kept my head bowed and my eyes closed and listened for the now familiar sound, the thump-tap, thump-tap of a cane and wooden leg against the floorboards as Junior walked onto the porch and heaved himself painfully into a rocker, the sound like bitterness.

"I did, Mama," Junior said softly. "It's wonderful."

When Papa's body arrived home, his casket was wrapped like a terrible present in red, white, and blue. In a town that was worn out with funerals and thought it had no grief left, Papa's funeral was a spectacle of mourning, attended by hundreds of people who all wanted to say a word, touch a hand, offer some comfort, recount a memory that would shore up the family through the sad, empty days ahead, as though that would have been possible. The effort of shaking each hand and acknowledging each well-intentioned, vague offer of assistance, of enduring the public ritual of our very private grief was draining. Church service, graveside service, burial, reception in the church basement, and visitors in the house long past dark.

When the last guest left, Mama closed the door and dissolved into tears, and we all ran to hold her. "Thank God it is over," she said, her eyes closed and a handkerchief held to them. "This was the worst day of my life."

I thought, yes, and felt a strange sense of relief. It cannot get worse than this. But I was wrong.

The day Junior came home was the worst day ever, worse even than Papa's funeral, because that day we were prepared for sorrow. We knew about Junior's leg, knew about the grenade and the surgeon-severed limb, but none of that mattered, because Junior was alive and coming home. We had such parties planned! Such celebrations!

We weren't prepared for the anguished, sad-eyed Junior-shell the porters had to lift down the steps of the train. We didn't yet know that he'd left much more of himself on the battlefield than a shattered leg. I ran toward him on the platform with my arms outstretched, but as I came near he leaned hard on his cane and reached out his free hand to clasp mine, stopping my ready embrace. He squeezed my hand, the hand that still wore his promise, and said it was good to see me, but his eyes darted away from mine, nervous, as though greeting a stranger. An awful thought pierced my mind—he blamed me.

That was the worst day.

We blew the month's sugar and butter ration to make a cake for dinner that night and slaughtered two of the older hens. The birds were a little tough, but they were big, and, for once, there was plenty for seconds.

We laughed and talked through dinner. Junior was quiet but not sullen and smiled at the jokes, even the corny ones. Mama announced she was going to brew a pot of real coffee to go with the cake. "I've been saving it for a special occasion. I think this is about as special as it gets," she declared happily and gave Junior the honor of opening the can.

As the blade of the can opener pierced metal, an intoxicating aroma of fresh coffee filled the room. Junior shoved his face up close to the can and breathed it in like it was air to a drowning man. "Mmmm," he groaned. His head lolled back and he shut his eyes, his face an expression of rapture. "Oh! I'd almost forgotten," he said in a tone that, for just an instant, sounded like the old Junior. "That is the best smell ever!"

Everyone agreed and gave a big three cheers for Mama and, if Papa had been there, it would have been just like the old days.

"Well, we've got a surprise, too!" announced Chip, raising and lowering his eyebrows like Groucho Marx and grinning at his twin.

"We do indeed!" Chuck agreed as he and Chip got up from the

table. They briefly disappeared into the broom closet and, after an interval of loud banging and the sound of boxes being moved and a floorboard creaking, they emerged.

"Tah-dah!" they shouted in unison.

Mama was aghast. "Charles and Chester Muller! That had better not be a bottle of liquor in my house! And cigars, too! No, boys! I mean it. Where in the world did you get that stuff?"

"Won it off of Otto Karlsberg in a card game," Chip replied.

"You were playing poker?" Mama exclaimed. "You were gambling?"

"Well, why not? Papa won Junior in a card game!" Everyone laughed, but I saw a stab of pain and memory flicker in Junior's eyes.

Chip waltzed across the kitchen floor, humming an off-key rendition of "Begin the Beguine" with one of the wrapped cigars stuck between his teeth. He lifted Mama off her feet and danced around the room with her while she laughed and slapped his shoulders harmlessly, saying to put her down, she meant it, no kidding, but not convincingly.

"Come on, Mama." Chuck said in a wheedling tone. "One little glass isn't going to hurt us. It's a party!"

"Yeah, Mama!" we chorused. "Just one little glass!" We pounded the kitchen table in time with our song while Chip carried her through the steps of an involuntary dance.

"Oh, for heaven's sake! All right! Put me down," she said, laughing. "Just one glass, but absolutely no cigars in this house. If you're going to smoke, you'd better do it outside, and you'd better not let me see you doing it. I mean it!" And we knew she did.

Chuck got down the glasses, and Chip poured sherry into six glasses. Though Curt complained about unfairness, Mama drew the line at letting him have any alcohol. When she got up to cut the cake, Junior put his finger to his lips to indicate the need for stealth and gave his littlest brother a tiny taste from his glass. Curt made a face and pushed the glass away.

We ate as much cake as we could hold and lingered around the table talking, drinking coffee, and sipping sherry. Actually, Junior and the twins drank it more than sipped—after all, it was a party. I didn't really care for the taste—it was kind of sweet and medicinal-tasting all at once—but I liked the way it felt so warm going down my throat.

It was late. Curt started yawning, and Mama sent him off to bed. The conversation lagged, but none of us really wanted to leave the table. It had been such a nice evening.

Mama brought the subject up first. "Elise and I were talking today," she began. "You all know that Papa left a pension and the church took up a collection for a small educational fund for you children." She threw a quick glance at Junior. "But the car is on its last legs, and the house is mortgaged. Until now, between the pension and Cookie's salary from the factory and Junior's government check—"

"Ah, yes!" Junior said sarcastically. "A token of thanks from a grateful nation!" Mama ignored him and went on.

"Between all that, we've been able to get by, but just barely. Elise thinks we ought to try growing tobacco." A murmur of surprise rippled around the table, but Mama continued, "It's hard work, I know, and we don't know the first thing about it—"

"That's not so," I protested. Junior shot me a look. "I know exactly what to do," I declared, ignoring Junior's skeptical expression.

Mama continued. "Before today, I wouldn't have considered it, but now that the war in Europe is over and it looks like Japan won't be far behind, we are going to have to come up with some way to support ourselves. Cookie's factory job will surely end with the fighting."

Chuck interrupted, "Mama, Chip and I will be graduating at the end of the month. We can get jobs and help out." He sat a little taller in his chair, as if to show that he was man enough for the task of supporting the family.

Mama smiled and patted his hand. "I appreciate that, Chuck, but think. When the war is over there are going to be thousands of GIs looking for work. The jobs are going to go to them. Nobody is going to hire you or your brother instead of a veteran."

The table was quiet for a moment as the truth about our situation sank in. Cookie toyed with her fork and gazed thoughtfully into the distance before speaking. "Are you sure it will take? The fields have never been cultivated. How do you know tobacco will even grow here?"

"Mr. Scholler's land is right next to ours, and his tobacco is fine," I said. "The quality is pretty fair, and he gets a good price for it. Ours might be even better because the land has been lying fallow so long; the nutrients haven't been leeched out. Also, Mr. Scholler said we could use any of his equipment we need, tractors and everything, and we can use any space left over in his drying sheds. That would save us having to put out so much money up front."

Chuck scratched his head, considering. "We got, say, fifteen acres out there. You want to plant all of it?" I nodded. "That means we'd still have to build at least one shed. How are we going to do that?"

"Well, I thought you and Chip could handle that part. You're so handy with tools and all."

Chip was doubtful. "Yeah, but it's going to take some real money to buy lumber for a shed. Where are we going to get that kind of cash?"

I bit my lip. I didn't know exactly how this was all going to work, it was true. Still, something deep in me said we could do it, but only if we all pulled together. I had to convince them.

Junior made a sucking sound with his teeth and said, "Well, I don't think we need to worry about money to build a shed just yet. Let's just cross the bridge when we come to it."

A little thrill of excitement jolted me. If Junior was for the idea, the rest of the family would get on board, I was certain. And it was so long since Junior had been for anything!

He spent his days sitting in chairs, reading or pretending to read, repeatedly opening and closing the cover of the pocket watch that Papa had left to him in his will, as if hoping that this time the clock face would show that hours had mysteriously passed and another day would soon be over. He didn't speak unless spoken to. His conversations were short, obligatory, and confined to bare, immediate exchanges of domestic necessity. He didn't want to talk about the future, or the past.

Mama said we needed to give him time, and I did. I still wore the garnet ring he'd given me, but we never spoke of it. I didn't press him. It didn't matter. It wasn't fulfillment of promise I was seeking from him, just . . . I don't know. Just the barest acknowledgement that he was still in there somewhere, a reassurance that Hitler had not been able to kill every man I loved.

I wanted to find a way to help support the family, yes, but more importantly, I wanted to find a way to bring Junior back to life. Surely, getting back into the fields, with the warmth of sun on his back and the smell of newly turned earth in his nostrils, would strengthen his unused muscles and heal the pain in his soul. I turned to give him a grateful, encouraging smile, but when I did, his eyes were cold. and the sarcastic edge had returned to his voice.

"I don't think we're going to have to worry about building a shed, because I don't think we've got a chance in the world of getting a crop! You have no idea what you'd be getting yourself into. Growing tobacco isn't like growing carrots in your victory garden," he snorted. "It's hard work. It's a man's work, Elise, not a girl's."

"First off, I'm not a girl!" I spat. "And I know all about growing tobacco. I've helped Mr. Scholler, and Mr. Jorgenson said I was the best worker on the place."

"He fired you!" Junior shouted.

Mama and Cookie gasped, and the twins looked down at their hands. I could feel angry tears at the back of my eyelids, but I blinked them back.

Junior spread his hands wide, exasperation dripping from his fingertips. "Look! I'm sorry, but it's true. It wasn't your fault, but Mr. Jorgenson fired you! You never even finished the season. You don't know anything about preparing the fields, or fertilizer, how to decide when to harvest, how to cure it. Elise, what you don't know about growing tobacco would fill a book!" The volume increased with each word, and by the time he finished he was shouting.

I was on my feet, shouting right back at him. "Maybe I don't! Maybe I'll fail! But at least I'm willing to take a chance and try. Maybe I don't know enough to bring in a decent crop, but you do! If you'd only get up out of your chair and quit feeling so damned sorry for yourself and help, maybe we'd have a chance!"

"Help you?" He screamed the question and shoved his arms against the table, pushing himself to a standing position, the veins in his neck throbbing with effort and anguish. The chair he'd been sitting in fell clattering onto the floor and he clutched the table lip for balance. "How am I to help you? Tell me how! I can't even walk across this room without a crutch. In the hospital I couldn't even relieve myself without help. I can't drive a car or hoe a field or do a decent day's work. I am useless!" He let out a tormented, trapped-animal cry of frustration and pounded his fist against the table like he wanted it to split in two.

"I can't even climb the stairs anymore, so I have to sleep in Papa's old study—surrounded by memories of him. The room still smells like him! Do you know that? When I was a little boy people used to come up and pat me on the head and say that if I was lucky I'd grow up to be half the man my father was. And I knew they were right. I admired him so much!" He was crying now, the tears streaming down his face, rivers of agony. "But I wasn't lucky. That's God's big joke on me, isn't it! Instead of making me half the man my father was, He just made me half a man."

His eyes screwed shut and his shoulders jerked like he was wincing from the pain of a hidden wound. His chest heaved as he swallowed all the air in the room and exhaled a damning self-indictment. "I go to sleep at night with the smell of him still in my nose, choking on the scent of the man I loved and helped kill!"

Junior turned, seeking escape, and kicked aside the fallen chair with his good leg, nearly falling himself in the attempt. He stumbled over to where his cane was propped on the wall and grabbed it, pounding it against the floor as he limped to Papa's old study, seeking refuge in the room he'd papered with his own accusations.

The kitchen was dead silent. Junior's pain stunned us. Mama whispered, "Oh, dear Lord," as she closed her eyes in prayer.

"Mama?"

Mama's eyes opened. "Curt! What are you doing up? You should be asleep." Curt stood leaning against the door frame, looking small and frightened in his pajamas.

"The noise woke me up. Is Junior all right? Is there anything I can do to help him?"

"You can pray, Curt. We can pray together."

"But, shouldn't someone talk to him?" Curt asked.

Mama looked a question at me.

"Yes," I answered. "Someone should go talk to him."

I opened the door a crack, hoping for an invitation to enter, but when none came I pushed the door wide and stepped inside anyway.

"You're right," I said to Junior's back. "It still smells like him."

He didn't respond, just stood leaning on his cane, looking out the window at empty fields. I waited for him to say something, but he just stood there. Silence divided us like a thick veil. I decided to take a chance, push through the barrier, ask the question that had been in my mind since his first day home, when he'd fended off my embrace and pushed me away.

"Junior. Do you want the ring back?"

"Yes."

One word only, but he cut me with it. I nodded to myself. Yes. I'd known all along. I took the ring from my finger. It slid off so easily, so much more easily than I'd imagined it would. Surprising. I laid it on the nightstand next to Junior's bed, in the spot where Papa's desk used to stand.

I turned to leave, but as I did, the other question slipped unbidden from my lips, the other question whose answer I was sure I knew, but whose answer I had to hear for myself. Just as the ring had come off more easily than I'd imagined, surely knowing the truth could not be more painful than the speculation.

"Why do you want it back?"

"I told you." He took a deep breath and let his head fall forward, resting on the windowpane, his back still to me. "I'm useless. I have nothing to offer you."

"What?" I didn't understand. "What are you talking about?"

He pivoted toward me, holding onto the window sash for support. "What do you mean, what am I talking about? You heard what I said in the kitchen. I can't marry you or anyone else. I can't take care of you!" His voice lifted in frustration, angry with me for forcing him to say it out loud.

His answer was simultaneously confounding and offending. "Well, that's a relief, because I don't want to be taken care of!" I retorted. "I can't believe you! Is that your reason, honestly? Is that the reason you're willing to throw away everything we had together, everything we might still have? For your pride?" I was incredulous.

He closed his eyes and raised his hand up like a cop stopping traffic. He looked tired. "Elise, you don't understand. A man has certain responsibilities and obligations. He has to fulfill them or he can't ever really be a man."

"So fulfill them!"

"How? Don't you have ears? Listen to what I'm trying to tell you. Open your eyes! Look at me!" He spread out his arms. "I'm a cripple! I'll never be able to do a decent day's work in my life. In the hospital they gave me occupational training. You know what they taught me? Caning chairs! Same thing they taught the blind guys." He laughed cynically.

"It's a nice hobby, Elise, but you can't support a family by caning chairs. Listen to me," he spoke slowly, spacing out his words to be certain I heard him. "Try to understand. I love you, but I can't take care of you."

I heard him. I heard the part that mattered. He loved me. That was all that mattered. I walked toward him, determined to make him understand, to touch him even though his wounds were still tender. We had to start somewhere. I moved in close to him, stretched out one finger, just one, and touched his face, traced a line from the base of his ear along the line of his clenched jaw.

"Listen to me," I said softly. "You are stubborn, Junior, and you're proud, and you're all the man I want. You're the only man I've ever wanted or ever will want—every bit as good a man as your father ever was. I know, because I loved him, too, like you did. But I know a thing about him that you don't."

I laid my whole hand on his cheek, leaned in closer, whispered urgently into his ear. "Listen! Papa took his responsibilities as a man seriously, yes. But he didn't take care of Mama. They took care of each other. That's what made their love so special. They each brought a piece of themselves to their union and fused the two parts into a whole, into something much better and stronger than they had been separately. They took care of each other! We could do that, Junior. We could be so much better together than we are apart."

I rose up on my toes to reach his cheek, but he collapsed onto me before I could kiss him. He leaned his weight onto mine, his arms wrapped around my shoulders for support, as if hanging on to a tree in a buffeting wind.

He bent his head down into my shoulder, his denials muffled in the fabric of my blouse. "No, Elise. It wouldn't work. You don't know. You don't know who I am. You don't know what I did."

My heart ached for him because I did know. I knew just what he'd done. "You let Papa die," I whispered. "That's what you think, isn't it?"

He nodded. I could feel his head rub against my shoulder, "I was supposed to protect him! It was my job to carry the weapon for him, to keep him safe, but I couldn't do it!" His tears fell hot and accusing on my shirtwaist as he told the story, letting loose all the demons that tortured him.

"The fighting was heavy that day," he remembered. "We were driving through this little village that we'd just captured. We were on our way to the hospital so Papa could visit the guys who'd been wounded. The burial squads hadn't even been through yet, and there were still bodies lying around. I was driving the jeep. Papa said 'Stop! There's something moving over there!'

"He jumped out before I could come to a full stop. I told him to give me a chance to scout around, make sure it was safe, but he didn't listen. Just jumped out of the jeep and ran over to the ditch. Papa was right. There was a guy lying there, hurt real bad, blood everywhere, barely breathing. He had a St. Christopher medal around his neck. Papa said, 'He's Catholic. Run back to the jeep and get my field kit. I've got to perform last rites.'

"I was halfway to the jeep and I heard a shot. I yelled for Papa to hit the dirt and he did. I crouched behind the jeep. Another shot rang out, and I spotted the sniper in an upstairs window of a house. I got off three shots, but missed on the first two. He threw the grenade before I killed him. I don't remember it hurting, just that I was bleeding and my leg wouldn't work. I crawled over to Papa. I said, 'It's all right now, Papa. You can get up. I got him.' But Papa didn't move. There was blood everywhere. The bullet hit him in the back of his head. Just below where his helmet ended. He was dead.

"It was my fault," he sobbed. "I tried to take care of him, but I couldn't do it. I couldn't do it." He crumpled under the weight of his own accusation, falling onto my shoulder, spent and exhausted.

I put my arms around him and led him to the bed, lay down next to him, and murmured forgiveness into his hair. "It wasn't your fault, Junior. It just happened. It wasn't your fault. You did the best you could. You tried. That is all that matters. Don't give up now. You have to try. We've got to try."

Chapter 22

"These new controls work great!" I yelled.

"What?" Junior said over the roar of the tractor engine. "Can't hear you!"

"I said the new controls work great!"

Junior frowned and shook his head. He shifted into a lower gear, brought the tractor to a stop near the shed and turned off the motor. "Now. What did you say?"

I smiled and jumped down from the fender that served as a passenger seat. "I said that the new hand controls work great!"

"Oh," Junior replied and grinned. "Yeah, they do work pretty slick. The twins had a great idea. All these years I thought Mama had given birth to a matched set of juvenile delinquents, and it turns out they were just a couple of inventors disguised as juvenile delinquents."

"They turned out to be pretty good workers, too," I commented, looking around at the rows and rows of tall, healthy broadleaf. We hadn't planted the full fifteen acres I'd planned. Junior had been right—fifteen would have been too much for a first crop on unbroken soil, but the ten we had planted were looking good so far.

"We couldn't have done it without them," I continued. "Or

without you. You're a pretty fair hand with that tractor." I smiled, and Junior reached for me, drew me close, and we kissed, leaning into one another for both strength and support, our caresses slow and savored because we knew this summer and the next and the next, we would always be together. I rested my head on Junior's shoulder and felt a flood of pure contentment that I never knew existed a year before but that was now as familiar as breathing.

"I love you."

"I love you, too," he answered and draped his arm over my shoulder. His eyes scanned the landscape, "Look at this!" he smiled in wonder and swept his arm across the vista of fields laid out green and growing before us. "I would never have imagined this! Without you, I wouldn't ever have tried. I'd still be sitting in that rocker feeling sorry for myself."

"We make a good team," I concurred.

"We do. Looks like our teamwork is going to pay off in a few weeks. Like Mr. Scholler always said, 'God willing and the creek don't rise, we ought to have a pretty good crop.' "

I smiled inwardly, thinking of kindly Mr. Scholler and the way his face had lit up as he shouted, "Girlie!" whenever he saw me coming. "It's so hard to believe he's really gone," I said. "It just seems strange to look at his house across the field and know that it's empty. Mr. Scholler's dead, and Mrs. Scholler's moved to Virginia to live with her sister."

"I know," Junior said. "He was a good man, but he was seventy-five. He lived a good, long, life and he died just the way he would have wanted to, tuning up the tractor and getting ready for planting—it's the only respectable way for a farmer to die." Junior bit his lip thoughtfully, missing the old man. "I was kind of surprised that Mrs. Scholler moved away, and so quickly, too, but I guess I can't blame her. She'll be less lonely living with her sister, and the weather in Virginia is bound to be better for her arthritis."

"Well," I said, patting the metal hood of the tractor like it was a horse's neck, "it was awfully nice of her to let us use all the equipment and the drying sheds until they find a buyer for the farm. I don't know what we would have done otherwise."

Junior nodded and said reflectively, his eyes moving over the horizon, taking in the abundance of green. "Yes. I wouldn't ever have thought it would have worked out. I guess God has reasons for everything."

"I guess so."

"Now we just have to hope nobody buys the place before we get the tobacco harvested, hung, and cured, but I think we're in the clear. Nobody will be looking to buy a tobacco farm at the end of the season. It probably won't sell until next spring. I just hope the new owners are as nice as the Schollers," he mused.

I reassured him. "I'm sure they will be."

Junior smiled at me and twisted around in the tractor seat, lifting his wooden leg off the edge. He braced one arm against the fender and the other on the edge of the metal seat, preparing to climb down.

"Want some help?" I inquired, offering an arm.

"Nope. I've been practicing—think I got it now. But better stand by to catch me in case I fall."

Always, I thought to myself, *and you'll do the same for me.*

Junior grunted with effort, lifting his torso with his powerful arms and sliding down to plant his good leg on the special step Chuck had welded onto the tractor's frame. He paused for a moment to steady himself, then hopped down to the ground. I noticed a few beads of perspiration on his brow, but that was all right. He was getting stronger every day; it would get easier, and even if it didn't, I knew he would never give up again.

I could smell Cookie's fried chicken all the way across the yard. We ambled toward the house with our arms draped around each other. I leaned my head against Junior's broad shoulder as we walked and silently composed a little prayer of thanks to God for driving all the demons from our lives and for the utter contentment of that moment. Junior leaned down and kissed the top of my head just as I heard Cookie shouting my name.

She ran out of the house, waving a piece of paper over her head like a flag and yelling, "Elise! Elise!"

I looked up at Junior. He face split into a grin, and he said what we were both thinking. "The war is over! It's V-J Day!"

We hurried toward Cookie as she ran up to us panting with excitement. "Elise! It's a telegram—and it's from Germany!"

The meaning of her words didn't quite register in my mind. Cookie held the paper out to me and I took it.

AUGUST 7, 1945

DAUGHTER:

AM ALIVE AND WELL. ARRIVING NEW YORK AUGUST 20 ON SS NORWAY. PLEASE MEET.

YOUR LOVING FATHER
HERMAN BRAUN

I thought I didn't remember what he looked like, but when he walked into the waiting room at the immigration station, through the same doors I had passed through a lifetime ago, I recognized him at once. He was wearing a suit and tie instead of a uniform and was much, much thinner, but the square shoulders, the ramrod-straight back, and the hair—grayer, but as close-trimmed as ever—told me immediately that, oh, yes, it was Father. I would have known him anywhere. He had not changed. I had known he never could.

I watched him approach but didn't move, wondering if he would be able to pick my face out from the crowd of waiting relatives. His eyes darted back and forth across the room, searching for his daughter, a quiet little girl with long brown braids, solemn dark eyes, and dressed in a blue woolen skirt and a cloak of loneliness and loss. He looked and looked for her, but she was gone, so I stepped forward instead.

"Father."

His head turned toward the sound of my voice, and his eyes narrowed a bit, as if trying to put me in focus. Then his face froze and his mouth dropped open just a little, like someone seeing a ghost. "Lale?" he breathed the question, holding himself very still.

I didn't know what to say.

He stared at me a long moment. "No," he corrected himself. "It is you. Elise." When I didn't answer, he asked, "It is you, isn't it?"

"Hello, Father." I put out my hand, and he seized it with both of his like a drowning man clutching a rope.

"Elise!" he cried over and over again. He threw his arms around me and began weeping uncontrollably. "My daughter! So beautiful! Safe. Oh yes, thank God! You are safe!"

I stood stiff as he embraced me and cried over me. My mind was blank, immobile and unable to reason, as disbelieving as Father had been just a moment before. Sobs racked his body. Without willing them to do so, my arms lifted to respond. I folded myself around him, my stranger-Father, whom I knew everything and nothing about. As he did me.

Yes, Daddy. It's me. It's your Elise.

Chapter 23

I took Father to the Automat because it was the only restaurant I knew in New York. He ate every bite, even picking up the crumbs of leftover piecrust with a wet fingertip and putting them in his mouth carefully, as though it were the most normal thing in the world for my formerly fastidious father to do.

He was impressed, as I had been, by the rows and rows of vending machines and the myriad choices of dishes, each sealed behind its own private door. "Very inventive, these Americans," he observed.

I walked with him to Grand Central Station to catch the train to Hartford, where Junior would be waiting to pick us up, retracing my path to Brightfield. I wasn't quite sure what to say to him, uncertain of how we were to relate to each other now, so I pointed out sights to him and tall buildings, reciting street names like a tour guide, though half the time I barely knew where we were myself.

It wasn't until we were settled in the train and had ridden some time in silence, each looking out the window at the passing scenery and thinking our own thoughts, that I worked up the courage to ask him what I really wanted to know.

What was he doing here? How did he survive the war? What

was a former officer of the Abwehr doing on American soil only months after the surrender of Germany?

And the questions I dared not ask aloud, the questions that, even in my brain, pulsed unspoken.

As we sat side by side on the train, he told me his story—all the things that had happened since we parted on dock at Hamburg. He told me almost everything, I am sure—at least all that he could bear to tell me.

As he had expected, the plans for the invasion of Poland were being finalized even as my ship left port in Germany. As he had intimated in his letter, Father thought the plan was foolhardy and that Hitler was a disgrace to his office and country, but he was the leader of the nation, and Father was a soldier, trained from childhood to do his duty. He would fulfill his orders.

The operation had gone quite swiftly, with a minimum of German casualties. As an aide to Admiral Canaris, "Uncle Wilhelm," he had accompanied the admiral on a trip to Poland. They saw terrible things there, the murder of civilians, the destruction of whole villages, like Mrs. Ludwig's ancestral home, not just the men but women and children, too. Father and many of the other career officers were horrified, but laid the blame in the lap of the SS, barbarians out of control and acting without orders, that must be it. General Canaris was outraged and flew back to Berlin to complain to the führer.

"The man is a pig, but he is the leader of the army. Surely he does not realize what has been happening." But he did know. Hitler ignored Canaris's complaints, and the admiral and many other officers began to understand that these atrocities were being carried out with Hitler's approval.

That was the beginning of the resistance within the officer corps. Father was sure there were other pockets of internal resistance, but he thought that the group he was part of, a group of officers within the Abwehr who'd been specially picked by Canaris, were the center of the organization. As the war went on, they learned more and more about the horrific things that were going on, terrible beyond belief.

Here Father stopped, and he looked at me with solemn, pledging eyes. "Shocking things have happened in Germany, my daughter. A carnage of innocents. Soon the whole world will know about it, and they will hate us for it. They will be right to hate us. We may not have pulled the trigger, but we stood by and watched as the gun was loaded, aimed, and fired. We are guilty, too. But, I want you to know, Elise—it is important that you believe I did not participate in these"—he searched for a word—"these horrors. I tried to stop them, but it was too late, and my efforts were too feeble."

He went on, explaining that as they learned more of what Hitler's true plans were, they decided that the führer had to be stopped. They made plans to assassinate him, even though they knew that if they were discovered, they would be tried and executed for treason. They planned several assassination attempts, but always something went wrong. Hitler seemed to have a sixth sense, often changing his schedule at the last minute, stepping neatly out of the noose they had laid for him.

They tried to make contact with the Allies, to let them know of their plans and possibly enlist their assistance. One of their number, Dr. Dietrich Bonhoeffer, a Lutheran minister, the man who had sent me the note in the candy box, had tried to open lines of communications through his old friend, George Bell, bishop of Chichester.

"He went to Switzerland to meet with him," Father related. "We weren't supposed to speak to each other of our plans, to maintain secrecy, but I could not resist. I asked him to get a message to you, to let you know I was alive. He sent the candy to you from Switzerland. I thought about you all the time—wondered if you'd found the note or thrown the box away without realizing it was there."

Father sighed and closed his eyes. "I am so glad you found it. Bonhoeffer was a good man, a brave man of faith."

"Was?" I asked. "What happened to him?"

"After the D-day invasion, we decided we had to try again to kill Hitler. We were desperate. One of our number, young Colonel Stauffenberg, planted a bomb in a conference room in the Eagle's Nest. It went off as planned. The room was destroyed, and several officers were badly hurt. One died. But Hitler survived with hardly a scratch. There was an investigation, and we were discovered. Admiral Canaris, Dr. Bonhoeffer, General Oster, and many others were arrested. Cousin Peter, too."

"Cousin Peter?" I gasped. "But I don't understand. He wasn't in the military. How could he have been arrested with officers from the Abwehr?"

"He was part of a different organization, the Kreisau Circle, whose resistance activity was based on Christian conviction. He was arrested and hanged in August of 1944."

"No!" I cried out. Tears welled in my eyes. Cousin Peter, laughing, handsome Cousin Peter, who was always late, who had given me the *Children's Encyclopedia of Animals.* He had been hanged in a Nazi prison? It couldn't be.

Father just nodded silently. His voice was flat as he continued his story. He had grieved for them all long ago and had no more tears in store. "Admiral Canaris and the others were executed in April, only weeks before the end of the war."

I held my hand to my mouth. My tears could only bring Father more pain, and I could see in his eyes that he had already known so much of it. "But, why weren't you arrested with the others? How did you escape?"

"I would have been among them," he said "but I was out of the office when the SS came. I saw the cars in front of the building, and I ran. I threw away my uniform, grew a mustache, and carried false papers I had prepared just in case. I went into hiding—always on the run, hungry, never able to catch more than a few hours' sleep before I felt compelled to move on. When they finally caught up with me in January, it was almost a relief. I was given a military trial in April, just before Canaris and the others were killed. I was found guilty and sentenced to be executed on May 15, 1945, but the war ended before the sentence was carried out.

"The Americans liberated the prison," he continued. "They interviewed me, corroborated my story, and said I was free to go. They were kind to me. After all that. After we had shot and killed so many of their friends, they were kind to me!" he marveled.

"One of them even said I was an officer and a gentleman, a hero," Father said, his voice dripping with self-loathing. "But I knew it wasn't true. I was a coward—a feeble, broken member of a failed conspiracy! We shouldn't have relied on bombs and plots. I should have just taken my pistol, walked up to Hitler, and shot him in the head. I would have died, too, but it would have been worth it to put a stop to Hitler—to regain a shred of honor for myself and my country, but I was a coward."

I wanted to reach out and console him, but I could think of no words that would help. Instead I just stroked his hand.

"General Canaris and the others were executed. At least in death they regained something of their honor. Only I was left alive, but I didn't want to go on living. I left the prison. Found a room in a hotel and made a plan to kill myself—sleeping pills. I swallowed the whole bottle and lay on the bed, so tired. I was ready to let go, and then, I don't know exactly why, I knew I mustn't do it. It would be too easy."

Oh yes, I thought. I knew. His foot brushed the sandy bottom and held on. I knew, even if Father didn't, that he was no coward.

"To face our destiny with unclean hands," I whispered.

"What?" Father said, a bit startled. "What did you say?"

"Nothing, Father. I'll explain later. Tell me what happened then."

"I pulled myself from the bed and staggered into the hallway looking for help. I collapsed, and someone found me. I don't know who it was, but they called an ambulance. When I woke up in the hospital the American officer, the one who said I was a hero, was sitting by my bed. Such a kind man. An honorable man."

"Yes, Father."

"He was worried about me. He said that I must find a reason for going on, that there had been enough deaths already—mine wouldn't change anything. It would just be one more casualty in a war that had gone on for too long. He said I must find the courage to go on, a reason to live." Father stopped and turned to me, a sad, small smile on his lips. "I knew already what my reason was. It was you, Elise! It was you! I told him that I had a daughter, living in America, and that I would like to find you. He arranged for my passage and immigration clearance. He said I could stay as long as I wanted, even apply for citizenship."

"That's wonderful!" I exclaimed. He bobbed his head and spoke before I could say anything more.

"Yes," Father agreed. "He was a very kind man. A gentleman, but I told him I would not stay. I just wanted to come and see my daughter, thank the kind family that cared for her all these years, and then bring her home."

"But Father," I protested. "We can't—"

"I know," he said. "I know. The house on Alexander Platz is gone. Destroyed in the bombing. Everything is gone, but we can start over, *Liebling*. You'll see. We are together again, and that is what matters. We can begin again."

Chapter 24

Father rode in the front seat and I in the back. Junior took the wheel. Now that the twins had installed the hand-controlled brake, Junior was able to drive as well as ever. Father was perfectly polite. No matter how strained the circumstances, Father was always polite; this was one thing about him that had not changed, but the car ride home was awkward at first. Junior cleared his throat self-consciously and tried to make small talk.

"Colonel Braun, sir. How was the voyage? You must be very tired after such a long trip."

"It was a good crossing, but, yes. I am tired. I'm not a colonel anymore, you know. I am simply Mr. Braun now."

"Mr. Braun," Junior repeated.

Another awkward silence ensued. This time Father was the one to break it. "Elise told me about your father, Junior. I am very sorry for your loss. So very sorry for everything," he said. His eyes rested on the spot where Junior's pants leg fell skinny and unnatural over his lifeless wooden leg. "I am sorry," he said again, as though he were personally responsible for throwing the grenade that took Junior's leg.

"Your father was a very good man. He was so kind to take Elise in. Who knows what might have happened if he had not? The bombings were so terrible. There is almost nothing left of Berlin. Your father was a good man, Junior." Father repeated, then paused for a moment, his brow wrinkling in a question. "It's such a strange name—Junior. I never heard it before. Does it mean something special?"

"Oh, it means something like 'the younger.' Junior isn't my real name. I was named Carl, after my father, but everyone called me Junior so they wouldn't get us mixed up."

"Hmm." Father considered this and shook his head. "But now that your father is gone, perhaps you should consider going back to your real name. Carl is a fine name. A strong name, and you don't look like a 'Junior' to me somehow."

"Well, I don't know, Mr. Braun. Papa is Carl, not me. Everyone in town loved him. I don't think they'd feel right about calling me by his name. I'm not sure I'd feel right about it myself."

Father tilted his head, as if he simply couldn't grasp Junior's objection. "Why not? I am sure your father would have been proud to know you were carrying on his name. He was a good man, and you are a good man. What is the difficulty?" Father gestured with one hand and then the other, weighing the equality of his argument on scales of logic.

"My father . . . well. It's just hard to explain, Mr. Braun. He was something very special. As I said, everyone in town loved him. He was the pastor in Brightfield his whole life."

Father bobbed his head. "Yes, I know, a minister. I knew another minister, during the war. I was telling Elise about him. He was a good man, too." Father paused a minute and looked out the window, thinking. Then he turned back to Junior. "You're very like your father, I'm sure. Elise said you were a minister, too, in the war."

"Oh no, sir," Junior corrected. "I was just a chaplain's assistant. I helped my father, but I wasn't a pastor. Papa was an ordained minister. I worked alongside him. Something like an aide, but I'm not trained like he was."

"Training, you can always get," Father said dismissively with a trace, just a trace, of his old haughty attitude. I smiled, glad to know that something of the old Father was still in residence. "I am sure you would be a fine minister. You need training? Go someplace and get some. You are very like your father, I am sure. Very like him in many ways, but not all, and that is best. You should train for the ministry," Father declared with conviction. "And you should change your name to Carl."

Father finished his speech, but Junior didn't comment. He just kept his eyes on the road, but when I glanced up to the rearview mirror, I could see him thinking.

"I am tired," Father said, turning to me. "I hope you will not think me rude if I take a nap."

"No, Father," I reassured him. "That's fine. Try to sleep. I'll wake you when we are home."

We drove in silence the rest of the way. When the car turned into the gravel driveway, Father awoke on his own. Mama came out on the porch to greet him, and the family joined her. Introductions were made, with Father greeting everyone individually, even bowing to kiss Cookie's hand.

He gave a manly handshake to each of the boys in turn. In a voice that could have been Uncle Wilhelm's, he said to Curt, "It's a pleasure to meet you at last, young man. I have a gift for you, in my suitcase." And turning to Mama with a charming smile, he said, "I have gifts for all of you."

Mama dipped her head in acknowledgement and opened the door for him. "Please come in, Mr. Braun. Let me show you to your room. Junior, will you bring in Mr. Braun's bags, please?"

Junior opened the trunk. "Did you tell him about us?" he asked out of one side of his mouth while keeping an eye on Father.

I shook my head. "Not yet. I will."

Initially I was concerned about how Father would react to the Mullers and their simple lifestyle: children running in and out of the house; doors slamming; men's dirty workboots lined up on the back porch; plain, homey meals around a kitchen table, with no one to serve; laundry hanging out on the line for everyone to see. But I needn't have worried. Father fit right in. The war had changed him, made him accepting, able to see and appreciate the good that was inside people rather than concentrate on the external. He was still Father, but he was different. Humble.

He was also very tired. He slept for days, it seemed. He got up and ate meals with us, but that was all he seemed to have energy for. But he was a delightful and appreciative dinner guest.

That first night he ate prodigiously, complimenting the cooking, taking seconds and sometimes thirds, as if he were trying to gain back all the weight he'd lost in one sitting. I had baked for him—an international menu of sweets: chocolate chip cookies, Mrs. Ludwig's *sernik babci,* and an apple strudel that he said tasted exactly like the strudel from the bakery on Willhelmstrasse.

"Delicious!" Father said, cutting into another piece of strudel with the edge of his fork and eating it with relish. "I cannot believe that you made this yourself, Elise!" And then, turning to Mama, he said, "You're an excellent teacher, Mrs. Muller."

"I had very little to do with it, I'm afraid," Mama replied. "A dear old friend who is now gone taught her. Elise is a very accomplished young woman."

Father nodded as if he knew exactly what Mama meant, "Yes. She was always a very clever girl. Even as a child—"

"Father," I chided him gently. There was no need to bore everyone with stories of my imagined childhood accomplishments.

"Well, it's true! You were always very bright. You loved to read, almost as much as this young man does," Father said, giving Curt an approving smile that Curt returned. "And how she could play the piano! Even as a tiny little girl! What an artist! You still play, don't you, Elise?"

"Yes, Father. I'll play for you after dinner if you'd like."

"I would like that very much," he said. "Very much." He turned to Mama again. "Her mother was also a pianist. She taught Elise herself. Lale said she was practically a prodigy. She wanted to send her to the conservatory to study, but I said no. I didn't like the idea of my daughter playing in public." Father sighed. "Silly of me. Now that I think about it, I don't know why that would have been so bad. So many things I might have done differently . . ." his voice trailed off.

I reached across the table and patted his hand. "No, Father. It was for the best. I wouldn't have wanted to leave Mother to go study, and I'm very happy with my life here."

"So many things," Father repeated, as though he hadn't heard me.

Mama spoke. "Mr. Braun. There are always different choices to be made. Other paths we might have taken. There's no way of knowing if they would have been better. None of us are completely innocent," she said gently, her eyes full of compassion, "or completely guilty."

Father nodded as if to agree, but I could see in his eyes that he couldn't quite believe her. A film of liquid flooded his eyes, and we all sat looking at our plates, trying not to notice. Curt spoke up to break the awkward silence.

"You should see what else Elise can do," he said. "She's a farmer."

"A farmer?" Father asked, not quite sure if he understood what Curt was saying.

"Yup. Those tobacco fields outside were all her idea," he reported. "And she works them herself, too. She can hoe and harvest tobacco as well as anybody. Faster than me, even."

Father turned to me with a curious expression. "Those are your fields?"

"No," I corrected him gently. "Those are *our* fields. We all work them together. The whole family helps."

"But it was your idea, Elise. Your plan," said Junior. "We would never have tried it if Elise hadn't pushed for it. We've got a fine crop out there, and it is all thanks to your daughter, Mr. Braun. You should go out later and have Elise give you a tour. I think you will be very proud of what she's been able to accomplish."

"I already am," Father said as he reached out to squeeze my hand.

"Would you like to see the fields, Father? We could go for a walk after dinner?"

He shook his head slowly, "Yes, I would, but not tonight. I think I will go to bed early. I'm suddenly very tired. It has been such a long journey."

We stood at the sink, washing the dishes after dinner. Mama said, "Elise, I was talking to your father. He says that you are going home together."

"I know," I said and sighed. "He wants us to go back to Berlin. He thinks he can make everything like it was, that we can begin again."

Mama was quiet, and for a moment the only sound in the kitchen was the sloshing of soapy water. "So you're leaving?"

"No, Mama! Of course not! This is my home now! You and Junior and the family. You are my new beginning! I just . . ." I faltered. "I just don't know how to tell him. He seems so tired and fragile."

"He has been through so much," Mama agreed, "but he's a strong man on the inside, Elise. The two of you are very much alike. He'll heal. He just needs time."

"I don't want to hurt him."

"I know, but you're going to have to tell him. Do you remember how I cut back the rosebushes every year?"

I nodded. "By the time you're finished, they always look like you hacked at them with a butcher knife."

"Yes, but I do it for a reason," Mama said as she rinsed another glass and put it on the counter for me to dry. "I cut away the old dead branches, all the parts that aren't needed anymore, because that's what I have to do to force new growth in the spring. I always hate doing it, it seems so cruel somehow, but after winter ends and the sun warms the ground, they sprout new branches and leaves, and the whole thing grows back. It is never quite the same as it was before, but it grows back stronger and more beautiful than ever."

I looked out the kitchen window at the fields. The wind had picked up and was blowing across the top of the tobacco plants, making the leaves wave in the wind, almost as if they were beckoning me. "I'll talk to him," I said. "I'll do it tomorrow."

We walked on the edge of the fields, along the south side, near the Schollers' place. Father seemed very interested in the process of tobacco cultivation and was fascinated by the design of the drying sheds with their adjustable louvers that let air pass freely through the shed without exposing the curing leaves to the weather. He asked very intelligent questions. I was surprised at how much he seemed to know about agriculture and told him so.

"You forget, Elise, we Brauns are not just soldiers, we also had estates in Silesia and grew all kinds of crops. As a boy, I used to spend my summers there and enjoyed helping in the fields. Or at least, supposing I was helping." He smiled. "I may have been more underfoot than anything else, but the farmworkers were always kind to me, and the estate manager, old Fuhrmann, was almost like a second father to me."

I was surprised. "Father, you never told me that story before. I had no idea."

"Well, there is a great deal you don't know about me, *Liebling.* A great deal we don't know about each other."

I continued the tour. "That is the Schollers' house over there," I said, pointing across the fields. "They were our neighbors before Mr. Scholler died and Mrs. Scholler moved to Virginia."

"Who lives there now?" he asked.

"No one at the moment. The place is up for sale." I chuckled. "I had this crazy idea in the back of my mind that if we made enough money from the tobacco I could buy it. Our tobacco should bring a good price at market, but I know it won't be enough. It was a silly idea." I shrugged. "But the boys are all good farmers, and they seem to enjoy it. I thought, if we had the Scholler land, too, there would be enough for all of them, and Mama would always be taken care of."

We were nearly back to the house but I'd still hadn't found the courage to speak of the things that were truly on my mind. "Father, I . . ."

Father turned to me, an expectant expression on his face. He looked at me and smiled, small lines like arrows pleating the skin at the corners of his eyes. "Elise, I know. I know what you're going to say. You can't go with me. I can see that." He lifted his arm and swept his hand across the fields. "This is your home now. It is where you belong. You are needed here—you found your destiny."

"Oh, *Vati!*" I cried and threw myself into his open arms. "*Vati!* I love you so much! Do you know?"

"I know," he answered, his voice choking with emotion. We held on to each other for the longest time, with the sun beating warm on us, and the smell of the earth all around. We cried from happiness, both of us.

"*Vati,* you should stay," I said, sniffing as I released myself from his embrace. "You could stay here in Brightfield!" I exclaimed, excited by the idea. "That captain said he could arrange for your immigration papers, and there is plenty of room here in the house. I know Mama would love to have you. You could help with the farm!"

He looked over the fields, and his eyes were wistful for a moment, thinking, but then a shadow passed over his face and he said, "No, Elise. I must go back. I couldn't move in with the Mullers. Mrs. Muller is a very fine woman, very fine, but it is too much of an imposition. Besides," he continued softly, "if I were to stay, people would find out who I was. They would hate me for it. They've lost sons and husbands and sweethearts. It will not matter to them who I am or that I tried to stop it. I was too late. Too late. They would blame me, *Liebling.* I blame myself."

He sounded so defeated, and for some reason, this made me angry. "Of course, there will be people who will blame you! There are people here who blamed me! Some still do! But not all of them would feel like that, *Vati,* not the people that matter."

He raised his hand, preparing to dismiss my arguments, but I forged ahead before he could object. "Listen. When Papa Muller was killed, when Junior came home without a leg, I thought the family would all blame me, but they didn't. Junior was so angry and sullen, and I thought it was my fault. When he wanted his ring back"—Father raised his eyebrows as I said this, but I ignored him and kept talking—"I thought it was because he blamed me. I was sure that every time he saw my German face and heard my German accent he was thinking I was the reason for all his pain. But it wasn't true! He was angry with himself, not me! He blamed himself for Papa's death because he didn't see the sniper!"

Father puffed out a breath, and his eyes bulged at my revelation. "But that is ridiculous! He tried his best to protect his father! He wasn't responsible for his death. He wasn't to blame, any more than you are to blame, for what that madman Hitler and his henchmen did. You were just a little girl when you left Germany. You bore no responsibility for what happened!"

He paused for a moment. His jaw clenched and his gaze grew steely as he looked off into the distance. "You were too young to know, but I was not. I was just like the rest. I didn't like Hitler, didn't trust him, but I did nothing to stop him. I couldn't imagine the things he was planning and even when I learned the truth, I couldn't quite bring myself to believe it. I just stood back like everyone else and watched, hoping someone else would do something. I didn't try to stop him until it was too late. No, you are not to blame, Elise. *We* are to blame, *this* generation. *My* generation, who stood by and did nothing." He shut his eyes tight, pushing back the painful memories. I reached out my hand and put it on his arm.

I was about to tell him, no, that none of it was his fault, that he had done everything he could do, but I knew he wouldn't believe me, and, sadly, I knew it wasn't true. "You are right," I admitted softly. "Some of it is your fault. Not all, but some. It is a guilt you share with a nation, and it will not be quickly forgiven, not by yourselves and not by the world."

"But, *Vati,*" I said urgently, "we are all guilty, each in our own way. There is always blame enough to go around. If you were to stay in Brightfield, some people will hate you for what you did or didn't do, and others will embrace you because, even though you didn't succeed, you tried to stop Hitler, even risking your life to do so. If you go back to Berlin, it will be the same—some blaming, some forgiving. That is the way the world is. I am proud of you, *Vati,* not because of what you did during the war, but because you didn't give up. When you were tired of life, tired of carrying the burden of guilt, hungry for an honorable death, you stopped and thought of me. You found the courage to go on! You could have chosen an easy escape, but instead you picked up the load, admitted your guilt, and decided to keep on going because you knew I still needed you. And I do, *Vati.* I still do," I whispered.

His head was bowed, and I could only see the top of it, a place that I had not noticed before, where his hair was thin and sparse.

"Someone once told me that courage, real courage, lies in facing your destiny with unclean hands. Once, I wanted to give up, too, but I heard those words, and I found the courage to go on. At the time I didn't know where I found it, but now I know where it came from. It came from you! I am, after all, a Braun."

Papa lifted his head and smiled at me through his tears.

"You could stay, *Vati.* Promise you'll think about it."

He nodded his head. "I will think about it."

We walked back to the house arm in arm. Junior was sitting on the porch, rocking. As we approached, he got up from his seat and bowed his head to Father, who bowed in reply.

"Mr. Braun, I would like to speak to you, sir. Privately, if I may."

"Of course, Mr. Muller," Father said formally. "I would be delighted."

Junior opened the door for him and said, "You can call me Carl, if you'd like."

"Good. Carl, you can call me Herman," Father replied, and they entered the house together.

Chapter 25

June 12, 1946

I got up early today, even before it was light. Last night I told Mama not to worry if I wasn't home for breakfast, that I was going to go out early and gather wildflowers to decorate the tables and the poles of the tents. But that's not the true reason I am walking across the dewy grass before the dawn.

I need to be alone this morning. Just for a little while more. I want to think. I want to remember.

It rained a little last night, and the ground is damp and spongy. I walk barefoot through the fields, between the rows of half-grown tobacco, my naked feet sinking into the soil, pressing down the cool, yielding earth, leaving deep prints so people will know I passed this way.

I walk, and the sun walks with me, ascending into the sky even as I ascend the slowly sloping path that leads to the lip of the valley. I come to the edge of the field and part the plants, pushing aside a curtain of leaves and stepping through them as if I were entering another part of a house with many rooms, a plain of untilled ground grown waist-high with wild grasses and sweet hay.

I move quietly and slowly across the face of the world, in satisfied silence, picking armfuls of wildflowers—yellow, blue, pink, purple—flowers that Cookie and I will tie into beribboned bundles to make beautiful the wedding tent. Adorning the tent with blossoms of the valley because they belong there as much as Junior and I do—a seed planted in the valley and a seed blown in on an alien wind, both burrowed deep in the soil, each pushing stubbornly through the fertile earth to stretch searching vines toward the light, drawing strength from the river and soil and sun and one another. We two are twisting green stems that wrap round and round each other, rising higher to bring forth two blooms, similar but separate, each made more beautiful by proximity with the other.

I hear a noise on the breeze, a sound of contended humming. I look across the field to see *Vati* outside his new house, the Schollers' old one, singing happily to himself as he cuts flowers from Mrs. Scholler's rosebushes. I notice he has planted something new in the south corner of the garden. Squinting through beams of the dawning day, I see it is a lilac bush. It is small now, the blossoms are few and underdeveloped, but every plant finds new soil shocking at first. Given time, sun, and nourishment it will grow and flourish, its branches bringing forth heavy, unruly blossoms to perfume the air and delight the eye. But that will not be for some time yet. These things take time.

Today Father concentrates on his roses, choosing the finest blossoms he will bring as a gift for Mama, as he does on so many mornings now. She will ask him in for coffee, and he will accept, and they will sit, talking and not talking, but none of it awkward because they are too wise and have seen too much to worry about what might come next. They are friends, and that is enough. And if someday they are more than friends, then that will be enough for then.

I don't call out to *Vati.* I don't want to speak to anyone just now. Ambling through the silver-green grass, I brush my hand across the tops of the blades to feel them caress my palms. I'm in no hurry to get to the water. I know the river will be waiting for me, as it always is and always was. Before I ever laid eyes on it, long before that day when Papa brought me to the ridge above the river, this place, this soft curve of the Connecticut, was destined to be my home.

The wedding will take place in the church, with the afternoon sunlight shafting through the plain, unstained windows, in front of the altar where Papa used to preach and where I embraced belief and exchanged fear for faith.

In a few hours, *Vati* will escort me down the aisle and place my hand in Junior's. We will repeat words that before God and men that will bind us one to another for life, though our hearts were bound long before. Afterwards, we'll come here, to this perfect place to dine and toast and begin a new day, sitting at tables with friends and family, feasting under the protection of specially built shade tents whose linen walls let in the breeze and the sound of the flowing river.

Another step, and the grasses give way to sandy riverbank, another door to another room, and I walk across the sand to bathe in the current, washing the dirt from my feet. I look up, marveling at how perfectly the water meets the earth and the earth meets the sky, admiring the way it all joins together, this world meeting the next without a ripple or seam.

We've invited guests to join us today, perhaps fifty, not more. The faces we love most will stand as witness to our first day together, smiling in celebration and solemn in commitment to stand as guides and shields in the days that will come after.

Standing side by side and flanked by those who love us, there is no possibility of our failure, but I had thought of leaving one chair empty—just one, in case old friends come by unexpectedly: Mr. Scholler, Papa, Mrs. Ludwig, Mother. I wanted to be sure to leave room for them, but as I look around, at the sky, the trees on the far bank, the fields on the near, at the river Jordan that divides us one from another, I realize there is no need.

They are here already, watching and waiting, rejoicing from the other side of the river, applauding the day with newly washed hands.

Acknowledgments

I've heard many authors say that writing their second book was ten times harder than writing the first, and now I know why.

For one thing, a published author is an author on a deadline and that puts external pressure on the writing process. But the greater pressure is an internal one: the small voice of inner doubt that fills writers with a terrible fear that their first success may have been accidental, that perhaps they had only one story to tell.

As I faced a blank computer screen many months ago and wrote chapter one, those were my fears. Now, three hundred plus pages later, I was able to write "The End" on the final page of the manuscript largely because of the support, advice, and encouragement of the following people:

As always, first and last in every endeavor of my life, I am grateful to my husband, Brad. You are my greatest love story—my partner, confidante, and friend in all that brings meaning to life.

To Jill Grosjean, my agent and friend, who talks me through the doubts and allows me to focus on writing, secure in the knowledge that she has the business end of things well in hand. To Audrey LaFehr, a wonderful editor whose literary judgment I trust and who has gone the extra mile for me on many occasions. Thank you both so much.

To my mother, Margaret, and my sister, Betty Walsh, who have been tireless in promoting my last book and who were such patient sounding boards as I worked on this one. To my father, Ray; my stepmother, Carolyn; my sisters, Donna Gomer and Lori Crace, and my friends Pam Helm, Beth Popadic, Marjie McCandless, Carol and Greg Fullerton, Susan and Glenn Wagner for their ongoing support and for bringing humor and perspective to my life. Many thanks to Adam Kortekas, webdude extraordinaire, and to Jeni Hulett and Juana Pena for helping me keep the home fires burning and more or less organized.

I owe special thanks to Reverend Steve Treash, whose own Christmas messages served as the inspiration for Papa's sermons in this book. Also to the wonderful women of Black Rock Church who have upheld me in prayer in these last months and years.

And, most importantly and eternally, to the God who hears our prayers and is faithful to answer, with gratitude that the love that binds us is based not on how I feel, but on who You are.

A Special Chat With Marie Bostwick

In the year since my first book, *Fields of Gold*, was published, nearly every day when I wasn't working on *River's Edge* was spent meeting and talking with readers. In that time I've chatted, in person or online, with hundreds of new reading friends and have been overjoyed to hear of their connection with my characters and impressed by the insight and depth of their questions. For me, this has been one of the most surprising, delightful, and humbling benefits of the writing life.

If I could, I'd love to sit down with each of you personally and have a good, long chat but of course that is impossible, so I thought I'd take some time to discuss a few of the questions some of my reading friends have had about *River's Edge*. Possibly you've had some of the same questions they did. I hope you'll find the answers you're looking for here. If you don't, please visit my website, *www.mariebostwick.com*, and send me an e-mail. I read all my e-mails personally and will do my best to answer any questions you might have. While you're there, be sure to check out the whole site—you'll find reader's guides, giveaways, contests, information about book signings and new releases, my quarterly newsletter and reader's spotlight, which features the stories of some of my reading friends, and even a DVD clip of me discussing *Fields of Gold.* I hope you'll drop by.

Like many of you, I am a voracious reader. I'm usually reading several books at the same time. In fact, as I write this there are exactly thirteen books sitting on my bedside table: four novels, three theological works, a book of quotations, a bible, a book on self-sufficient farming, a biography, and two nonfiction historical titles. Even though my choice of reading materials runs the gamut of genre, style, and subject matter, the mish-mash of things I'm reading has a way of connecting in my mind and adding texture to whatever it is I'm writing. However, once I have a new character in mind, history tends to be my jumping-off place. This was exactly what happened when I began working on *River's Edge.*

I knew my main character for this book was going to be a young girl who, for reasons beyond her control or understanding, found herself separated from her family. At the same time this girl made her appearance in my imagination, I was reading a series of books about the underground resistance within the officer corps in Hitler's Germany. I was fascinated by these men who were public participants in Nazi aggression while simultaneously plotting Hitler's assassination. How did they live with themselves knowing that, even if they were not directly active in Nazi genocide, they certainly were complicit in the deaths of countless innocents? For the safety of their families, they must have had to keep much of what they were doing a secret; perhaps they found it necessary to push those they loved away in an effort to protect them if their plot was uncovered. I wondered—in trying to wrestle their country and children from the clutches of a madman, did they lose the respect and love of those they were trying to protect?

Nothing in the books I was reading could answer these questions, and when historical fact cannot answer questions of human motivation that is when I begin to rely on imagination. Some writers outline their plots before they ever begin to write, but not me. I don't like to outline any more of the story than is strictly necessary to help my publisher believe there really is a book hiding somewhere in my mind. This may be stubbornness on my part, but I really believe the work comes out better when I let the characters lead me where they want to go without binding them to the constraints of some pre-constructed plot. For me, the best books are sewn from threads of imagination and it was in my imagination that Elise, Hermann, Carl, Sophia, Junior, and the intertwining tapestry of their stories were woven.

Before we move to the fictional side of the *River's Edge* story, you probably want to know more about the factual side of it. There were many soldiers and citizens who were involved in the underground resistance movement in Hitler's Germany. The most well-known of the military resistance groups was centered in the Abwehr, a military intelligence unit. Admiral Wilhelm Canaris was a real person and one of the key players in the resistance. He was a career officer and began his military service long before Hitler's arrival on the scene of German history. Like many career officers he was very unhappy with the conditions of surrender imposed on Germany after World War I but had no real admiration for the Nazis or their leader and, in fact, held Hitler in contempt. However, trained from an early age to be obedient and loyal to superiors, he followed orders (how enthusiastically or reluctantly I cannot guess) and played his part in the German war machine.

When he witnessed numerous atrocities and the wholesale slaughter of innocent citizens during the Polish invasion, Canaris was horrified. He initially believed these were the uncoordinated actions of a few ruthless renegades within the army, but soon came to the realization that these atrocities were condoned and even ordered by Hitler. This marked Admiral Carnaris's conversion to the resistance movement. As the war progressed, dozens of other high-ranking officers would undergo the same transformation. His involvement in the resistance was suspected as early as 1940, but he was not arrested until 1944. He was hung in a concentration camp on April 9, 1945, just weeks before the end of the war.

Elise's beloved cousin Peter was also an actual person. Count Peter Yorck von Watenburg was descended from an old Prussian family, the tree upon which I decided to graft Elise's fictional ancestry. Peter was a lawyer, a charming, handsome man whose deep religious convictions led him to become part of the Christian resistance that was known as the Kreisau Circle. He played a role in the July 20, 1944 attempt to assassinate Hitler, was arrested when the plot failed, and executed on August 8. The well-known protestant theologian, Dietrich Bonhoeffer, whose writings I have admired for many years, was also part of the Kreisau Circle as were many others from diverse Christian denominations. Bonhoeffer was killed in the same place and on the same day as Canaris.

As I read about these men and many others, I was torn. Certainly not all of their motives were pure, but I couldn't help but admire their willingness to risk everything in an attempt to stop Hitler. Still, I grew impatient and even angry at their inability to carry out their mission. During Hitler's reign, there were fifteen attempts on his life—all failures. The July 20 bombing during a meeting at the Wolf's Lair headquarters inflicted the most damage, but though the bomb had been planted directly at his feet, Hitler walked away unscathed. Why, if the plotters were actually in the conference room with Hitler, didn't they just walk up to the Führer and shoot him at close range? Why rely on something as unreliable as a bomb? Surely, after the plan failed, they must have asked themselves the same thing. The weight of their guilt must have been hard to live with. That is where Hermann Braun comes in and *River's Edge* moves into the world of fiction.

Elise's father, Hermann Braun, is completely a product of my imagination. My thoughts about this book began with a girl who is sent away from her family for reasons she cannot understand and thrust into a new family whose traditions and lifestyle are utterly confusing to her. But why would a family willingly send their child away to live with another family? Hermann provides the answer.

Hermann has many reasons, some well-intentioned and some misguided, for sending Elise to live with the Mullers but the biggest is his growing realization that eventually he will have no choice but to join the resistance. Though he will try to resist it, the pull of morality will eventually win out over a lifetime of ingrained obedience to authority and when it does, Hermann knows his daughter will be in danger. When he leaves Elise on the dock at Hamburg, Hermann himself doesn't entirely understand his reasoning and he certainly can't explain it to Elise. From an early age, Hermann was taught to obey without discussion or question. Because of this, his communication skills, even to the wife and daughter he loves, are painfully underdeveloped. He cannot express his love, his fears, his desires, or even his grief. It is a legacy he passes on to his little girl and consequently, the Brauns become a family of secret keepers.

Though Elise doesn't realize it at the time, the boisterous, joyous, demonstrative Muller family is just what she needs. Otherwise she would have grown up to be a hard, judgmental, and bitter woman instead of the strong, forgiving, and loving person she becomes.

Shall I tell you a secret? As I began working on this story, I didn't much like Elise! Her superior attitude coupled with her insecurity made me grow impatient with her. And yet, I understood her. In fact, the unlovely parts of Elise's character are not too different from the unlovely parts of my own character, so I suppose that explains my reaction. What is more to be despised than our own bad habits? But still, I do understand her. Like Elise, I have lived as a stranger in a strange land. My family and I lived in Mexico for almost five years, so I understand Elise's culture shock only too well. Even as she appreciates the warmth, generosity, and essential goodness of the Mullers, she can't quite help but feel that their way of life is at best confusing and at worst simply wrong. She will come to appreciate and even love her adopted country, but it will take time. In the beginning, she feels lonely and abandoned and that, coupled with the difficulty she has in expressing herself, causes her to say and do things that don't exactly endear her to some members of the Muller family, like Junior, who are less inclined to give her the benefit of the doubt. Elise the girl is not the most loveable of children.

However, by the time I'd finished writing, I not only loved Elise, I admired her. As she grows into womanhood, Elise attains the type of feminine maturity I think most of us aspire to—she is strong and gentle, forgiving and moral, capable and generous, discerning and visionary, able to give love and receive it. And because she starts out life with so many strikes against her, her ultimate transformation is even more of a triumph.

But, as you know, Elise's transformation is not a sure bet. There are many people in Brightfield who, even though she is just an innocent girl living thousands of miles from the center of Nazi power, are more than ready to lay the blame for the war and the terrible crimes that came with it squarely at Elise's feet, perhaps none so much as Elise herself. The greatest challenge Elise will face is in dealing with her own sense of guilt. She must separate feelings of shame that stem from the soul of an abandoned child who is sure that her abandonment must be her own fault from the things for which she is truly to blame. She must learn to live with and learn from her regrets and mistakes. Having done that, Elise is finally able to move to a place of faith, to be forgiven and forgiving of herself and others. It seems to me an act of supreme courage.

But Elise isn't the only one who must come face-to-face with guilt and shame. All the men Elise loves—Hermann, Papa, and Junior—

are all confronted with the reality of their own failures and each, in their own way, is in danger of being crushed under the weight of remorse. Having learned to carry this load herself, Elise is able to help Junior and Hermann face their faults, call them by name, and embrace life. She is a true heroine and that is what I love most about her.

Of course, Elise could not have become a heroine without the help and guidance of so many people. Though her tragic death from tuberculosis separates her from her daughter at a young age, Elise's own mother gives her love and the gift of music that will supply Elise with a sense of worth and a voice that help her through some difficult days. Additionally, the love and acceptance she receives from Mama, Papa, Cookie, and so many other people in Brightfield, including the loveable, curmudgeonly Mrs. Ludwig, (one of my favorite characters!) are crucial in molding Elise's character and helping her become a woman.

I suspect that I've written another book that is liberally sprinkled with wonderful, supportive secondary characters because I recognize the importance that loving family, friends, and neighbors have had in shaping my own character. I cannot imagine writing about a place where, even in the midst of tragedy, especially in the midst of tragedy, there were not people that brought rays of hope and words of wisdom, forgiveness, and compassion to those who need it.

Sometimes in life we are lucky enough to receive that type of love, sometimes we are privileged enough to give it. I hope you have the opportunity to do both.

Blessings,
Marie

DON'T MISS MARIE BOSTWICK'S HEARTWARMING DEBUT

© Kerry Long

Marie Bostwick Skinner was born and raised in the Northwest. Since marrying the love of her life twenty-four years ago, she has never known a moment's boredom. Marie and her family have moved a score of times, living in eight U.S. states and two Mexican cities, and collecting a vast and cherished array of friends and experiences. Marie now lives with her husband and three handsome sons in Connecticut where she writes, reads, quilts, and is privileged to serve the women of her local church. Visit her at www.mariebostwick.com.